ROOTS OF ALL EVIL

PAUL CARRO

CHAPTER 1

B ob Hawking sang along to the country song on his truck radio, much to the chagrin of his dog, Butler. Butler was of the mutt variety, as were Bob's last two wives he would say to any who would listen. Most did not. That was just fine by him. The general population did not enjoy Bob's company much, and Bob didn't like theirs either. Truthfully, he preferred his alone time.

He had plenty of like-minded friends on social media, people who still appreciated a long night of drinking interrupted by bouts of porn, which was God's gift to the internet, Bob also always said. Bob always said a lot of things, repeatedly. It had been decades since he added any new words of wisdom to his repertoire, which left him what one would call, 'set in his ways' at sixty.

Because he identified with so many songs, country music was his favorite. Tunes of honky-tonk bar shenanigans, failed relationships, and been done wrong scenarios fit him to a bold, italicized, capital letter T. At least he could say (at what he considered the midway point of life because *misery lives forever)* he had his dog. Except if his dog had the ability, Bob reckoned, Butler would have divorced him over the singalongs long ago.

When the next song started, Butler lowered his head as if trying to vanish. The mutt had learned the more it protested, the bigger the forthcoming show would be. Bob gazed into puppy eyes, which begged the man to stop before he started. The unspoken request failed. Bob enunciated words at an uncomfortable volume. To call what came out of his mouth singing would serve as an insult to auto-tuned pop phenoms.

"*I'm not big on social graces, think I'll...* shit, forgot that part." Bob hummed through the lyrics he did not know.

Butler's stoicism faltered under the vocal onslaught. He howled in protest. There were ambulance sirens, and then there was this guy—draw. Bob handed off the vocals to Garth Brooks, then smiled at his mutt.

"Since when did you become so discriminating with your country? What is it But Face? Me or Garth? You don't like the song or is it my singing because I might take that personal, shortchange your dinner later and such. Which is it? Oh, wait, here we go. *I've got friends in...*"

As Bob crooned on, Butler found himself in a low place. They navigated an ornery pothole filled straightaway heading home. The back road connected to the downtown proper, but the terrain was a bitch on vehicles. Townsfolk used it for safe passage when they drove while nursing open containers. Bob kept his tall boy between his legs. Cops were loath to patrol the narrow stretch because it required a department policy car wash after driving through. Townies understood it to be the safest way to travel if one had a few too many. *Which was just the right amount,* Bob thought.

Trees lined both sides of the street. Even in farm country with enough flatland to hypnotize a cow, forests thrived. Branches reached out from the trunks like spindly arthritic hands eager to catch passersby. The autumn foliage gasped last seasonal breaths as fiery colored leaves sought the cold ground in order to become mulch. The fiery colors in their prime brought flocks of tourists to New England. Seasonal visitors keen on picture taking coined the term 'leaf peeping.' Locals called it, "shit, winter's coming."

Because the road was so narrow, avoiding the many potholes of the poorly maintained road required concentration. Bob had none. By the time he realized a doozy was coming, it was too late. The teeth crunching bump created an epic bounce.

"Shit on my Aunt Petunia's shingles!" Bob cursed as half a beer found his lap. He chugged the last foamy remnants, tossed the bottle into the backseat, then looked to his dog. "Why didn't you remind me about that dip? I'm three sheets to the wind, what's your excuse?"

Butler wagged his tail once Bob switched from crooning to gabbing. Anything that interrupted the vocal onslaught was fine with the dog, except Bob showed he was not a one and done kind of guy. With practiced flair, the man used one hand to flip the cap off another Budweiser before locking eyes with his pet and belting out lyrics. Even though he gave every line its own key, none approximated that of the song on the radio.

"*When I taste Tequila...*"

Butler growled, low at first then gradually louder. Normally the dog harmonized along with a whine minus any cheese, so the growl caught Bob off guard. He fluffed Butler's head.

"I take it you're an old country versus new mutt. I understand. That Blake Shelton is a little too pretty, if you know what I mean. And these 'Tequila' guys don't get me started on them. Good song though."

Butler bit Bob's hand. Bob yanked it away and sucked at the wound. It bled. The nip broke the skin. He glared angrily at his pet.

"What was that Butt Face? I was kidding about your dinner earlier, but you think you're getting anything now, you're crazy!"

Butler growled deeply, verging on a full bark. He fixated on an area outside the truck. Bob tightened his legs to prevent another drink from spilling, then checked every direction.

"What is it, boy? I don't see nothin'."

Wham! Butler slammed his head against the passenger window. The animal looked as though it was attacking its own reflection.

"Oh no, Butt, tell me you haven't gone rabid."

Fear fueled the dog's antics. Something terrified the poor thing. Bob failed to identify a source of worry.

"It's okay Butt, it's..."

With a disturbing smack, the dog bashed its head again, cracking the non-tempered glass. The action drew blood, which matted into the fur on the animal's face. The injury failed to stop the dog who continued the face versus glass routine.

"Oh Lord, stop it. What's wrong?"

Bob hit the brakes. Unable to afford a truck with fancy electric controls, he leaned across the seat and turned the crank handle. The glass crackled and popped and threatened to shatter by the time he rolled it halfway down.

That proved enough for Butler, who forced his body through the small opening. The dog fell ungracefully in a heap, but quickly recovered and trotted away from the road. Once the animal reached the forest edge, it turned back and barked, returning to the role of protector. But protecting from what?

"I don't understand, boy. What is it?"

As if the dog provided an answer, the truck jerked so violently it launched the beer from between Bob's legs. The bottle jetted around near the pedals as wildly as a whitewater raft in an eddy. Rolling around the floorboard, it signaled the ride was just beginning.

"What the...?"

The vehicle bounced into the air like a prize-winning low-rider. Bob grabbed the wheel and through it felt a thunderous pulse of rumbling earth below. In the rearview mirror, he glimpsed a spray of debris blast up as a massive crack opened in the road, heading straight toward him.

Bob hit the gas. Tires spun in the loose dirt, almost sending him into trees, but he compensated and shot forward, narrowly avoiding the growing chasm at his six. He finally looked ahead again only to find an even larger hole waiting.

Without a chance to brake, Bob vanished instantly.

CHAPTER 2

Tyler Whatley, on the bean pole side of athletic, squeezed a ball tight in his glove. Kicking dirt off the pitcher's mound, he twisted his cap slightly off kilter and readied the pitch. The world fell silent. No crowd, no cheers or boos from competing crowds. Nothing mattered except that next throw. He started his rotation, rising to full frame, and shook off the catcher. *I call my own pitches, thank you very much,* the superstar thought.

"As Whatley winds up, even the unborn children of the opposing team go weak in the knees. Tragically a generation will be born bowlegged over fear of the greatest pitcher who ever lived," Tyler announced before throwing the pitch.

The ball (tennis variety) flew with all the velocity the twelve-year-old could muster. It struck the side of a large colonial home. The well-kept house sat atop a massive front yard of exquisite upkeep. The picture postcard environment suffered a single flaw. That of a stretch of grass eroded to soil where Tyler played his baseball variant. (A different fantasy sport than his older brother enjoyed online.)

The pitch added a fresh skid-mark on clapboards already blemished from countless innings of play. The ball ricocheted through the air, threatening to float over Tyler's head. Once he made the catch, he turned to an invisible crowd and supplied his own cheering sounds.

"The crowd roars. They know the man is unstoppable!"

The side of the home acting as his opposing batters was unique in that it offered only second-floor windows, none on the first. If he remained within an approximation of a strike zone, the glass above would survive. There were, however, soiled spots perilously close to the sashes. Whenever he tossed a wild pitch, he prayed to the baseball Gods they might spare the window, and therefore, his allowance. Tyler threw once again. The ball bounced back as a grounder. As he leaned in for the catch, a window opened. Kate, beautiful, a hayseed ten in her thirties, poked her head out.

"Goddamnit Tyler. I asked you to stop that fifteen minutes ago!"

Tyler bobbled the ball, groaning as it rolled through his legs. A Buckner miss. "Geez Mom, I was one out from a perfect game."

"And I was one more bounced ball away from a perfect headache. You know you're only supposed to play when someone isn't in the house."

"Someone's ALWAYS in the house."

Kate shrugged before waving hands in a 'what are you going to do' gesture. Then she smiled conspiratorially at her son. "Besides, we need to get ready. Your girlfriend is on her way over."

He rolled his eyes. "She's not my girlfriend. I mean, nothing's official. She's a friend. She's a girl."

"Whatever," Kate said and closed the window.

"My Mom just 'whatever'd' me."

Tyler chased after the ball, corralling it before it could roll too far down a lawn that angled steeply to a dirt road fronting their property. A massive barn rose in the distance at the youth's back. While its large red walls would have served as the perfect backstop for his games, the grass surrounding it grew too high. There were already enough assigned chores related to cutting and watering their front yard for him to bother tending a budding jungle along the base of the weathered structure. Plus, his father regularly parked the tractor there.

Dozens of acres stretched toward the horizon. An immense cornfield occupied most of the impressive landscape. Cornstalks grew over the largest portion of the family-owned farm. The tall green stalks rose high midfield and stretched all the way to the property line on one side. Various other crops grew in sectioned gardens across the balance of the farm. A thick forest filled the skyline in the distance with fiery orange and red leaves offering a pop of color against a gray skyline. A chilled breeze confirmed the season.

Tyler scooped up the ball with disappointment. While upset at the abrupt end to his game, he was eager for Jenny's arrival. Most girls were gross, well more annoying than gross. Jenny was more like a guy, except she was nothing like a guy, and anyway, he was excited to see her. He dropped the mitt on the front stoop and entered the house.

The kitchen appeared nearly as rustic as the barn but offered modern conveniences. The refrigerator was stainless steel. A trendy instant pot sat atop a granite counter alongside a sleek coffee maker. Hanging over the convection oven, a rack adorned with a metal rooster held a mix of copper and cast-iron pans. The bird fit in with several animal pictures hanging on walls, and with the barn animal influenced kitchen towels and potholders scattered through the room.

After checking the food was ready, Kate pulled a Le Creuset casserole dish from the stove and placed it on a trivet. The color of the stoneware matched the kitchen's copper and cerulean décor. Her khaki capris and chambray shirt over a light blue halter blended into the surroundings. A perfect fit.

Kate's oldest son, Matt, dug through the refrigerator. The eighteen-year-old foraged like the racoons in their backyard garbage cans. While sniffing everything in sight, the teen appeared oblivious to whether dinner was forthcoming. She snapped a reminder at him.

"Get out of there. We are eating soon."

He stepped away from the fridge, hands raised to prove they were empty. "As you wish."

"You could at least close the door," his mother said and did.

"What can I say, I was brought up in a barn."

"For that smart remark, table setting. Our guests will arrive shortly."

Kate handed off dishes to her son, who frowned but accepted the load. Tyler bounded into the room. She presented him silverware, which he took without complaint. He followed his brother to the dining area just off the kitchen.

Matthew dropped each plate with a 'thunk' designed to draw ire from his mother. She failed to notice, too involved in prep. Matt's appearance was more polished than his table manners. He wore a navy Polo shirt and linen pants not commonly found amongst country living denizens. His hair appeared perfectly groomed, the chestnut tufts salon cut and frozen in place with styling product. Retailers offering an 'I don't want to live on a farm' clothing line would identify Matt as their target demographic.

Tyler set the silverware carefully at correct angles in designated spots. His denim jeans bled green and brown from fielding balls. He wore a simple grey tee along with an ever-present Boston Red Sox baseball cap.

"I can't wait until the Hennigan's arrive," Matthew said.

"Is that so? Seems to me you've been on all week about how crazy little Jenny is," Kate said.

"Oh, Jenny's a whack job all right, but come on, her sister is major babeage."

"Are you sure you're my son?"

"If he's not, can I have all his stuff?" Tyler chimed in.

"You stay out of my things and my room."

Matt hit his brother on the head. Their dad, Roger, entered and repeated the move on his oldest. Matt grimaced, less from the gentle tap than from being busted. He attempted to slink away.

Roger called him back. "It is time for a family meeting."

Matt returned, leaning against a wall while his father held court between the kitchen and dining area. Roger's clothing hewed more closely to his younger son's look than his older. The man's ensemble of jeans, work boots and a tee displayed a muscular frame that combined with calloused hands suggested farm life versus a gym kept him fit.

"Listen, this dinner is a huge deal. Jenny has been absent a long time and it is important we do not treat her any differently than we used to."

"Come on, Dad, it's not like she's been backpacking through Europe. Loco chick has been in a sanitarium," Matt said.

"A hospital," Kate replied.

"Yeah, with bars on windows and rubber in rooms. Any idea why they don't call them in-sanitariums by the way?"

"Shut up. Jenny's my friend. You say one more inappropriate thing about her, and I rat you out to her sister Cassie."

Matt eyed his brother nervously. "You wouldn't."

"In my mind, I already have."

"Behave when they get here. Both of you," Roger said. He rose from the chair at the sound of a car on gravel.

Tyler ran to the living room window and pulled the curtain to reveal a truck sitting in the driveway. He raced outside first, followed closely by the balance of the family. They all gathered on the porch. No one exited the vehicle. Roger mused aloud that his friend was likely offering a similar talk to his daughters that he just gave his sons.

Roger worried about Joe. The man suffered an unfathomable loss. The 'incident' became a part of all their lives and changed the dynamics of their lifelong friendship. A lifetime of familiar banter and shared inside jokes disappeared when Joe's wife did. Rebecca vanished without a trace.

The two families came together in the early days to help search for the missing woman. They even took turns babysitting Jenny before they sent her away. The young girl witnessed the abduction and remained in a fragile state. Soon after all the craziness, Joe retreated into a world of privacy. The distraught father hunkered down with his girls. Until recently, the two men never spent any significant time apart during decades of friendship.

Along with the pause on their almost daily in person get togethers, the friends maintained only minimal phone contact. Conversations were brief when they did speak. Joe apologized frequently, insisting he acted in such a manner to benefit his daughters. Roger understood, but felt Joe held something back, which made little sense given their history of sharing the most intimate secrets. Between them, they already shared a dark one of which they swore never to speak about again. Given that history, Roger failed to fully understand his friend's hesitancy to talk it out.

For the first time in months they were about to meet in person, and he wondered which friend would exit the truck. The best buddy or the aloof husband who refused to talk about his wife? Joe stepped from the truck flashing an affable smile reminiscent of happier times. The man looked, in a word, good. For that Roger was grateful. Kate felt the same based on how tightly she squeezed Roger's hand. The couple shared quick, tight smiles.

Cassie exited the vehicle from the shotgun position and beamed upon spotting Matt. Matt breathed deep as if his heart suddenly skipped a beat or three. Cassie was a stunner with long golden hair and an athletic body borne of years on the track team combined with working a family farm. In her sundress, backlit from the very thing that gave the garment its name, she could have stepped straight from a movie set. She slipped a stray lock over an ear and grinned wider. She appeared the type who could have fun in a hailstorm.

Tyler rushed over and opened the rear door of the extended cab pickup. Jenny peered into the sun with the fragile countenance of one wishing to hide from the world. Still, her friend's smile was as contagious as a yawn. She smirked in return.

"Hi," Tyler said.

"Hi," Jenny replied. Then they were good. He helped her out of the vehicle.

While Joe indeed looked well considering circumstances, he appeared older than Roger despite their identical ages. A few gray hairs set up shop on the real estate atop the man's head. Even with the subtle difference, there was no stopping a machine, and Joe's grin suggested there remained plenty of gas in the man's engine. Joe cast aside the weight of this and several other worlds (all having hitched a ride on his shoulders) to barnstorm the porch and embrace Kate.

"What's a gorgeous middle-aged woman like you doing with an old bastard like him?"

Kate gripped him tightly, trying not to crack. She fought tears as they released. Joe avoided the moment by shaking Roger's hand.

"How's it going, buddy?" Roger asked.

"Damn near perfect, you know?" The men pulled themselves into an embrace. They patted backs, then broke apart.

Kate rubbed Joe's arm affectionately. "I remember when you used to ask what a **young** woman was doing with a guy like him."

"We've both got eighteen-year-old kids. That ship has sailed, huh? Besides, you're prettier now."

"Don't say that to my husband, he might get jealous."

"Please. I've assumed an affair between the two of you for years. You want to make me jealous, tell me again about your new giant screen TV," Roger said.

The three wrapped arms around shoulders and headed for the house. Kate spoke over her shoulder to the kids.

"You guys catch up. But don't wander too far, dinner will be ready soon."

The parents went inside while the younger couples paired off and walked in opposite directions.

A twelve-inch metal blade sailed through the air and nailed the bullseye painted on an aged wooden shed. The tiny building stood in the barn's shadow. The shack rested at an angle. Weeds sprouted along its foundation as wildly as an old man's nose hairs. Tyler ran and pulled the object free of the target then returned to his friend.

He offered it to Jenny. "Dad gives us his older ones. It's like Ninja throwing stars. You wanna' try?"

She scrunched her face and shook her head. "You said you had a surprise. Is this it?" Jenny asked.

"No, that comes after dinner. I can't wait to show you."

Tyler fired the blade, dead center again. Kid was talented. He waved to the same invisible crowd that attended his baseball game before remembering Jenny's presence. She giggled over the goofiness as he retrieved it once again.

M att and Cassie walked along a dirt path parallel to the cornfield. Stalks rose above them at peak height, ready for harvest. The pair stood so close they occasionally bumped into one another. Matt warmed under every touch of the woman he knew his entire life. When they were younger, he considered her the biggest pain in the universe. Such a bookworm, so stoic. Uptight, one might say.

She constantly corrected his English, which 'weren't too good' back in the day. Over the years, he watched her grow into a beautiful woman who bloomed around others. She shared her easy (and stunning) smile with all their friends, mutual and otherwise. Cassie traveled in cooler circles than him from a much younger age. It was not until he reached his Junior year in high school and developed physically that he finally gained traction in the acceptable to hang with category.

It often frustrated Matt how she was so open and fun with their other friends, yet so serious around him. They fought occasionally over the years as sleights turned into lover's quarrels, minus them being lovers. They acted like an old married couple, but truth was they had never kissed. In fact, he witnessed her kiss plenty of other guys and his heart broke each time as if he had some claim to her.

Their non-relationship fell apart one night in their sophomore year at a school formal. Cassie partied with a wild abandon, even appearing slightly drunk. It pained him to realize she excluded him from participating in the rebellious act. What hurt more was how she bristled when he tried to dance with her. She stiffened up physically and mentally. He attempted to instigate minimal bodily contact. He desired at most a hug for the thrill of the touch. But she repelled his advances while embracing so many others, including people she barely knew.

They fought on the dance floor where he asked what he had done so wrong that made her always treat him that way despite their lifelong friendship. Why was she more fun around their other friends?

"Because I expect nothing from them. I do from you. That's why!" She stormed to the girl's room, after which she avoided him the rest of the evening.

They did not talk for a full month after that. She ceased accompanying her family during their weekly visits to his family's farm. On those miserable days, Cassie's parents sadly suggested their daughter would come around some time, but Matt was giving up. Such a long break from the most beautiful woman he had ever seen in his life weighed on him. The fighting pair fell into an unspoken rule at school. Whoever connected with their mutual friends first got to spend the balance of the day with them. The other steered clear.

Their classmates urged them to make-up, but that seemed unlikely. Neither could even articulate why they were fighting. Matt learned to ignore the visitors when they arrived. He loved them nearly as much as his own family, but it pained him to see them without her in tow. One day, his parents called for him to come down and join them. He refused as he was far too busy sulking. The fight was nearing a two-month anniversary.

Matt resigned himself to a permanent separation, which was why it shocked him when Cassie appeared in his doorway. She looked more beautiful than he remembered. Before he could blurt a greeting, she stormed across the room and kissed him. He fought through the shock to kiss back. A warmth flooded his entire body. Hormones urged him to take things further except she pulled away, leaving them both breathing heavyily in excitement.

"Are we good?" When he nodded, she jerked her head toward the door. "Let's go."

He followed her past parents who were happy yet curious about the reunion. The pair walked alongside the cornfield, catching up on lost time. Despite attending the same school, they learned much had changed for each since last speaking. Reconnecting proved bittersweet as they realized the extent of what they had missed out on in one another's lives.

They did not kiss again that day or since. Matt never pushed because as badly as he wanted to taste her again and again, he missed their friendship terribly and feared messing it up. Their mutual friends relayed their annoyance at how the pair acted as though nothing ever happened, despite all the drama. Matt took the lumps gladly, happy enough to be back in Cassie's good graces. School became tolerable again.

And he always had the memory of that kiss.

The memory lingered while Matt walked alongside her again in the cornfield. Since their last time, things had changed in dramatic fashion. The incident involving Mrs. Hennigan occurred during the last month of summer break, so Cassie never returned to school with the rest of the students. Her father picked up her daily lessons and worked out a home-schooling situation. Cassie remained on the track team, but the coach interceded in any looky-loos, including himself. All he could do was watch her from a distance.

The laissez-faire attitude he displayed around his parents in the kitchen earlier hid a truth. Matt was crazy about the woman, but also concerned for all she went through. There was a part of him that figured if he could only tell her how he felt she would finally embrace him, kiss him again. Because that made too much sense. He played it cool instead.

"Has it really been three months since I saw you?" Matt asked.

"You've been keeping track?"

"Maybe I have. That's too long—for the record."

"That's sweet—for the record."

She leaned into him, and he maintained the contact, pleased to discover she was not eager to pull away from him. The closeness delighted Matt. He felt the urge to roll through literal hay with her, but they continued along the path they were on. "So, are things returning to normal?"

"I don't know how anything will ever be that way again. My mother is still missing. The only lead the police have is Jenny, who swears a monster abducted Mom. In my family's case, I believe normalcy has left the building and set the place on fire." Cassie stopped. "I've heard things around school. I'm sure you feel the same. My sister is crazy."

Matt blanched, either from the proximity or accuracy. "No. I would never suggest such a thing. If she said Lord Voldemort, or the Care Bears took your Mom, now that would be insane."

"You know, I think the time off did us some good, you're less of a jerk than I remember."

Matt smiled, internally his heart did a fist pump. He was growing on her.

"Wait, she didn't say it was Lord Voldemort, did she?"

Cassie groaned in the lost moment and started off again. Matt followed, trying to catch up to his stupid mouth. Neither noticed a row of corn stalks suddenly vanish underground one after the other, as if something pulled an invisible thread.

CHAPTER 3

The parents nursed beers in the living room, sipping nervously as the animated small talk of the porch gave way to awkward silence. As they sat there, the trio appeared as if meeting for the first time. Lifelong familiarity abandoned them when faced with recent circumstances. Someone clearing their throat broke the quiet, but it only highlighted the awkwardness. Joe raised a finger as if to speak, then changed his mind and guzzled the last of his beer. Kate discreetly nudged her husband to break the ice.

"How's your crop coming along?" Roger asked.

"Best I've ever had. Can't expect less since all I do is tend to the fields. Every second of each day. All I do is work while I wait for updates from the authorities."

"That is what we are here for. If you wish to talk." Kate said.

Joe set the empty bottle down and shook off the thought. The man straightened in his seat, then displayed his contagious smile. "Actually, all I want is to get drunk and have a grand time, which is exactly what I plan after leaving you boring people."

"Only here for the free meal, huh?" Roger asked.

"Well, it's not the company."

Kate rose. "The freebie is ready. I hope you are hungry."

"I'm thirsty for sure." Joe gestured to his empty.

Kate crooked a finger for him to follow while calling over her shoulder. "Honey, can you fetch the kids?"

After Roger left to do so, Kate led Joe into the kitchen. Once there, she opened the fridge for her guest before checking on the dinner in the oven. Joe grabbed a beer of choice, closed the refrigerator, and dropped the bottle which shattered with a loud pop. Foamy residue hissed and spread over shards of glass. Kate turned to find him staring at a photo hanging from a magnet on the appliance door.

The image showed the two couples together during better times. Rebecca, buoyant, sexy in hiking gear, draping herself over Joe in a manner suggesting there was no place she would rather be.

"I'm so sorry. I thought we took all those down."

"Oh God, Kate. Rebecca is gone. I've lost her."

"There's always hope."

"Is there? After all this time?"

"Crazier things have happened."

"Crazier than monsters like Jenny suggested?"

"She's young, impressionable, she…"

"Why can't she just say it? 'Dad, Mom ran off with another man. She was so infatuated with the new guy and so over you she voluntarily left me in the middle of downtown with no supervision.' Jesus. Why not say that?"

"It's not that simple sometimes. I'm surprised to hear you lean into the willingly part. Someone abducted her, of that I am certain. Why Jenny sees it the way she does, well, you're her father."

"Yeah. I have considered that. In that scenario, even the evil man who grabbed Rebecca would be a monster to my poor kid. She's not wrong per se, but her failure to recall details keeps us from nailing down a description. And she mentioned several abductors, versus one. Said they were small and hideous, like burnt children. A gang? Is that it? A bunch of teens? One tattoo. If she could remember one tat, the police would have something to go on."

"Like I said. Crazy. But the situation, not her."

"You want insane? I hear Rebecca's voice."

"I can't blame you. It is natural when you're dreaming."

"No, it happens when I am awake and alone. And I'm always alone. Rebecca whispers my name." He shook his head, releasing his tenuous hold over the image. "But I understand it cannot be real."

Kate touched his shoulder, but he pulled away, making a fuss over cleaning up the glass. She stepped aside to give him space. He went to work as if there were no other way to numb pain.

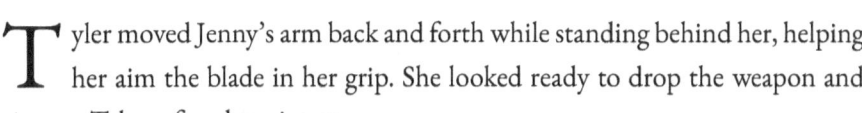

Tyler moved Jenny's arm back and forth while standing behind her, helping her aim the blade in her grip. She looked ready to drop the weapon and give up. Tyler refused to give up.

"One throw. It's fun, I promise." Tyler egged her on.

"I don't know. I can't really toss things very far."

"They fly. Trust me. It will make you feel better. Pretend you're shooting at the monster who got your Mom."

Tyler grimaced at the stupid comment. Yet it produced the desired effect. A look of determination crossed the girl's face. She hurled the object with a long simmering rage.

"Kids, dinner's..." Roger barely dodged the spinning metal that whooshed millimeters away from his head! It stuck into the trunk of a nearby shade tree with a loud thunk.

Tyler slapped his hands over his face. "Dad, I didn't know you'd be near..."

Jenny stepped up. "Mr. Whatley, I'm sorry. I was aiming for the door, honest."

Roger breathed deep. He kept his temper in check for the already traumatized girl. He did, however, share a harsh look with a son who understood. Repercussions. Later.

"That's okay. Things happen. Tyler, we'll talk. No more saw-blades, huh?"

"Who needs em? I'm off them, I swear!"

"I have no appetite now, but if either of you do, dinner is ready."

Roger stepped aside, allowing the kids to pass. None of them noticed a thick liquid pour from the underside of the blade. The fluid (most likely sap) looked very much like blood.

The group chatted during the meal. The gathering served as a welcome respite to recent events. Cassie and Matt stole frequent glances at one another. Occasionally he slipped a foot under the table to caress hers. After nudging him away, she would bite her food sensually. They kept the flirtation discreet, none at the table appeared the wiser. Tyler ate like a forager. A little of this and that. Variety was the spice of his zero table manners life. Both parents scolded his antics more than once, but there was only so much time in a day.

"Should we call you Professor now?" Roger asked.

"Ah, the home-schooling." Joe rolled his eyes.

"I still run track at the high school. We worked it out so that I report after classes let out," Cassie said.

"Why can't **we** be home-schooled?" Tyler asked.

"Because you need smart parents." Matt faltered under the stare of death from his mother and father. "That came out wrong. Smarter ones who have teaching backgrounds, for example."

"We don't home-school because it would be nothing but twenty-four-hour detention with you two." Kate toasted her beer bottle.

"Well played, Mom!" Matt leaned over to fist bump her.

"I only instruct Cassie. Waste of everyone's time as she could teach herself," Joe said.

"I teach my sister now that she has returned. She's an exceptional student."

"Cassie gives me stickers more than at my regular school, and the other place. I hated it there. I never wanted to go."

Guilt crossed Joe's face. "Anyway, everything is temporary, while we adjust, until we get our sea legs back."

"There's no sea near here. Only a lake." Jenny scrunched her face, confused.

"It's a saying, honey."

"It's weird."

"Adding colloquialisms to the course list," Cassie said.

"I figure next quarter they return. In the meantime, they are around to help finish the harvest. That way they earn money toward their college funds."

"Matt is knee deep in applications himself." Roger sat up straighter, a booster shot of pride at play.

Cassie and Matt shared a sorrowful look. Whenever the subject came up, they could not help but face the reality that collegiate life required leaving. The two of them weren't a thing per se, but they shared the shorthand of *I like you bunches and wish we could figure this entire thing out because I kind of need you in my life.* She broke the gaze first.

She turned to the adults. "So, are you all still going to the State Fair next week?"

"The plan is to check in Tyler's..." Roger started.

"Dad! Ixnay. It's a surprise." Tyler jerked his head toward Jenny.

Roger course corrected. "Yeah, Kate and I are. Joe?"

"I don't know."

"Come on, Dad. You need a break," Cassie said.

"Sounds like you girls need one from me."

Glancing around the room, the sisters looked everywhere except at their father. Each whistled innocently. Once their eyes met, the giggle fest began. Joe shook his head.

"Conspiracy corner with my kids there. Yeah, it's the plan, but it comes down to the arrangements. I want everything dialed before I consider leaving."

"Dad, Matt and I are technically adults." Cassie pleaded.

"Listen, did you all hear that?" Heads shook around the table, signaling negative. "That was my heart snapping. Let's just pretend when we go out that I'm leaving my two baby girls behind and I will worry."

Cassie gripped her father's hand. "I love you, but we'll be okay. And yes, we need a break!"

Jenny pushed food around with her fork. The amount left on her plate showed barely touched the meal. Kate noticed.

"My cooking is not that bad, is it?" Kate asked.

"No."

"So, what's wrong?"

The girl gestured to an empty spot near the end of the table.

"You forgot to set a plate for Mom. We do it every night at home. She will be starving when she returns."

"Jenny, don't," Cassie scolded.

"I'll add another dish if it helps you eat." Kate rose from her seat.

"No, enough. Dinner is over. Girls go outside, I need to talk to my friends in private."

Oblivious to the meltdown, Tyler leaped to his feet. "Now I can show you my surprise." Tyler led his morose friend out the door.

Cassie stood in the doorway waiting for Matt, who scarfed down food until realizing all eyes were on him. His mother pointed toward the exit. He shrugged a "what?" before finally swallowing.

"I'm still hungry." Roger glared at his son. "Fine." Matt grabbed a roll and bit an enormous chunk in protest.

"We are adults, we should be able to take part in the discussion," Cassie said.

"Yeah." Matt spit crumbs when he talked.

"You are right, sweetheart, but this is more about reminiscing. Besides, with all that has happened, would it kill you to hang onto childhood for just a little longer?"

Matt stood in solidarity with his friend. He took another defiant bite and choked when it went down the wrong pipe. Roger spoke to his son's posturing.

"There is a proverb which may interest you. 'When I became a man, I did away with childish things.' You want to be an adult? Let's start with no more video games."

"Yeah, conversation looks boring anyway. Gotta go. Come on, Cassie, I have my own surprise to share." Matt led her up the stairs.

The adults moved to the living room with drinks in hand. Kate curled up on the couch, legs under herself, yoga lithe. Joe sat on the other end of the couch. Roger occupied a chair across from his friend, who picked at the label on his bottle.

"Our trip to the county fair is a big test for me. Leaving the children alone is a gigantic step after all that has happened," Joe said.

"I understand. We will always worry about ours too, but we all still deserve a life. We've left them before," Roger said.

"Not with the fear that whoever took my wife could come back for them."

Kate blanched. Someone had to say it. "We can hire a sitter if it makes you feel better. On our end we can't cancel the trip, we need to meet with buyers. I'm sure you are in the same boat."

"It's not about that. Our kids are old enough. Answer me this. If anything happened to yours truly, would you take care of my girls?"

"Of course, we would. Why say such a thing? Do you know something we don't?" Roger asked.

The men locked eyes in a stalemate unrelated to who would blink first but over who would speak. It was a loaded question asking Joe what he knew when the pair shared a secret long buried. Roger expected his friend to expose the truth about the horrific day. Would he do so in front of Kate? Roger shared some details with her after they married, but not all. Not the worst of it.

Roger feared Joe's sudden silence was the man's way of steeling himself before blurting everything out. He sensed Joe needed to unburden himself and share it all. Could the tragic day when they were teens relate to more recent events? Had it played a part in Rebecca's disappearance? Roger feared Kate's reaction to discovering the truth in such a manner. Would she walk away after learning how much he withheld? Would she be furious their friend came clean about the past rather than her own husband?

Joe cleared his throat and took a hard left turn. "I think the police are about to arrest me for the murder of my wife."

Kate gasped. Roger did not see that coming. He did not see that coming at all.

CHAPTER 4

To passersby, the second-floor hallway appeared immaculate. Normal tell-tale signs of brothers sharing a common space failed to materialize. Cassie asked whether the area was always so spotless. Matt scoffed, answering no instinctively before posturing into an affirmative. He asked his guest if she considered him an animal. She answered with a knowing grin, then nodded, showing her appreciation of the effort related to their visit. They moved past the first door on which hung a sign designating it as Tyler's room, accompanied by a sign warning people not to enter. Below it someone had scrawled, "Already did, butt-munch." The teens next passed the guest room before arriving at their destination. A *Stranger Things* poster covered the door.

"That's new."

"A lot has changed since you were last here."

"If you're hoping I follow you into your bedroom for a repeat of that kiss, then…"

Matt froze with his hand on the knob. "You kind of trailed off there. Were you about to say if I'm expecting one, I will so totally have my expectations met? Or were you planning the whole sorely disappointed thing?"

"Parents are downstairs. What do you think?"

"It might surprise you how little that matters to me."

"Keep it in your pants cowboy."

"I wasn't even thinking that until you just said it!"

"Go." She shoved him inside.

They entered a room of dubious upkeep as the fake promise of the hall crumbled. Matt cringed, suddenly aware that a beautiful woman was entering an equally unbeautiful location. He scooped up evidence of a teen life well lived and stuffed everything into the closet. As the teen raced about in damage control, Cassie pressed herself against his desk to wait out the storm.

She glanced down. Applications for NYU, Hampshire College, UCLA, Miskatonic U., and Hofstra covered the desk. She examined the brochures promoting fun times on sunny campuses. The Miskatonic students looked more serious than other coeds. They must be studious types, Cassie thought.

Hurricane Matt finally touched down on the desk, sweeping all the collateral into a drawer, and slammed it shut on his future. He spread his arms wide to welcome a queen to his castle and pointed out a forty-inch wall-mounted screen hanging above a miniature drum set and electric guitar. Matt switched the game on. The title *Music Maestro* lit up the screen.

"Cool." Cassie said.

"I bought it with money saved from working for my Dad. This is my practice equipment until I form a band and leave this cowpoke town. Possibly for L.A. or New York. Here, take these."

Matt handed her drumsticks. She demurred. "No, I can't play."

"Come on, it's fun, just a game. Fine, if you'd rather watch me rock solo."

She reluctantly took the sticks. "Okay, let's bring it."

Matt lifted the guitar with dirty underwear dangling from its neck. He shook the instrument, launching the undershorts across the room. Cassie appeared oblivious of the faux pas, too busy settling into the kit. Matt hit start, and the pair jammed to the song on the screen.

Joe peered out the window, searching the fields. (for kids or police?) He remained stoically quiet as he scanned the distant landscape. Roger and Kate stood by in stunned silence.

Kate finally spoke, breaking the spell. "You can't be serious, Joe."

"I am. They have been monitoring me, surveilling my house."

"For what? How about they knock that off and find who took her, huh? Why don't they focus on that?" Roger fumed.

Joe turned and raised his beer in a toast. "It angered me when I realized what they were doing, but I've moved past it. I am too worried about my kids to bother with what law enforcement thinks. Besides, a police presence might be the best thing. What if whoever abducted Rebecca plans to come back for them?"

"There's no reason to believe that. You think law enforcement might arrest you? They haven't even found Becca," Kate said.

"It is possible. I do not want to burden Cassie with having to tend to her sister long term. I'll take my lumps with the cops, but I need reassurance you will be there for them in my absence if it comes to that."

"Without question. No worries there, buddy. Until they present some evidence, we don't even know if she..." Roger froze, realizing what he was about to say.

Joe called him out. "What?"

"I mean, is there some slight chance she ran off?"

"Roger!" Kate snapped at her husband.

"Before we get in the weeds on this, we have to admit Jenny saw something other than a monster. Was it a male companion? If so, perhaps she could not process the disappointment, the shock..."

"I won't even..." Kate started.

"No, he's right. We need to consider everything. You and I already talked about a man could have abducted her. What about one she willingly left with? You were closest with her. It's okay if you have something to tell me, if she wasn't happy," Joe said.

Kate rose in anger. "Like that you pissed her off sometimes? That maybe she gets bored around our backwater town? Want details on your love life? You want me to bring that up?" Roger reached out. But she raised a finger to warn him off. "No. Let's get this straight. I search my memory, then sure, I'll find plenty she complained about. But if either of you believe even one second Rebecca willingly left her daughter, then I don't know what to say. God damn it Joe, you know better." Kate crossed her arms, stepping away from the men, openly pondering the exit.

"Wow. You get this often?" Joe asked Roger.

"Only on days of the week ending in the letter Y."

Kate started toward the exit before circling back, angry. She raised a finger. The index. "Do not brush me off on this. The cops are wrong about you. She may be out there. You fight for her! No matter what, because she would fight for you. This I know about my friend."

"Thanks Kate, I needed that."

Suddenly all the lights went out. The world turned black.

CHAPTER 5

The tenebrosity of the Whatley home appeared absolute, a residence transformed into a void. Cassie rose blindly from behind the drums. Once on her feet, she stood in place waiting for a rescue from one who knew the layout better. Her sudden blindness heightened her other senses. A swish of cloth fluttered by as gently as a whisper. Footsteps fell softly, passing by her where they suddenly stopped. Something squeaked. A drawer? She turned toward the source and screamed. A face materialized, lit harshly from below.

Responding to her frightened cry, Matt pulled it from himself and pointed it straight at her. "Sorry, didn't mean to do the campground scare thing."

"Kind of can't see." She raised her hands, blinded differently.

"Matt, fix it!" Roger yelled up the stairs.

"On it!"

Matt handed the flashlight to Cassie, then fired up a second. As Cassie swept the room to acclimate herself, her beam landed on an open desk drawer. It housed an absurd number of candles, batteries, and flashlights.

Matt explained. "Old house. We keep backup light everywhere. I blow fuses half the time I play. I think it was your epic drum solo, you ask me."

"Please, I was just pounding away. The rhythm was never going to get me."

"No, I saw true talent. Another four or five—decades—of practice and you could showcase for a local bar."

"Only local, huh?"

"Hey, we all level out somewhere."

The two shared a laugh. The pair leaned into one another. Cassie realized he made her comfortable, even in a creepy situation. She felt secure in knowing they had each other's backs if something more serious ever occurred. Because of that, she pondered a second kiss. The first had been terrific, but like all things Matt, a little went a long way. Her lifelong friend did not possess a casual-relationship gene. Too much kissing would lead them both to distractions that could alter their planned career paths.

The light sparkled in his eyes. *The boy sure was pretty*, she thought, and felt her will slipping. They gently pressed their foreheads together.

"Matt! Do it today, not tomorrow!" Kate yelled.

Cassie smiled languidly and pulled away, minus the contemplated smooch.

"Guess you have to go?"

"Seems so."

Matt stepped into the doorway and extended his arm. "Better take my hand. These stairs are treacherous in the dark."

"Are they now?"

"Oh, they'll take you out before you know what hit you. Vicious, vicious steps."

They gripped hands and exited the room, both excited by more than the darkness.

As Tyler and Jenny walked along a dirt path adjacent the cornfield, the girl fidgeted with a nervous energy. Despite the late hour, rows of string lights dangling from poles at equidistant intervals kept the immediate area well lit. Jenny grew nervous at the diminishing size of the residence they left behind. She spread her fingers as if trying to expand a picture on a phone. It failed to work.

"We're getting kind of far," she said.

Suddenly the house went dark. The girl burped, a nervous reaction. Tyler followed her gaze.

"Video games. See? We have generators on timers here, they don't there. My surprise is only a little further. It's worth it, I promise."

"I guess. I don't like the dark," Jenny said.

"By the time we're finished, Matt will reset the circuit breakers."

Corn gave way to other crops as they continued. Multiple shacks dotted the landscape, standing out as silent sentries in the void. The barn in the distance morphed from a common structure in the light of day to that of a shadow monster at night. The massive beast if it broke free could easily run rampage over the county. Tyler shivered upon viewing the ominous outline which always jumpstarted his imagination. He fought to hide his unease from his friend.

Making the trip solo always left his nerves on edge, but it was necessary. Someone needed to check on his prize every evening. Tyler refused to provide his dufus brother the satisfaction of admitting the trek scared him. For that reason, he kept secret the fears about the barn sprouting demonic red eyes and rising from its foundation.

With Jenny present, Tyler felt different. Rather than worry about his own unease, he wished to protect her. She was quick to startle and bounced her head as frequently as the Star Wars bobbleheads back in his room. She appeared on a constant search, leaving him to wonder, searching for what?

Tyler understood her apprehension. He still encountered moments where the snap of a twig could clench his bowels. He developed coping mechanisms to ignore his fears. One was stargazing. The million billion pinpricks above gave him something to focus on. The vastness allowed him to imagine worlds beyond the farm where aliens thrived and enjoyed grand adventures with blasters and spaceships. Those daydreams (despite it being night) distracted him long enough to reach his pride and joy.

They were almost there. He wanted to run the last hundred yards, but out of excitement, not fear. He greased the wheels for the reveal, giving her a hint of what was to come. "Every year I plant a heart seed."

"What's that?"

"The last clinging seed from a jack-o'-lantern. The one that refuses to let go of the guts."

They arrived at a pumpkin patch. Orange skins glimmered in the night. Upon first glance in the dimness, the gourds could be mistaken as the heads of poor souls deposited into the ground by a predator. Perhaps done in by the barn monster. Tyler mostly imagined that scenario, but occasionally leaned into the opposite. They were predators, an orange-headed army with bodies maintaining formation underground. The oversized leaves and vines sprouting from their necks would become arms with which they could lift themselves from the soil upon receiving orders. From there, they would march on the unsuspecting farm and town.

"Why plant the gut clinger?"

"Some say it is the one that most wants to be a pumpkin. That is why it refuses to let go. I've had some success before, but never anything like this." Tyler swept the beam past a shack where two massive eyes popped into view.

Jenny yelped in fright. "What is that?"

"It is what we're looking for. A utility vehicle. See?"

He waved the light back and forth. The resulting strobe revealed headlights of a transporter facing the pumpkins. The transport was a four-wheeler ATV with a tow-behind attached at its rear. Tyler pointed out the shed.

"The shack is for fertilizer. We keep it far from the house because—boom!" He made an explosion gesture with his hands.

"Not helping."

"My Dad lets me drive sometimes. It's legal without a license if I stay on our private property. We both live on farms. You don't seem to know this stuff. What do you do all day?"

"I take care of the animals," she said defensively.

"Oh. We used to have some. Too much work. Points to your place."

Tyler turned the key and headlights cascaded over a tarp covering something large. He plugged a cord into a socket in the trailer bed. Several heat lamps on tripods hummed to life. He gripped the edge of the fabric and yanked it off, revealing a pumpkin of stunning proportion.

"Wow! It's amazing."

"We expect it to take top prize. Entering it into competition and reserving a space is the reason my parents are going to the fair with your Dad. Night two is when I get to attend. I can't wait. I want to go on the rides I'm finally tall enough for this year for sure, but mostly I want to watch people's reactions when they see this bad boy."

Tyler caressed the surface, cooing to it like a pet or a child. Jenny arched an eyebrow, but Tyler waved her over. "Come on. It doesn't get this big by itself. It likes attention, it helps him grow."

Jenny joined him. "Him? Hello Mr. Pumpkin."

"Whoa, Mr. is our parents. This is Cool Dude Pumpkin. Cool Dude P for short."

"Hello Cool Dude P."

Jenny raised a fist for a bump, but the fruit unsurprisingly refused to return the gesture. She tapped it on her own. Tyler laughed. The pair swept their hands over the curves, praising its shiny coating. For a moment at least, darkness receded, vanishing behind the light of unbridled enthusiasm.

Matt navigated into a dark which fed on his flashlight beam as if it were a snack. Cassie remained back in the living room where the flickering candles in the common space felt romantic until he noticed his parents' displeasure over his blowing a fuse while hosting guests. He understood the possibility when booting up the game, but there was a woman he wanted to impress. Aware his stunning good looks, *which did not belong on a farm, thank you very much,* never prompted a second round of making out, he hoped the gaming system would earn him points where his charm failed.

Fine, Matt knew well models were another genus, and he would never be part of that club. He fell more on the sapiens side of homo sapiens. He would never be the best-looking kid, though Cassie was. Despite her being out of several of his leagues, he had grown on her like a fungus. Matt knew his time to impress was running out. He planned to leave for Los Angeles, to go where life happened. And he expected Cassie to do what? Accompany him? Without so much as a second kiss, why would he expect her to travel to a place that beckoned to him, not her?

He had an odd connection with his preferred destination. Local TV stations ran programs years behind bigger markets because they could only afford syndicated programming. Cable did not reach most sections of town, thanks to the angry television Gods. Local internet relied on a community Wi-Fi hub set up for farming businesses, which made it hit or miss. That left streaming out as it required too much bandwidth. Matt considered himself lucky when he could score a YouTube video that did not freeze during the lead in ad. Satellites were a thing but parents and their budgets. What could he do?

For those reasons, Baywatch repeats (running two on Tuesdays) became a staple for him and his brother. When not goofing together about the ridiculous plots, Matt often shared his desire to run off to women like those on screen. His butt faced brother would ask if he planned to do so in slow motion as on the show. *Would he hoof it or Hasselhoff it*? Nerd.

Yes, Matt spoke of fantasy women in what might as well been a foreign province, but there was always a major issue floating out there. Cassie. He remained uncertain what he wanted from her. Currently, he would not have minded some company on the dark stairs. One thing Matt would not miss from country living was the stunning depths of darkness which blanketed their world when the sun took its daily nap. With the city too far away for light pollution, blackness ruled the land. That was why he normally avoided late night power consumption. It was worth it to see Cassie pound those drums, though. He descended the steps, remembering how cute she looked, banging with abandon. Fine, maybe not so much cute as totally hot, he reflected.

With outages so common, the family adopted doomsday prepper habits by storing candles and flashlights in many places. It always fell on him to restore power, even if Tyler instigated the outage. The parental unit deemed the basement not kid brother friendly, so Matt had to flip the switch. The so-called adults had no problem with the boy walking nightly to his stupid pumpkin. Hypocrites.

By now Matt could make the trek using only muscle memory as a guide. Once at the panel, he flipped the lever with his eyes closed. Occasionally the job required changing a fuse. That process still unnerved him as it left him feeling he might do it wrong and receive lethal jolt for his troubles. Yeah, his brother could be a snot, but he did not want him near the panel.

Matt crossed an expanse of concrete to reach the massive metal box. He flipped the switch. A hum filled the air as energy flooded back into the house. A lone bulb dangling from the ceiling in the distance turned on. Mission accomplished. The jaundiced light cast an oversized shadow of a spider across a nearby wall. While the sheer size of the outline proved unnerving, failing to identify the location of the arachnid was scarier.

More than once Matt fell victim to a face full of web while traversing the basement. The sticky face wrap often drew cries of protest from the teen along the lines of, "couldn't you build the webs higher than six feet? Do we have to go through this every time?" The spiders never followed his agitated suggestion.

Something cracked as he neared the stairs. He halted to attempt to make sense of the noise. It took another step for him to realize it came from underfoot. Snap! Fissures spread across the cement underfoot like buckling ice on a pond. Then, with a horrendous pop, his leg broke through, sinking to the knee. With his other leg still on solid ground, he found himself painfully contorted with an extra dose of agony centered around his hyper-extended groin. Then his situation got worse.

Matt screamed as something tore at his lower limb. Whatever had hold of him tugged hard, eager to bring him down. The attack punctured his skin, drawing new cries of pain. The ferocity suggested a starving beast deciding it was dinnertime and his calf the main course. *Now serving fresh meat*, he thought. The stairwell became a lifeline. He grabbed the railing and fought to free himself. The terrifying turn of events caused him to worry whether he might never make it to California, instead fulfilling a destiny to become worm food. Or more accurately, whatever had a hold of his leg food.

CHAPTER 6

A cry in the distance alerted Kate. From the cellar? She asked the others if they heard it. Before anyone could answer, a second yell removed all doubt. Everyone scrambled to their feet. Once the power returned, everyone ditched their flashlights, but Cassie grabbed one to brandish as a club. Roger bolted down the narrow hall past the master bedroom and laundry room. The basement door hung open at the end of the hall. Matt tripped over the top step as he emerged from below. Blood poured down his calf beneath a shredded pant leg.

Roger caught his son who struggled to stand and asked what happened while guiding him to the living room. Everyone in the hall backtracked to make room for the injured teen. Kate jumped in and helped her son sit on the couch.

"I think the barn rats got into the house," Matt said.

Cassie gripped his hand in sympathy. Kate lifted the torn fabric for a better look, then rose without a word and exited the room. Joe made a cursory exam of the damage.

"Long abrasions versus deep. You got lucky. That means claws not teeth. Keeps us from worrying about rabies."

Cassie eyed her father questioningly. "You sure Dad?"

"Yes. I have done the wild animal bite doctor's office tour several times in my life. I know a thing or two about the situation."

"Joe is right. You'd be wearing it still if one bit you. They don't let go."

"Gee thanks Dad, I was doing fine until that thought."

Kate reappeared with alcohol, gauze, and scissors. She cut the leg of the pants off above his knee.

"Mom, these are my favorite pair."

"We'll order you a new one. Brace yourself. This will sting." Kate raised the bottle over the gash.

Matt looked at Cassie. "If I scream like a little girl, please leave the room."

Kate poured liberally. Matt stiffened, grimacing through clenched teeth. Then a girl screamed.

"That wasn't me!" Matt yelled.

Roger and Joe bolted out of the house with Cassie close behind. When Matt stood, intending to join them, Kate pushed him back down and continued tending to his leg. While dressing his injuries, she glanced out the open door with concern.

Jenny screamed again. The three adults raced to the source of the commotion. Tyler peered into the field. Jenny threw herself at her dad, hugging him as he arrived. Joe caressed his daughter's head and scoured the area for threats.

Tyler answered the parents' questions before they could ask. "We were coming back from my pumpkin when she freaked. Said she spotted something."

"I did. I saw the monster that took Mom. It even had red eyes."

Corn rustled. Joe pointed at Cassie. "Stay with your sister."

Joe stormed the field, listening for any signs of life. After hearing snapping stalks on both sides, he picked a direction and ran. Soon he broke into a clearing housing a corn thrasher. There was no sign of anything besides the machine. He listened, his breath caught in the chilled air, and floated away as steam. Then more rustling off to one side. No mistaking the sound of something large approaching. The tips of stalks wavered, acting as an early warning system. Joe braced himself, only for Roger to emerge. The friends traded a defeated look.

The men called out in advance when they returned. They did not wish to further scare the children. Cassie eyed her father in anticipation. He shook his head, answering without a word. The subtlety failed to escape Jenny's notice.

"It was out there. I swear. You saw it, right, Tyler?"

"I'm sorry. I didn't even hear anything."

Joe kneeled and took his youngest by the shoulders. "Sweetie, barn rats just now went after Matt. His cries would have driven them away, likely into these very fields. I'm certain that's what you saw."

"Dad, you're talking to a farm kid. I think rats are cute. This wasn't that. The eyes stood as tall as me."

Joe shook his head. "There is nothing out there. This must stop. There are no monsters. Rebecca... Your Mom has been missing for too long. I'm afraid she won't be coming back."

The tough love caused the young girl to catch her breath. Joe pulled her tight, hoping if he squeezed tightly enough tears might not flow. Cassie joined in. The three remained a unit until they felt strong enough to rise. When they arrived back at the farm, Kate and Matt waited anxiously on the porch. Joe herded Jenny into the rear seat of the truck while Cassie rendezvoused with Matt out of earshot of the adults.

"Your leg is okay?"

"I'll be fine. I just hope your sister gets better."

"Thanks."

"See you next weekend when our parents hit the fair?"

"I'd say those plans are up in the air." She hugged him, then got into the truck and rolled the window down. "Thanks for being so supportive."

"I am nothing if not sensitive and attentive. You know me."

"Thought I did. Who are you and what did you do with the real Matt?"

Kate spoke to Joe through the driver's side window. "Keep us informed on how she is doing,"

"Yeah, hang in there, buddy." Roger clapped his friends on the shoulder.

"I've let her live in her fantasy world too long. It is time we work through the reality of this." Joe pulled out of the driveway.

The Whatley's waved as the truck departed. Matt fell into a pageant wave as the vehicle faded in the distance, then he turned to his family.

"Somebody call NASA. We have finally contacted Mars. Man, was she out there or what?"

"You're lucky your leg is already hurt..." Tyler started.

"Knock it off, you guys. Time to call it a night," Roger said.

The brothers entered the house. Roger and Kate looked out across their vast property. Nothing stared back at them other than the stars in the sky.

"You think she really saw something?" Kate asked.

"Only vermin and a child's overactive imagination."

The couple shared a sorrowful smile, mourners of two friends lost in much different ways. Neither spoke, only existed in a quiet moment. Soon they repaired inside.

Back outside, Joe drove parallel to the cornfield while his girls gazed out the windows. As much as it concerned Joe that Jenny kept seeing things, his own irrational behavior concerned him more. Something occurred out there which he decided not to share with anyone. Roger chased more than rustling plants earlier. Rebecca's voice guided him. She called to him from somewhere deep in the corn. There was a part of him that hoped speaking about it out loud to Kate back at the house would make it all fade, yet once in the cornfield he heard her louder than ever. He decided not to share details of the situation with his friends, figuring it would only worry them more than they already were. Enough going on without him giving everyone a reason to send him to the adult version of the hospital Jenny spent time in.

Joe buried his thoughts as he noticed his girls visibly exhale after passing the edge of the farm. He exhaled also while shaking off the impossibility of what he heard. What mattered was his girls were okay. They had navigated through grief for one more day. As they drove to town, none noticed a set of red eyes watching them go.

CHAPTER 7

Any relief Joe felt over the upbeat demeanor of his daughters earlier in the evening quickly faded as the night wore on. The permanent gabbing, which his kids regularly partook in, never surfaced during the ride home. That was unlike them. Even in the immediate aftermath of Rebecca's abduction, the girls argued at several inappropriate moments. Now during the drive, they remained silent, showing no signs of consoling one another, or even fighting amongst themselves. Worse, neither so much as glanced at their phones since they got in the truck. That alone warranted a visit to a doctor, he thought.

Jenny fidgeted in the backseat, a child forever on edge. She squinted at something in the rearview mirror and gasped. Spotting something caused her to grip the front seat as if seeking a return to normalcy through factory installed fabric. The vision of twin red eyes trailing their vehicle went unnoticed by her family. She cried out a warning.

"Dad!"

Joe met her gaze in the rearview mirror and quickly identified what spooked her. He turned the wheel and slowed the vehicle. "Shit."

Jenny turned, finally aware there was blue mixed in with the red. A police cruiser tailed them, a familiar staple in recent months. Joe pulled over and turned to Cassie.

"If they take me, drive right back to the Whatley's, okay?"

"What are you talking about, Dad?"

His and hers officers approached the truck, the woman on the passenger side, the male on the driver's. An obnoxiously bright police-issued flashlight lit up Cassie. It did not take the teen long to realize the beam performed a light show over her chest, so she crossed her arms to block the intrusion. The female officer was tall, fit, with dark frazzled hair but remained mostly hidden behind the bright beam. The woman could have been mistaken for a witch based on her silhouette.

"Hands on the wheel, you ever get stopped. You girls remember that." Joe turned to his oldest. "No matter how much they might deserve a punch in the teeth."

Joe rolled down his window. The approaching man appeared roughly Joe's age, but fitter. The muscles appeared too tight, a sign of steroid abuse. Despite being armed with such musculature, he kept one hand on his gun. After performing an inventory of occupants, the man returned his focus to the driver.

"Nice night, wouldn't you say, Joe?"

"Was Mitch."

"Now Joe, here I am being friendly. I believe that comment to be a knock about my presence."

"Specifically, it was a reference to your breath."

Mitch cupped a palm to his mouth, breathed and sniffed. The look on his face suggested agreement. The officer angled his head to peak at the child in the back. "How are you, Jenny?"

Joe shushed his daughter before pointing twin fingers at his own eyes, then at the officer's. "She's fine. How about you talk to me?"

"How about you watch those hands?" Mitch replied, emphasizing his own on the butt of a gun.

"We've known each other since grade school, and you think I'm a threat?"

Mitch backed down, releasing his hold on his weapon. "No, I do not, and I am not the enemy. It might serve you well to figure that out."

"I appreciate that Mitch, but it's been a rough day..." Joe ran his fingers through his hair. "In a horrible month of a terrible year. What is this all about?"

The officer noticed the strobe light shenanigans of his partner. He spoke firmly over the roof of the vehicle. "Stand down, Nadine."

Once the woman extinguished the device, Cassie could finally see who she was dealing with. The woman of indeterminate age filled out her uniform too well. Buttons on her shirt fought to hold back the tide of bosom. Whether the top one gave up the fight or the lady preferred it open, cleavage made an appearance. Cassie thought it strange given the occupation of the individual. Still, the generous nature of the woman's proportions made reading the name Rand on her badge hard to miss.

Since the work issued shirt was short-sleeved, it left her toned biceps on full display. On the surface, the partners appeared to share more than a vehicle, at minimum they used the same steroid source. Sporting a permanent pout with artificially plumped lips, the officer's entire appearance leaned into the carnal. She winked at Cassie, who turned away, disgusted.

"We had a report that Bob's dog was loose. We all know he's married to that mutt, so out of concern, we have been driving some back roads," Mitch said.

"Find anything?"

"Yeah, you. We need you to come on into the station, Joe."

"Now? It's late, the girls got to get to bed."

"We have enough to pop you and truth be told, that has been the ongoing conversation at work. They will move on you soon unless we give them an excellent reason not to."

"I would never hurt Rebecca!" Joe gripped the wheel as if to tear it off.

"Calm down. Your girls, remember? Listen, Jenny suggesting monsters is what we call a mental block. For example, she sees her Daddy, who we all know she loves so much, do something to her Mommy who she loves equally so. In such a case, her mind might supply a description of Godzilla instead of you."

"It wasn't Godzilla. It was monsters. Lots of them, and they were small but super scary! And one big one that did the bad thing," Jenny yelled through the window.

"My, my, my, what good ears you have. Tell you what, follow us in and everyone can give one more go to their stories." Mitch lowered his voice so only Joe could hear. "I'm your best shot. I urge you to take up this offer."

Joe nodded. Before the father could change his mind, Nadine yanked open the passenger door. Cassie turned to her father in surprise.

"What the hell?" Joe reached for her.

Mitch raised his hands to calm the man. "Station's a long ass way from here. Can't have everyone synching stories. They will come with us."

Cassie exited the truck and interceded when Nadine attempted to assist Jenny. "I've got it."

She let her sister out. The siblings approached the squad car. Jenny climbed in. Cassie attempted the same until the officer interceded.

Nadine gripped the teen, pulling her close. "Uh, uh, got to frisk you first."

The woman patted Cassie's arms quickly before shifting to her chest where the woman lingered. Cassie grimaced, but remained still, attempting a different version of gripping the wheel like her father taught her. Nadine then went for the dress, scrunching the material in a bunch, lifting it high enough to give her access as her free hand slid toward panty town. Cassie finally yelped in discomfort.

Mitch noticed the protest. "Officer Rand, what are you doing?"

Nadine bristled under the tone of her partner, but stopped, then postured. "I am frisking before transport. Workplace policy."

"Are you out of your damn mind? I'm asking her father to trust me. Jesus, get in the car."

While brushing her dress back down, Cassie shivered in disgust. She leaped into the backseat of the cruiser and slammed the door. Nadine got in the front and they drove away. The red lights kicked in as it went.

Inside the truck, Joe pounded the steering wheel repeatedly and screamed. Before the cop car vanished from view, he put it in gear and followed the flashing lights into the night.

CHAPTER 8

The cruiser parked directly in front of the police station upon arrival. The station occupied a former bank in the center of town. Because land was precious in farming communities, most of the town's businesses set up shop along a single street. Main Street comprised a church, the lodge hall, Miss Kitty's Yarn Barn, a hardware shop, drugstore, bowling alley, laundromat, and grocery store. Bars anchored the eastern and western ends of the business district. Because of its selection of imported beers, people considered the westside pub the fancier of the two. Companies requiring more square footage built their businesses on dust bowl plots. That left the lumberyard, a feed store, Ricky's Garage, and a John Deere retailer set up on the outskirts of town. Because they were all destination businesses, their random locations did not hurt them any. The schools were all located south of downtown.

Farm communities held the country hostage to daylight savings time. A glimpse of the area after nine PM offered a snapshot of why the antiquated concept lingered. Besides the police station, all shops appeared dark except the bars. Those remained open until the last drunk fell off his stool. Otherwise, the town resembled a post-apocalyptic zombie film. Most residents were already less than eight hours of sleep away from waking for the day.

The exited their vehicle. Mitch opened the door for Jenny. Cassie tried to exit, only to find the doors locked, leaving her at the mercy of Nadine, who opened it with a smirk. Cassie could not avoid rising into the officer's body because of how the woman positioned herself.

"Bet you'd love a go with these cuffs now, wouldn't you?"

"I want nothing from you."

"You will soon enough. I promise," Nadine replied.

Nadine pressed in on the teen (a difficult feat given how they were already atop one another) and touched a hand to Cassie's side in a gesture meant to titillate. An invitation. Cassie gasped in surprise yet stood firm while probing the woman's eyes. The woman appeared too perfect, too pretty, and based on a cursory search of the windows to her soul, too empty.

"Officer!" Mitch barked. "I've got this. Why don't you return to the bar, check if Bob has returned for round two of his drinking?"

"Sure. Pleasant night for a walk."

Nadine walked away, almost sashaying, making a show of her rearview. Mitch joined Cassie. They watched the woman leave.

"She had a rough go on call a couple years back and since has been a little..." Mitch started.

"Forward?" Cassie asked.

"I planned to say authoritative but can't argue. Don't stare at her ass, it only encourages her," Mitch said.

"You said ass!" Jenny yelled.

"Jenny," Cassie scolded as the three entered the station.

The lobby opened into a row of teller windows. An older woman sat behind one, knitting. She looked over her bifocals and blinked.

"Oh my. Let me guess. Cow tipping?"

"Now Cora, only city folk think that's an actual thing. These girls know better."

"I suppose they would. Hello, Cassie. Jenny."

"Hi Mrs. Winston," the sisters collectively chimed.

"Mind taking them to the lunch-room? I need to have a chat with their father."

"Of course. Snack machines galore. You all enjoy Twinkies?"

"I love them!" Jenny responded.

"We only carry them raw here, not deep-fried like at the fair, but they sure will do in a pinch, wouldn't you say?"

Cora smiled warmly, then tussled with her knitting project. She grabbed her supplies and led the siblings away. Mitch turned and leaped at the sight of Joe in the doorway.

"Jesus and shit in my pants, man, you scared me."

"Sorry. I heard you putting them at ease. Thanks."

After acknowledging the sentiment with a nod, Mitch gestured for Joe to go ahead. They walked down the corridor, passing offices until entering one not much larger than a broom closet. The windowless room contained two chairs with a desk between. The interrogator's seat sat two inches higher than that of the suspect's chair. Essentially a poor man's intimidation tool.

"Let me start with something, Joe. I ride with my partner every day. You've seen her, right?"

"Who hasn't?"

"Wears that bikini while at Dundee Beach. She likes to flaunt. Damn near perfect body, wouldn't you say?"

"I'm married."

"Marriage is not a synonym for dead. It's an honest question."

"She is hot if you're into that kind of thing."

"I know your wife. You are." Mitch waited for either a thank you or fisticuffs. When neither arrived, he continued talking. "Let's be frank. Rebecca is stunning, just saying. So is Nadine. Fact meet fact. Yet, most folks around here would never look at your spouse sideways because of your marriage. We respect that. Nadine, however, is eternally single, and makes her availability known."

"Are you trying to set me up on a date?"

"Don't have to. My partner in all her Pansexual ways has conveyed her thoughts on your general appearance. She's a fan. You say go and you've got yourself a ride wilder than anything at the fair, except for the Vomit Comet. How does that make you feel?"

"No different than before you uttered that sentence."

Mitch steepled his fingers in thought before leaning in. "Principled man. That makes you a decent person. I'm not. I enjoy this badge. I appreciate the authority. I work diligently at a gym, two towns away, every day, to maintain this physique. I like when women look at me and cheat on pretty much all my relationships."

"Aren't I the one here to confess?"

"In time. It is difficult for me not to lose control around Nadine. She is objectively hot and somehow stays in better shape than me, despite her fondness for the snack machines. We have a lot of them. My point is, there is no reason for me not to roll in the hay with her."

"I'm really not interested in your personal life, Mitch."

"You should be because I am terrified to get involved with her. I sense everything would change for me if I made that leap. Sometimes a person experiences The Dread."

"I am aware of what that is. Trust me."

"I don't mean simple dread. 'The Dread.' A knowing certainty of an unfortunate conclusion. For example, if I hooked up with Nadine there would be a negative impact on my life and wellbeing. That is factual. I cannot explain how I know, only that I am fully aware there is no possibility of a decent outcome besides a night of mind-blowing sex. Anything after that would be the shit hitting the shit."

"The Dread." Joe tried the words on for size.

Mitch collapsed the steeple, pressing his palms flat, as if praying. "The man who taught me about the concept experienced it while working a certain case. That person was my father. You remember him?"

Joe did. After the horrific slaughter in the pasture, the responding officer was Mitch's dad. The cop was the first to shake his and Roger's worlds by announcing the field appeared unspoiled. There were no remnants of a bonfire. No tire tracks, and no blood. Except there had been. Sickening splashes of it. Joe shook off the memory and leaned forward. Now Mitch had his attention.

Tick, tick, tick. Cora clacked metal needles while pulling at a ball of yarn located somewhere to one side. The older woman occupied a cafeteria style chair behind a six-foot banquet table. The girls sat opposite her. Jenny cheerfully chowed on Twinkies. Cassie ignored the bright pink package of Hostess Sno-balls in front of her. The door opened and Nadine entered. Cora kept knitting. The officer appeared to undress Cassie with her eyes.

"Time for interrogation, missy," Nadine said.

"I'll wait for my father, thank you," Cassie replied.

"Tsk. Smart mouth," Cora said.

"Excuse me?" Cassie blinked, stunned. Surprised by the sudden attitude of an older authority figure, she thought she knew.

"You need to answer questions, my dear. The kid is in excellent hands. Better Cora than some men around here. Those men would love a crack at your... well, do not want to say more in front of the child."

"Aren't you supposed to be our protectors? If you are the police, then act like it!" Cassie yelled, rising from behind the table.

"Okay. Come with me, or we put you AND your sister into a cell. How's my acting so far? You want me to do my job? Then I will lock your father up for a long time. I went into this thinking you might have some info to exonerate him. Exoneration means..."

"I know the meaning. Let's go." Cassie stormed past the officer into the hall.

Nadine saluted Jenny, who frowned at the odd behavior. The cop exited. Jenny eyed her sister's untouched snack. Cora nodded, and the child slid it over.

A metal table bolted to the floor centered the interrogation room. Chairs rested on either side with one anchored and another free standing. Nadine gestured to Cassie, who sat and instinctively placed her hands at her sides. In a smooth motion, the cop slapped cuffs connecting each wrist to corresponding chair legs. Cassie yanked at the restraints.

"What is this?"

"It's this or a strip search, sweetheart. I'm not as trusting as my partner."

The officer turned the other chair backward and sat, making a show of her breasts resting over the furniture-back. Nadine licked her lips. Cassie cringed but had nowhere to go.

"Let us talk, you and me. I look at you, wondering how you appear so pure while wearing a skin for sin."

"Why are you like this? What does this have to do with my dad?"

"You don't get it, do you? It has everything to do with him. Is he innocent? Or is he hiding a dark secret? Has he strayed? Cheated? Has your father been a wicked boy?"

"Never!"

The officer rose from the chair. She leaned her face into Cassie's and searched the young woman's eyes. "And what about you? You look at boys, think of them? Or do you lust after women?"

"What?"

Nadine lifted Cassie's bangs. "So beautiful. You are sexy. That's the accurate word, objectively. You move and I quiver inside, but you know that, don't you? You understand your power."

"Dad!" she struggled against the chains.

"You could learn to love restraints, discipline. I could teach you so much." Nadine traced a hand along Cassie's cheek.

"I will report you. I'm going to..."

"Shh," Nadine said, pressing a finger to the teen's lips. "Report me?" The officer raised an arm at startling speed and gripped Cassie's throat! "You're not reporting shit, silly girl!"

T

ick-tick. Tick-tick. Tick-tick. Cora knitted faster, the clacking increasing.

The woman worked blindly. Her gaze remained fixed on Jenny, not on her knit one pearl two action. "Monsters, huh?"

Jenny looked confused but nodded. Her mouth too full of snack cake to answer.

"Sounds awful, dear. Also, fantastical. Monsters. Pfftt. We all talk. Word gets around in a town like this. At the park, was it not?" Jenny ceased chewing. Cora smiled over her bifocals. "You were swinging with your Mother pushing you. I am certain you laughed, enjoying how she rocked you on the swing, right child?" Jenny nodded. "And then she wasn't there anymore. She just stopped. How strange. For surely she would know how much you loved to swing. Obviously, she would push you forever if she could. I would wager it made her as happy as it did you. Stopping meant something went wrong. She would never wish to disappoint her favorite girl. Oh, no."

Tick, tick, tick. Cora knitted ever faster. The yarn fed into the project at a startling speed. Jenny gulped nervously.

"You are old enough to swing on your own, but your mama can't help herself. She longed to make her little one happy. Her initial pushing kept you in motion even after she mysteriously stopped. The wind in your face normally would have thrilled you so. Oh, how you love to swing. But you felt a difference in that breeze, did you not? You understood a change had occurred. Something in the wind sang to you. A song, but you could not hear the lyrics, could you? Simple, really. It said, 'join us.' Had you failed to hear properly?"

Jenny involuntarily squished the pastry in her hand. The white innards shot out like someone's guts. A whimper escaped her lips.

"I suppose you are too young. Too innocent to know why your mother left. Monsters? Strange how you call them that. You described them as your height. Am I to take you as a monster then? They sound cute. Oversized heads with no facial features other than fiery red eyes. I would assume someone your age would consider that cool. You understand the word, do you not?"

Jenny sat frozen, rooted in place, reliving memories that previously visited her only in sleep. A tear formed in one eye and tracked the curve of her cheek. She hiccuped a sob.

"I'm sure you do. You call them monsters, but everyone is someone's child, no matter what world they are from. The swing still lifts you high into the air. Your height off the ground raises nerves in your stomach. Those butterflies soon fade, overtaken by a strange wonder because of what you glimpse over your shoulder. Because their shape makes no sense, you attribute the oddity to the speed and angle of your flight. You grip the chains tighter, thinking somehow it will slow you down. When it doesn't, you dangle your feet to drag yourself to a stop, but are too petite to reach the grass. Then you hear the screams. Don't you?"

Jenny nodded, tears flowing down both cheeks now.

"There are so many of them. They wrap their arms around her neck, legs, and torso. I bet your mom looked small to you as they carried her away. Your mother is screaming and flailing. Tears flow down her face while snot runs from her nose in fear. And you? You just sat there and swung without a care in the world. So. Who is the monster now, sweetie? Huh?"

Cora offered one last smile, then lost herself in the knitting as Jenny trembled in memory.

"What do you know about my father?" Mitch asked.

"They assigned him the case from when I was a teen. It was..."

"The accident. I was there, at both funerals as a kid. They put two people in the ground, and yet you and your bestie raved all over town about some crazy story."

"Bestie?"

"Just because we live on the farm doesn't mean we don't get the internet. You need to catch up to the world, IMHO," Mitch said, spelling out the acronym. "You and your best friend made charges about a lot of students back in the day. I'm worse than a PK. That's pastor's kid before your brain explodes. I was a CK. You think I had anything to do with your crazy story?"

"I couldn't know because of the robes. We never stated everyone attended. But many did. We saw their cars."

"Nate Felder, Mark Scott, Sheila Nelson. All three died within a year of the accident. One from farm equipment failure, two to overdoses. Were those accidents as well? Or could we say it sealed their fates when you identified their vehicles at the scene? They were all interrogated repeatedly."

"Is there a question anywhere in my future?"

"My Pops. I asked what you know about him other than him being assigned your case back then."

Joe shifted in his chair, uncomfortable. "I'm sorry to hear what happened."

"I'm not." Joe looked surprised. Mitch continued. "He beat my Mom out of our lives. He was a bastard and a hard man; harder than even the land here raises. So why would such a person clam up whenever I asked him about your case? Why would such a man's hand tremble so much when he tried to end his own life that the bullet went wide? Him being a vegetable now keeps me from asking. So how about you tell me? How about telling me exactly what you think happened that night all those years ago?"

CHAPTER 9

Young Roger and his best friend Joe roared down a country lane in a sixty-five Chevy. At age seventeen they possessed enough energy to seek adventures even after an interminable day of classes and farm work. The pair traveled a road of endless possibilities while dusk chased them in their rear view. School and chores would return before dawn, but that came tomorrow. Now was their time. The sun struggled to remain in the sky, flickering orange waves over distant plains, though the onset of night appeared more than capable of beating the day's glow into submission. The boys whooped it up while the celestial war raged.

"I can't believe you unhooked Marcy Cupertino's bra right there in class! Through her shirt, no less. That takes mad skills. How did you do it?" Roger asked.

"I practiced on my sister."

"Gross. Is that where you learned to kiss too?"

Joe punched his friend. "Don't make me sick. Besides, you're the kissing fiend. You and Denise. Suck face much?" Silence filled the car as levity escaped through an open rear window. "Oh, oh, trouble in paradise?"

"She said nothing about the last mix tape I sent her."

Joe guffawed while Roger sank deeper than should have been possible into the driver's seat. Upon noticing the extent of his friend's melancholy, Joe fought to stifle his laughter. With his crack wise gene firing on all cylinders, he struggled to keep it in check.

"Improper music reaction. That is tough. You ever consider there was a song she despised on there and did not wish to break it to you?"

"I am aware of her tastes. You know how long I sat next to a radio to record some of those?"

"Honestly? I have no idea." Joe smirked.

"It was a lot, asshole."

"Look, I'm the last person you should ask about relationships. I can't hang onto a girl. Hey, have you noticed the way Rebecca looks at me lately? She's hot, right?"

"Stupid hot."

"Oh yeah, back to you. So, what is up with Denise? Are you thinking long term?"

"I am the marrying type. At least that is the plan. I thought it would be her until..."

"Until?" Joe asked.

"That strange kid who recently arrived. Granger. What kind of name is that? No one has ever seen his parents. It's like he runs wild. Denise acts different since he came to town." Roger glimpsed something in the rearview mirror. A dust cloud?

"Tough break there, pal. Remember when we had that exchange student Toby from the Netherlands last year? All the girls latched on to him until Kate got her hooks in him. Man is she a looker too. Look, we've all been friends since kindergarten. If we suddenly had an unfamiliar woman in our midst, we'd be excited. If Olga came to town, we would be all over her."

Roger laughed. "I would not be all over Olga."

"You would be so infatuated with Olga. 'Marry me, Olga' would be out of your mouth before she stepped off the bus."

The goofing lightened their collective load, and the night of fun was back on. They agreed on a Dairy Queen run. The car picked up speed.

Roger attempted to put the argument to rest. "I draw the line at Olga."

"You're so in love with her, you don't even know it. You will have kids and an Olga Jr.," Joe chided.

Roger laughed. The distant sandstorm grew in size and proximity, something bordering on impossible based on their speed. The velocity required to catch them would place it on hurricane level. Joe followed Roger's gaze and looked back.

"What the hell?" Joe asked.

The swirling soil matched the path of the road, adding a layer of mystery meat to their impossibility sandwich. The phenomenon made little sense. While common in the soil rich county, dust devils were not prone to stick to back roads. But this one did.

Roger searched for signs of a tornado. That force of nature was as unpredictable as it was destructive. Still, twisters rarely made a habit of chasing down a single Chevy. Joe rolled down the passenger window and stuck his head out for a better look. The wind whipped so hard, he quickly pulled himself back into the vehicle. Joe noted the noise at their rear appeared too loud for a dust storm.

Then they saw it.

From within the curtain of swirling particles, light filtered through. Twin orbs of headlights burst through the cloud cover. A convertible Mustang raced toward them.

"How fast is he going?" Roger checked his speedometer as the other vehicle threatened to overtake them. "I'm doing sixty, he's catching up!"

"How does he have his top down at this speed?" Joe finally spotted the driver. "Holy shit, it's Granger."

The car fell onto their back bumper. Granger maintained control while steering with a single hand, almost acting blasé about the pursuit. Despite being the approximate age of the other teens, the youthful man possessed a gravitas not common in high school students.

The student was objectively handsome and sported a wild thick main which defied the whipping wind. He wore sunglasses, the frames of which sparkled red under the reflection of Roger's taillights. A devilish grin (the talk of local females) occupied most of the real estate across his face. The man also appeared immune to bug teeth. Roger often heard people mention Granger's good looks, but he felt the strange kid's smile suggested an 'abandon all hope ye who enter here' vibe.

The mustang drew close enough for their bumpers to be lovers, moving so uniformly it would appear to bystanders as though one towed the other. The passengers leaped when Granger leaned on the horn.

The surprise blast caused Roger to swerve before over-correcting. "Why doesn't he just pass?"

"Give the a-hole more room."

The street comprised a single wide lane for miles, forcing townies to navigate via gentleman agreements over who would move out of whose way. Roger steered as far to one side as possible. The Mustang pulled alongside them.

"What are you doing?" Joe yelled through the window.

"Inviting you to Thompson's field. All the cool kids are coming," Granger said through his cocky smile.

"No thanks, weirdo," Joe replied.

"Really? You should ask your friend. I believe he will wish to attend."

Granger motioned to his rear seat, where a large sack rested in repose. The fabric fluttered violently. Despite the vortex cascading through the open top vehicle, the contents proved substantial enough to remain in position. Granger reached back and pulled a drawstring. The burlap spilled down to reveal an unconscious woman. Drugged? The bag lady appeared in her teens, blonde with pigtails. Her exposed blouse whipped so hard it threatened to take flight.

"Maniac! Pull over!" Joe yelled.

"What is it?" Roger asked from the driver's seat, struggling to see.

"It's Denise."

"What about her?"

Before Joe could answer, Granger nudged the Chevy, which veered off-road and spun into donuts. Roger fought for control of the vehicle. Eventually the car came to a stop. The boys leaped out, coughing dust which filled the cab. Dozens of other cars passed at unsafe speeds. The procession proved to be the catalyst of the storm.

Headlights within the cloud cover flashed like lightning while engines roared like distant thunder. The artificial storm promised the worst of what real ones offered. Chaos. The vehicles faded in the distance. The quiet that descended on them felt less the result of a storm ending than that they now stood in its eye.

"He could have killed us," Roger said.

"Denise was in his car. Not willingly."

"What do you mean? There was something in the back, but I didn't see a passenger, I..."

"It's bad. She looked unconscious."

Roger leaped into the Chevy. Joe barely climbed in before Roger gave chase. The drive proved short as the convoy ahead of them had stopped. They slowed, driving past vehicles parked alongside Thompson's field.

The pasture comprised dozens of acres stretching from the base of a steep hill. The nutrient depleted soil was useless for farming, so it remained unoccupied. Locals made use of the lot, hosting barbecues, celebrations, or touch football games. A dense forest bordered the land on the furthest perimeter.

Roger U-turned midway along the queue and parked facing town. They exited and crept past cars.

A large percent of the town's population had gathered based on the number of parked vehicles. A gunning engine drew their attention, but not from any of the parked vehicles on the road. It sounded below. The buddies moved closer and spotted dozens of people congregated in the field. The identities of the individuals remained hidden in shadows.

Red embers burned in the center of a circle of bodies. A car sat parked near the fire with headlights off. Shadows bled together, obfuscating the scene, yet something stood out about the masses. Their clothing covered them from head to toe, which made little sense given the warm evening. A flame ignited, bursting high into the sky. A bonfire. The light revealed the true nature of the dress code. Everyone other than Granger wore dark hooded robes.

"Do you see Denise?" Roger rose from his covered position. He protested when Joe pulled him back. "What? Besides the fact she is down there somewhere, I owe him for what he did to my Chevy."

"We need to figure out what is happening first. We don't even know who is down there," Joe said.

They continued observing. Granger stood atop the roof of the car. The engine revved again beneath his feet as the teen spun while taking in those gathered around him. His arms extended out at his sides with fists closed. (Hiding something?) He addressed the eager crowd.

"Salt of the earth. That is what some call those born of towns such as this. Salt of the earth is an ancient phrase cribbed for a blasphemous book of lies. That tome prompted humanity to abandon the Timeless Ones to worship false gods of light. The ignorance of their actions delivered a twisted version of morality on humankind. They formed councils to mete out punishment within the ill-conceived societies. Whenever the collective flock deemed one to have strayed from community norms, they punished the individual by salting his land, ensuring crops would never grow again. Hence 'salt of the earth.' What delivered the wrath of the society at large? The simple act of embracing chaos. Take lust. Do you believe in punishment for partaking in gifts of flesh?"

The crowd roared disapproval, which blended into a strange murmuring chant. The circle tightened around the vehicle. All eyes on the speaker.

"To lust is the essence of humanity. Who does not wish to visit sin upon skin? All secretly desire the glorious dance of darkness that comes with celebrating carnal urges. Why should that bring on punishment? Celebrating skin through taste, touch, sweet torture, or instilling pain upon others is why the Timeless Ones birthed us into fleshy vessels! Those who dared partake of hedonism often found themselves judged by those secretly guilty of the same. Do not all men and women fornicate?"

The group collectively affirmed the statement. Meanwhile, moans of pleasure rose from the crowd. A sexual fervor took hold of the obscene congregation. The moaning blended with the chant.

"Your presence proves they do. Humanity is not born without a prior generation fucking them into existence! Yet those fornicators would deny you your right to do the same. They can do as they please while insisting you remain chaste! Worship anything other than their false Gods and one could find themselves at the mercy of a mob. With a mere accusation, judges destroyed a sovereign person's property. Salt their earth! Are those judging not hypocrites? Are they not the true sinners?"

Affirmative chants harmonized with his words. Granger continued circling. Whenever he turned toward the ridge, Joe and Roger acted on instinct and crouched further. Neither discussed it, but they sensed Granger's gaze fall directly upon them despite the distance. The clarity of the man's voice from afar further unsettled the pair.

Roger and Joe shared a nervous look while Granger's words boomed through the air as if speaking over their shoulders. The mysterious man spoke with a deep rumble absent from how they knew him to talk. Roger shook his head, attempting to dislodge the idea that he heard it all in his mind rather than in the distant pasture.

"The punished suffered the indignity of having land salted, destroying any ability to feed a ravenous soul. The action destroyed all future crops, leaving a cursed farm. For what? Pierce your body? Salt! Tattoo? Salt! Covet thy neighbor's hot slutty wife? Salt! Explore the glories of the same sex? Salt! Touch yourself or others when the mood strikes? Salt! This is what the masses think of you! They deem your wild rebellious nasty desires as worthy of this!"

Granger ceased rotating, leaving him facing the ridge. He opened his fists and spilled salt from both. The white crystals poured at a volume and velocity exceeding the size of his hands. The pour continued endlessly, like a clown trick with a ribbon in a mouth. Eventually it depleted, the last remnants carried away in the wind.

As he dispersed the last, the crowd went wild. The engine at Granger's feet roared back to life, revving as if planning to race. The rumble echoed across the pasture. Granger smiled. The chant built.

"Fear not. As is their way, the Timeless Ones intervened. The true keepers of the universe rewarded the wicked by spreading the cursed salt over the lands of the so-called righteous. Through this, deserts were born. It forced the masses living on previously fertile plains to fight for scraps of food. Self-proclaimed moral citizens soon committed vile acts for tiny bits of bread, performing atrocities of skin for mere crumbs. The Timeless Ones restored the natural order by replacing false ceremonies with something more worthy, the rise of chaos. Are not hearts of dignity designed to leak? Are not inhibitions built for crumbling? Your skin shells bind each of you with a self-consciousness born of hypocrisy. Your ritualistic and communal leaders raised to higher societal status fornicate more often than others while decrying the same. No longer. These are your bodies. Your choices. The Timeless Ones demand each of you to free the flesh!"

"Free the flesh, free the flesh, free the flesh!" The crowd chanted as a passionate fervor grew. Since they wore robes, their identities remained a mystery. If the individuals did not know one another well to start, they did as the show went on. The masses groped themselves and others during the ceremony in wanton displays of lust. The robes only hid so much, making it clear women fell into the fervor with a zeal equal to that of the men.

"Yes, free the flesh from the confines of the small-minded nature of this community. You break backs planting seeds to feed others. It is time to gorge yourselves, to embrace the gluttony of sin, to taste the pleasures of violated spirits and skin. It is time to salt this earth!"

"Free the flesh! Free the flesh! Free the flesh!" The crowd roared over an undercurrent of sexual gratification.

Roger and Joe watched in stunned silence as the masses danced in communion. Shapes writhed under some cloaks like snakes slithering en masse. Attendees groped themselves or others. Granger appeared to feed off the onset of depravity. His cadence rose to the occasion.

"Tiny towns grow a cancer which metastasizes into terminal boredom! Where were you before I arrived? In bed by nine every evening, only to rise before dawn. Why? To work the fields, bringing life to soil only for it to steal the same from you? Is that all you desire?" A rapturous no sounded. "I spent my time amongst you exposing the disease, and now I alone offer the cure. The treatment includes heavy doses of greed, lust, gluttony! Can any man or woman crave anything more?"

Joe looked from the crowd to the nearby vehicles. "I know many of these cars. These are all townies. How long have they been hanging with this freak?"

"It's all weird, but I just want to check that Denise is okay. If she is in a robe, then maybe she went willingly. She liked him, a lot. I can tell," Roger said, defeated.

Then Roger grabbed his ears as Granger's voice boomed, throbbing within his skull. The thunderous baritone synchronized with the pulse in Roger's temple. Chanting circled the air around him as if in theater surround sound, filling him with the idea that he should reveal himself, stand up, join the party. Why be any different? Maybe that was Denise having sex below, maybe she waited for him.

Roger rose, stepping into plain view of those below. Joe tried to wave him back, but Roger continued forward in a dead legged walk. Soon he stood atop the ridge.

"More greed, more lust, more gluttony! Live by this creed. Azlagoth demands it! The Timeless Ones feed on depravity. Violate others as you wish to be violated yourself! I ascended to this pathetic town to reveal truth, and to rid this realm of false gods. We are overdue to return the celestial to the Ancients. But more than anything, you lecherous townsfolk, I came to raise a little Hell. Gentlemen, start your engines!"

Granger leaped off the roof of the car, and the row of people widened their circle, revealing three additional cars facing out in a quad formation. Denise lay spread eagle on the grass in between the vehicles, her limbs tied to the bumpers!

No longer unconscious, Denise wailed in terror. She struggled against her bonds, pulling as the engines revved all around her. Four robed figures, the statures of which suggested female, stood alongside the cars with arms raised as if ready to start a street race. The dangling sleeves of their robes took the place of traditional white rags.

Denise's cries transitioned into a fearful whimper. She spotted Roger on the ridge and screamed his name. Granger nodded, and the women dropped their arms. The four cars drove off and Denise blurted a strange "ugh" before bursting into pieces. Roger yelled, reaching out toward his lost love. Too late to stop the horror. His outburst drew the attention of the crowd. The robed figures scrambled up the hill, dozens, all eager to confront a witness. Roger balled his fists, ready to take them all on, make them pay for what they did. Joe had other ideas. He dragged his friend to the car.

Joe jumped in, yelling for Roger to hurry. Roger stood frozen with his door open as he gazed out upon the impossible. Somehow Granger stood straight ahead, staring at him, his head bobbing above the oncoming crowd.

Stood would be the wrong word, Roger thought. The man remained the same distance away as moments earlier, leaving him in a valley. To exist in a sightline above the hill-climbing masses was unfeasible unless the teen was prone to float. It made no sense. Joe hit the horn, breaking the spell. Roger glanced to the car, then back. The classmate had vanished, if ever there at all. The pursuers, however, grew dangerously close. Roger jumped in and they sped away.

R oger woke to a scream. His own. Kate slipped out of her slumber as if shedding a jacket. She embraced her husband, who searched the room for an emotional anchor within the familiarity of a bedroom shared for decades. He finally focused on Kate—his North Star.

"The dream again?" Kate asked. "It's been years, I had hoped it was over."

"It will never be over," Roger said.

"Honey, we've gone over this. Denise died, yes, but in a car accident alongside Granger."

"You still don't believe me?"

"I understand someone close to you passed, and it scarred you. They buried her in a single piece. You and I weren't a couple yet, but I was at the funeral. No one in the field ever came forward."

"People knew the truth. Their guilt kept them from looking me in the eye. There are those who never talked to me again after that day."

"Tiny town, tinier grudges. I had a best friend before Rebecca, and she and I no longer speak. Things happen, honey."

"They forced me off the road, it damaged my car."

"Honey, I don't have all the answers. Except, yes, there was something about Granger that unnerved me. He appeared more foreign, stranger than my exchange boyfriend back then. Had I not been so crazy over Toby, I might have fallen into his orbit. Having said all that, I know of no one who showed any loyalty to Granger. No matter what occurred, he perished that day. It's over."

Except it wasn't. It never was. Roger smiled dutifully to appease his spouse while silently acknowledging there was more to the story. Something else happened that he never shared with her, only Joe. In moments of doubt, he thought he should tell his wife. He never did though, because he worried that she would not believe him. And on some dark days when doubt settled in, he wondered whether Kate was there that day, wearing a robe along with other friends and neighbors.

The couple held one another in silence until finally sleep reclaimed them both.

CHAPTER 10

J oe waited for Mitch's response. During the uncomfortable silence, Joe could not help but consider how loathe he was to discuss the subject. A strange phenomenon attached itself to the memory. Not long after the incident that changed their lives, Joe and Roger discovered that if one recounted the story to anyone, the other found themselves subject to nightmares. It happened without fail every time. The concept made no sense, but anecdotal evidence proved solid. They eventually swore one another to silence to minimize further traumatizing one another.

Joe read a news report once about nearly identical movies being released simultaneously. The reporter called it 'parallel thinking.' Joe adopted the term. If one suffered a nightmare, they phoned the other demanding answers. Why was the issue being raised again? Why talk about it now? What good could come from talking about it? Though Joe mostly believed in the strange tethering that entwined he and his best friend in a battle over who suffered the worst from the memories, as he grew older he wondered if their odd conclusion covered for something else. If they refused to talk because they believed it would hurt the other, then that locked them into silence. That meant never speaking to anyone, not even therapists. A convenient excuse for two men not known for showing vulnerabilities.

Whether the theory was sound or not, based on history, Joe felt guilty knowing Roger would now suffer fresh night terrors. His friend was likely already sleeping and had no reason to expect the violation of their pact. Joe came clean to a cop, one who had fallen strangely silent. He would worry about Roger later. Mitch's strange demeanor held his attention.

The cop chewed the skin on a finger. A tell that would destroy him in poker, Joe thought. If it were Jenny, he would slap her hand before prying into the source of her compulsion while trying to put her at ease. The man was not a child though, at least not his. The officer was a peer, one who could place Joe behind bars for the disappearance of his wife. Mitch chewed away then rose from his seat only to sit back down.

After finishing his skin sandwich, the man caressed the table like a drunk searching for steady land. Once he found a spot he liked, he pressed hard, which flexed his muscles. Probably a security blanket for one who lived in a gym. Joe finally shared details of his past with someone other than Rebecca. There was more information to the tale, but the rest only involved Roger. It was not Joe's story to tell. He swore an oath of silence to his best friend and stuck to it. Not that he needed more details. He already gave the cop plenty to ponder.

"I was there at the funerals. Plural," Mitch started.

"As was I. Correction. I attended one."

"You said your peace. My turn. One piece. As in single. Denise rested intact, as did Granger. How could anyone believe your story knowing those facts? There are pictures, for Christ's sake! Buried whole, both. My Dad had connections at the funeral home. Between you and me, no one else..."

Joe nodded, unsure of the direction of the conversation. Mitch looked around as if searching for witnesses. He leaned in closer, spoke lower.

"Denise was a looker. Occasionally I viewed tits at the parlor. I believe it thrilled funeral director Shelby to allow young ones like myself to catch a peek. The old man had passed by the time I became a cop, so I never got to interrogate the bastard. May he rot in peace. Point is, if I ever ranked my preferences for a bare boob show, Denise would have topped that list. Don't mention that to Roger."

"Christ, he's married, Mitch."

"Jealousy dies a slow death. You are friends is all, so I ask discretion. When my Pops gave me the okay to pay a visit to Ole Shelby, I was aching to see the girl. Shelby always wore the shits grin when I dragged my horny ass into his place of business. But something was different. The geezer greeted me white as a damn sheet and looked near as though his heart were about to go. I almost called my Pop to check on him, but worried it would diminish my chance of seeing our classmate butt-nekkid. I thought to myself, *hang in there, old man, I need two seconds of your establishment's time and then I'll see about getting you some aid.*"

"What happened?" Joe leaned forward, hungry for information. Excited that after so many years, someone might hold a piece to a puzzle that long haunted him.

"Son of a bitch told me to check on Granger."

"The hell?"

"Exactly. My interests defaulted to the female persuasion. I had zero interest in examining such a scoundrel on his way to the afterlife. I hemmed and hawed about my titular mission until Shelby rose with a fury. His face raced from pale to red, might quick. '*You ever hope to glimpse the cooch of that fine thing, you will first go in there and tell me what you see!*' Shelby yelled. I reluctantly agreed to his request and entered the room. I found the dead kid lying in repose under a sheet from the shoulders down."

Mitch fell silent. His head twitched unnaturally, as if the cop attempted a mental reboot after encountering whatever the human version of a hard drive error was. The officer shook it off and continued.

"Through the windshield, they said. Man flew through glass with Denise by his side. A twofer. Story went she was blowing him on a straightaway when they struck a tree. Yet, the bastard had not a scratch on his face. Why Shelby wished me to examine the kid, I could not understand. I only wanted to get back in his good graces for all future titty tours. Taking Shelby for a perv, I figured he expected me to check Granger's junk. It took little to convince me. Our classmate was a hit with the ladies, leaving me curious about all the fuss. Except as I neared the body, a sense of foreboding flooded me like none I ever felt before."

"The Dread."

Mitch nodded. "The same. Course I did not know the term yet. Once the Dread washed over me, I left without a below the waist peekaboo. That is when it happened."

"What happened?" Joe asked.

"I had my hand on the door ready to exit when I heard a rustle. I turned and damned if he wasn't sitting upright. I ran. When I glimpsed over my shoulder, his face appeared as if in a photo where the flash hits you just so, making them red eyes. They have apps that fix that stuff now. Wished I had an app back then. Shelby grabbed me on my way out, damn near scaring me as much as an active dead boy. '*How ancient is he*?' Shelby asked. Except in a way that felt more akin to a statement. Like he knew something and wanted confirmation."

"How ancient?"

"Yep. I ran from the crazy coot and burst into the next room which turns out held Denise, laid out nude with no covering. Pervert for sure, that guy. I put her corpse between us. The man rambled the same garbage continuously. Once I drew him away from the door, I bolted. He knew he lost me but kept yelling the same question while I fled."

"Jesus," Joe said.

At the mention, Mitch made the sign of the cross. "Talked to my Pops, and he promised to check it out. He never told me what he found. Clammed up whenever I asked about it. Then, well, you know how things turned out for my father. Doctors never expect him to un-vegetate. They say more officers fire a gun at the end of their career than during."

"I'm sorry," Joe said.

"The total mess has me open to believing something more is going on. But the officer in me attributes Granger's movement back then to nothing more than gasses releasing in the body. The red eyes merely a fluke of my youthful discomfort. As for my Pop closing the case involving crash victim lovebirds, what else could he do? She was in one solid piece, tits and all. I saw her myself. That leaves me unable to believe your story. At least as told. I believe you experienced trauma, which caused you to think you witnessed a tragedy. We could say the same for your daughter's version of events."

"There were two of us watching them quarter the poor woman. We had to escape a violent crowd."

"I don't want to go to the grave mulling over a case like my Pops. Others are looking to jail you. My partner being one. Folks here appear a bit off, different from when we were growing up. It's not my job to determine why. Opiates, I reckon. Ain't half the world aboard that train? I've already explained I can't come to your side of the table on the story. But I also understand it bothered my father enough that he sought a way out. It may not shake out as you stated, but for Pop's sake, I wish to help you. Thing is, I need more from you and more from your daughter if I am to fight the tide aimed at arresting you."

"It's late. Well past the girl's bedtimes. If I'm not under arrest, then I want to take them home."

Mitch nodded, gesturing to the door.

Tick, tick, tick. Jenny looked at the elderly woman who glared back over her bifocals. The lady's smile vacillated between that of a sweet old gal, or a cat who swallowed a bird whole. She gripped the needles so tightly it exposed almost every vein and bone under her papery skin. The possibility that someone of her advanced age might suffer arthritis fell in line with Vegas odds, yet the needles clacked together at a blurred pace.

"Tsk, tsk, tsk," Cora said, shaking her head, her mouth noises matching up with those of her needle. "Shame to waste such a fine snack. I hear guilt messes with the appetite. I'm nearing completion on this, what do you think?"

Jenny trembled upon noticing how much the blanket grew since she arrived at the station. Her mother used to knit, and it would take days to produce what Cora somehow did in less than an hour. Worse, the emerging black on grey color scheme looked familiar and frightening.

Cora noticed the girl's sudden interest and attempted to display the afghan, but her reach fell short. The image lost in the folds of the fabric appeared almost as a living thing, seeking to steal a glance at the child. What little Jenny could identify disturbed her. The height? Not much larger than a child. The eyes? Too big. The single exposed arm? It fell too low on the body. (And was that a claw?)

The desk clerk struggled with the fabric. As one portion of the image exposed itself, others fell away, showing the work in bits and pieces. Jenny assembled a mental puzzle of what she saw and trembled. The images sparked memories. Cora looked down at her handiwork, then back to the child.

"Looks like that guilt train is roaring into your station. Tell me what you saw that day. What took your Momma?"

Jenny pointed at the blanket. The folds suddenly revealed a single fiery eye (where did the colored yarn come from? Was that there before?) Cora's arms stretched, moving beyond what should have been possible, and the image grew clearer. Before Jenny could scream, the door burst open. Jenny raced into her father's embrace. He caressed her shoulder while scanning the tight space.

"Where's your sister?"

"The lady took her."

"What lady?" Joe asked.

"Officer Rand took the suspect in for questioning."

Joe turned on Mitch, gearing for a fight. "That your plan? You pretend to be on my side so you can sneak my daughter out and question her without my consent?"

Mitch lifted his arms to wave off the fight. "She's eighteen, ain't no consent needed. But yes, out of courtesy I would have asked if that was the plan. It wasn't. Nadine is out of line but you raise hands to me, you got genuine problems, that I promise you."

Joe pinched his nose to bring himself under control. Then he and Jenny followed Mitch down the hall while Cora continued to tick, tick, tick.

Cassie struggled to breathe. Nadine squeezed Cassie's windpipe and searched the girl's eyes. Once Cassie's face reached a certain shade, the officer finally let her go. The teen gasped for air.

"You're not into breath play. There's an excitement that flashes in those who appreciate the nuances and nastiness of it. You mostly looked ready to pee your pants. Give it experience, give it time, it'll be your thing. Call me a farmer. I just planted a seed."

"You're crazy." Cassie choked, surprised how weak her voice sounded.

The woman maintained her close contact, leaning in as if gearing up for a lap dance. "Are you a righty or lefty?"

"What?"

"Which hand do you... do things with?"

"Right." Cassie said, desperate to change the subject.

Nadine reached over Cassie and released that arm from the cuffs. Cassie made a fist. The officer noticed and nodded.

"You need to finish anything you start. Are you ready to take me on, darling? You might find I enjoy it rough." Cassie relaxed the fist. "I didn't think so. Now reach into my shirt. Grab anything you like."

The officer's shirt pocket showed the outline of a cellphone. The woman's breasts stood out so prominently they threatened to crack the screen. Cassie pulled it free. The cop appeared stimulated by the contact.

"Nine-one-one routes here, so don't bother. Unlock it." Cassie did so in a practiced motion. The officer took the phone and typed. "I'm sending a few texts from you to me about how much you enjoyed our time together. How it was good for you too. Call it my insurance policy. Now in return, I plan to send you some interesting correspondence in the coming days, which I believe will pique your curiosity. A girl like you is too big for this tiny burg. With the gifts you possess, you can get anything you desire."

"I don't think so, because you're still here."

Nadine grinned lasciviously. "Oh, how I want to taste that smart mouth. Before you get too mouthy, maybe check the last text you sent to law enforcement."

The officer handed back the device. Cassie's eyes widened, and her lip trembled. The screen read, 'My father killed my mother.'

T he door burst open. Nadine sat opposite Cassie, who remained seated, her cell phone lying in front of her, left hand still handcuffed. Joe appeared ready to leap across the table to get at the cop.

"Officer Rand, what is the meaning of this?" Mitch asked.

"I had some questions. It fell short of a confession, but just barely. Productive, you might say, gained solid insights. A little woman-talk capped off the conversation."

Mitch uncuffed Cassie, who rose and hugged her Dad.

"You okay?" he asked.

His oldest nodded in a daze. Joe gestured his daughters to exit. Nadine winked at Cassie on her way out the door. Joe turned on the officers.

"Now Joe…"

"Don't now Joe me. We're done. You plan on taking me in, do so. But anyone goes near them again, and badges won't mean a thing!"

Joe left the cops behind to quarrel while he went to check on his girls.

CHAPTER 11

"Where are my boots? Has anyone seen my boots?" Roger asked, spinning in a search party circle around the living room.

"In the bathroom where you left them, where you always leave them," Tyler said before handing them off.

Roger shook the hair on his boy's head. The youngster shrunk away in protest, as if to announce, *I'm not a kid.* Tyler wandered over to Jenny, who conversed with her dad. Cassie and Matt stood by eagerly awaiting the departure while Kate rushed around verbally checking things off a mental to do list. Joe remained immune to the chaos and focused on his youngest.

"Are you okay with me going out tonight?" Joe asked.

"No," the young girl replied.

All activity ceased. The adults shared a look, suggesting a change of plans was imminent. She crossed her arms and harrumphed.

"I want to go to the fair too."

Everyone returned to prep mode while Joe comforted his daughter. "Honey, you will go several times. But opening night is about securing deals and contracts and…"

"Okay, I'm bored already. When it's my turn, do I get deep fried Twinkies?"

"Twinkie. Singular, not plural. Maybe some cotton candy if you are extra special good tonight. You better be nice to your older sister because she will report back. That makes Cassie the keeper of the candy."

Jenny hugged her sibling. "I love you!"

Joe rose to engage his oldest with a munchkin newly attached to her hip. Cassie stepped toward her father, dragging a sister who refused to let go.

"How about you?" he asked.

"Love you Dad, but if you don't leave, then this relationship is over."

"I raise and feed you for eighteen years and then just like that it's over?"

"If you are really nice, I might allow you to help me pay for college."

Matt deflated upon hearing the 'C' word. College was a passport to escape farming. But it also meant distance. Matt and Cassie discussed the topic many times. They agreed on skepticism related to distance making anything fonder. Cassie was so busy she failed to notice Matt's onset of melancholy.

"I've got Dr. bell's number in case there is an emergency," Cassie said.

"Good. That's good, I hadn't thought of that. Good parenting on my part. Or is that TV wisdom?"

"If it helps you walk out the door, let's say it was all you."

Kate slipped Matt some cash. "Pizza money. Remember to tip, we live in the middle of nowhere, they come a long way."

"Don't be a jerk, got it. Thanks for the reminder, without it I default to A-h..." Matt started.

"Language," Roger scolded.

"A less respectful person. Geez, what did you think I was about to say?" Matt sneezed the word asshole which slid under his parent's radar.

The trio of adults bottlenecked at the front door, all eyes on the kids. Roger squinted in concern. "It's a lengthy drive, we will be back after midnight. Flashlights everywhere. I'd prefer you avoid candles. Maybe keep the power on? How about you don't play your games, huh?"

"Dad, we got this," Matt declared.

"You know I'm actually nervous. This feels like a date. Is this a date?" Roger turned to his wife.

She placed her arms around his neck and kissed him. "Yes, it is, you lucky man."

Tyler slapped his face. Jenny giggled at the display.

"Okay, now we demand you go. Take it outside, please. No one wants to see that," Matt said.

Roger and Kate walked through the doorway, holding hands. Joe gestured to the mobile love birds as he followed.

"Third wheel." He left, closing the door behind himself. Cassie parted the curtains and looked out the window.

A tarp covered the rear of the Whatley's vehicle. Roger peeked under, checking a load of regular size pumpkins while Kate tested some knots. Confirming the load was properly secured, they climbed in the truck, Kate taking the back. Joe's truck blocked theirs, so he jumped in and backed out, parking alongside the dirt road, partially on the front lawn.

The Whatley's backed out after and Joe jumped in shotgun. The father waved at his girls, who waved back. Then the truck honked and drove away. Matt pocketed the cash. Tyler frowned.

"Pizza?"

"Got it covered, don't worry. Come on Cassie, I want to show you something." Cassie followed him up the stairs.

Tyler called out. "Pizza. I want meat. All the meats!"

A door slammed above. Tyler groaned in annoyance before joining Jenny, who claimed the couch and remote. She turned the station to a cartoon.

Outside, the parents drove the dirt road fronting their farm. The cornfields whizzed by. They all instinctively looked back as the farmhouse receded in the distance. By the time they reached the end of the property line, the house vanished from view. No one in the truck noticed someone in the fields watching them depart.

CHAPTER 12

With the pickup truck fading from view, dust swirling in its wake, the watcher turned attention to the house in the distance. Stalks timbered and crunched underfoot as the unknown individual moved toward the house. Heavy breathing accompanied thunderous steps.

Tyler and Jenny laughed at a cartoon. Tyler occasionally glanced at his friend, happy to notice laughter lived on in the girl. Things had been so crazy lately; he was grateful for a respite. A loud knock on the door startled the pair. He attempted to appear blasé so as not to alarm her. The second round of pounding liquidated his feigned sense of coolness. Grabbing the remote, he hit mute.

"What was that?" Jenny asked.

"It's called the front door. Be quiet, maybe it will go away."

"I know what it is. I meant it was way too loud."

Wham! She was right. The room shook, and the two leaped to their feet. Tyler attempted to relay an aura of calm as he followed the noise. Jenny sought refuge behind the couch. Tyler opened the door, and his face went pale. He yelped and slammed it closed. The pounding began anew.

"Matt!" Tyler yelled.

"What is it?" Jenny asked.

"It's bad."

Matt and Cassie raced down the stairs. Matt yanked open the door, then yelled. "Hell to the yeah!"

Dozens of teens covered the front porch and lawn. The revelers marched through the living room, carrying cases of soda, beer, and snacks. Brad, handsome, black, entered first, followed closely by Heather, a sporty-looking woman.

The couple arrived together, both weighed down with party essentials. Other students diverted themselves around the pair bee-lining to the back of the house.

Despite Brad's massive size, which explained the thunderous knocking, the man struggled with his load. A mini keg dangled from one hand while a stack of pizzas rose high in the other. The weight differential kept him off balance. He eyed Tyler with annoyance.

"Thanks for slamming the door on me, Tyler," Brad said.

Brad spotted Cassie and kissed her on the cheek. Heather lit up at the sight of her friend. The women struggled to hug over cases of soda. Cassie lightened her friend's load by taking two and they headed toward the back, merging into the sea of bodies. They punctuated their conversation with bouts of laughter and several OMGs along the way.

Matt performed a meet and greet with everyone flowing through, all while working his way to his struggling buddy. Those rushing past appeared blissfully unaware of Brad's predicament. One jock pounded it out with Jenny over her cartoon choice. Brad looked relieved when Matt finally drew close. Then Tyler intercepted his brother.

"You are so roadkill when Mom and Dad find out."

"How would they? Besides, even if they did, that would make me grounded. If that happened, I would be stuck in the house all day, which would leave me nothing but time to plot and plan what to do about the individual who ratted me out."

Brad grimaced, turning color as he awaited rescue. The teen's overall look offered a study in contradictions. The way in which he carried himself along with how he interacted with those around him gave off a nerdy vibe while his muscular frame and size suggested jock or MMA enthusiast. The teen would be obligated to beat himself up regularly if he were to live up to both his surface stereotypes. Matt reached out to aid his friend until another guest filled Matt's hands with bags of snacks. Matt refocused on his brother, waiting for an answer.

"Fine, just keep them out of my room. Come on Jenny, I have a computer upstairs we can watch on," Tyler said.

The kids ascended the stairs. Matt departed, following the throngs of people. Tyler stopped on a step where he matched Brad's height.

"Here, let me help," Tyler said.

The boy grabbed a few pizza boxes, almost causing Brad to spill the remaining stack under the shifted weight. Tyler scanned the ingredient stickers and snatched one before placing the others back atop the pile. After climbing the stairs, Tyler leaned over the rail and offered some sage advice.

"You know you just could have set the keg down the entire time, right?" Tyler vanished down the hall.

Brad suddenly realized and dropped it. He grinned in relief, that expressive face suggesting life had vastly improved. He used both hands to get a handle on the pizzas, but as he examined the somewhat lighter load he frowned.

"He took the one with all the meats!"

Joe watched Kate in the rearview mirror as they drove to the fair. Kate stared out a window, focused, searching for something? This was the 'Other Kate' as Joe sometimes thought of her. Other Kate was the attractive woman not married to his best friend, who was not also one of his closest friends. Another time, another place sort of thing.

Kate's night at the fair ensemble comprised denim shorts with Timberland boots topped off with a madras plaid button down over a white V-neck tee. With her outer shirt fastened only halfway, the mirror provided Joe an unobstructed view of cleavage. The Other Kate only appeared when the kids were not around (the rarest of occurrences). He was thankful for the limited exposure. While his inappropriate desires were frustrating and ones he would never vocalize or act on, they still existed. Amongst the plethora of barnyard animals common in their county, Joe figured himself to be one of them.

In the mirror, Kate noticed his gaze and held it. Her acceptance of his lustful gaze failed to make things easier. She never once scolded or pushed back when

certain comments or looks danced right up to a line. He never sought such moments, but they happened occasionally, leaving him to wonder about how much
it bothered her, if at all. Perhaps because their love ran deep, all transgressions were
pre-forgiven. They were as comfortable as a married couple. That allowed them
to be knuckleheads in one another's company, Joe reckoned. Still, that stare, that
half-opened blouse combined with how long Rebecca had been absent, brought
Joe to an uncomfortable place.

"You, okay, Kate? Having bedroom troubles?" Joe said, diving right into the
should not have said it fray.

"Yes," Kate answered.

Roger swerved the truck while attempting to look back at his wife. He
course-corrected and refocused on the road. "Jesus, honey, he was just kidding.
At least I hope you were."

"Not that kind of bedroom problem. It's the dreams," she said.

Roger stiffened in his seat. "Honey, we agreed not to talk about this, especially..."

"Come on, Roger, save the protector bullshit for my kids. I talked with law
enforcement about it the other night, laid it all out."

"Explains my nightmare," Roger groused.

"Sorry that. Should have warned you. Add it to the circumstantial evidence file
on our strange juju, though." Joe shifted, changing his position so he could speak
to both at once. "Maybe we should not have fought so hard to fight the memories
of Denise's murder. What has that brought except more nightmares?"

Kate crossed her arms, leaning forward. "How do I put this? My resistance
to this, understand, comes not from jealousy. I won. We got married. All my
thoughts about Denise relate to my experiences. I went to her funeral. I cannot
discount your experience in the field. But they buried her whole. I saw her in the
casket."

"I did too, which only confirms something unnatural occurred. They interred
her in near perfect condition. Forget being quartered, which is what happened.
If you believe she perished in an accident, where was the bruising? How did she
appear so angelic?"

"It's what the funeral director does, honey. How many farmers went down to machinery over the year but were still presentable for the open casket. They have tricks. That is a different conversation. You and I have discussed this plenty, but not with Joe. I want to get these thoughts out with the two of you present. Forgetting the condition of the body, she died alongside another student."

"Roger and I never attended his funeral. Based on what we experienced, neither of us dared be round those mourners. Mitch claims he saw something odd in the morgue. The pastor at the church mentioned he never held a service for Granger. We have no proof he ever died," Joe said.

"There was a funeral. I attended it." Kate stiffened in her seat, awaiting a reaction. She got one.

"You never told me this." Roger turned to her, as the vehicle drifted.

"Road," Kate said, speaking in marriage shorthand.

Roger broke their gaze. His experience suggested if he stared her down, she would shut down. He refocused on the dark lane ahead, trying not to whistle a tune to signal feigned indifference. She continued.

"I, well, my date, the boy I was with? He was in with Granger's crowd. Hell, half the town worshipped the guy. They invited us to a party that night, but I wanted some alone time with Toby. We would have been there otherwise."

"Jesus, Kate," Roger said.

"The church thing was correct, something about they would not have him, or he would not have them. They held the service in the lodge hall. You always mention how many townsfolk were in the field. I have to say the attendance at his funeral versus hers was off the charts. To be there, you might have thought you were in line for a rock concert. Young and old. I got a weird vibe, so I left before it was over. What I know as the truth does not match up with what the two most important men in my life tell me."

"So how am I supposed to feel about that?" Roger asked.

"I guess the same way my daughter feels when no one believes her," Joe said.

"Except we're not scared kids," Roger said.

Though suddenly they were. Roger spotted it first in his mirror, followed by a rumble. An engine gunned, moving fast. Joe peered out the side window, noticing a black mustang gaining on them. Kate turned in her seat. The windows of the Ford remained too opaque to identify any occupants.

The car closed the gap, swerving into the opposite lane as if to pass. Roger searched for a trail of other vehicles, any hint of a local parade. He maintained speed but gripped the wheel, braced for impact as the Mustang pulled alongside them.

A tinted window rolled down, then a young female leaned out flashing her tits. Hoots and hollers echoed inside the vehicle. After a quick show of the goods, the woman slipped on her top and into the car. It honked, then sped off, leaving them in the dust.

They all leaned into their seats, breathing in relief. "I'll assume at least one of you looked away," Kate said.

"One of us did for sure. I'm proud of you, Joe."

Kate punched Roger. The couple noticed the pensive look on their friend's face. Joe tilted his head against the window as if deep in thought. Kate touched his shoulder. He appeared oblivious to the gesture. The man spoke into his own reflection.

"You know, there is another explanation for what we experienced all those years ago. One thing that might make sense. Maybe we're..." He sat up. "Crazy. Crazy for feeling so lonely! I'm crazy for trying, crazy for crying," Joe sang.

The trio broke into laughter, relieved after their scare. Ahead, the lights of Ferris wheels and other rides shimmered in the distance. They joined the queue of cars four deep, all lining up to park in a field.

Joe absorbed the enthusiastic energy of his friends even as he fell into a renewed melancholy. Any desires to be with 'Other Kate' dissipated. It was his destiny to remain alone. They were about to embark on their first county fair experience since his wife vanished. Joe put on a smile, hoping they would not spy the heartbreak hiding underneath.

CHAPTER 13

The party raged in Matt's backyard. The headlights of twin trucks parked at angles lit a grass dance floor. One blasted music alternating between country tunes and urban dance numbers. Mason jars filled with tea lights dangled from a clothesline, tied off at random intervals. Makeshift nightlights hung above coolers of drinks. Empty pizza box carnage covered the picnic table. Most of the action had moved to the dance floor. Minus adult supervision, coeds ground against one another freely. Cassie danced with Lisa, a blonde in a "Spiritual Gangster" tee. The pair moved in an energetic synch. Plenty of males watched.

"Thanks so much for coming out tonight, Lisa. I've missed you all," Cassie said.

"Sames. While you were absent, we voted you best boobs for the yearbook committee."

"Couldn't recognize my record number of field and track wins this season? Had to go with that, huh?"

"Hey, perfection is perfection. You lost a race or two, I doubt the twins ever lost anything."

Cassie laughed and twirled. A different time she might have protested, but she needed some fun. She spotted a big lug in the crowd and hugged him. "Chester!"

The stocky classmate oozed charm. He wore a trucker's cap over a high and tight haircut. Chet gently nudged Cassie away from the embrace and her variant of his name. "Chet, it's just Chet," he said.

"You'll always be my little Chester.," Cassie took off his cap and rubbed his fuzz, which failed to move.

Chet snatched the hat back and flipped it back on. "Be careful which friends you make at age six. They never let you grow up," he said to Lisa.

"Oh, you've grown all right. Going to grow plenty more tonight too, I guarantee it," Lisa leaped onto her boyfriend and grabbed his crotch.

"Sorry, Cassieliscious. There's a beer bong with my girlfriend's name on it." Chet hauled her away.

Lisa cried out playfully. "Help me, my boyfriend is an enabler!"

Cassie laughed. Then her phone chimed. She checked the text and reacted with disgust. The screen bore the image of Nadine's chest almost fully exposed in a fishnet top.

"Whoa! You been holding out on me? I had you pegged all wrong," Heather looked over Cassie's shoulder, eyes wide in appreciation.

Cassie fumbled with her phone, making it worse as the next pic revealed even more flesh. The progression suggested a strip tease in progress. Cassie stopped before swiping again.

Heather grabbed the phone. "I have many types. This is one. Who is she? How long have you two?"

"What? No. If I were gay, I would never hide it from you. I was so proud when you came out. This is something else."

Heather looked at it with fresh eyes. "Wait. Is this unsolicited?"

"You could say that."

"Yeah, well, I'm not interested anymore. That makes this as bad as a dick pic. Here, let me put her on blast."

Heather typed, but Cassie took the phone back and cleared the screen. "Please. Just leave it be."

"You sure? Because I've got you boo."

Cassie changed the subject. "Like Brad's got you?"

Heather followed Cassie's gaze. A group of letterman jacket jocks huddled in the distance. Brad was near them, not with them. Matt's friend stood with a group who looked like D&D enthusiasts. Brad toasted the women from afar. Heather blew him a kiss.

"He's my ride tonight and my shining night. Wish I liked guys sometimes because I'm head over heels for that dude."

"And you know he is crazy for you, even though he, uh, knows. You know?"

"If things don't work out for you and Matt, maybe you give him a shot?"

"A man who only has eyes for you. No, thank you. Wouldn't want to compete with that lifelong unrequited crush."

"Speaking of." Heather gestured to Matt in the distance and backed away. She pointed at Cassie. "For real. That woman gives you trouble let me know. I've got you."

"I love you, Heather."

"Smooches cuz." With that, Heather faded into the crowd.

A rap song gave way to a country ballad. Cassie positioned herself to face Matt. He extended a hand. She nodded. He crossed the yard and spun her once before pulling her intimately close, but with enough room to talk. They gazed into one another's eyes.

"Thank you," Cassie said.

"For what?"

"This. All this. I needed it, needed a break."

"Hey, I didn't do it for you."

"Oh, no?"

"No, I live for the danger of my parents coming home too early, discovering I've thrown a party and then punishing me by sending me more often to my room and working the farm more than I already do."

She attempted to smile but failed. "You're going away," she said.

He nodded. "First chance I get. Los Angeles, or New York."

"Why? What do those places offer?"

"Excitement, adventure."

"Living dangerously by throwing a party doesn't fill that void?"

Matt pulled his hand free, showed his fingers inches apart. "The tiniest of bits."

"You must answer better than that. You leave your family, you leave…" Cassie couldn't bring herself to finish the thought. She smiled melancholy, then pulled Matt back into dancing, both moving in synch. "There has to be a better reason."

"Hope. I can't explain it. Those places call to me. I don't even know what I want out of them, but deep down, they give me hope. Hey, you're going away to college too."

"Yeah, but plenty of local schools will offer me a track scholarship. It's an education, a chance to grow, to experience things, to meet different people. But I'm not seeking escape. I love it here, I love..."

Cassie stopped short again. The pair pressed their foreheads together and rocked their heads gently, as if shaking their heads no. They danced while speaking a whispered breath apart.

"We can't start the goodbyes this soon, we can't. I can't... I don't want to start. Can we not start this?" Matt asked.

Cassie's eyes filled with tears. "I think we're in trouble."

Matt looked at her quizzically, pushing a strand of her hair free from her wet cheek.

"My parents won't be home until late."

"Not that. We're in trouble because neither of us noticed the song changed at some point."

Matt looked around and sure enough, the rest of the group grooved to rap while Cassie and Matt continued their slow dance.

"See? Trouble, you and me. What are we going to do?"

"Well, for tonight we will not say goodbye. I'm okay with how we are right now. You?"

She wiped her tears, nodded, then leaned into his shoulder as the pair continued to waltz to Jay-Z.

CHAPTER 14

A food vendor handed Joe a large, breaded block on a stick. While Joe's eyes lit up from the smell, the calory dense treat elicited a groan from Kate. Lights and music emanated from every direction, accompanied by the constant murmur of congregated masses. Kate tugged tufts of cotton candy from a pink paper bouquet of sugar. She grimaced when Joe bit into his greasy concoction.

"You are disgusting," Kate said.

"Me? Or my food choice?"

"Careful, do you really want her answer?" Roger asked.

"Come on, deep fried Ring Dings. Who would not enjoy this amazingness?"

Kate raised her hand. They crossed the concession and games concourse which bled into the rides park. Their ultimate destination loomed further ahead. Tall permanent structures rose in the distance. The massive county owned buildings housed exhibits for swine and cattle, botanical gardens, (a favorite of Kate's), cooking demonstrations, and a harvest arena where the biggest produce would battle for ribbons and bragging rights. They felt Tyler would be a lock this year. The plan was to deliver his prize on the last date of entry to leapfrog to a win in dramatic fashion.

The group strolled while eating and reminiscing over a place they attended every year since childhood. Crisp fall air elicited memories of simpler times. County fairs represented a break from hard work. The nostalgia of the surroundings brought comfort to the troubled souls.

A roller coaster loomed high in the distance. Rider's screams followed the motion of the cars on the tracks. A Ferris wheel rose to the highest point in the park. The center of the ride displayed a light show as it spun languidly in the night. The bursts of color were not for those in the gondolas (they had their own majestic view) but for passersby.

Balloons popped in multiple booths. Kate spotted the game where contestants sprayed water into clown mouths. A father aimed at nothing in order to allow his young daughter to win. The child giggled infectiously. More latex exploded from the tips of tossed darts. That booth advertised oversized stuffed animals as prizes. Locals understood spotting Bigfoot was more likely than someone walking away with anything larger than a woven bamboo finger trap or plastic snake whistle.

The smell of pretzels, popcorn, and fried dough reached every corner of the fair. Gentle wafts of smoke shifted directions under an uncertain breeze. Roger bit again into his snack cake, despite the groans of his friends.

"Hey, you're eating about a month's worth of sugar, so pot kettle alert." Joe tossed the bite around in his mouth with his tongue, battling liquid lava heat.

"Sweet is something else. It's what this time of year is for. That thing in your hand is an abomination. Would you let your kids eat that?" Kate asked before devouring another tuft of cotton candy.

"No, but I also draw the line on them and whiskey. Doesn't mean I don't indulge."

A young couple stepped away from a nearby ring toss game booth. The man frowned at his prize of a single goldfish in a plastic bag. His date fought him when he tried to dump it in a wastebasket. A college aged group passed by causing a ruckus. One was the girl from the Mustang.

"Hey, I'm a fan of your work," Joe said.

A person pulled her away, grumbling about that being the reason she should not do that kind of thing. The woman winked at Joe as she slipped into the crowd.

"Mustang woman doesn't mind my eating habits."

"Yeah, well, maybe you two should get married." Roger winced as soon as the words slipped out.

Kate hit her husband. They traded a look, the eggshell one, and they just stepped on several dozen. Joe seemed oblivious, staring into the distance.

Roger apologized. "I'm sorry. I didn't mean that. Just a joke."

Joe suddenly realized his friends were still there. "Huh? Yeah, whatever. Think I will check this out." He walked away.

A calliope blasted its drunken sound as Joe passed the merry-go-round. He dumped his unfinished food into a trashcan. A painted sign rose high in the distance. Even in a sea of sights and sounds, one exhibition stood out. Large red letters splashed across the top of the building spelled 'Freakshow.'

The exhibit was a square two-story structure with railed porches lining the front of each level. Attendees entered through a door and never crossed the open space. Joe assumed the area was for talent to appear to drive ticket sales.

The color scheme itself was part of the show. Bright canary yellow covered most of the exterior, while blocks of equally garish colors dotted the facade. Each block advertised a 'freak' with the Lobster Boy featured prominently. A blank mask high on the front tilted in a manner to look down on the crowd. Several painted stripes suggested its surface was that of a mirror. Underneath it read, "The World's Ugliest Woman."

The mystery of the disguise captured Joe's attention, serving as the beacon which called to him. The furious activity of the concession stands faded in the distance, left behind with his confused friends. There was something about the place. He could not articulate what drew him to the location, only that he felt it promised answers.

A ticket booth rested on ground level below the exhibit. The boxed structure was no larger than a toll station, with the same mission in mind. Collect money. An enormous sculpture of a mustached sorcerer wearing a jewel encrusted turban glared down from above as if daring people to enter. A carny barker worked the crowd from inside. The young man sported piercings and tattoos in several creative places and wore an ill-fitted suit jacket over a rock band tee. He spoke in a 1940s radio voice.

"Step right up and look at the amazing Lobster Boy. Half boy, half crustacean. Check out the bearded lady, and the two-headed cow!" Despite the number of people crowding the exhibit, the carney appeared focused on Joe. "All that and more inside. See the world's ugliest woman with a face so terrifying she must always wear a veil."

Joe stared at the enormous mask, tilted as if it too sought him out. While the face remained hidden, the painting showcased a stunning figure in a red bikini, leaving little to the imagination. Joe assumed the impressive physique was for show, designed to draw in the rubes. Here he was, one of them. Except in his case, the mystery of the mask called to him, not the overabundance of tit.

Roger finally caught up. "You're not going in there, are you? You know these things are a scam."

Joe spotted Kate nearby, ditching the paper cone of her candy into a waste-bin. He handed over cash to the ticket taker before his friends could gang up and change his mind. "I need to. I'll catch up with you guys." He entered the exhibit.

The entrance led him up a set of stairs on one side of the building. Signing indicated the tour started on the upper level. Joe followed a young couple through the door. The pair wore twin cutoff denim shorts, hers with a square in the pocket from a cellphone. They collectively stopped short inside to allow their eyes to adjust to the sudden dimness.

Thick velvet curtains hung over entrances of half a dozen rooms lining the hallway. Along the furthest end of the hall, a red neon arrow pointed down a narrow staircase directing attendees to the rest of the show. Joe maintained a social distance behind the couple. The woman stopped and relayed her nervousness to her date. He flopped an arm over her shoulder and cupped a breast. The second base move prompted an excited laugh, so they moved forward, maintaining their flirty contact.

He waited a few seconds after they entered before doing the same. Blacklight flooded the nondescript room. The words "Lobster Boy" glowed bleach white on a far wall, matching the female's teeth. Her mouth hung open in a nervous grin upon spying the subject of the signage. The youth sat behind a roped stanchion atop a high bar stool. The boy appeared to be in his early teens and wore a 'Skillet' tee. On the surface, he looked normal enough, though his limbs and lower half remained hidden in a permanent twilight.

"You think people ever offer to eat lobster?" Mullet hair asked his date.

She bumped him with her body. "Ew, gross, he's a kid!"

Lobster Boy rose from the stool revealing a massive, misshapen leg, one which appeared red under the UV light. The way the foot fed into a wide club, it emulated a lobster tail. The girl screamed. Then the teen raised a hand. It looked like a claw and snapped open and closed. The couple ran. Lobster Boy clipped at the escaping teen's mullet.

Joe found himself alone with the carnie. The boy eyed the man sadly, as if encountering a kindred spirit before slinking silently to the stool. Once seated, the youth leaned away in a practiced manner until vanishing into shadows. Joe exited.

The curtain of the next room fluttered from someone entering, probably the couple. Joe did not follow them into the room labeled 'Snake Man.' Loud hissing inside prompted screams. Multiple voices, more than just the two kids inside.

Joe moved on. A family of four startled him when they exited a room speaking Spanish. The group dressed as if attending a more formal event than a fair. They shared an easy familial warmth as they bantered. The father apologized for the near collision while the youngest smiled at Joe.

"If you don't like spiders, I would NOT go in there," she said.

"Is it as scary as the Lobster Boy?" Joe asked.

"Way worse. My sister thought the crustacean kid was cute."

"I did not!" The older girl slapped the younger, forcing the mother to intercede.

"Girls, girls. Miha tu para!"

The father held the next curtain open. "Okay kids, bearded lady time, come on."

"She will look like Daddy," the youngest chimed.

The kids entered. The mother smiled at Joe as she passed. Joe watched them all enter the room as they fell back into excited Spanish. He thought of his own girls. The young couple from earlier bumped into him without even an 'excuse me' and followed the Latina family in. Further down, two female teens left one exhibit engaging in a playful battle of who could freak the other out the most.

Joe felt suddenly foolish. He wondered what came over him that prompted him to visit the Freakshow. They designed the place as a bonding experience for lovers, friends, or family. There was no reason to attend without his girls, which was an unlikely scenario. He would have to drag Cassie. The place was far from her jam, but boy would he have fun watching their reactions. Scare the snot out of both in an enjoyable manner. If Jenny was ready. The exhibition was strange, sure, but mostly a goof.

He pressed himself against the wall furthest from curtains to avoid running into anyone else. He proceeded forward, glancing at signs along the way to catalog what he was missing for his five dollars.

Midway down the stairs he interrupted a different couple making out, doing their best to contribute to the teen birth rate. Why not? Could never have enough new farmhands around these parts. Joe tried not to act fatherly, but he lingered long enough for them to split. A parent somewhere just thanked him, he thought.

The wannabe lovers had vanished by the time he reached the ground floor. Joe located the exit sign at the end of the hall, though its use required him to pass the balance of exhibits. A moo sounded in a tight repeat. He peaked through a curtain housing a two-headed cow. Its right side mooed, followed by its left. A family of three engaged the mammal. A parent in overalls frowned while a mother and son attempted to pet the animal.

"Great, another mouth to feed," the father griped.

Joe slipped out and beelined for the exit. He spotted the curtain announcing the world's ugliest woman. A miniature version of the mask hung over the drapes. Though the exhibit initially drew him in, he shrugged it off and leaned into the crash bar of the door.

"Joe," a voice whispered.

He squinted into the darkness and backtracked. The teen lovers reappeared near a distant corner, kissing and groping. The girl noticed him. She pushed her boyfriend while straightening her skirt.

"Creep," she said. The pair grabbed hands and entered the next exhibit.

"Touché," Joe replied. He turned away and heard another whisper.

"I'm here."

He looked back. Rebecca? The thump of bass from an outside ride boomed through the walls while screams and laughter rose from behind various curtains. The location should have made whispering impossible to hear, yet he did. Twice. At the least, it meant the whisperer had to be near. He stepped through the last curtain.

A crimson bulb dangled over a woman on a stool in the center of a small open space. A simple rope stanchion separated the talent from the audience. There was no false advertising related to her body. The woman's breasts were on full display under a skimpy black bikini (not red like the picture).

The colored bulb reflected off the silver mask. It started wide at the top but tapered toward the jaw line. The model sat with her legs crossed, enticingly lean and toned as if she worked out every moment away from the job. She tilted her head at him. Shoulder length hair jutted at odd angles from underneath the face covering. The locks appeared the same color as his wife's.

She rose, gripped the velvet rope, and leaned toward him. The movement showed cleavage to her solo audience member. The exposed flesh did not go unnoticed. Joe visually mapped the curves on display. In them he spotted the familiar, the body of someone he knew very well, one he had seen in far less clothing many times before.

"Rebecca?"

The woman lifted the mask. Her luxurious hair burst free and cascaded across her face, acting as a fresh veil. She flipped her head back and pulled away from the stanchion, the sexy move of a model on the shoot. The motion cleared the hair away. The woman met Joe's gaze and winked. Standing before him was none other than the one from the picture on the refrigerator.

"Rebecca!"

Joe advanced while Rebecca slipped the mask back on. He stepped over the rope and she backed away, slipping through a hidden rear door. He followed her into a tight walkway designed for employees to reach their workstations. She deftly navigated the familiar area.

Joe gave chase. "Rebecca, wait. Stop!"

She burst through an emergency exit. Joe caught the door before it latched, thrusting it open and leaping out. The cacophony of carnival sounds and bright lights gave him pause. Protests from a jostled crowd drew his attention. She fled in the near distance. Joe ran. The masked figure looked back, somehow able to see through the eyeless covering.

People parted as she ditched high heels to run faster. Joe caught up and grabbed her shoulders. She stumbled. Their combined momentum drove them to the ground, Joe atop her.

"Rebecca, stop. I just need to see you."

The only thing he saw was his own crazed reflection staring back. The mirror showed the wide eyes of a madman, yet he could not stop himself. She shook her head while pushing and kicking to free herself. A soft garbled whine mewled under the mask. Joe pulled it off.

The crowd gasped. The unmasking revealed a tragic visage. Her skull warped in odd directions, the skin swollen, bubbled, a boiling pot frozen in motion. Large knots of flesh jutted at random angles as if tumors held portions of her face hostage. One eyebrow rested several inches higher than the other. A knobbed approximation of a nose pulled tight against a bulbous portion of cartilage over one cheek. The limited air passing through her nasal passages hissed with every breath.

Her upper lip was a botched version of bee sting lips favored by reality show housewives. The top of her forehead rose high into misshapenness. A bald strip lined the center of her dome. Shoulder length hair hung from both sides in a reverse mohawk. She groaned through mutated vocal cords. Tears rolled down her one working eye. The second remained frozen in a permanent squint under a bloated brow long past crying. She struggled to fight him off.

Roger and the barker arrived at the same time. Roger pulled Joe off while the employee helped the woman up and handed her the mask. He urged her to return to her station. The lady walked a gauntlet of attendees who paved a path for her. She retrieved her shoes from the ground and placed the mask back on as she left. The carnie noticed the size of the assembled crowd.

"That's right, folks, see all this AND more, inside!"

Dozens followed him to purchase tickets while Roger and Kate tended to Joe.

"What we have here is a situation," the security guard said.

His name was Phil based on his name tag and that everyone in town knew everyone. The youth was eighteen and wore a mustache designed to appear more authoritative in the chance his oversized badge which looked like a skee ball prize did not do the trick.

"I swear I saw her," Joe reiterated to his friends, not so much the guard.

"We were there. She is who she is," Roger said.

"Poor thing. Joe, how could you?" Kate asked.

"Are you all listening to me? This is serious. This isn't a code yellow or code brown situation," Phil said. Roger eyed the teen inquisitively. Phil gestured with his hands while explaining. "Scared by the Freakshow or the Funhouse so they have an accident, you know they piss, or they... Code brown. That is a huge deal. We kick those people out, send in the cleanup crew. Man, I hated that job. But this? Wow, this is next level. Do you understand what the penalty is for something like this?"

Kate stood straight up to the teen, invading his private space. His hand instinctively went to the Taser at his waist.

"Phillip Reynolds, I've known you since you were a boy and I am friends with your Mother. Now if you plan to walk around with a certain thing in your pocket, at least hide the plastic of the baggie."

Kate reached behind him, retrieved a bag of weed from his person, and dangled it before him. Phil went red, trying to grab it. The mother to boys, she easily kept it from his reach.

"I confiscated that from somebody else. It is not mine."

"So, you have no problem if I flush it then, right? I'm sure it would give your mother peace of mind. What do they call this? Code green?"

"No, don't!" The guard noticed all eyes on him. "Fine. Everyone get out."

She dropped the goods into his shaking hands. The adults exited. Phil opened the bag, sniffed.

"Code green. I like that."

CHAPTER 15

The backyard had seen better days. All the partygoers had departed leaving a sea of waste in their wake. The debris field resembled the aftermath of the County Fair when it pulled up stakes. Carnies loved to slip away under cover of night. They understood folks would be too excited when they returned the following year for anyone to ever bother holding them accountable for the mess they left behind. Matt, Cassie, and Heather walked through their version with garbage bags already overflowing.

"Thanks for staying, Heather. Nice knowing who our true friends are," Cassie said.

"I love you, but I'm only here because my ride is MIA," Heather said.

"Well, thank you anyway. We're looking better, right? The 'rents will never guess what went on here." Matt postured, trying to remain calm.

"Keep telling yourself that. I read on the internet that getting busted by one's parents is a great bonding experience," Heather said.

"Really?"

"No, total making that up. You're screwed cowboy if we don't get these bags filled."

Tire tracks graced a section of the lawn, perfect enough to take prints for forensics. Matt went to work kicking the green over the exposed brown, desperately trying to bury the evidence. Mid-task, he bumped into his friend who cradled a beer and wobbled on unsteady feet.

"A little help here, buddy?"

"Sure, yeah. Wait, helping with what?" Brad asked.

"Cleanup in aisles five through a thousand, Einstein."

"Nah, I only came to say what I think of you and Cassie."

Matt scrunched his face and shook his head, trying to warn his classmate off. The girls stopped to listen.

"She and I are friends. Normal neighborly stuff. No need to elaborate. You're drunk, Brad. Absolutely zero reason to expand that thought process," Matt said.

"No, someone has to say it. I want you to know what I and all the students think. First off, that months long split? Douche move!" He pointed to Matt. "Douche move!" He pointed to Cassie. "Now that said. The two of you? Everyone can see it. That being the both of you…"

Brad danced a finger back and forth between the non-couple. Cassie blanched under the scrutiny. Brad settled on Matt, who rolled his eyes, waiting for another shoe to drop. Something else dropped all over the lawn when Brad hurled. The group collectively groaned, fighting their own gag reflexes.

"Does this mean he approves or disapproves of our friendship?" Cassie asked.

Matt smiled at her joke but felt the sting of the friend zone declaration despite his stating the same moments ago. In his case, it was for cover. He didn't really believe it. But what about her? Where did she stand? How did she feel? Disgusted based on the look on her face.

"I'll get the hose," Cassie said.

"No, no, this is not good. He can't be here when my parents return home, yet he is in no shape to drive. Help us out, Heather?"

"Sorry, no license. The ride thing I mentioned? He's it."

"Okay, maybe someone else is still around. Come on Brad, let's hurry."

Matt grabbed his friend and rushed through the backdoor of the house. They bumbled their way into the living room. Tyler and Jenny watched TV, paying no mind as Matt staggered in with his drunken load. Burdened with the weight, Matt leaned his drunk classmate against a wall. The motion proved too much for the youth, who slumped to the floor, moaning. Matt rushed the porch, yelling for a rescue only to spot taillights vanishing over the hill. He was too late. He returned to the foyer, frantic, grabbing his hair, willing his brain to find a solution. Tyler walked over.

Matt looked to him for a lifeline. "How am I going to explain this?"

"A passed-out Neanderthal in our house? I'm sure Mom and Dad will overlook that. Maybe they'll think he's a new piece of furniture."

"Coffee. Then he'll be okay by the time they get home."

"So even if he is, what about the two out cold in the guest room?"

"Shit!" Matt raced upstairs.

Tyler stepped to the front door and called over his shoulder to Jenny. "I need to go check on my Pumpkin, want to come?"

"Nope, all kinds of nope. Say hello to Cool Dude for me."

Tyler exited and grabbed a flashlight from the porch, turning it on as he crossed the yard. Where it met the road, he noticed fresh tire tracks with turf missing, dirt exposed. No way Matt could fix that in time. *Busted*, Tyler thought with glee. His brother wasn't entirely a goofball. They did lots of cool stuff together, but his brother also tortured Tyler every chance he got. Given Tyler's age, size, and lack of resources, he always felt any payback was inadequate. For once, he could witness Matt's torture at the hand of their parents without being labeled a rat. Matt did everything to himself.

The corn stalks stretched out as if to infinity under the glimmer of stars. Tyler swept his lamp across the field. Nothing. Why would there be? He made the trek multiple times since the evening with Jenny. In solidarity with his friend, he searched the area each night. He failed to spot anything on previous trips. But what about now?

On the surface everything looked normal, yet he felt an overwhelming nervousness creeping in. For no discernable reason, he wanted to hide. Tyler feared many things in life, such as darkness, horror movies, old men with excessive ear hair, and bullies to name a few. While each of those fears comprised portions of his psychological repertoire, most seldom came into play. And none of them explained his sudden burst of discomfort, except perhaps the dark. But he was relatively used to that by now. So, what was it?

Tyler struggled to understand the gnawing unease which made no sense. Circumstances recently reset his baseline to one of excitement during the walks. Every day closer to judgement day found him bouncing on his way to visit Cool Dude. Aware the limited time remaining before his orange friend would grow up and leave the nest (or the patch) changed the nature of the night. Since there would not be many more such visits, he abandoned primal fears and found excitement in the nightly journey. He came to enjoy the visits.

But not tonight.

Something was different. Tyler scanned the cornfield again, somehow recognizing it as the source of his discomfort. Rigid husked soldiers stood in formation, for what? Marching orders? Tasked to free themselves of soil to storm a castle? Or in this case, the barn? He fantasized about such scenarios many times.

A cursory exam of the troops revealed the lonely stalks to be an army of peace. They were a regiment prepared to feed the community with cobs for all. Still, danger nagged at him. Tyler picked up the pace. If life were a comic book, he would attribute the sensation to having developed 'Spidey' sense, except Tyler was neither superhero nor mutant. *What a horrible thing to have,* he thought. To always know harmful things were imminent. *No thank you, sir. You can keep all the web slinging and other awesomeness that comes with it. I prefer devastating news to whomp me upside the head unexpected like. No early warning system for this kid.*

He realized the only difference, besides a strange electricity in the crisp fall air, was the return of his female friend. This was her first time back since her meltdown over red eyes. Could her presence be influencing him? Tyler knew her well, kind of liked her as much as he appreciated any girl. Forgetting how he felt about her, what he knew of her is what raised his hackles. Jenny claimed to have seen something. There was one certainty about her. Jenny. Did. Not. Lie.

That meant a monster abducted her mother, and red eyes existed in the cornfield. Acknowledging those truths elicited a shiver which rippled along his spine and lifted hairs on his arms. He power walked toward his target, eager to disperse some nervous energy. Then it hit him. A feeling of being watched. He desperately wished to call his brother, but cells did not work once past the barn. Their property comprised one mass dead zone for electronic lifelines.

Tyler began a fake conversation, hoping to convince any within earshot that he traveled deep. If that mattered. Maybe the watcher preferred a buffet.

"Wonderful night for a stroll, wouldn't you say, Charles?"

Charles? Where did he come up with such a nerdy name? He felt foolish. He shivered again despite the flushed heat of embarrassment. Why? Why did he feel so scared? The dread gnawing at him finally formed words in his brain. *Move or die!* He ran for his prized gourd without looking back.

"No red eyes, no red eyes, no red eyes," Tyler chanted while running.

He arrived at the shack and turned the key for the transporter. The sudden brightness gave him the courage to look back. Nothing. He breathed deeply, then yanked the tarp off his large companion.

"You missed me having an epically dorky moment, Cool Dude. I don't know how you spend the night out here. It would freak me out. You are braver than I, oh orange one. I think we will give you a change of scenery this weekend, allow you to mingle with your own kind at the fair. I understand you live among your own out here, but I meant size wise. How do you feel about that? Maybe meet a Mrs. Pumpkin."

As in any scenario, his overweight friend appeared cool with it. Tyler caressed the surface. He told Jenny he did so to help it grow. That was not accurate. He performed daily inspections for cracking. Even a small one could cause the under-pressure fruit to burst while transporting it. If anything external ever helped it gain size, it was likely conversation.

"Want to hear a scary story Cool? In coffee shops all over America they are serving pumpkin spice lattes! Bum-bum-bah! I drink your milkshakes! That wouldn't make any sense to you. Maybe I should get you a TV. You'd love the Charlie Brown special,"

Tyler sniffed. Impossible. He detected the aroma of the very beverage he jokingly mentioned. It hung in the air so heavy, closing his eyes would be enough for him to believe he really was in a coffee shop. Then he felt it.

Warmth.

The orange flesh under his hand grew warm. Very. October nights were frigid, global warming or not. He turned electric heaters on at night for a reason, to keep frost at bay. The pumpkin fever made no sense. Unless...

Tyler spun, searching frantically for a fallen heat lamp. One had to have tipped and landed on his orange friend. Except he had not powered them up yet, only the headlights of the vehicle. A quick visual inventory revealed all remained in place.

The odor intensified. *Venti Pumpkin Spice Latte, no coffee, extra whip*, was Tyler's go to at the cafe in town. The drink gave off an unmistakable and pleasant odor. Heck, many of their backup candles at home were of the same scent. He knew of what he sniffed. There was only sweet pumpkin, no hints of espresso.

The presence of roasted beans might have explained away the mystery. A hayride could have crossed their property with passengers nursing lattes. There was zero chance that riders at such a late hour would have all ordered caffeine free beverages. Yet the smell matched his coffee free version exactly.

Until it did not.

The air soured. His Mom burned a pie or two in her day, and a pumpkin was one. He remembered such a time in their kitchen. While hurrying to cook for a school event, she raised the temperature higher than her norm and things went south from there. The memory stuck as it was the first time that he heard her curse. She had plenty since, but the first time stuck.

Tyler swept his hand over the surface only to pull away upon encountering a hot section of skin! Could there be a fire within? Everything external appeared normal. There were no signs of smoke.

Wham!

The ground shook. He staggered. Was that an earthquake? If so, it caused a sharp drop versus a rolling motion. A rhythmic clink sounded nearby. The string lights danced against their poles on the tow behind, proof the earth moved.

Splitch. The unusual sound drew his attention and tightened his guts. His family coined the term 'splitch' to explain the noise when carving a jack-o'-lantern. After some debate in their house (okay, only he and Matt debated) they made up the word to best represent the penetration of fleshy orange skin. Hearing it meant only one thing.

Shining his light in the directions of the splitch, he caught the tip of a sharp object glistening in the night. Like a call coming from inside the house, the cut was coming from inside his pumpkin! The tool appeared less a blade than a claw and was slick with fruit guts. It sliced down high on the surface. Once it completed a set length, the cutter retracted only to reappear elsewhere to form an angle off the first line.

The third splitch brought completion. A triangle! The internal carver created a matching one a short distance apart. Eyes! With a loud squish and plop, the wedges dislodged and dropped to the ground. A flash of something dark appeared briefly. Innards and seeds fell across the twin openings concealing the identity of the mystery cutter.

With a few quick jabs, a nose was born. Splitch! The curved tool receded only to reappear as it jutted out well below and to the side of the nasal cavity. Perfect position to begin a mouth. Tyler believed that to be the most important facial feature. Every year he weighted whether to create a goofy grin or a terrifying one (though one year he carved a large O and spread the innards out like it puked). The decision informed the overall look on any given year. Creating a wicked smile required sharp outer angles to start. Teeth came later. The hidden carver's new cuts suggested an evil grin was forthcoming.

Reality crumbled before his very eyes. Tyler long believed the powers that be would reveal the world's secrets to every youth who turned eighteen. *Sorry kid, Area 51 is a mystery, but when you hit that age eighteen mile marker, we'll finally loop you in on the scoop.* Now mysteries unraveled around him despite his being far shy of eighteen and less than eager to face this unknown world.

Historically he believed parents held children hostage behind a strategic veil put in place to keep kids from seeing the entire universe until they reached that specific age. Somehow, he scored an early ticket, a sneak peek at it all as that curtain ripped open. Not just part way, but all the way off. Rather than plinks of defeated shower rings, this reality drape tore away with a splitch, splitch, splitch.

The sharp pointer making quick work of his produce glistened under the moon, slick with sloppy innards. A smile no less enigmatic than Mona Lisa's took shape. Before it could complete its masterpiece, the claw sliced through the full length of the gourd's front. Guts spilled from its belly, followed by a garbled screech. The inhuman cry spouted from something with a mouthful of pumpkin sputum. Prior to that, a wounded rabbit was the worst sound Tyler ever experienced. He covered his ears to block the horrific wailing.

Innards poured out. Once the inside partially hollowed out, red eyes peered through the twin triangles! The furious wail ceased, replaced by a sloshing gurgle. Cool Dude rumbled.

Whoosh!

Pumpkin slime shot through the openings, bathing Tyler in slime, spraying with the force of an opened fire hydrant. The flow knocked him off his feet.

He screamed until tendrils of stringy pith flooded his throat. Then he choked, snorting out seeds lodged into sinuses, tearing chunks of slop free, gasping for air.

The thing within screeched anew. The horrific sound echoed in the newly hollow fruit, instilling more fear in the already terrified youth. With a thunderous pop, the top of the pumpkin exploded, and a series of tentacles shot into the sky, each one tipped with a curved claw. The fiery red of a monster's eyes cut through the dark.

Jenny did not lie!

And Cool Dude was cool no more. Flashes of something impossibly shaped writhed within. Dark feelers rippled in motion as the exposed creature leaped free of its orange cage.

Tyler scrambled off the ground into a run. The tip of a claw swiped at him, tearing cloth. Tyler glanced back as the shape (still indeterminate, though roughly the size of a bear) launched itself into the cornfield where it ran parallel to him concealed partially by the enormous stalks. The violent motion of the green indicated the beast's proximity.

The monster course corrected and angled toward the road. Tyler monitored its progress by watching the tips of the corn. The thing angled itself for an intercept. He came to a hard stop. The beast did not.

It shot across the roadway barely missing him on its way to the distant barn. The fluid shape with twisted angles made no sense. Darkness limited his view of the creature. It defied normal biological classification and moved too quickly for him to absorb its unnatural anatomy. Fast and big was the only thing clear.

The beast smashed through the side of the barn with explosive force. Tyler instinctively shielded himself despite remaining a safe distance away. The impact blew a massive hole in the structure. *Smart enough to carve a pumpkin but not intelligent enough to use a front door*, Tyler thought. His brain threatened to overload with too much input.

He ran, yelling a warning while assuming the effort would prove futile. If no one heard the barn explode, they were unlikely to hear his measly cries. The teen no longer worried for his own safety. He sprinted faster, desperate to warn those in the house.

CHAPTER 16

Rebecca danced in the rain. The beautiful woman gyrated with abandon, shimmying and shaking so suggestively it would not have surprised Joe to discover her moves instigated the showers. The downpour saturated her clothing all the way to her tight denim cutoffs (the one with the rip along her left ass cheek) which had no business fitting so well after two children. But boy did they, Joe thought. Rebecca paid no heed to the elements. She stood out amongst a sea of writhing bodies with her wet tee confirming an absence of a bra to the world. The firmness of her breasts even in motion highlighted an uncanny ability to defy age.

Their youngest, Jenny, recently turned six. That magic number provided them the courage to enjoy their first getaway since the birth of their youngest. They trusted Roger and Kate as babysitters. The couple's sons were close friends with his girls, leaving all involved happy with the arrangement. The children's ages matched up because the couples somehow did everything in synch. This half of the fantastic foursome finally earned a vacation.

They needed it. The couple argued frequently in recent months. Mostly about chance encounters with past lovers. Such encounters were unavoidable in a small town. It was not only the chance encounters of past lovers colliding that caused rows between the couple, but it was also their reactions to the situation. After years of marriage, compliments coming from someone other than a spouse often caused the recipient to fluster and act a fool. The other half of the couple could only stand by and nod through social niceties while their spouse flirted shamelessly.

Out of respect for all marriages involved, participants at least usually kept the reminiscing brief. A simple, "You look great," was enough to start the whole uncomfortable situation. Things went south from there. The simple sentence became fighting words once the reunion ended. The longer the time since the past loves broke up, the more they tended to fawn over one another in the present.

Hurt feelings drove the disputes, and the only time-tested way to end the situation was for the guilty party to declare the person meant nothing to them. There was truth to that. If Joe examined his past dalliances, he would cop to memorable sex, but beyond that, not much else. Endless drama reigned in his immature years, driven by youthful passions. Truthfully, at that age he longed for sex and stayed with those who offered it. Hell, he despised Norma Milton and still slept with her. He hated her then, hated her now. Hoo-boy was the sex unbelievable though.

That was the conundrum in a casket. Rebecca and Joe lived an honest life, which meant when one asked a question, the other answered, sometimes to the detriment of the questioner. They often put the common refrain of 'sharing is caring' to the test because of their candor. Such honesty resulted in Joe's knowledge about the size of Charlie Walker's package. He could have gone through his entire existence not knowing, yet he inquired about who her largest partner was. Obviously, both had their fun prior to meeting the other. Without question, Joe had his in the day, but it always led to lovers, never love.

Love began with Rebecca.

Now it threatened to die with her while he watched her dance in the rain, wondering if she was still his girl. Their chosen destination for the weekend was an annual music fest they frequented prior to having children. The event catered to current generations and in their absence, much had changed.

The size grew exponentially since they first attended. Only one band used to play at a time. Now DJ's played one end of the field while bands rocked the other. Multimedia displays filled the skyline in every direction. The festival promoted beer and pot as necessities. Stimulants once classified as underground became mainstream. Booths offered tasting flights of micro-brews and weed.

Joe imagined they stood out in the overwhelmingly college-aged crowd but hoped they did not appear too far out of the ballpark. He prided himself on his decent physical shape born of fieldwork and kid chasing. No gym required. He did not care if his general outward presentation proved acceptable to the hot young coeds who flooded the fields. He only wanted to ensure they did not stand out so they could blend in and enjoy themselves.

Rebecca, she of the good genes, (and jeans), somehow remained youthful. The woman was subjectively sexy and stunning. She worked as hard as him, which explained her fantastic shape. The mystery was how time avoided wearing down her surface as it did his. As the years grew after their nuptials, the couple occasionally discussed broadening their activities in the bedroom to include their best friends.

Joe found Kate attractive. Roger felt the same about Rebecca. The women often made their attraction to one another's mates known. While many fantasies came from such discussions, jealousy stopped them from acting on anything. Joe and Roger already shared a tragic secret, so sharing wives would be a bridge too far.

Where it came to flirting and fantasizing, they left jealousy behind regarding their best friends. If no lines were crossed, they allowed lines to blur into a different kind of foursome. One where fantasies ruled, and familiarity was allowed if the buck stopped somewhere. The love ran so deep that they banked any slipups or impure thoughts in an 'all is forgiven' account. Ironically, their arguments involved individuals who meant far less to either of them. Since those encounters happened locally, the couple vacationed out-of-town. They drove their truck towing a camper. Once at their destination, they parked in a remote spot within a makeshift tent city.

They overindulged the first evening at the festival, abandoning parental role modeling behavior for an evening of unadulterated fun. The booze and weed quickly caught up to the born-again lightweights. Even as bands played into the night, the couple stumbled back to their camper only to find their ability to open a door stunted.

Their efforts to do so were further hindered based on their positioning. Rebecca leaned face first against the trailer with Joe pressed against her as one hand wrestled the knob. Failing to gain entry, he turned his focus to more pressing needs. His and hers. Joe kissed her neck, eliciting moans. He shifted his hands from the original task and discovered it easier to enter something else. He lifted one of Rebecca's legs, thrusting against her while she turned her head to kiss passionately. She breathlessly asked him to fuck her there.

Joe yanked his shorts down. She arched her ass and urged him to take her. Then Joe noticed the visitors. Two men stood nearby, watching. One rubbed his crotch through his shorts while the other gawked in amazement. Joe whispered to her about the audience.

"I want it now. Let's do it right here," she said.

Joe glanced over his shoulder. The guy rubbing himself stepped forward and rubbed one of Rebecca's breasts through her top. She groaned at the unfamiliar touch. The individual, maybe twenty-one, smiled like he won the lottery. Joe sobered and stepped back. Rebecca immediately noticed his absence. She turned and pushed the stranger away, gently, to ensure his presence had not been entirely unwanted. Then she grabbed her husband and kissed him deeply, drawing him toward the door. They finally figured it out and fell through the threshold.

They groped and kissed in the opening as the stranger stood by awaiting round two. Rebecca winked at him and maneuvered herself and Joe until they could close the door. The two men high-fived one another and then went on their way. Stumbling themselves from a night of fun that almost got more fun.

Inside, Rebecca straddled Joe, and they raced one another toward climax. The round on the floor was only the first. They made love throughout the night, fueled by the aborted group scene and lingering effects of weed. Rebecca unleashed her vocal cords with no children to worry about. During one bout where Joe took her from behind, she pressed her face down into a pillow and moaned a mantra.

"I've been very bad," she groaned over and over.

While the sex was the best Joe ever experienced, her words haunted him in the light of morning when the afterglow of their wild coupling gave way to hangover pains. What did she mean by she had been bad? Also, how far would she have gone with the strange men had he left that option open? Was she disappointed they stopped? The two drank all the next day, dancing to bands neither ever heard of. Through it all, Joe stewed in the cancerous emotion of jealousy.

Her bedroom pronouncement performed its own version of the Watusi through his mind while they surfed in the crowd. When they danced, several young studs touched Rebecca in intimate places. They acted as though the contact was inadvertent. Joe tensed over every stolen touch or glance. Rebecca repeatedly asked him what was wrong. Rather than answer, he withdrew into himself, wrapping a blanket of insecurity so tight it choked off any sensible answer.

In his head he replied, *I'm afraid I will lose you.* But what he spoke each time was one word. "Nothing."

Their second night at the festival brought with it a massive fight. It sprung from a transgression that Joe forgot almost as quickly as it occurred. Whatever the spark, it lit a fire. The last thing Joe yelled before storming out was, "Maybe you should hookup with those college studs!"

"Maybe I will," she replied.

Sleeping bag in hand, he kicked open the door which bounced closed on his face, removing any modicum of dignity he might have hoped to abscond with. That night he slept on the ground amidst the sea of tents. The makeshift abodes surrounding him supplied a festive soundtrack where lovers laughed and enjoyed one another's flesh. Overheard snippets of conversations and moaning from groups larger than two suggested many couples took strangers up on their offers, unlike he and Rebecca at the trailer.

Any downside to such couplings fell off his radar that night. To a person, everyone but him seemed to enjoy themselves (well minus the one man somewhere in the distance who kept rushing from his tent and puking into a bucket.) Despite his age, the cries of lovers still excited him, leaving in a frustrating position considering his butt hurt state of mind. He did his best to focus on puke guy until eventually he succumbed to sleep.

Rain woke him. What started as a sprinkle quickly gave way to a downpour. The sun hung high in the sky, albeit behind cloud cover. The lateness of the hour shocked Joe. It stunned him to discover how long he slept out in the open, especially when crowds must have trampled around him on their way back to the event. He had not woken past noon since college. On the farm, he traditionally rose at four AM.

He thought of what to say to Rebecca while returning to the trailer. He failed to come up with anything noteworthy, though it proved moot. Rebecca was not there. A cursory search produced no note. He returned to the mud-soaked grounds on the last day of the festival. The crowds appeared larger than ever. Celebrating a last hurrah. After an hour of wandering, he finally spotted her. Or them.

Rebecca danced alongside a young couple he never met. The girl wore a two-tone bikini top, one color for each enormous breast. The disparity in color scheme between the two somehow exaggerated each individual boob as if by design. A tall, lean male without a shirt, a keeper of six-pack abs, ground on one side of Rebecca, the woman on the other. He wondered when the trio formed. Had she spent the night alone?

Joe approached. Rebecca kept dancing even as he closed in on her. She subtly monitored his approach. The two women ground together. It should have excited Joe, but only saddened him. Joe beelined for his wife. She finally noticed him. The stranger appeared upset at his presence.

"Rebecca." Joe stood in the rain as she continued to dance inches from him. "I'm sorry."

The younger female traded a sister security check look. Rebecca nodded. The woman returned to her own guy. The stranger's connection to Rebecca suggested there had at least been a conversation about Joe. Whether it occurred in the field or back in the trailer during a group sex romp played out in Joe's head. He tried his best to ignore the demons sitting atop both his shoulders, whispering into each ear how Rebecca was unfaithful.

Rebecca matched his gaze with a sadness that tugged at his chest. They stared at one another until Joe couldn't hear the music anymore. His heart broke right where he stood, as he felt overcome with the certainty that he had lost her.

"Are you with them?" Joe asked.

"I could be."

"He's a good-looking guy. Are you attracted to him?"

"Very much. More so to her. Sarah is her name."

"So, you could be with her."

"I could, yes. She wants to be. You love Kate that way. I see how you look at her. You could be with her."

"Rebecca, I..."

"No, tell me you don't lust for Kate."

"Fine. I do. Sometimes. We've talked about this."

"My point is you could be with her." Rebecca pointed to another coed dancing nearby. "That woman over there. I know your type. I bet you could be with her."

Joe glanced over. She was right about his type.

"I could be with those two anonymous men at the trailer last night."

"Did you want to?"

She stared at him for some time before answering. "Yes." Joe shook his head, devastated. She grabbed his shoulders. "At that moment. I don't think about them now. When you talk about sex, you always call it 'be with.' It's called fucking, Joe. We can fuck others, but who I want to be with..." She made air quotes with her fingers.

"Who do you want to be with?" Joe asked, repeating the finger quotes.

It was her turn. Her heart appeared to break. "Kids, Joe. We have kids. Jesus, can you believe Cassie is twelve? She will be in high school before you know it. Sweet Jenny is six. They are our children. I had them with you. Not Roger, not the guys at the camper, not Sarah."

"I don't think that's possible," Joe said, searching for levity as a lifeline to bring them back at least partially unscathed. It failed. She shoved him.

"Don't do that! Don't joke this away. You always do that. I can have them. I can have those guys over there, but you don't get it. Our kids, our children. We have children. Our kids, they need their Father. They need you, Joe, don't you understand that? They need you. Our kids need you. Our kids, they need you, they need you... I need you. I need you, Joe, I need you."

Joe pulled her into a kiss. They groped through a mix of raindrops and tears, neither willing to let the other go. They kissed less with passion than need. Once they finally came up for air, they locked fingers and stood a whisper's breath apart.

"So, we're in this together, forever. This adventure of life. It is the two of us?" Joe asked.

"Always," she said, gripping him tighter.

Joe turned and crouched. She leaped onto him and he piggybacked them through the mud to their campsite. The couple climbed into the truck and drove home to spend a lifetime together.

The memory faded as Joe bounced awake. He had demanded the rear seat on ride back from the fair so he could be alone with his thoughts. His companion's concern over his inexplicable behavior caused him to feign sleep, which quickly turned real. A bump in the road stirred him. Upon opening his eyes, he glimpsed the rearview mirror and saw Rebecca seated next to him.

He looked to his side only to confirm that which he already knew. She was not there. Yet as he woke further, he heard a whisper, one likely the fragment of a quickly fading dream. The soft voice repeated words he had not heard since a field in the rain long ago.

"Joe, the kids need you," the voice said.

He leaned into the front seat.

"We have to hurry!"

CHAPTER 17

Tyler burst into the house, out of breath and out of his mind. Jenny laughed at cartoons as if the world still tilted on a normal axis despite knowing better given her recent brushes with the unknown. Tyler scanned his surroundings frantically, searching. For what? The barn monster? Friends of the barn monster? His excited demeanor initially rang no alarm bells at first for his couch surfing friend. His shuffling around without speaking finally caused the girl to take note. Tyler was nothing if not a babbler, so his utter silence signaled something was wrong.

Jenny rose from the seat and turned off the TV. She looked at him expectantly. He nodded an affirmation. He gripped the banister and screamed his brother's name. Cassie and Matt appeared on the second-floor balcony. Matt spotted his sopping wet brother, covered in something. Slime? Matt took the stairs two at a time. Cassie followed and instinctively corralled her sister.

"What is going on?" Matt asked.

"Jenny was right. There is a monster."

"Told you. I told everyone," Jenny said.

"There are no monsters, doofus," Matt grumbled.

"Are you suggesting I routinely sneeze vast quantities of orange snot?"

Matt placed a hand to his chin, thinking. Tyler rolled his eyes and gestured toward the front door. When his brother failed to pick up what he was dropping, Tyler exited in a huff. Matt begrudgingly followed in full scolding mode.

"You're pissed that I had my friends over. I get it. But I don't have time for whatever con you are running. Mom and Dad will be home soon. I still have unconscious people in the house, and... Oh crap! Are those tire tracks?" He rushed over to twin lines of damaged turf.

"There's more near the end of the driveway. That doesn't matter. Do you believe I did this to my proudest accomplishment?"

Matt scrutinized his brother. "That's your prize pumpkin's guts?"

"Prize? Not anymore. Cool Dude is officially out of the running." Tyler neared the barn.

"It has to be something else. Monsters do not exist," Matt said.

"Yeah, well, something that does not exist did redecorated."

Matt gazed at the massive hole in the building's side. He clenched his fists. "I'm going to kill my friends. What were they thinking? How can I explain this to Mom and Dad?"

"They don't have this much imagination, it can't be them. All offense intended."

Matt walked through the opening and gestured for Tyler to light up a workbench which ran along one side of the barn. He retrieved an electric lantern and twisted the knob to full intensity. The two scoured the space, each checking different corners, spotting nothing out of the ordinary. Matt turned his ire back on the nearest target.

"Seriously Tyler, I don't have time for this."

"It was in here. You truly believe a section of wall walked away on its own?"

"No. I think my butt munch so-called buddies figured out a way to break something I can't fix by midnight. As collateral damage, they jacked your pumpkin too. I am sorry. It sucks and isn't fair. When I see them..."

Hay fluttered down from a loft. They lit up the overhead space, revealing only stacked hay bales. A rickety wooden ladder leaned against the railing above. Matt clenched the handle of the lamp in his teeth, then climbed. He ducked under the rail and swept the lantern across the length of the storage area.

Everything appeared normal and mostly in the open. One corner housed bundles of hay stacked higher than the rest. Matt approached but could not see over or behind it without moving adjacent bales that blocked his path. Unwilling to put in the work, he drop-kicked the tall stack. It wavered, then stilled. Nothing revealed itself.

He struck harder. The stacks rocked, then settled. Matt leaped in fright when his brother shouted for him to put effort into it. The actual verbiage included a version of growing some balls. An unsettling feeling poured over Matt, but he refused to show fear. He responded to the taunt by body slamming the pile.

The stacks tumbled. There was nothing there, not even a barn rat. Nerves gave way to frustration. Matt checked his cell. Almost midnight! Had his brother played him? Made him waste time he could have spent fixing damage? He cursed himself for being so gullible. He stepped on the first wrung and lifted the lantern handle to his teeth. Before biting down, he lashed out in frustration.

"Told you, jerk wad, there is nothing here. When I get down there, I am going to…"

Something cut off Matt's words. A tentacle shot from the rafters and wrapped around his throat! The red, slick appendage ran thick with veins like a thick umbilical cord. Matt inadvertently kicked the ladder away and fell until hanging! His hands shot to his throat, which launched the lantern into the air. It landed on the edge of the loft, illuminating the horrific scene.

The source of the organic noose remained hidden in shadows. Matt kicked furiously, seeking elusive, solid ground. His face ran a gamut of colors before settling on a deep purple. His eyes bulged. Matt saw sparks of white. He understood that meant imminent unconsciousness.

Abandoning the battle at his throat, he reached out for his brother. His eyes widened in shock when Tyler ran away. One of Matt's legs went slack, while the remaining one continued fighting the good fight, kicking at nothing. One of his arms drooped, useless. The world faded.

Thunk!

A saw blade barely missed his face and struck a wooden slab on the loft. Matt eyed enough to identify the metal object that almost ended his torture via beheading. He nodded frantically at his brother.

Tyler dropped his flashlight and double fisted blades. He threw both forcefully into a dark corner. Dull wet thuds announced twin bulls-eyes. A whiny pitch sounding through vocal cords of something non-native to the area, or perhaps Earth. The tentacle retracted, dropping its prize.

Matt fell to the barn floor, unable to gasp in pain at the landing as he had no voice or breath. He struggled for air and pointed toward the workbench. Tyler lit it up again. A large footlocker rested underneath the workstation. Matt found his feet and opened the makeshift toolbox, yanking items out. He tossed a first aid kit, small gardening spades, and several flashlights. Matt lifted a machete and another flashlight.

They looked back to the last known location of the tentacled abomination. Two glowing red eyes glared at them. Matt tested the weight of the blade in his hand. Grabbed his throat as if considering vengeance.

"So, what do we do?" Tyler asked.

"This is the part where we run."

The boys sprinted through the open hole. Matt kept himself between the barn and his brother the entire time. They reached the house and burst through the door. They slammed it shut and fastened the deadbolt. Matt added his body weight against it for good measure while Tyler vanished down the hall. Cassie and Jenny looked on.

Jenny noted the machete. "Are we going to carve pumpkins?"

"What kind of crazy pumpkins do you carve?" Tyler asked upon his return. His face and hands were clean. He wiped himself down with a towel.

Cassie eyed the blade, then met Matt's gaze. She nodded discreetly toward her sister before speaking in a measured tone. "What is happening?"

"We are experiencing the proof that Jenny is not crazy," Matt said, failing to be discreet.

"BIG proof," Tyler chimed in.

"Huge," Matt agreed.

"They are out there?" Jenny asked.

"We know about one. You're saying plural? Wonderful! Could use some muscle. Where is Brad?" Matt asked.

"Still passed out. Lisa and Chet too," Heather said from atop the stairs.

"Roust them. All of you upstairs. Now!"

"You are kind of freaking us out," Cassie said.

"Join the club." The front door shook, the knob rattled as something struck the other side. Matt leaned into the thundering slab, a bulwark against inevitability. "Go now!"

Cassie grabbed the children and raced upstairs. Heather waved them on from above. The pounding grew loud enough to drown out their footsteps. Once everyone crested the stairs, Matt made a stand. He raised the blade over his head.

"Yippee ki yay..." he yanked the door open. "Mom?"

His parents instinctively retreated from the raised machete. Roger recovered and grabbed the weapon. "What the hell is going on?"

"Mom, Dad! While you attended the fair, I threw a major party. It was epic. It could have been a hot club in L.A. kind of thing. My generation will talk about it forever, or at least until next Tuesday. I'd like to think for eternity. It raged."

"Matt, focus! I can tell there is a major 'but' coming," his Mother said.

"Sorry, nervous. There is an actual monster out in the barn, and it tried to kill us."

Joe burst past the others deeper into the foyer. "I knew something was wrong, Rebecca warned me. Where are the girls?"

Matt waved him on and ascended the stairs. Joe followed. Matt stopped midway along the staircase to yell. "You guys, it's all clear!"

Cassie stepped into the hallway. Joe breathed in relief upon spotting his daughter. The relief proved short-lived. The house rocked violently. Everyone reached out to grab something as the world churned below their feet.

"Dad? What was that?" Cassie asked.

With a thunderous rumble, everything shook harder. A sharp jolt segued to wild rocking. Roger yelled for everyone to get down. Joe and Matt found themselves trapped on the no-man's-land of the stairwell. The stairs danced like a roped bridge in the wind. They leaned into the wall as the risers below their feet bucked wildly.

Parts of the ceiling broke away in a thunderous crack. Chunks of material rained down. Lisa and Chet emerged from an upstairs bedroom, sobered by an adrenaline surge. Something under the staircase cracked like a gunshot, and it tilted to one side, building momentum. Matt leaped and caught the ledge of the hallway by his fingertips. Chet and Cassie pulled him up. He rolled onto his back and gave them a thumbs up.

Joe rode the tipping staircase like a surfer, leaping before it smashed across the floor into the living room. Roger and Kate dodged the falling structure. The shaking continued, growing by the minute. Matt stopped himself short of tumbling over the ledge. Heather shielded the children near the end of the hall. The youngsters screamed in unison as the home announced a goodbye to structural integrity. Pops of cement crumbling, wood snapping, and metal buckling roared in waves. The second floor tilted as if seeking to toss everyone into the wreckage below.

Matt grabbed Cassie and pushed her through an open bedroom door, corralling Lisa and Chet on the way. Heather followed suit with the kids, shoving them into a different entryway.

Chunks of ceiling rained down in a house ready to crumble. Furniture glided around the living room. Pictures flew off a wall that cracked from the top to bottom. A section of drywall exploded in a blast of gypsum. Roger threw himself atop Kate.

Then the world went black.

Outside, a barn rat discovered a piece of pizza in the garbage. It dragged it along like a certain New York cousin until the rumbling ground caused it to halt. The vermin watched with some curiosity as the large farmhouse sparked electricity from collapsing power fixtures. With a loud blast, the house shifted, dropping several feet. It stopped momentarily before descending at a slow pace.

The groaning of defeated man-made materials accompanied the house as it sank into the ground until vanishing from sight. A gaping hole took the place of the spot where the family once lived. Once the rumbling ceased, the rat returned to its bounty only to squeal as a viscous tentacle lashed out. It lifted the creature and its pepperoni prize into a drooling mouth full of fangs.

The rat's cries gave way to the sound of crunching bones, then everything fell silent. Another night in the country.

CHAPTER 18

Young Roger pulled into the driveway of Denise's house. Keeping a car dirt free in farm country was a chore ignored by most, but he wanted to impress, so washed and waxed his vehicle until it sparkled in the afternoon sun. He grabbed a chamois cloth from the glove compartment, then stepped out to give it a final once over. Buffing out a couple of spots, he then tossed the rag aside. The only thing more spit shined than the Chevy was his hair. He checked it in the windshield while gathering his courage.

Denise was a stunning beauty with an infectious laugh. The two knew each other since childhood, but were only friends. Innocent friendships of youth often changed as the kids matured. By their teens, locals looked at one another differently. Roger first noticed her at age sixteen. She was a stunner and grew more so with every month that followed. At seventeen going on eighteen, the stars appeared to have aligned for the two of them. Prior to Denise, Roger long had eyes for Kate, a beauty and brains combo in his chemistry class, but she dated a foreign exchange student. Heck, her foreigner intrigued half the women in the school up to and including some teachers. He tapped out quickly on those prospects.

A handful of townies moved away over the years, never heard from again. Since those who ventured beyond the borders never returned, it left a void of information regarding life in the outside world. The exchange student, Toby, filled that gap by sharing tales of adventures in foreign lands. With a drinking age of sixteen where he was from, he had impressive stories about drunken antics. Toby was a fun dude for an outsider. The town embraced him.

Then there was the other stranger. Emphasis on strange. The newcomer named Granger arrived with a muddled back story about his origins. With no hard facts, many theorized the youth belonged in the witness protection program. Roger paid the stories no mind because he did not care to learn more about the new kid. He only wanted to know where he stood with Denise. Since Granger's arrival, Denise frequently stole glances at the man. She appeared infatuated.

Granger was eighteen (leaving him too old for Denise, Roger constantly reminded her) and over six feet tall. He was lean, yet rugged, with taut muscles screaming of blessed genetics. His hands lacked the telltale callouses signaling hard work. He wore his raven hair mopped at the top like the Beatles at their height. His eyes were gray, but under certain light almost appeared black. Granger's smile stretched wider than his friend Joe's.

When Granger smiled, his pupils shifted strangely. It gave the appearance the man knew a secret of some sort. His teeth were always dentist visit pearl white. Sadly, most women fawned over the student. Oddly, most guys in school acted okay around him, as if he posed no threat to relationships. Roger felt certain Granger's presence threatened his standing with Denise.

Roger understood what many did not. The visitor was not what he seemed. Those who focused on Granger's charms were blind to a core of depravity under the surface. Roger learned the lesson well one day in the school gym.

"I'd love to take a turn on those tits," Granger said.

"Excuse me?" Roger asked.

The women's basketball team practiced on the court. Roger stood on the sidelines waiting for Denise to finish practice. When he arrived, Granger already stood waiting and watching from the sidelines. Granger fixated on Denise. She ran the court sweaty and in the zone. A physical player. Granger watched the girl while engaging in conversation.

"Doesn't take a blind guy to see how you look at her. You get anywhere with her yet?"

Roger fumed. His face blanched. He was angry at Granger for objectifying his love interest. But it also embarrassed him they had not been physical. There was no way for Granger to know that, but with that shift of pupils, Roger felt as though the student knew exactly that, and many other things.

"Don't talk about her like that." Roger faced the new kid, but Granger continued to watch the court.

"See how her tee-shirt clings? Sweat gathers near her breasts. One cannot look away."

"Yeah, well, you better."

"Ah, the imminent promise of violence. I do so love my Podunk threats."

"What does Podunk mean?"

Granger smiled that knowing smile. As if sensing, Denise glanced over. Granger winked, and she stumbled, losing possession of the ball. It took her a moment to notice Roger. She eyed him as if an afterthought, before shaking her head and emerging from a fugue. She blanched red in embarrassment before waving awkwardly at him. Roger returned the wave, but she was already back in the game.

"I can ensure she hooks up with you."

"You can? No thanks. It's called free will, buddy," Roger said.

"Please. Free will is a constructed concept designed to designate a will without a purpose. Deep down people long for someone to push them, nudge them toward..."

"What?"

"Behavioral changes."

"Yeah, well, I'll take my chances that my charms aren't lost on her. Yes or no will be her choice when the time is right."

"When a woman touches her neck, it signals physical stimulation. Horniness, as they say."

"What? Why are you telling me this?"

"Observe. Hey Denise, looking good out there!"

Denise stopped mid-play to meet Granger's gaze. The young man winked. She touched her neck instinctively. The game continued around Denise, who appeared lost, struggling with her focus. The coach yelled for her to come out. She made the walk of shame while eyeing Granger the entire time until reaching the bench. The coach grilled her about her flub. Roger found himself on the sidelines in more ways than one. She never noticed his presence, too focused on the new kid.

Granger raised his arms in victory before heading toward the locker room. Roger fought the urge to question Denise in front of the team, but the coach was already doing that. Mid-conversation, the coach and Denise watched Granger stride confidently away.

Even the teacher seemed flustered at the sight of the transfer student. The woman nodded to Denise as if finally understanding. She blew her whistle and Denise returned to the game. Roger followed Granger, if for no other reason than to hear the rest of his pitch. He considered asking the classmate why he was heading to the locker rooms. No men's teams practiced that day. It was as if the youth staged himself to interact with Roger. Granger spoke over his shoulder without looking back.

"I can deliver her to you or take her for myself. I don't ask for much in return, only the promise of certain behavioral changes on your part relating to character. Defiling that pretty thing would be a good start. There are pleasures you have never dreamed of available to you if you commit. Join me and you would have the time of your life."

Granger exited. The coach whistled to end practice. Denise raced to the locker room without acknowledging Roger. She appeared in another world, as in not his.

The memory of that day in the gym surfaced when Roger parked in Denise's driveway. He saw her several times after the practice, but things were never the same. Denise grew aloof regarding Roger. She even changed her makeup.

Where she previously wore minimal product, (unnecessary because of her natural beauty) she since made herself up heavily. Guys and girls noticed the change and appeared happy with it. The reception was as if she suddenly joined a club, and one which would not invite him to join.

The offer Granger presented in the gym returned frequently to Roger's mind. What exactly would Roger have to do? How could the dude make anything happen Roger wondered? Denise changed. Did she form a pact with the man? What did he promise her?

So many questions fluttered through his head. The fact Roger never crossed paths with Granger since the gym cemented his declining of the offer. Whenever Roger could assemble his thoughts clearly, he reminded himself how angry his classmate made him. The words spoken that day were disgusting.

Yet despite the anger, a part of Roger did not want to strike back, afraid of angering the one person who could help his situation. Denise had drifted away. One way to win her back was to have Granger act as his Cyrano. Maybe the shit-talking guy could become the smooth talking one who could convince Denise to shine toward him like before.

Before giving into that desperate ask, Roger decided on a last romantic push. It started with washing the car, buying flowers, and securing enough money to show her a grand night out. He intended to fix everything on his own by reminding her what a catch he was. At least that is what he practiced in the mirror. Now as he stood in front of her house, he remembered she was the catch, and he just another dirt worker.

He gave it his best go with his wardrobe. Roger wore a skinny tie under a jacket from Chess King, both of which he purchased on sale during one of his family's too rare trips to the city. He bought flowers for the packaging. There were plenty free to pick where they lived, but he coughed up the dough for baby's breath and red foil. She was worth it. Bouquet in hand, he rang the doorbell of the tidy two-story Victorian home. The door opened.

Roger gasped at the sight of Denise's Mom. Wanda Nelson was quite striking like her daughter, but she usually hid behind baggy jeans and baggier tops. She looked far different from her norm. She stood in the doorway bordering on naked in a silk robe dangling so loosely it threatened to fall away under the gentlest of gusts. A dangling sash appeared as ready to fall open as the fabric. The weak knot left the garment draped loosely the entire length of her body. While her cleavage was hard to miss, the woman's legs fought for attention, along with the promise of something more. The outfit ended barely below her waist. The crease under the sash promised to reveal hidden secrets if she moved an inch in any direction. Roger gulped nervously.

He stumbled through a hello which drew a smile from the older woman. She lowered a hand toward her breasts. Roger followed the motion, unable to avert his lustful gaze. She snapped her fingers to regain his attention. He looked at her face.

Her hair, normally collected in a bun, draped over her neck and shoulders. The bangs of her brown bob dangled over one eye. Her makeup appeared smudged as if recently soaked, possibly sweat from too much exercise. She sipped from a heavy crystal tumbler full of a dark liquid and grinned lustily, hungry, ready to take a bite out of the glass, or something else.

"Mrs. Nelson, sorry to catch you like this."

"Like what?"

"Um, well, the way..."

"Spit it out. The word you are looking for is—satisfied."

That is exactly how she looked, Roger thought, based on movies he'd watched. He had no actual life experience with which to back it up. He glanced past her, looking for her husband, assuming the man was around given her current state. She noticed him searching.

"My husband is not home, if that is who you are looking for."

"What? No. Well, sort of. I assumed... Never mind. I'm here for Denise."

"Hm, yes, looks like my daughter is quite popular. You are her second suitor today. Please come in."

Roger followed her, intoxicated by the scent of her perfume. He struggled to look away even as Wanda refilled her glass.

"I enjoy how you look at me."

"Pardon me. You said another suitor?"

"I stand before you like this, and you still ask about her? I'll chalk that up to lack of confidence. Never pass up the now for the later, you will miss out on much in life."

"So, Denise is where?"

"Thankfully not here."

"Thankfully?"

"Yes, it allowed me to spend some quality time with her other beau. He's obscenely good looking. Plain obscene, now that I think about it. I'm afraid when I speak to my daughter, I plan to suggest she date Granger the moment she reaches the proper age. We agreed I would keep him satisfied until then. Though I believe I received the best end of the deal on that front. I will encourage their courtship because I would very much enjoy having him around more often."

"Granger? Mrs. Nelson?"

She set her glass down, approached him and stroked his tie. She pressed herself close to him. Roger squirmed in contradiction.

"My name is Wanda. Can the formalities. I know you lust after my daughter, don't hide your intentions under formal clothing and flowers when all you want is a fuck. Maybe I loosen that necktie and wrap it to wrap around your wrists, give you the chance to show me you have what he doesn't."

Roger pulled away, panting with excitement.

"Mrs.—Wanda. How can you let him near your daughter? He just rolled into town, no one has even seen his parents if he has any. I mean, what do you really know about him?"

"I am aware he is not timid. I understand he takes what he wants. And he knows me too. Things I've kept secret, and the rough ways I want men to touch me." Roger fell back stunned while she pressed her attack, moving in on him again. "See something you like? I've opened my mind to my own desires. I refuse to hold them in check any longer. Flesh is for consumption. I understand that now."

"I think I should go."

"And just when my engine is revving. Need I say more about my new friend and his boldness? He would never leave. In fact, he hasn't. I needed the break. Guess I'm almost ready. His stamina knows no bounds, though. His energy is endless, timeless. He is tending my garden as we speak."

"Granger is here?"

Wanda swallowed the last of her drink before using the empty glass to gesture to the rear door. Wanda yelped in excitement when Roger appeared to storm her castle, only to deflate as he bypassed her for the back door. She harrumphed in disappointment before filling her tumbler and toasting herself.

"Boys will be boys."

Roger exited into the backyard where he found Granger, shirtless, clad only in shorts. The man poked the soil of a garden with a pole, then dropped a strange marble sized seed into the ground. He covered it with dirt, then moved a few inches and repeated the process.

"What are you doing here?" Roger asked.

Granger continued planting. "Like you, I came for Denise. Unlike you, I found her slut mother instead. Willing and ready. Maybe not at first. But now and forever."

"Don't talk about Mrs. Nelson that way!"

Granger turned. His hair slick with post coital sweat lay plastered across his forehead. His wily grin took up half the real estate of his dashing face. He tilted his head in wonder. "You can't be this naïve, can you? While I find it—interesting—it already grows tiresome. You chose not to take me up on my offer with Denise. I have a new one for you. I give you her mother. The woman has come around to my ways of thinking and wishes to use her skin in the manner the Endless intended. You may partake here, right now."

"She's married."

Granger laughed, a raucous tenor which quickly slipped into a deep baritone, before abruptly stopping. He squinted at Roger as if studying a new species. "You're for real. Hm, two sides of a coin, I suppose. No darkness without light? Until death do they part? She is now a different woman than when they exchanged vows, I've made certain of that. Her relationship is irrelevant. She is unconcerned about her spouse any longer and will grow less so with every vile act I expose her too. The next person I place in her bed shall hasten the decline of any pretense of morality she once embraced. Her smuttiness was always there, I only exposed it. The bastard husband cheats anyway. Now she needn't care."

"If you've corrupted Denise..."

"On the contrary. My interest in the offspring requires her to maintain innocence. You know how hard it is to find a virgin in a country bumpkin town like this? Little jackrabbits, you people. Maybe I should have set my eyes on you, but too late, my plan is in motion. You've already seen how Denise has upped her presentation. She is fishing for physical contact, needing it to be dirt. Nasty. She begged me for it, but I need her to remain pure a tad longer. We are going to have a coming out of sorts for her. You're welcome to join the party."

Roger lashed out, punching Granger. Granger barely moved. He grinned wider under a newly split lip as the blood poured into the pile of seeds in his hand.

"Blood spilled in anger. An accelerant. Despite this fortunate assist, your arrival has interfered with my planting. Be a good sport and help me out?"

Granger tossed a black seed. Roger instinctively caught it and raised it to the sun for inspection. The small orb appeared to swirl with motion. A blackness within shifted, ever moving, like a piece of the night sky swirling. Then a redness flickered. Fire?

The seedling suddenly melted, taking on an inkiness which quickly spread. It spilled over his support and up his arm. Roger yelped as the contact burned his skin. The intensity grew the further it moved. He eyed the open soil at his feet.

Roger thrust his arm into the tilled soil to his elbow. The dirt clamped down, as if trying to absorb his limb. He struggled until finally yanking himself free. The oily blackness drained into the earth. Roger examined his limb. The red blotches over his skin faded as he watched. Granger chuckled while continuing to plant.

"We all reap what we sow. Every. One. Of. Us. This is my town now."

CHAPTER 19

Roger woke from the haunting memory. He never shared details of the incident with Kate, only Joe, mostly because of his desires for Mrs. Nelson. Had things not gone so crazy in the garden, if the strange seeds had not frightened him so, there was every chance he would have succumbed to the woman. Such a dalliance would likely have set his life off on an entirely different path. Who knows what direction his life would have taken? Would there have been a violent confrontation with her husband? Would they have had a child together? No matt, maybe a Ted, or a Dave, which were the only names coming to mind when he considered such possibilities. Despite sharing the more horrific tale of Denise's murder, Roger always kept the other story a secret from his wife.

That day with Denise's mother spoke to his own desires, his own doubts on whether to be an honorable man or a failed one. During the conversation in the garden, Granger's language had been so raw and revealing he chose not to share it with Kate (never mind her sailor swearing capabilities were at full peak). The dark black seeds might well have been secrets being buried, for that is what he and Joe did with their knowledge of events. After their tale of the quartering of a classmate in a field fell on deaf and doubtful ears, neither thought it wise to talk further about a rogue citizen and his evil machinations. Besides, the kid was dead.

Roger groaned under the weight of fresh memory and fallen debris. A flicker of light stirred him from his stupor. A flame touched the wick of a candle. Kate sat against a nearby wall, her mussed hair wore a dusting of plaster. Worry lines road-mapped her face as she eyed him from a distance. She tried to blow out the match but struggled to find the breath. She weakly waved it out instead.

"Are you okay?" She gasped.

Roger attempted to answer, only to cough dust. He nodded through the coughing jag and shoved a remnant of the staircase off his legs. He slid over to his wife. She winced as he sidled up. An upturned table rested alongside her with a drawer open which had spilled candles and matches. She raised an unlit candle to him. He shook her off.

"I think I see a flashlight." Roger turned on all fours. "Shit!" An exposed nail met his hand. He lifted the injury to the flickering light, revealing merely a scratch.

"I'm fine. We need that torch."

The couple crab walked to a flashlight resting under a chair. Roger lit it and aimed the beam upstairs. Despite all the damage, their home remained intact, though it looked like an image minimized with the pinch of fingers on a phone. There was no sign of the kids.

"Matt, Tyler!" Roger yelled.

A groan sounded behind them. They turned. Under a portion of fallen sheetrock, Joe stirred. He rose to all fours. Alive.

"Joe!" Kate yelled.

He ignored his condition and pointed to the upper floor. "The kids?"

"No answer. Come on, big guy."

Everyone stood on unsteady feet. Roger and Kate leaned into one another. Joe followed the trajectory of a stumble until he fell against a wall which kept him up. Kate broke from her husband and lit more candles. She poured wax from her initial candle on various surfaces, then placed others into the hot anchors before lighting them. The men yelled in vain for the kids.

A soft glow filled the room. While the lighting could have been romantic in another time and place, all it did was reveal the extent of the damage. The earthquake overturned most of the furniture, lamps, and TV. Pictures lay scattered on the floor in an absurdist art gallery.

Joe located a bright halogen lamp. He scanned the ceiling for structural integrity. Earthquakes were uncommon in their state, though not unheard of. They just experienced the mother of them all. Joe thought it reminiscent of the dreaded "big one" Californian expected for decades. Fracking was new to their region. There were reports of a causal effect related to temblors.

Ultimately, the reason behind the quake did not matter. It happened. They survived. Now they had to find the children. With every unanswered call, chills poured down Roger's spine.

"Why don't they answer?" Kate asked.

"We're on the first floor and it is intact as far as these things go. They are above us, which means they should be okay," Roger replied.

"Unless the roof came down," Joe said.

"Don't even think about that," Kate said.

Joe gestured to the exit. "One way to find out. We check from outside." Joe stormed to the front door, opened it, and froze.

Roger quizzed his friend. "What is it?"

"It wasn't an earthquake."

Roger and Kate approached. Instead of a fertile vista, a massive tunnel aligned roughly with the doorway greeted them. The stone catacomb stretched as far as they could see.

"We are underground. We are freaking underground," Joe said.

CHAPTER 20

Red flashing of a reset digital clock served as a beacon for Tyler. The four zeroes blinked on the chest-plate of a Darth Vader clock missing a head. Shadows as dark as the movie villain's cape flooded the room. The battery backup brought the device back to life minus the actual time, which left Tyler unaware of how long he remained unconscious. If he ever lost consciousness at all. He remembered things shaking and then things got fuzzy. He crawled to the device and flicked a switch. The toy cast a light show across the ceiling, a spinning circle of a Tie-fighter chasing an X-Wing. Tyler noted with disappointment the decapitation of his functional toy.

"What is that?" Jenny chirped.

"Darth Vader chasing Luke. Don't worry, they just circle. No one ever gets caught." Tyler scrambled over debris and joined her. "You okay?"

"I'm tired of people asking me that. After all that's happened, let's assume no."

Tyler used Vader to scan the surroundings. The damage was extensive. The bed had overturned, tossing the mattress and blankets across the floor. Cracks lined the screen of his open laptop, which found its way to one corner of the room. He continued the sweep, but both cried out when the spaceships landed on a face. Heather sat against a wall opposite them. Upon spotting the kids, she pressed her back to the wall, using it to help herself stand.

"Don't move. I'm coming to you guys," Heather said.

Jenny pointed to her own head, then Heather's. "Bad hair day."

A mounted mirror remained somehow intact. Tyler aimed the light so Heather could catch her reflection. The young woman's hair reached for the sky as if electrocuted. She laughed.

"I know how to dress for a party, huh? Don't think I will find a girlfriend looking like this."

Heather grabbed her head, puffing the tufts higher as a goof for their benefit, putting them at ease. She raised her hands and snarled like a monster drawing laughter from the children. The chuckling died when Heather stepped onto a blanket and vanished from sight.

A loud crack sounded as Heather landed on her back atop the dining table one floor below. Air jetted from her lungs. Tyler and Jenny leaned over the hole. Heather tried to speak but couldn't catch her breath. The floor shifted under the children's combined weight, dropping in a quick jerk. Jenny grabbed Tyler and pulled them backward. They looked down from a safer distance. Heather waved them off while finding her voice.

"Not safe. Don't get too close. I'm okay." She rolled off the table.

Tyler used his flashlight to point out one side of the dining room. "You can reach my parents through there."

"I can't see."

He lit up a nearby China cabinet, now empty of dishes. Glass littered the floor. He waved the beam over a pull handle under the display shelves.

"Candles. We have them everywhere."

"Same at my place. You guys lose power a lot too, huh?"

"Video games," Tyler replied.

Heather pulled at the drawer, struggling with it until it jerked open at an uneven angle. The violent motion prompted a box of matches to fly up. After bobbling them, she finally secured it tight against her chest. She retrieved a thick red candle wide enough to stand without a holder and stood it up in the cabinet. Her hands shook violently while she tried to light a match. Turning away from the kids to hide her fear, she lit the wick with trembling fingers.

Turning back to the children, (who smiled at her success) she waved them off again. "I've got this. Find Brad. He should be in the next room. Stay with an adult until your parents find you. Watch where you step."

Tyler and Jenny vanished from view, leaving Heather all alone.

CHAPTER 21

A nightmare about near death in the barn at the hands of an unholy creature woke Matt with a start. The waking world offered him no respite from his intense dream. First monsters, then an earthquake? What were the chances, he wondered? The culmination of two such horrific events caused him to consider whether it all had been a horrible dream. When he moved, pain visited him and brought with it clarity. A beast had strangled him and the earth had shaken. For how long the world shook, he remained uncertain because things had quickly gone dark for him.

When a portion of their group sought refuge in his room, he witnessed his beloved TV dancing a jig against the wall. The house lights went out as he leaped to save it, then his own followed as something connected with his skull. Finally awake, he attributed the big screen resting atop him as the cause of his unplanned nap. The painful lump on his head confirmed as much. A part of him welcomed the blackness so he could not see the extent of the damage to his hard-earned device.

Matt used the nearest wall to guide himself to where his desk used to sit. Strewn papers at his feet identified it as the correct location, even if the object had moved. He crouched down, swept his arms in an arc over the floor. His head found what he was looking for with a thump. He cursed at the pain produced by the sensitive lump near his forehead. The piece of furniture remained upright.

He fumbled open the top drawer. His clumsy efforts roused the others. Groans filled the tight space. Matt retrieved a flashlight and switched it on. The beam landed on Lisa and Chet cradled together in one corner. He swept the room in a panic at what he did not see.

"Cassie! Cassie!"

A scrape drew his attention to a hand fluttering to life from under the mattress. The bed remained pressed against a wall, but all the bedding made ground. He lifted it off, helping Cassie to her feet.

She tested her legs and nodded. "I think I'm okay."

Matt kept an arm around her just in case and because he liked it. He led her to the exit. Chet and Lisa finally rose. The couple took a step and stumbled against each other. The tilted floor gave them pause.

"Am I drunk?" Chet asked.

"Yes, but that is unrelated to the quake damage," Matt said.

"Still, I'll never drink again."

Matt pushed the door. It failed to budge. Cassie joined in, followed by Chet. It might as well have been a wall. Lisa informed them how the frame appeared twisted. A tiny gap in an upper corner along with a bulge near the bottom confirmed the slab had wedged in place.

Lisa stepped away from the others, surveying their situation with a frown. "I don't like this. I've got a terrible feeling. I want to go home."

"We will soon, honeybunch, we just need to get out."

"How about the windows?" Cassie asked.

They moved to the closest of the two, hoping to use it as an escape route. Glass crunched underfoot. He pointed his flashlight at the opening and squinted in confusion. Minus the broken pane, there should have been no reflection hindering the view. Yet something seemed to swallow the light, leaving him unable to see their yard. Strange how he could not see stars either. It made no sense. He reached out and yelped as his hand jammed against a solid surface. The collision jolted pain down his arm, rivaling the throbbing in his skull.

His eyes shot open wide, and he suddenly realized their plight. "Jesus. It wasn't an earthquake."

"What are you talking about, we all felt it," Lisa said.

"Well, you all did. I was a little passed out. Score!" Chet yelled in victory upon discovering a flashlight on the ground. He turned it on with the grin of a man who was a fan of minor victories.

"Sinkholes. They have been in the news." Matt slapped the stone for emphasis. A massive sheet of rock covered the entire window. No cracks, no crevices, no openings, just a pure boulder. The group stared in disbelief.

"What are you talking about? What does that mean?" Lisa asked.

"It means we're underground, Baby. It means we're fucking underground."

"No way," Cassie said.

Lisa freaked as her fight-or-flight mode slid over to hard flight. She grabbed her throat as if she could no longer breathe. "We will suffocate."

"The other window," Matt suggested.

The guys rushed to it, discovering the glass miraculously intact despite the frame having shifted like the door. Beyond the pane, a tunnel stretched into the distance.

"Do you think all this has anything to do with the monster?" Cassie asked.

Lisa lost what little shit she had left. "What are you talking about? Monsters? What is happening?"

Chet turned to scold his friends. "Knock it off with the creature feature stuff, you guys. An earthquake is bad enough. You are freaking my girlfriend out with all that garbage."

She smiled at her big lug, sniffling away some of her fear, finding some normalcy in his protective nature. "Thanks, sweetie."

"No problem, honeybunches," Chet said.

Glass and wood exploded as a hideous creature crashed through the window and grabbed Chet. The beast bore no resemblance to the barn monster. The oversized biped was sickly pale and bloated like a week-old corpse pulled from a lake. Despite its imposing size, it moved frightfully fast. It snorted wildly, which was when everyone noticed the frightening pièce de résistance.

The head mimicked a pig's but drooped at an odd angle, as if a person wore the helmet of a pig skull. Blinking red eyes proved it was not a mask. Long sharp upper and lower teeth overlapped into an overbite within its wide maw, an assembly of boar tusks. Raised veins pulsed the length of both arms, which ended in tipped claws on sausage finger hands. The thing sprayed dollops of drool while wrangling the drunk student.

Chet tried to escape, but the grip proved too tight. With one clawed hand, the creature lashed at the teen's midsection. The young man's eyes widened in shock. He stared at Lisa, but it became clear the boy no longer saw anything when his legs took a single step away from his newly separated body before falling to the ground. His lifeless hands dropped the flashlight. The beast retreated into the tunnel with a torso as a snack.

Everyone screamed at the bloody scene. Matt hauled the mattress and thrust it against the window. Lisa slid down a wall, as close to fetal as she could manage. Cassie grimaced and tossed a blanket over Chet's legs.

Lisa covered her ears and shook in place while screaming out in confused horror. "What was that thing? It just took him. What was that thing?"

Matt ran to his closet and tore at the junk inside, tossing it into the bedroom. The mattress bounced from the window. Something wanted in. Cassie threw herself against it as strange gurgling sounds emitted from the other side, muffled by the fabric. The intruder struck opposite her, bouncing her back. Matt finished his task, then rose and got a head start. He rushed to the closet, slamming into the interior wall. The force caused him to stumble back into the room.

"Come on!" he yelled.

Cassie retook her position as something pushed back. She leaned into it with determination. With every jolt away from the wall, she glimpsed flashes of black fur. Whatever was on the attack appeared different from that of the pig creature. She screamed as a claw briefly slipped alongside one gap, but vanished back to the other side. She cried out to her friend.

"Lisa, help me!"

The frightened woman shook her head fast enough to resemble a spinning gnome pencil. Cassie yelped under the increasing pushback. Matt took another go at the closet and burst through into the next room in an explosion of lattice work and gypsum. Towels and other household items spilled over him, and he slammed his tender skull into the closed door of the guest room. He went down to his knees and looked back.

Cassie roared but appeared on the verge of losing the battle as bubbles rose on the surface. Rather than pushing any longer, it appeared the attackers burrowed into the mattress. The frenzied nature of the onslaught made it clear there were multiple entities at work. They were making their way through the obstacle.

Gnashing sounds accompanied the furious activity within the fabric. Shredding noises sounded as their makeshift wall shifted its weight. It became front heavy and Cassie could no longer hold off the storm. She fell onto her back. The mattress came along for the ride, landing atop her. Foam danced in the air from the frantic chewing of unknown creatures clawing and biting frantically inside the large cushion.

The attackers finally came into view as several more appeared at the window. Matted black fur and pale pink skin came together to form the abominations. The blend looked similar to wildlife burned in forest fires. They were roughly the size of wolverines, with elongated faces that tapered into pointed snouts. They had multiple sharp appendages. Their teeth jutted from wiry jaws and each paw culminated in jagged talons of various sizes. The amount of claws varied on each beast, as did the amount of skin versus fur. The hideous vermin displayed a disorderly appearance, as if someone slapped puzzle pieces together wrong.

Cassie screamed anew when a beast chewed through the material facing her. She lifted the mattress up to give some distance. She also planted her legs and then with a powerful thrust, she kicked it off. The creatures went airborne, trapped inside the filling, screeching at the momentary separation from a free meal. Cassie grabbed Chet's dropped light and used it to whack an oncoming abomination.

Matt arrived and shoved her into the closet. One creature bit Lisa's leg. The attack forced the paralyzed woman into action. She shook her limb furiously, trying to dislodge the gnawing animal. Matt kicked it off and yanked Lisa to her feet and led her through to safety as the bloodthirsty gaggle regrouped. The hissing horde followed their meal.

"Go, go, go!" Matt screamed.

Matt leaped through and Cassie slammed the door, locking it. A flurry of clawing and hissing sounded from the other side. Cassie handed her light to Linda, who shined it on her injury. The teen gasped at the sight of a sucking wound that bled in time to her own breathing. Cassie gathered towels and wiped the blood off before tying one off around the bite.

Matt nodded at the triage. "You'll be fine, trust me. I didn't know then, but one bit me last week in the basement."

"Fine? I'm far from fine!"

Something sounded nearby. Cassie and Matt rose back to back, ready for battle. Matt raised his flashlight like a club, Cassie grabbed the nearest thing she could find, a coat hanger. They scoured the room, prepared to strike.

"Do you think one of them got in?" Cassie whispered.

Matt shushed her. All fell silent. The initial relief at finding shelter turned into uncertainty. They locked themselves into a space without knowing what might be inside. The silence unsettled them. Suddenly a monstrous-sized figure appeared. It lashed out, grabbing Matt's flashlight.

The figure placed it under his chin and grinned. "What's going on, guys?" Brad asked.

"You almost made me crap Twinkies!" Matt took the tool back.

"Gross image, Dude. Hey, where is Heather?"

"She is with... Oh no, the kids. We need to get to them, warn them, if it's not too late," Matt said.

Brad finally noticed Lisa rising on her injured leg. "Whoa, no offense, but you look like crap. Mad party, am I right?" He raised a fist for a bump. She left him hanging.

Cassie's hair fluttered. She followed the air to the nearest window. "I think this one goes outside."

Lisa joined her friend and lit the opening. The beam danced uncontrollably under her shaking grip. Cassie thrust open the sash. Another tunnel stretched into the distance. The breeze was noticeable. Matt tested the door to the hall. Brad remained in the no-man's-land between the two groups.

Brad raised his hands in exasperation. "Uh, guys, same questions still floating out there. I might have napped a little. Turns out I'm a lightweight. I come from a family of lightweights. They have one glass of wine once a year at Christmas gets the place rocking until they fall asleep by seven PM. Yeah, I'm proud."

Matt looked over his shoulder to his friend. "Don't freak out, but a sinkhole opened under the house. We are underground. Chet is dead."

Brad furrowed his brow, trying to understand. The closet door rattled. Then a loud crack announced a breach as the barrier split down the middle. The wolverines poured in, crying out for flesh. The first beelined toward Matt. Brad tipped a chest of drawers onto the furry figure, snapping something inside. It went still as silvery liquid spilled from its body like blood.

The advancing creatures split the group with the men on one side, ladies on the other. Matt yelled for Cassie to run. The women escaped into the tunnel. Matt leaped to the center of the room to draw attention from the fleeing ladies. It worked. The beasts turned on him and Brad, the larger lunch meat. Brad stepped onto the overturned dresser and kicked at the hissing horde.

Once Cassie left, Matt bolted for the exit. It opened immediately. Brad leaped through, then they slammed it shut. Scratching and hissing continued on the opposite side. Despite being fearful, Matt was happy for the sounds as it meant they had not yet gone after the others. The guys leaned against the door to catch their breath and hold back the onslaught.

"When were you going to mention the monster part?"

"My bad. We're underground AND we're screwed."

The beasts continued their claw-a-thon, drooling so much in hunger it spilled through the gap and into the hall. Matt closed his eyes and silently wished for Cassie to be okay. Meanwhile, his own fate rested on the strength of the slab standing between him and dozens of abhorrent creatures from Hell.

CHAPTER 22

Heather waited until the children were out of view before sucking in much needed oxygen. She blinked, stunned at the pain of landing so hard. Everything ached. A solid table broke her fall, but luckily not her back. The surprise fiasco stole all the air from her lungs. She fought through it long enough to calm the kids. Now that they were in search of an exit, she took time to recover. Her hands shook, not unlike the house earlier. She no longer believed the maxim about life flashing before one's eyes in the face of death. When the ground shuddered for what felt an eternity, she remained fully in the moment. Every violent sway seemed endless. The cracking of walls and support columns tore at the fabric of normalcy with thunderous booms. Time slowed during the entire event.

Movement during the chaos was that of being on a ship in the worst of storms. Despite the proximity of her friends, they might as well have been on another continent based on her inability to reach them once the ground moved. The world rumbled so ferociously it drowned out all voices. She saw Matt and Cassie's lips move but heard nothing but thunder.

Townspeople nicknamed a bend in a street midway through town "tickle belly hill" for the feeling it gave one's stomach when driven over at a high speed. She felt that effect on steroids as the house roared with movement. The terror initially rooted her in place, but seeing the children forced her into action. When running proved impossible, she leaped, clipping each child and yanking them through the door.

The enclosed room offered no respite from the ongoing destruction. It was foolhardy to believe a few feet could make a difference. Their world continued to roil around them. Getting everyone under the bed became her goal. She shoved the children harder than intended (or perhaps the earthquake amplified their trajectory). The kids tumbled into a wall. Before she could join them, a violent jolt ripped her legs from beneath her, causing her to face plant.

Her skull bounced off the floor, her teeth crunching painfully together. The door slammed of its own accord, placing a button on the house's angry protest. It swung shut so forcefully it struck the bottom of her feet, jolting her with a blast of pure agony up the legs and into her spine. Before she could tend to the injury, their world went black.

The candle now provided comfort. Heather leaned over it as if praying in a church. She breathed, calming herself, centering her thoughts. She examined the mostly destroyed room. The sooner she identified an exit, the faster she could reunite with the children. Once free, she would call for Brad, her bestie. He had a way with kids. She hoped he wasn't still too drunk to assist. She loved the big lug like a brother. He liked her more than that. His obsession over her was the town's worst kept secret.

She didn't much mind. He would totally be her type if guys were her thing. He was objectively handsome, tall, dark skin, piercing eyes when he took off the glasses. Sure, his thumbs tipped heavily on the nerd scale, but his heart was enormous. She considered him trustworthy except for driving when alcohol entered the picture. The man seldom drank. She should have inquired if he intended to imbibe before accepting the carpool. It would have been easy to catch a ride home with someone else, but she remained behind to make sure he sobered up. The act of waiting for him guaranteed to stoke gossip about them dating. It did not bother her. Heather was out, but many seemed intent on 'shipping' the two of them. She could see why. He was good people. If her classmates focused on her relationship with him, it left her free to date women under the radar. Once she found true love, she planned to make it official with the world.

Heather shook her head to rid herself of memories leading up to her situation to focus on the task at hand. Tyler relayed the location of the living room, but there was an obstacle. A major one. The same floor she fell through dangled perilously against the exit, along with other crumbled portions of the ceiling. She was glad the kids found a safe passage from a room with swiss cheese flooring. The children were lucky they too had not fallen. She investigated the other exit.

Debris covered that also, but it appeared more navigable. A pile of boards, shifted furniture and portions of a crumbled wall pressed against the door. The messy mountain was not unscalable, it only covered half. The top remained visible. Timber lay scattered throughout the space. She marveled at the juxtaposition of how some exposed boards looked new despite the age of the house. Destructive shaking opened a time capsule of construction bones. It revealed long hidden sections of architecture. The thought calmed her. The place proved sturdy, and so was she.

The wreckage spread wider than it did high. So while the upper half of the door remained clear, she could not easily reach it. She decided it smart to first test it before beginning the hard work of digging. No point fighting through destruction, only to discover more of the same blocked the exit on the other side. She grabbed a loose two by four and raised it to shoulder height. She jabbed it against the closed door and screamed.

She dropped the wood, and her cry of pain segued into cursing. She nursed her palms. A painful vibration rocked her world when she made contact. She played on the softball team and understood how a poor grip on a bat could produce a surprising amount of agony to one's hands. The board gave her a good dose of lesson learning. Tighten that grip, she thought, flexing her fingers.

Tap.

A knock from the other side startled her. She scrambled up the pile and called out. "Mr. Whatley, Mrs. Whatley, are you there?" She pressed her ear against the door. "Are you hurt? Knock once for yes."

A single tap answered her plea. She pushed at the door but found it stuck. Leaning into it, she pressed harder, which caused the debris to shift. Heather rode the wave as it slid, falling back further, stopping close to the board. She grabbed it once again and gripped tight, anchoring it part way under one arm. She attempted to strike like a joust.

"Hang on. I'll try to break through."

A solo knock followed, affirming the plan. She ran and struck the door with her wooden lance. The surface cracked, but the impact knocked Heather to her knees. She rose, then stepped back for a greater head start. She rushed the target. With a thunderous clop, it broke through, creating a hole exactly the size of the board itself. Heather yelled in victory. Luckily the interior door was an inexpensive hollow core.

The tiny space would not offer an escape, but it would give her a way to identify the injured party. The rupture also gave her hope she could eventually break through the barrier, even if she could not push it open. She attempted to yank the board but discovered it wedged tight in the hole of its own making. Scrambling back up, she steadied herself, gripped it more firmly, ready to pull only it pulled her. Before she could react, her feet left the ground.

The board yanked through from the other side!

The immense force ripped her free of her precarious perch. It happened so fast she had no chance to let go. Her face smashed into the wooden slab, splitting her lip and nose with a sickening pop. Blood sprayed as she grunted in pain and surprise, leaving her completely stunned. Heather leaned into the door, bordering on passing out. She moaned, struggling to understand what transpired.

Her vision blurred as she looked up and noticed the open hole. She touched her face and cried out in agony, waking her from her stupor. She peered into the small opening. Red glowing eyes looked through from the opposite side! She screamed and attempted to flee. The debris shifted underfoot, causing her head to smash into the door again. Wooden shrapnel exploded around her.

Splintered wood turned her face into a pincushion. Bubbles of blood poured down her cheeks, tears of red. A massive hole replaced the smaller, where something had punched through the hollow core. The sizeable gap revealed the silhouette of an immense creature wearing the face of a pig hanging slack.

It snarled through wild boar style tusk teeth. Spittle spraying while it groped for her. The door broke unevenly, leaving jagged strips of wood composite jutting up from the bottom half. The monster moved in starts and jerks, grunting animalistic noises with every twitch of bloated muscle. A large massive hand caught her by the hair. She twisted her body only for her locks to wrap tighter in its grip. She grew fearful it might scalp her.

Its free limb, topped with sharp claws, blasted through the hole, stabbing deep into her stomach. Heather gasped a bubbled breath while her body spasmed involuntarily. She lay on her back, faced away from the creature. The gluttonous monstrosity yanked her through the opening as the jagged edges sliced her as cleanly as shattered glass. She grunted under the invasions of flesh.

Fading quickly, she glimpsed a window in the kitchen. Despite noticing how a stone wall blocked escape behind the glass, she latched on to the sight as hope. A slight chance for freedom. Then the brute opened its maw wide. Its drool splashed her face with the foul smell of sulfur. She raised her hands in impotent defense. Her screams echoed throughout the tight confines of the room until the beast brought its fangs to bear. Soon there were no sounds other than teeth on bone.

CHAPTER 23

Kate spotted Matt along the second-floor ledge. Had he leaned inches in either direction shadows would have swallowed him. After experiencing what they thought was only an earthquake, their plan was to race outside to climb up and free the trapped children. They would have come out if they were able. She refused to believe the worst; instead thinking they might be unconscious. Even that thought terrified her. Since the whole thing started, her legs shook as much as the house had. She did not tell her husband or Joe, figured they would see it, but then they opened a door.

Such a simple act changed everything. She did not believe any of them would have understood what they looked at in what used to be a front yard if they had not seen so many news reports lately. The incident had already stolen her legs, which quivered over fear for their children. Seeing what lay beyond the threshold stole her breath. The men examined it with awe while she turned, trying not to be sick as circumstances grew more dire the moment they turned that knob. That was when she spotted her oldest. She had never felt such relief, such joy. She tried to dry out but her voice froze as she considered perhaps she looked upon a mirage.

Kate squinted, making sure the vision was real. She called out. "Matt!"

Matt beamed at seeing his mother, but quickly placed a finger over his lips. The youth appeared distracted, scanning the dark surroundings. Something sounded down the hall. Matt tapped Brad in warning. The duo braced for a round two fight while the adults huddled below, yelling in unison. Matt gave up on shushing them. Thunk! Again, the noise. A door opened. Tyler and Jenny stepped through it.

Matt dropped to one knee and accepted the running hug from Tyler. The teen wiped a tear at the sight of his baby brother, but quickly fell into bravado mode like any good older brother would. He feigned indifference as he broke the hug.

"Sup?"

"Nothing," Tyler replied, and they were good.

"Dad!" Jenny yelled down.

"Sweetheart, are you alright?"

The child nodded. Kate ran her fingers through her hair before shoving them into her back pockets. The mother spun in a circle, kicking air and mouthing a 'thank God.' She completed a full turn before looking up again, as if needing a moment to ensure all was real. She shook her head in anxious relief when suddenly their world shook again.

Wham! The house dropped several more feet. The jolt knocked Jenny off the ledge. Brad leaped and caught her arm. She dangled midair as Joe rushed over and collected her, lowering her into an embrace.

Roger looked up at the others. "Let's get the rest of you down before the entire thing collapses."

"If that is what we're expecting, shouldn't we stay up here?" Matt suggested.

Roger pointed a finger down in a no arguing signal. The older boys lowered Tyler first. Roger gripped his son's waist and pulled him from dangling into a hug. Matt lowered himself and dropped unassisted, springing up deftly into the arms of his waiting mother. Brad followed Matt's lead and gripped the edge and hung in place, ready to drop. The ledge shifted under his weight.

With a loud snap, it broke off. The parents pushed the kids clear as Brad fell along with a portion of the upper hall. Brad landed with a thud, debris crashing atop his chest. The adults lifted the section off while Matt pulled his friend free.

"You okay?" Matt asked.

"I don't like your house."

Brad sat up, waving at everyone to give him space. Kate ignored him and rubbed the youth's back. He nodded in appreciation. Joe stared up, searching.

Worry crossed the man's face. "Where is Cassie?"

"And Heather. Where is she?" Brad asked.

"We all owe Jenny an apology. There are monsters here," Matt said.

"What are you talking about? We don't have enough to worry about the aftermath of an earthquake that we need to talk about monsters?" Roger scolded.

"Dad, they're real," Tyler chimed in.

"Super real. My friend, Chet, is... gone."

"Gone, as in the quake killed him?" Kate asked.

"You're not listening," Tyler said.

"Someone died? Cassie. Is she?" Joe asked.

Matt shook his head, shrugged. "She and Lisa were alive when I last saw them, but the creatures separated us. The women went out into the cave."

"There are tunnels upstairs too?" Roger asked.

"Monsters. Plural?" Kate asked, pulling Tyler close as she searched their surroundings for answers.

Brad finally rose to his feet, frantic. "Heather. I asked about Heather."

"Tall, pretty?" Tyler asked.

"The prettiest, yeah."

"That was her name. She fell through a hole in the floor," Jenny said.

Roger called for a huddle. Everyone gathered quickly, as if eager for the contact. None shied away from touching. Individualism gave way to a sense of team, a sense of family. Roger acted as the quarterback.

"Look, we are talking about an earthquake, because technically it was. But it is more than that. All the news reports of sinkholes suggest we are in one. As for monsters, I am sure everyone is conflating barn rats with something more dire. We are aware of the presence of the vermin. Matt encountered them the other..."

"If that is what we are dealing with, they are the kind that can bench a truck," Brad said.

Roger closed his eyes, breathing deep to shake off the interruption. Matt recognized the look on his Dad's face, the determination, like getting a harvest in before sunset. Matt slugged his friend into silence.

"My point is, no matter whatever one might have seen in a moment of chaos, we can't worry about that. We need to stay focused on each other. My only goal is to get us out of here..." Brad stiffened in protest until Roger addressed the youth's unspoken concerns. "And find Cassie, Linda, and Heather, in the meantime."

"People we would not have to search for if there was no party," Kate chimed in.

"I tried to tell him," Tyler said.

Matt knuckled Tyler's skull, as was their custom. The boy rubbed his head, grinning at the return of normalcy.

"First, we locate a route to the surface. The most important thing is for us to stick together. We are already missing some people. No need to make it any worse," Roger said.

Kate tapped her husband on the shoulder. He followed her gaze to the front, noticing Joe abandoned the group. Roger approached his friend, who stood outside the threshold in the tunnel. Joe's head swiveled, listening for something. A sign.

"What are you doing?"

"Don't mind me. Just planning a little spelunking," Joe said.

Kate gestured for the kids to remain where they were. She joined the two men. Brad leaned into Tyler's face. Tyler raised his arms as if fending off a monster.

"The pizza earlier, yeah, sorry about that," the boy pleaded.

"Not that. You say Heather fell. Where?"

Tyler pointed to the dining room. A pile of debris blocked the closed door. Brad rushed over and tossed planks. Matt joined his friend. They went to work trying to forge a way in, all while calling her name. The younger kids leaned in, hoping to eavesdrop on their parents.

"What's the plan, Joe?" Roger asked.

"No plan. Just go out there. That's where the answers are."

"Your daughter needs you," Kate said.

"So does my wife and Cassie. They are out there. I sense it." Joe looked at Jenny, who waved the tips of her fingers sadly, as if she understood. No words needed to read her Dad like a Harry Potter book. He offered a melancholy smile before turning back to his friends.

"That promise you made to take care of my girls if something were to happen to me?" The couple nodded. "I want to cash that favor in."

CHAPTER 24

Roger walked past the boys, digging frantically in search of Heather. Brad grunted under the heavy lifting as if releasing pressure from a valve. Roger let them be as he passed them to enter the kitchen. There was a second entrance to the dining area there, and he planned to check it out. His son knew that, but likely failed to remember in the heated moment, too focused on the option in front of him. It concerned Roger how long the woman was missing. There had been plenty of time since the quake for her to have reappeared if she were able. He feared the worst. The house was unstable, a miracle as much of the structure remained upright as it did. He worried what befell their unexpected houseguest. That was why he allowed the boys to continue the dig. He would investigate before confirming his growing suspicions of dread.

He entered the kitchen. Checking on Heather was not his sole reason for entering their formerly cozy cooking nook. The goal was to gather items for Joe's own misadventure. The search for the student would take precedent over a quest for tools. Despite his underlying concerns over her status, he hoped to find her well. It would be nice to surprise the boys, give them some relief.

Brad was a good friend to Matt and a constant presence around their house. The youths spent most of their time together at school, however, as Brad's father was stringent about his child's whereabouts and preferred his son remain on their farm. Technology kept the guys connected (internet Gods willing). Without that, their friendship might have faded. The demands that parents put on their kids to work in an agricultural community were daunting. Plus, there were all the obscenely early hours involved. Roger understood why his oldest was so eager to run away to college. The ability to sleep in alone would be worth it, poor kid.

The kitchen had seen better days, meaning every day prior to the present one. The doorway summed it up. It stood at a crooked angle, a visible representation of the immense force visited upon their homestead. He swept his beam over what looked like a battlefield in the aftermath of a war fought over their Corningware. A two by four leaned against the still upright refrigerator. The piece of lumber unsettled him, feeling incongruent to the surroundings as if someone placed it there. Heather?

She was the priority. He lit up the dining-room entrance and gasped. Only the lower half of the door remained intact. He peered through the ruptured top. Rivulets of red drooled over the jagged edges leading to puddles at his feet. The copper notes wafting about made it clear someone was in trouble.

"Hello! Heather?"

A glance inside revealed a burning candle. She had been there. He yelled again. No answer. His foot slipped in the liquid. He looked down and discovered a wet crimson trail which led directly to a cabinet which housed cleaning supplies. Why there? Did she seek towels? Maybe a first aid kit? Farming life meant storing kits everywhere. Had the youth kept one at home in a similar floor to ceiling closet? In an injured delirium, did she forget where she was and seek the familiar? Even if she had, why was the door closed?

Roger approached cautiously. The blood suggested serious injury but could also mean foul play. If someone did harm, it could have been at the hands of the person who abducted Rebecca. Roger remained in the camp that an evil man took his friend's wife. It was easy-to-understand Jenny attributing the incident to something fantastical. It did not take actual monsters to do harm to man, humans were plenty capable. He and Joe understood that well from experience. They still found themselves haunted by the act visited upon poor Denise.

Yet his own sons suggested something was out there. He trusted his boys, but also recognized Matt inherited plenty of Roger's "ability to screwup" DNA. The most recent example being the unauthorized party. His son could make bad choices with the best of them. Though Matt was not prone to delve into such oddities as tales of creatures, the youth needed a story to avoid punishment for his ill-advised bash. He thought his eldest could cover better than that.

Roger shook it off. There was no such thing as monsters. Jenny encountered a maniac, human one. End of story. As for Tyler, he was only looking out for his older brother, went along with the wacky excuse. Good kids, both. And now he worried about them.

They had suffered a sinking ship called their house. Everything they owned and treasured now lay buried underground minus caskets. The sheer insanity of such an occurrence guaranteed they would need therapy. He struggled to think if the town even had a therapist. As much as he and Joe could have used one, they never would have trusted the individual. Who wore those robes? Who to trust when at least a quarter of the population likely took part in a barbaric act? Each other's family. That was it.

Roger struggled to remember Heather. He was happy his boys were so well adjusted they had plenty of friends. Girls everywhere with Matt. He mentally tried to picture the woman in his mind. Instead of isolating a memory of his son's friend, he remembered Denise looking at him, making that weird sound as the engines gunned and they hit the gas. Okay, monsters existed, but as a man. Granger. Long dead, Roger told himself. *Yeah, then why am I following a trail of blood in my kitchen?* He gripped the pull handle to the supply cabinet.

He yanked it open. Relief washed over him when a body did not fall into his lap. But the minor victory quickly gave way to worry. The floor of the tight space opened into a miniature sinkhole. While the gap appeared too small for someone his size, it could accommodate a female teen. The blood which led him there in the first place ended along the cusp of the fissure. The trail likely picked up below, but his light proved too weak to pick it up.

Roger speculated that no matter the injuries in the initial fall, the jagged escape route caused plenty of damage. The poor woman only had to look up at the kitchen entrance and she would have found help on the other side. Instead, she sought towels or first aid and discovered a missing floor. The darkness would have hidden the opening. It would only take one step.

"Heather!"

Roger yelled down, searching for signs of her legs, figuring she could lie unconscious where she fell. Had she risen and stumbled from the view of the kitchen? Mere inches from sight? He leaned in and listened. It was a misnomer to think seashells at beaches sounded like the ocean. They amplified sea breezes in a confined echo chamber transposing sound into a dull white noise. A similar tone greeted him as his head rested within a wall of stone. Then he heard a subtle change.

Skritch, skritch, skritch. Roger lowered his head further, attempting to identify the strange sound. It repeated. Skritch, skritch, skritch. Was she tapping a message? Or scratching one? It sounded like nails on a rock.

"Hello, are you okay?"

Then he glimpsed a flash of gnashing teeth. It hissed before vanishing from view. But vanished where? It was right there and then disappeared. His eyes adjusted to the dark and then he spotted it. Movement. An undulating form, large, expansive. He refocused his beam, which revealed the ground below writhing, rippling like a rushing river full of eddies. The hissing grew, building to a crescendo of screeches. Recognition sunk in. He reeled backward only to stumble, crashing onto his back. His flashlight dropped into a roll which illuminated the opening, then away from it before repeating the cycle. Screeching cries echoed along with claws scraping over stone with primal ferocity.

Barn rats!

Masses of them. They poured through the hole in massive numbers. Claws clacked vilely against linoleum. The furry army stormed forth. Whatever their intended destination, he served as the freeway. The horrendous mass of agitated critters swarmed over him.

He wanted to scream but dared not, fearing one might set up home in his throat, explore all his innards could offer. Barn rats traditionally bit deep and often with an ever-present hunger. Roger imagined the nasty animals gnashed their teeth even in sleep, always awaiting that next meal. Yet none chomped down on him. Still, the foul cascade of critters passing over every inch of his body caused him to tremor with revulsion.

As quickly as it began, the horde vanished. Tufts of dusky fur twirled in the air, accompanied by the sour smell of a diet rich in scavenging. Rat droppings served as a telltale sign of the invasion. The hideous animals loosened bowels liberally when frightened. As if they had anything to be afraid of, Roger thought, taking stock of himself. Everything appeared intact. A relief, but a conundrum. Were

Roger in a cartoon, the vermin (hey look everybody, with Disney eyes for the kids!) would have taken the shape of his form while swarming only to leave a skeleton behind as they finished their biz and moved on.

Roger rose on unsteady feet, limbs trembling. Experiencing a palsy in one arm, he flexed the hand to shake it out. The numbness fading, he felt a breeze. The kitchen housed two windows. Checking the first, he saw solid stone through shattered glass where the rough surface bowed the frame. The other suffered a crack running the length of the largest pane, beyond which appeared a wall of soil threatening to pour in like quicksand, held in place by the fragile barrier. Neither showed any obvious openings. He followed the breeze to the stone backed aperture. A closer inspection revealed a slight gap of mere inches between the frame and the rock. Stunning to think rats could squeeze through such a tight opening.

"They say those critters can fit in an asshole." Roger spoke the axiom of locals aloud. The more crudeness old-timers added to warnings, the bigger the danger. Roger repeated the button farmers applied to the vile vermin. "Grab your butt cheeks, you see too many of them things." The thought being they climb into any available hole. He examined himself down there just to check.

A lack of biting failed to compute. Those things bite. It's what they do. Their DNA comprised a Hatfield and McCoy style feud against humans for interrupting their dominance over the planet. Many of the fleeing fuzzballs should have chomped down on him in multiple places, yet none did. They only ran. What could make the nastiest creatures on Earth so afraid they ignored their favorite food group?

Roger shined the light back into the hole. All the answers were below. Heather's condition. Whether an escape route to the surface existed. And what frightened the fury horde? He turned his attention to the drawers in the kitchen. He could only hope Heather was okay and was even now seeking a way out, after which she could send the cavalry.

Joe's fixation on exploring the underground on his own would be their next best bet for rescue. The two friends struck any uneasy truce about the plan, but someone had to go for help. He knew his friend had another agenda for leaving and he could not fault him, but he also feared the man might have left already.

The search and its aftermath caused him to take longer than expected to gather supplies for his buddy.

Roger raided the cutlery. He stuffed a blade into his belt at his back, then found what he was looking for, a meat cleaver. Initially Roger planned to weaponise his friend purely as a precaution, but now he worried it might be necessary. Would a cleaver be enough against something that scared a mass of the most fearsome predators on Earth? Forget crocodiles, bears, piranha, Roger stacked the barn varmints up against any of them which raised the question. What frightened them? What exactly was down there?

CHAPTER 25

Roger stepped from the kitchen to find the guys at an impasse with their task. A beam blocked the door, one too heavy for the two to move it. They struggled but kept trying. Roger did not to share his newfound knowledge. There stood a chance, however slight, the woman remained in the dining area out of his view. That was unlikely. The room was not too big. He liked to think Heather already reached the surface to get help after inadvertently falling into the gap he discovered. If events proved more tragic, it was his duty to shield them from the horror, at least for now. He would pull the boys aside soon enough but had another thing to deal with first.

Joe waited in the tunnel's mouth. Jenny stood guard on the threshold. Roger raised the meat cleaver in the air, well out of view of the girl. Joe nodded and dropped to a knee.

"You're going away?" Jenny asked.

"Only taking a walk is all."

"I'm not a kid anymore, Dad. Don't lie."

"You are too a kid. Don't **you** lie."

She burst into tears, hugging him. "I'm afraid I'll lose you."

"I know, kiddo."

Kate fought not to cry while watching the two grieve in advance. There were no goodbyes when Rebecca went missing. Father and daughter had one now. Tyler sniffled and kicked the floor. Matt ceased digging, leaning on his knees as if catching breath, but mostly he watched the goodbye.

"Why do you have to go?" Jenny asked.

Joe wiped strands of hair out of Jenny's face as a feint to wipe away tears. "Because I do not have enough money to pay the rent here. We will be broke if I don't find a way out."

Jenny looked accusingly at Kate, who shrugged. "Casa Whatley is a very high-class establishment in case you hadn't noticed. It takes a lot for us to make this place look this good."

As if on cue, Brad tripped up and stumbled into the pile, sending boards clattering across the floor. Matt leaped away from the shifting mess. Kate disguised her concern for her son, instead smiling at the youngster who giggled at the destruction.

"If we stay here then we're getting swindled?"

"Do you see a water park? Because I don't see a water park."

"I want to visit one."

"That's what I'm working on, honey. Now go with the Whatley's and I'll do my best to make that happen real soon."

She nodded. Kate took the girl's hand and led her away. Roger discreetly handed over a knife and the cleaver. Joe held the larger blade and slipped the smaller into his belt.

"Protection, just in case. Minimum there are vermin, trust me. Keep eyes out for Heather. I believe she fell. She has left a trail. It does not look good. I get it, your wanting to search out there but might I remind you how you are venturing into a place which could collapse any minute."

"I don't believe it will. This is all by design. You and I both know there is more to this tunnel than a random act of nature. As crazy as my actions were at the freak show, this is different. Tell me you don't feel it."

Roger answered by ignoring the question. "I understand you have Cassie on your mind. But haste to the surface helps all of us."

"Solid plan."

"Which you'll ignore the second I close the door."

"She's out there."

"We're still talking about your daughter, right?"

Now Joe refused to answer. "Lock it behind me for all the good it will do."

Roger complied, closing off his friend. The teens shifted the door a few inches. They fought over the view in the room. They swept the interior with a flashlight. Brad yelled through the opening.

"Heather! Heather, are you in there?"

"Boys. I need to show you something."

They followed Roger to the kitchen. Matt muttered about forgetting the back entrance to their situation. His father lit up the crimson trail leading to the cabinet. Brad called out into the void.

"I tried that. There was no answer. No sign of her. I let you two keep digging in case I missed her. I was wrong. I should have told you right away. I fear this opening holds the key to her fate."

Brad leaned too far and fell, wedging in at his shoulders. He kicked violently to dislodge himself. Roger and Matt pulled him free. The young man jolted to his feet and scrambled across the room, drenched in sweat. He spread his arms wide in search of open space. Once he caught his breath, he danced in place like prepping for a wrestling meet, attempting to give off a *no big thing* vibe.

"Not claustrophobic, nope. Would go right in after her, but no way I can fit."

"Question is, could she?" Roger asked.

"Yeah, for sure, she's petite. She cut herself on the door, then saw a monster like we did, ran down there to escape," Matt said.

"Or took shelter from the quake. How about we leave monsters out of this?" Roger implored.

Matt leaned further into the gap than Brad was able. Brad shivered at the sight of anyone squeezed in like a sausage. Matt called out over his shoulder.

"I think this goes through into the basement!"

The teen slipped on the slick redness, his planted knee slipping away. He fell with a jolt and lost the lamp. It tumbled against a rock and skidded across the floor below. Roger grabbed his son by the belt and pulled him free.

"Smells bad down there, like Tyler's socks."

"Hey!" Tyler protested from the doorway where he stood alongside his mother and Jenny.

Brad tugged at his friend's shirt. "Show me the basement."

"As in the place where the entire house might come down on?"

"Exactly that. You said you believe the hole leads to the cellar."

"I believe a lot of things. Why do you think I'm always in trouble? Your current thought process, however, is bordering on two words. Cray and Zee."

"Fine, I've visited enough. Hallway down by your parents' room, right?" Brad rushed the doorway, easily shoving Tyler aside, but Kate blocked his path.

"No, I want everyone to stay in my sight," she said.

"No disrespect, Mrs. Whatley, but you are not my mother. Heather is my best friend and I'm stressed from a hot round of not being totally claustrophobic just now. It will be unpleasant if anyone tries to stop me."

"I vote we let the caveman go," Tyler said.

Roger grabbed a knife from the silverware drawer and approached Brad, who raised his hands. "You've convinced me to stay."

The man flipped it to present it hilt first. Brad took it. Kate gazed angrily at her husband. He shrugged and tried to explain.

"If it was you, no one would stop me. At least we send him off with protection."

"From what? A collapsing building? How will a knife stop that?"

Matt searched drawers, retrieving a sharp utensil of his own.

Kate pointed at him. "You, I can tell what to do."

"I can't let him go down there alone, Mom. He's right. Heather needs help."

"Exactly. Pretend I believe you about the monster attack," Kate started.

"Do you?"

She shook her head no even as she answered. "If I did. I would assume whatever hurt her is still down there."

"Look, the house sinking thing is not my fault, but my friends being trapped here is. I should go with him."

"You're using the fact you threw a party as an excuse for me to let you do what I do **not** want you to do?"

Matt raised his eyebrows while considering a retort, but found nothing in the tank. He gave over to puppy dog eyes. Roger nodded to his wife, who finally stepped aside. Tyler grabbed Matt's arm.

"I don't really want all your stuff, if you know what I mean."

"And I don't want you to have it if you know what I mean."

The two teens left the others behind. They rushed down the hall leading to the basement. Matt gripped the knob and discovered the door wedged tight. Brad sidled over and threw his weight into it. It opened instantly. His blade flew into the air as he released it to grab the jam to stop from tumbling down the stairs. The knife landed upright, stabbing the floor, narrowly missing a toe. Matt retrieved it and handed it over.

"Might want to hold tighter?"

Brad nodded, then stepped forward and almost tumbled again. His toes dangled over the ledge of a third and last step. The balance of the staircase was absent. Something reflected their light back with abnormal intensity. It reflected off water rising just shy of the last step.

"Wow, it flooded," Matt said.

"Makes sense. Everything flowing through the pipes and tanks went somewhere. There's a dry patch over there. Heather!"

Matt lit up the spot, but they remained too far from the location for a good look. "Nothing we can do. We should go back."

Brad reluctantly nodded, looking out upon lost hope. As the pair turned to leave, they heard a snap. The step broke off, splashing them into the wash. They sank over their heads. Matt surfaced, choking. He reached for his bobbing waterproof flashlight. Brad splashed nearby, treading water.

"Dude, the floor is missing over here. No way this should be over my head. You?"

"I'm on solid ground, still deep though."

Brad jerked in fright. "Something touched me. What's in here?" An empty paint bucket bobbed up alongside him. He laughed in relief. "Wow, almost my turn to shit Twinkies."

The water behind the teen bubbled, gurgling like a slow boil, intent on becoming full. An object of considerable size sluiced through the surf. Matt watched it unfold while his friend remained oblivious.

"Get over here. Now!"

"Dude, it's only my buddy Sherman Williams. Or is it Colonel sanders? Which one is the paint bucket and which is the chicken bucket again?"

"For real, move."

Brad jerked in a fluid, violent motion. The youth sank, then resurfaced, hacking out foul liquid as he treaded water again, searching for the source. "What was..."

Another jerk. He reached out too late, vanishing into the mire. Matt swam toward his friend, splashing to scare off whatever hid below the surface.

"Brad! Brad!"

Matt attempted a dive but soon swam back up, rubbing irritated eyes from the dirty liquid. Something brushed his leg. He reached and pulled at the object, yelping in terror as Heather's bloated torso surfaced, squishing against him as if a lover's embrace. Only half her face remained intact and offered a sick grimace with a solo egg white eye staring into his soul. Her breasts proved buoyant as they floated, offering an unobstructed view below that with exposed ribs running the length of one side. Her arms stretched rigidly in mortis.

Matt pushed her off while scrambling away. His feet found purchase on a firm section of floor. He remained in chest high flooding but finally stood on solid ground. Another arm dropped on Matt's shoulder from behind. He turned, intending to push the corpse again, only to find Brad slipping from consciousness. The battered teen's face was bloody, his eyes closed, but he appeared to be breathing.

Matt struggled through the wash to the concrete island they spotted earlier. The ledge of cement jutted at an angle, a buckled foundation wall. Matt fought to drag himself and his buddy to shore. Once he manged to get them both in place, he yelled through the floorboards overhead, hoping his family might hear.

"Dad! There are monsters! There really are!"

Silence greeted him. No adults yelling back and a friend barely hanging on. His parents made the huge mistake of not believing the kids. Now they themselves were vulnerable. If they refused to believe, something could easily catch them unaware, Matt thought. Without a doubt, something was in their house. And that something was on the hunt.

CHAPTER 26

Cassie and Lisa raced through the seemingly endless sublevel, chased if not by monsters, then at least by flashbacks. Lisa struggled to keep pace. Alcohol sloshed in her guts. Sloppy gurgling noises sounded the alarm that the vomit comet was about to pull into sour stomach station. The teen stopped, leaning on her knees, battling the imminent hurl. Lisa watched her friend go and thought of herself as an anchor, the twisted ankle coed who could not outrun a serial killer who only ever seemed to walk in all the movies. Despite the danger, she was out of gas. If her friend left her in the dust, so be it. One less person to witness the inevitable spew that she felt in her throat.

Cassie, used to watching her sister, noticed the absence quickly and returned to her friend. "We need to keep moving."

"I am about to be sick," Lisa said through spittle.

Cassie rubbed her friend's back while the woman wept in between bouts of dry heaving. Cassie pulled Lisa's hair aside in the event her friend puked for real. Even while she took care of her friend, Cassie kept an eye out for signs of the snarling abominations. They appeared to be in the clear. Maybe the monsters remained back at the house, cavorting in her former life. Their presence became a record scratch moment in her existence. Everything changed when she encountered the horrid beasts. Beyond the terror they instilled, Cassie recognized nothing would ever be the same. Despite the forced mental reckoning over a shifted universe, Cassie vowed not to give in to despair.

"I think I'll be okay, but not if we run," Lisa whimpered through a string of drool running a straight path to the floor.

"Fine. But we need to keep moving. Let's walk for now."

They continued into the depths. Lisa eyed Cassie as if she were stranger than clawed furries and pig-men. "How are you doing this?"

"What?"

"Keeping so cool."

"Maybe because my sister counts on me, because my Dad needs me."

"So, what do you need?"

Cassie stopped. She pretended to do so as an excuse to rest. Truthfully, the question stumped her. What did she need? Her family. More so since her Mom vanished. Cassie took on the position of mother figure in the absence of the real thing. Jenny suffered a traumatic event of some sort for certain. Cassie believed the situation to have regressed her sister to a younger age. Jenny displayed behaviors and a sensitivity to her surroundings, mimicking earlier adolescent stages. Once upon a time, her sibling longed for adulthood. No longer. Then there was her father, who did his best while riding a spiral of grief. Cassie grieved along with everyone but dealt with it by throwing herself into her new role.

There was Matt. He was a thing. Okay, maybe not a thing, more like a person, a concept at the very least. What about him? Did she need him? He was not long for the country life, eager to leave a lifestyle she quite enjoyed. Country meant family, friends, and until recently, peace. Matt never hid a desire to escape from the trees, the fields, the lakes and rivers she called home.

There were so many reasons the two should not be together. His departure would aid their ability to move on with their lives. She imagined how they might eventually run into one another's families a decade later. Perhaps reminisce over coffee at a halfway point between their new homes. Did she need Matt? She hated that somehow the answer always seemed to come back to a single word. Yes.

She abandoned the introspection to answer her friend. "The biggest thing I've needed for some time is answers to what happened to my mother. Things had been so weird for so long now, that as bad as all this is, I believe answers are on the horizon. I am scared though, trust me. I'm terrified. Don't dare think I am not. How about you? Are you going to be okay?"

"No, I have to pee."

They laughed, reveling in a shared moment of levity, happy to bury terror if even for a second. Cassie quickly returned to the role of protector. She was not as worried about themselves anymore; she wished to get help for the others. That meant moving.

"We now have proof that my sister saw monsters. She witnessed them above ground, which means there is a way to the surface. The quicker we find it, the faster we can help the others. Are you with me?"

Lisa nodded. Cassie stepped forward and vanished. Lisa screamed as she watched her friend fall into an open pit. A wide chasm stood where a floor used to be. Cassie dangled by her fingertips, body swinging from the momentum caused by the unexpected fall. It was miraculous she turned in time to save herself at all. The miracle did not last long. Cassie's hands slipped free! Gravity took over and the young woman fell.

Tributaries split off in multiple directions through an underworld vast as the plains above. Joe occasionally yelled into offshoot caverns while maintaining a course in the main tunnel. If a forest offered a well-worn path, one could be certain it led somewhere. He applied the same theory to the underground variant by remaining on the straight and narrow. More like wide. The enormity of the subterranean complex stunned him. He hollered into smaller tunnels in case his daughter had investigated some arteries, but he taught her better than that. She knew to follow the dominant pathway. He could only hope their paths would cross.

Whiffs of rotten eggs led him forward. The obnoxious element, familiar to anyone who ever took a basic chemistry class, was that of sulfur. Science professors enjoyed subjecting the yellow rocks to Bunsen burners. The result could clear a room. Joe and Roger once joked teachers used it to cover their own farts after sloppy Joe day in the cafeteria. Long gone were days when he and his friend goofed about anything.

A literature teacher taught him more about the subject than any science class ever did. Her name was Mrs. Wise. The teacher had fantasy grade looks that captivated male and females alike. What made her a great educator had nothing to do with appearances. She made every student feel special. Students griped to her one day about the obnoxious smelling experiment from their previous class. Mrs. Wise ran with the subject, relaying it to literature. She spoke of common lore related to demons but challenged them to think the reverse.

While there were untold stories of the foul smell accompanying the foulest of beings, what of angels? Would they not have an odor? One produced by the act of entering the human world. The bulk of the students argued an angel would smell like Mrs. Wise. She changed the subject to keep it from going off the rails, but she spoke of a quote which stuck with Joe.

"Follow ye not the Devil, for the mephitic vapors of his cloak are but a ruse. The malodorous packaging deters the virtuous from gazing deeper into eyes burning of flame, which reveal the genuine nature of the beast. The abject cruelty beating within the blackest heart."

She explained the quote to them. An entity such as the devil would choose such a foul odor to keep others at bay. If kind-hearted people avoided him, they could not determine his true nature. She further suggested people needed to remain vigilant. Evil is unafraid to announce its presence. If men and women do not to confront it, that leaves it to grow. 'If someone tells you who they are, believe them.' That was a similar quote that Joe could not remember who to attribute to. He felt it held the same meaning. Avoiding the reality of darkness out of convenience or fear could lead one down a path that might darken their own heart, eventually.

Joe wondered whether any heart was as black as his own. It fell into disrepair after losing his wife and continued to beat only from muscle memory. Part of the reason he so easily left the others behind in the house and ventured out on his own was because the destruction wrought by a sinkhole supplied him with an idea too long missing. Hope. The unbelievable nature and turn of events that thrust them into chaos acted as a sign that anything was possible. He was underground. If he believed his youngest, and he did, they dragged Rebecca into a hole. Hope visited him simply because the earth split under his best friend's farm. The devastation instilled in him a strange belief: Rebecca was here.

He could no more explain the feeling than he could the instinct which drew him to the masked woman at the fair. Hopefully, his current situation would produce better results. And if not, were he to prove himself a fool again, he would do so alone, with no witnesses.

Every step brought him closer. He felt Becca guiding him. Not through whispers any longer. Those ceased since the ride home. She called to him in another impossible way. Between wafts of sulfur, he swore he detected her perfume. Something gurgled nearby. What first sounded like the growl of an angry beast revealed itself to be a small spout of water cascading over rock, the dripping amplified by cavernous acoustics.

Something fluttered to his right, then left. He spotted nothing. Was Rebecca trying to communicate? They used to play a game where one would sneak up on the other and place hands over eyes from behind. The common surprise greeting varied in that it signaled the start of their unique gameplay. Rules were simple, the blinded individual could not speak.

That gave the one clasping hands over the other's face the only one with a voice. They had the floor until they instructed they released the blinders. The one in the rear position could talk about any subject in any manner they chose. If Becca wished to convey it angered her when he failed to wash dishes, he could not respond. Or, better yet, if she whispered how badly she desired his body, he could only listen as she went into graphic detail.

Joe closed his eyes. He could almost feel her hands spread across his face. He waited for a sign and felt one as air on his neck. A breath? More likely a draft, but he remained still, understanding if there was a way she would discover it. She would whisper to him.

Then she did. "*Open your eyes, you silly boy.*"

It proved to be a warning. Joe opened his eyes to a perverted monstrous version of a dog. it snarled but not in a domestic animal way. The growl formed a canine chorus, as if it came from multiple demonic dogs, not just the one. The sizeable beast came front loaded. The muscular black front legs comprised stacked musculature impressive enough to compete against human bodybuilders.

Its hindquarters were leaner with stringy muscles pulled taut. likely designed for speed. Its bared fangs crisscrossed at such wild angles that it likely nicked its own flesh with every bite. The enormous head bobbed like a punch-drunk prizefighter. One ear stood upright while the other ended in a stub. Each paw had five-digits culminating in sharp claws, but they were free of fur so resembled human hands. The beast drooled liberally.

Joe ran, but too late. The creature sprang, leaping onto his back and sinking teeth into his shoulder. A cascade of fire ripped through his body. He fought to remain standing as the weight of the creature threatened to take him down more than the attack itself. He understood that to fall meant death.

The horrific entity thrashed its head, enhancing Joe's agony. Blood poured from his wound. Despite the black of the tunnel, his world faded toward white, which he understood as a signal of imminent fainting. He would surely become kibble and human bits if he succumbed.

He spun, using the weight on his back, following the momentum it provided. He careened at a stone wall, causing the creature to release its bite. It howled in what could have been a thousand barks. The strange chorus effect of the monster unnerved him to his core. The devil dog recovered and bit him again near the same spot. Joe noticed a jagged outcropping.

He yelled a battle cry and raced forward. Turning at the last second, he jammed the beast against the sharp stone. He heard a pop as if a walnut cracked. The thing on his back wailed in apparent disbelief that a food source could cause any discomfort beyond indigestion.

Its legs drifted into slackness before it slid to the ground. Joe turned and stabbed a blade into one of its eyes. The creature moaned in a descending chorus of cries until all the voices in the thing's head went silent. Then he dropped alongside the defeated animal. He pulled his shirt open to examine his wound. The appearance of something so foreign to this world to any sense of normalcy ironically fueled Joe's odd outlook leading to renewed faith. Anything was possible. He would not stop now.

"I'm coming for you, Becca."

CHAPTER 27

Roger and Kate competed in an unspoken contest over who could outpace the other. Remnants of a living room no longer livable served as the arena. The kids held court on the couch. Earlier, they dusted it off, repositioned it, and checked everything for safety before handing it over for a sit. Tyler straddled the sofa arm like a saddle, occasionally miming the motion of pressing a remote. Jenny slept on the cushions in a fetal position. Kate wondered whether that was normal or resulted from all that had rocked the poor child's world over the last several months. Jenny spent the night with them plenty, but Kate never noted the girl's sleeping habits. At least the child rested.

Her thoughts turned to friends in town. She had many more than her husband, who trusted only Joe. As she thought of her friends, she could not help but worry that some of them too succumbed to vanishing strata beneath their homes. She remembered little of her geology, but that word came to mind. She believed strata meant lined sections of rock. Local anchors mentioned it with some frequency during recent news reports. The population had been fortunate that all previous ruptures occurred in remote areas, at least until one scored a bullseye on their farm. There was every chance other people suffered the same. That was why she worried about her acquaintances. It was a matter of time before one hit. Well, pay dirt.

Succumbing to the worst of small-town stereotypes, Kate gossiped with neighbors at the hair salon. It served as their local TMZ. The crumbling ground recently became the topic du jour. The others never seemed as interested as Kate as to the cause for the swiss cheese landscape spreading across their community. They preferred to discuss who cheated on whom and which relationships were beginning or ending.

Kate had an accomplice who took no prisoners during the group therapy sessions. One woman was not afraid to veer off the heartbreak express and get back on track with the good stuff. That woman was octogenarian Connie Willow. The old bird always brought the heat regarding the direction of conversations. Not too long ago, the woman stormed into the shop and created a stir which stuck with Kate.

Their aged neighbor wore a wig. She popped in one day, paying no mind to signing up for a turn with a stylist. She simply lifted the whole fuzzy kaboodle off her head and thrust it at Wanda Foster for styling. Connie seated herself and steered the conversation to whatever conspiracy theory buggered her butt that day. Kate enjoyed Connie's visits. At least the chatting always proved interesting.

Connie had inside sources at both bars and was quick to share what people were drinking and thinking. She started that day with which businesses were floundering, and which farms were on the brink of failure. Kate disliked wallowing in misery, so tuned out and texted her kids during those conversations. When the topic turned to sinkholes, she reengaged. Word was the sudden lack of solidity below their quaint town flummoxed community leaders. They were considering calling in state officials for a look-see. Kate mentioned it was about time. Big city engineers would know better how to handle things. The notoriously independent salon patrons scoffed at the mention of outsiders. Kate let it drop, but Connie had more to say.

The old woman waited for the scuttle to die down and then lowered her voice. (Which was still loud since the woman was hard of hearing.) Connie suggested a big party years ago related to the current sinkholes. Conversation ground to a halt. Not a chirp sounded from the local birds. Only the clink of Wanda snipping at Connie's removable 'do continued. Kate noticed not one lady would meet her gaze. Time seemed to stand still until Wanda screamed.

The employee slipped with the scissors and cut herself mighty deep. Her proximity to the wash-bin was fortuitous. She ran her bleeding finger under the faucet while dangling the hairpiece in her other. Sherilyn Franks rushed to assist the stylist. The tinfoil in Sherilyn's hair made Kate think of a conspiracy hat.

Connie, meanwhile, had her fill of the activity and yanked her wig from Wanda. The stylist protested, but winced and refocused on her hand under the wash.

Connie placed her mop back on top and looked in a mirror. The trim was half complete and visibly lopsided. The old geezer shifted it and smiled at her image, tufting her hair as if she owned a perfectly coifed sixties bob.

"I dare say you have outdone yourself, Ms. Wanda. You understand I'm on a tight budget, so the tip is unavailable, but I always remember you at Christmas with the crisp dollar bill." Connie headed for the exit.

The customers collectively urged the woman to stop, but the lady strutted through the door proudly, ready to show off her fresh look to the world. The women gasped at the sight of the blood smear on one side of the wig. Suzy Osgood, a shift manager at the grocery store, made the most of the moment.

"You outdid yourself with the highlight, Wanda," Suzy said to a room full of laughter.

Kate needed to return to the boys that day, so she left before quizzing the others about Connie's proclamation. She could not fathom any way the collapsing stretches of landscape could relate to the field so long ago. She was curious why the group collectively clammed up when Connie raised the subject. Without knowing why, she felt as if she tried to bring it up, the women would clam up again. Kate was on the outside on this one, as oblivious as the old woman with blood smeared across her head. She wanted to know more and vowed to return.

With her curiosity piqued, she considered visiting the only other gossip hub she knew of in town (besides the bars). The nail salon. She wondered what the response would be from that crew. She never paid the visit, however, as she was not a regular customer. There was no reason to bother with her nails. Farming too quickly stole any elegance related to fingertips. She considered herself lucky they all still had their digits intact. Life on a farm was hard.

And perfect.

She loved her situation, always had. There were times, sure, where she thought of leaving everything behind to travel with her family. When the kids were younger, they drove to Washington DC. Kate made it educational and fun by insisting her children write reports in advance about different monuments they planned to visit. The boys presented their project at assigned destinations. Matt surprised her with the level of detail he put into his presentation, despite his utter rambunctiousness at that age. Her oldest was the wilder of the two.

As the children grew older, their family found less reason to travel. The boys had friends and wished to spend time with them, so the furthest they went anymore was to the nearby city or to Dundee Beach. The boys became less interested in roaming than in hanging out with local girls. Even Tyler had a soft spot for the ladies, though he would never admit as much.

Nothing but guys all around, and she was okay with that. She was motherly by nature and enjoyed her role as peacekeeper, felt her words of wisdom offered a fresh point of view versus that of their father. Roger's job was to toughen them while hers was to soften their edges. Matt could be a cad, often exasperating her to no end. Though his heart was far from pure, it was noble. She was proud of her sons.

Then there was Roger. Kate relished her dalliances in High School with the foreign exchange student, Toby. She enjoyed him greatly—thank you very much. Once upon a time she considered following him to his country. When the deadline came to decide, she chose the soil below her feet. Oh, how she missed her pretty boy, but this was home. Making the mature decision did not immunize her to heartbreak. The situation primed a miserable and lonely Kate to seek a rebound. She found it in Roger. When she first kissed him, she knew he was the one.

She had sex with Toby. The foreigner took her virginity in a truck bed parked in a field. He was an experienced and yummy lover. Upon dating Roger, she expected to pick up her physical needs where they left off, but her farm boy would not have it. Everything proceeded slowly. Roger was a "shucks and gee whiz, ma'am" kind of guy who believed in courtship. He fumbled plenty, almost dropped the pass when the two of them finally made love, but he quickly recovered. Woo-boy, did he recover. She got over Toby by getting under Roger and never looked back.

Roger made it clear she was his "gal" and promised he would never stray. Around the same time Kate connected with Roger, she also became best friends with Rebecca. Becca had long been a thorn in Kate's side prior to their newfound bonding. 'Frenemies' her sons would call it. Rebecca was a smartass, athletic, wild girl who never met a button she did not like to push.

Heck, Becca continued her one-woman rampage even after the two tapped out on conflict and decided friendship was the way to go. Becca went from pushing

Kate's buttons to trying to unbutton them. Rebecca was sexually adventurous and made her desire to explore her new bestie's landscape known. Kate threw up every no thank you sign she could, even while admiring how hot her friend was.

Rebecca attempted to get Kate to play the field. A very wide-open one. Her young friend always goaded Kate toward promiscuity. Kate never took the bait and never cheated on Roger. She understood there would always be temptations, that she would develop sexual urges for others. She was human. They could embrace every urge or bury them alongside the corn and tomatoes. She and Roger were good farmers so they could bury anything, including temptation.

Kate and her husband agreed fantasies differed from reality, so allowed them into the bedroom. As close to home as some were, none ever instigated conflict. Their fights related to discipline. Not bondage style bedroom talk. They argued over family discipline.

She believed in standing firm as a team concerning their children, which was why it infuriated her whenever Roger gave in to the boys. The boys were well-versed in dividing the parents. Something about all of them being male created a different bond than she shared with them. Roger was more open to certain indiscretions. Her anger over Roger's forgiving nature did not stem from feeling left out. Her only intention for wanting to stand united was to ensure the safety of their tribe. Their two loveable knuckleheads were dowsers for danger rather than water.

Such fights came to Kate's mind while she paced their destroyed home. Kate found herself on edge over more than a natural disaster. Her nerves danced along a tightwire of emotions fostered by worry about her family. They were a unit, and it stood fractured. Kate protested her oldest leaving earlier, but Roger overrode the decision without the agreed upon consulting. As a result, Matt was missing. Moments like these were ones that prodded, poked, and tested the bonds of marriage.

"Why isn't he back yet?" Kate asked.

"I don't know, honey."

"Something must have happened. Why are you just standing here?"

It didn't take a slap to suffuse Roger's face to red. The sting of her words hit harder than any open palm. "Because I have to look after you and the kids is why.

I am worried. But I will not leave you alone. Maybe I shouldn't have let him go. They never covered something like this in parenting 101!"

Kate knew her husband well, so understood the rage her comment would produce. Despite that, his face displayed more than fury. Knots of tension hid below worry line wrinkles so intense they would likely become part of his permanent look as he grew older. Those lines traveled to dark places, ones where a parent could imagine the worst outcome for a child. Their mutual fears could drive them apart, test their faith, or they could come together as a team to battle such dreadful thoughts. She preferred they unite, so stepped away from the abyss of striking out further in anger.

"You're right. If they taught it, I must have skipped that class myself."

She smirked at her husband. Roger remained aggravated. She wounded him with her words and understood healing takes time. She turned to an end table, another outlier piece of furniture which stayed upright in the storm. A lamp lay alongside it on the floor. She lifted it, wiped a layer of dust off the surface, then placed it where it once stood. Tyler scrunched his face.

"What are you doing, Mom?"

"I don't know, straightening, I guess."

"Why?"

"The place is a mess."

"No duh, we're underground! Our entire house looks like Matt's room now."

"It is horrible, isn't it?"

"If someone in the neighborhood saw this, they would shuttle me and Matt off to an orphanage. Even TV makeover shows would turn this project down."

Kate smiled. Despite her psyche matching the state of their surroundings, she giggled. The sudden laughter caught Roger's attention. She smashed the lamp onto the floor, breaking it into pieces.

"Like a different reality show, the object never gave me joy, so it had to go. I had to change its bulb too often," she said.

Roger embraced his wife from behind. "Careful, that may be the straw that breaks our insurance agent's back."

"You went from one item not giving you joy to about five individual pieces of lamp not giving you joy. Not sure you fully understand the concept, Mom," Tyler said.

The three laughed in release. Let the world test their faith. They would remain a family, let nothing, not even monsters tear it asunder. Circumstances brought them quickly back to reality when Jenny screamed.

"Daddy, Daddy!"

Kate rushed to the child. The girl appeared caught between wakefulness and a dream. "It's okay, sweetie, it's okay."

Jenny offered a cryptic message. "No, it's not. Mommy isn't alive anymore. Don't let him find her!"

Kate shared a look with her husband. Another class the two had missed. Kate did her best to soothe a child who could not stop shaking.

CHAPTER 28

Lisa leaped and caught one of Cassie's hands. Cassie lifted her other and gripped her friend's clothing. Lisa lay sprawled on her stomach, but she could not muster the strength to pull. Cassie swung her legs until finding purchase along the lip of the fractured surface. Using the planted leg and her hold on her friend, Cassie wiggled her way onto solid ground. Mostly solid. Rocks crumbled under their combined weight. The pair scrambled away from the precarious edge, collapsing in a heap, exhausted.

"Thank you," Cassie said.

"I don't think I can keep going." Lisa wept. A snot bubble formed and popped.

"You can. Aren't you the badass who just saved me?"

"I was your ladder. You crawled over me. I'm not strong enough. I can't do this."

Cassie took her friend's face in her hands. "This is all kinds of messed up. There is no guidepost on how to deal with something like this. But you witnessed your boyfriend being taken and still you fight. I could have died. Who saved me?"

Lisa murmured a reply. Too softly to hear. Cassie demanded an answer.

"Who saved me?"

"I did."

"Yeah, you did! You've got this. Fighters don't give up. Are you with me?"

They rose and Lisa nodded. She wiped her tears and nose with her shirt. Her stomach sloshed again. The woman was a mess, but still alive. Lisa grabbed the only remaining flashlight. Their other one fell so far they could not see its light if it survived the fall. A narrow ledge stretched to the other side of the open pit. Cassie eyed the pathway, but Lisa shook her head.

"No. All kinds of no. Are you kidding? We have to turn back."

"We know what's there. Monsterpalooza. If we wish to get help, we need to move forward. I'll go first."

Cassie sidled onto the edge, leaning into it as much as possible. Lisa trained the flashlight on her. The walkway was no wider than the girl's feet. The expanse was several yards wide but might as well been a mile given how slowly she moved, barely an inch at a time. A rock crumbled and her foot slipped. She grunted and recovered.

With a sudden burst, Cassie finally navigated to the opposite side and leaped off. She faced away from Lisa long enough to close her eyes and silently pray a *thank you*. After battling her shaking hands to still, she turned to her friend. She plastered a smile across her face to entice her buddy to take a spin on one of the most frightening of state fair rides.

"Your turn."

"I don't know. I..."

Something growled ferociously from Lisa's side of the pit. The hollowed-out acoustics amplified the warning. Lisa rushed to the chasm, ready to run for her life, ledge or no ledge. The growl repeated. The teen stepped on the narrow stretch and inched forward. Guttural rumbling sounded again, right where she balanced herself.

Lisa laughed. "It's my stomach."

Cassie waved with both arms. "Good. No monster. But use the adrenaline while you still have it."

The teen faltered and threw her arms against the cavern wall to recover. In doing so, she smashed the flashlight. The light flickered, threatening to go out. Cassie's face drooped. If they lost the tool, it would seal their fate. Lisa maneuvered at a slow pace but soon reached the end.

Cassie grabbed her friend by the wrist, a move designed to assist but also to control the torch. They could not afford for it to drop into the chasm. Lisa leaped onto solid ground. She did a similar quick prayer without trying to hide it.

"Sucked, I know. You did good. Is it working?" Cassie asked.

Lisa shook the device. It continued flickering but worked. They exchanged nods and advanced. Lisa took the lead, unwilling to share the light, her own version of a security blanket. Shadows were so dense on their journey it threatened to swallow any illumination whole. They struggled to see even with hardware at their disposal.

"What do you think those things were? Aliens? Chet believed in them and ghosts and all that shit. He streamed like a million ghost-hunter shows."

"These aren't spirits. They have teeth."

"Aliens?"

"If they were, government people would have stormed what used to be Matt's backyard. They would have rescued or imprisoned us in Area 51 or whatever. No. This all relates to the sinkholes and our community. All this GMO stuff they have been working on for foods. I think maybe a lab went too far. Everything we have seen holds semblances of animals combined with something foreign. And not like French, but from another world."

"Yeah. Sure. Makes sense."

Cassie noticed Lisa's reaction. The teen eagerly speculated on their circumstances moments ago. Now she acted as if wanting to change the subject. Why the sudden change? Lisa was hiding something. Had Cassie's words jogged her memory? The women reached a crossroads. Twin tunnels loomed ahead. Lisa danced the beam between the two.

"Lisa, tell me."

"Later. We need to decide which tunnel."

"Either direction. You choose. Don't hide things from me. You went from sixty to zero on the theories train. What are you not telling me?"

Lisa sighed in resignation. "You know my mom, right?"

Everyone in town did. Lisa's mom got around. The stunning woman used to model, though recent years had caught up to her. Vanessa was her name. She dangled blatant sexuality as a lure, using it to trap men in committed relationships. Her own parents raised the woman's name during a fight once. Cassie never asked them about the issue, too afraid of learning things she wished not to know.

"Yes. I know your Mom."

"Let me explain why I loved Chet. I walked in one day, late from school, and he sat waiting for me in the living room with my mother. They had not noticed me enter. She made a move on him. Sick. Not okay for a million reasons. But he said,

'Sorry. I'm not interested. I love your daughter.' Trying to steal my boyfriend. Can you imagine?"

Cassie could not. The thought sickened her. She could not fathom the devastation she would feel if Mr. Whatley did the same to her. She loved Matt's father, found him attractive even. But he was her second dad. It would break her heart and shake her core if ever he approached her in such a manner. Honorable people existed in the world. The Whatley's fell in that camp. Lisa's mother did not. Cassie respected Lisa for transforming herself despite the constant stream of men in her life playing stepdad, none sticking around for more than months at a time. She wished to comfort her friend but was too eager to get at the information.

"No. I can't imagine."

"Then another day I returned home to find a police car in the yard. I ran inside, worried, following sounds to her room. Once there, I peeked through the open door and spotted a female officer watching my mom go at it with some guy in handcuffs. I've seen him around but had no idea who he was. A farm hand, I think. Only the cop noticed me. She smiled in a way that made me sick. It was like she planned for me to be next. I rushed from the house."

Cassie couldn't believe it. Deputy Baker. The situation lined up with Cassie's own experience at the station. But what could the officer have to do with any of this? She felt horrible for her friend after hearing the story, but she could not piece together how it related to their current circumstances. There were many questions she wanted answered but kept quiet to allow Lisa to finish.

"When I came back that night, my mother was drunk. I confronted her and asked who the man was and why the cop was there. She said the police arrested him. For what, I don't know. He apparently was religious, a family man with a new wife and newer kid. This officer promised she would let the guy off if he got off. The woman intended to force him to commit adultery. Why, I cannot imagine. I blew up asking Mom how she could do such a thing and that's when..."

The light went out. Lisa tapped it on her palm. It lit up but still flickered. Lisa flashed down both tunnels again.

"Never mind. Right or left?"

"Lisa, you suggested it might have something to do with all this. You can't stop. I've met that cop. She is seriously damaged."

"How do you know her?"

"I'll tell you after you finish."

"Mom claimed her actions were altruistic. It kept the stranger from being locked up. But the guy started crying at the prospect of such an act. Then by the time my mother finished with him, he cried for a different reason. That he liked it so much. This individual by the end was a hanger on begging for her number. She called him in front of me and set up a date. Loss of innocence turned the cop on more than the sex. I'm mature enough to understand that now. My mother claimed there was a darkness in this town. One planted long ago, and the reaping was imminent. She mentioned how soon I too would succumb and eventually would not be innocent any longer."

"Darkness? What did she mean?"

Lisa shook her head. "I blew up and yelled about how I would never be like her. But what if she is right? What if I become a vulgar person? I only know now that we are facing such awful things it makes me think of that day the cop undressed me with her eyes. It wasn't normal. This isn't normal. Something is happening. I believe the source of all this feeds on innocence. Maybe the way to stay safe is to give into the inevitable. I should just follow in my mother's degenerate footsteps. Do I even have a choice? What if it is in my DNA?"

"No. You have an entire world ahead of you. You decide who you will be. You are a phenomenal person. I am proud to call you my friend. And if you ever started acting anything like that cop, trust me, there would be a huge intervention coming your way."

"Promise?"

"I promise."

"Okay. Let's go." Lisa uttered a childhood decision mechanism while dancing the beam back and forth. "Eenie, meenie, miney... Shit!"

The beam extinguished while pointed at the left tunnel. Cassie froze in the dark, afraid to drift too far from their position. The telltale smack of plastic against hand sounded as Lisa smacked the device on her palm. Light returned at the exact moment Lisa's went out.

Crunch!

Something bit Lisa's entire face. It all happened so quickly at the hands of what appeared to be a morbidly obese man. Layers of fat cascaded over a thick body feeding into massive tree trunk legs where much of the flaccid skin settled. A tiny penis dangled from folds below the belly. It appeared to be more human than monster, except for its head.

Cassie spotted only a quick glimpse before it sprang into action. The entire skull and face were regular sized, but hairless and featureless. The front split vertically down the center, opening sideways to reveal a tremendous mouth. Teeth cascaded in descending layers of gums, all leading into the throat. The largest perimeter of jagged ivory ran the full length of the gaping maw while smaller rows descended from there.

It snapped its vertical jaw closed over Lisa's head with a crunch, enveloping her from ear to ear. Lisa remained standing momentarily until her body timbered on its back. A bloody mass filled the void that was once a beautiful face. Skull fragments crunched loudly as the killer chomped on its morsel.

The thing that was once Lisa (Cassie hated to think of her that way, but defaulted to the notion for her own sanity) maintained a tight grip on the flashlight. The fat man swallowed, then stepped forward, twisting its head, searching. She launched herself against the nearby cavern wall, fading into a shadow. She caught a better glimpse of the horrendous being as it fell into Lisa's light.

The massive form squished with every step. Sweat dripped liberally from its body, forming a slick liquid coating. The dribbling sweatiness gathered in pools at its feet, causing it to splash through its own filth while walking. The horrific entity searched the area. Could it sense her? Smell her? How?

It faced her. She suddenly understood. Resting in between serrated layers of teeth were two beady black eyes. Their positioning ensured the foul thing would see its food as it ate. Something approximating ears rose on either side of the open skull, just shy of its throat. All its facial features existed within the beast's mouth like a mad version of a Russian nesting doll.

Bioluminescent plaque covered its teeth, which explained how it could navigate underground. While studying 'Lord of the Rings' in one of her classes, the filming of the movie in New Zealand came up. That country had a native species called glow worms. The pictures the teacher showed on her tablet matched the color in the walking blob's mouth. The light did not extend far but served its purpose.

Cassie froze, rooted in place as it looked directly at her. The head opened and closed as it searched. (And sniffed?) She heard the huffs of air, but it failed to spot her. It grabbed Lisa by one leg and dragged her down the same tunnel it came from. The grotesque killer squished with such heavy footfalls she could not understand how they missed its earlier approach.

They were likely too deep in the story about Lisa's mother. A parent who sought darkness while her poor daughter found it. The flashlight receded as it grew further away along with her fallen friend. Cassie scrambled from her hiding spot and gave chase. She followed the nightmare as it dragged her friend. The light shifted with every bump.

Cassie fought her gag reflex upon nearing the thing as the smell finally hit her. Whether from the dead body or the abomination itself, noxious fumes filled the air. She moved stealthily but quickly. That which she sought to retrieve threatened to reveal her position. Lisa's body collided with an obstruction, causing her arm to shift. The beam landed on Cassie.

One backward glance from the fat man and he would spot her. Cassie bolted forward and grabbed the flashlight. Lisa refused to let go! Rigor mortis? The tug of war jerked her friend's corpse. With no apparent neck, the loathsome monstrosity stopped and turned its entire body to investigate the commotion. It opened and closed its face down the center. Teeth clomped every time its maw snapped shut.

Cassie pressed against a cavern wall, hiding in a shadow. The coolness of the rock nothing to the frigidity she felt in her heart over her friend and the fear it raised for the rest of her family's safety. The thing failed to see her and squished back into motion. She dashed forward and grabbed the torch. She maintained a grip on the shaft and allowed the beast to pull the corpse away. As it did so, Lisa finally showed love one last time by releasing the item.

The fat man opened and closed its face. The acoustics of the cave exaggerated the noise, which resembled that of self-closing jewelry boxes. She and Jenny used to drive her father crazy by flipping them opened and closed whenever he gifted them trinkets. Now the sound horrified her.

The grotesque monstrosity did the shuffle turn again. Body of a dead girl? Check. Flashlight in the dead girl's hand? Check. No other food source nearby? Check. It circled back forward to continue its bastardized trek, dragging its prize behind. Had it a neck, it might have turned to notice the flashlight remained on the cave floor, no longer traveling with the deceased. Cassie waited until the blue from its mouth faded into the distance. Once she felt it safe, she retrieved the light from where she staged it to appear as though it still rested in Lisa's grip.

With no one left to slow her down, and with terror building in her soul over thoughts of being hunted, (two friends down) she defaulted to her track skills. Needing no cap gun to get off the blocks, she sprinted down the second corridor without looking back.

The jaundiced beam of light swept the basement. Matt calculated escape options while Brad recovered. Occasional bubbles on the surface caused him to swish in search of the source, only to find ripples settling.

"Man, it really hurts," Brad moaned.

"Don't worry, we will find a way out of this."

"Last time I come to party at your place, Dude."

Matt landed the beam on a far corner of the basement. "The bulkhead! That's the only other entrance. Formerly wacky, no longer crazy Jenny, witnessed monsters topside. That means even prior to this sinkhole, they had a route to get to ground. Some tunnels must reach the surface. One even made it to the pumpkin patch to chew its way through Tyler's prize."

"Maybe that's how Heather got out."

"Yeah, about that..."

Before Matt could break the news to his friend, the same pig creature responsible for Heather's demise burst from the water and grabbed Matt's throat! It lifted him into the air. Matt choked, clawing at the feral clawed hands draining him of his life. His world faded, his arms drooped to his sides. The loops of alien intestines in the barn had nothing on this massive grip. The pressure on his neck felt as if vertebrae were about to pop.

Wham!

Brad smashed the monster in the head with a piece of ruptured pipe. Brad struck repeatedly until the beast let go. The pig-faced predator turned its attention to Brad. Brad swung at the center of its face. Blood spurted, accompanied by squeals of pain.

"You freaking thing! What the hell are you? I'm tired of you freaking things!" The creature collapsed halfway between concrete and water. Matt scrambled away as Brad bashed it repeatedly. "Worst of all, you ruined our party!"

Brad struck several more times for good measure, though the creature had since gone still. It slid into the water and suddenly the surface went slick with silver. The dirty water made it impossible to tell if the body sank or if it turned into the metallic hue riding the ripples like an oil spill. In the periphery of vision, Brad sensed another threat and raised the club for round two, only to discover Matt back on his feet.

"Okay, Van Helsing, time to go."

They followed the wall to where the bulkhead used to be. The cellar had collapsed on itself but left a narrow opening for escape. The ground shifted in an aftershock. A rock tumbled past, splashing into water. The structural integrity appeared questionable.

"No way I fit in there," Brad said.

"I noticed you freaking up in the kitchen, but this is bigger. Look, it's tight but we can fit."

"Claustrophobia, big time. I can't go in there."

"You just killed Godzilla Junior and you're afraid of a hole?"

"I killed pig face. And yes, I am terrified. You got a problem with that?" Suddenly the pipe in Brad's hand appeared menacing.

Matt raised his hands in surrender. "No, I'm cool. I'll send help as soon as I reach the surface."

Matt squeezed in. Brad shuddered at the birth canal style excursion and turned away. He raised the pipe like a Samurai sword, scanning the cellar for threats, waiting for the next monster to arrive.

CHAPTER 29

Sloppy wet suction rose to a clamor in the distance. Joe picked up the pace despite his injuries. Heavy rains often reduced fields to mud, which forced farmers to don rain boots. During the rainy season, earthen sludge sucked shoes off feet. Even footwear designed for the elements did not ease the difficulties of walking in such conditions. Trudging through nature's goop took great effort and produced grotesque sucking sounds that delighted many a child.

Something made such a sound somewhere ahead. He struggled to determine what might make such a noise. Large quantities of liquid seemed unlikely so deep underground. Besides, Roger's land was notoriously dry. Water distribution was a problem for many farms. Sadly, his best friend's situation was worse than most. Besides the lack of bodies of water near his property, the topography of his land fed runoff to his neighbors to the south. Given those realities, such splashing nearby made little sense.

As he neared the source, he grew nervous, as if sensing something unnatural. The earlier encounter with a fanged furry happy to take him down already confirmed the world as he knew it had changed. There were plenty of threats he needed to protect his daughters prior to recent events. Sad he now had to add snarling behemoths to the list. As unnerving as the creature was, he compartmentalized it within a solvable category. A monster he could put down. Whatever loomed before him felt different. Worse, despite his worries, it drew him with the same strange feeling he encountered at the fair.

The force drawing him onward cramped his guts like the day long ago with Denise. He shook his head, trying to forget, but he could not. Never could. He never spoke of his initial fears in that moment to Roger or anyone. Seeing the townspeople clad in robes unnerved him to his core. Watching them grind in an erotic frenzy caused him to feel as if he stepped into a parallel universe. He was a popular kid in school. How was it he had not known in advance about the event, never heard a hint that such a horrific plan was to take place?

Who was down there that day? His own parents? Teachers? Only students? Were the cops present? After it all unfolded, he realized there was only one left who he could trust. The person who witnessed the ritualistic murder alongside him. He often questioned why he never sold the farm and moved somewhere where neighbors didn't wear sacrificial robes, but only jorts. He could not explain why he stayed. The fact he remained a townie had long instilled an existential worry in him. What rooted him in place? His psyche or circumstances? Why remain amongst people he no longer trusted? What sort of invisible influence held sway over him? While plodding through the subterranean corridor, he imagined the same intangible puppet strings guided him to a world not of his choosing. Yet he continued.

For all his irrational fear, Joe understood answers loomed ahead. Ones hidden in the bowels of a stone society built (How long ago? Years? Decades?) below their unknowing town. A strange shimmering glow came into view. Joe looked back to ensure nothing followed. Deeming it clear, he extinguished his light, deferring to the overwhelming blue brightness now guiding his way.

The tunnel narrowed to a jagged slant. Without the sparkling intensity, he likely never would have noticed the slight gap between tilted boulders that hid in shadows. It would prove tight, but it was squeeze through or go back. As if luring him on, the blueness flickered, calling him out. *We have your answers, Joe. Get your answers here! Answers here! We've got em'!* Joe ascribed words to the foreboding mystery ahead, imagining the goading coming from a peanut pusher in a ballpark.

He was ready for answers, thank you very much. Or thought he was. Gripping the edge of the crevasse, a chill overwhelmed him, rippling along his spine then cascading through his body until it numbed the tips of his fingers. While the rock formation proved cool, (expected given its depth) that alone did not account for the frigidity overwhelming him.

A border. He was about to cross one. Joe had always thought of national borders and state lines as blatantly arbitrary. An exercise designed to divide people. Live on that side of the tracks makes one special, while south of the same would label someone a "Southie" or worse. Borders as a meaningless construct was a philosophy he embraced in his regular life, but this one felt substantial. One more step would deliver him to—what? An 'Other' was the only way he could describe it.

The possibilities of what he might face lied ahead, though they remained partially blocked by a large fallen stone. He scrambled over it and squished through. The twisted opening limited the view of his destination. He navigated through the narrow gap. The sloshing grew in intensity. It provided an ominous soundtrack as he crossed over from a natural world to the supernatural.

He emerged on the other side (again feeling it as 'Other') and found himself on the shore of an epic landscape. The tightness of the tunnel opened into an enormous cavern, dazzling in brilliance.

The ground sloped gently from the miniscule beachhead comprising stone, pebbles, and a touch of sand. The portion of land fed almost immediately into the wash. Stalactites hung from the cavernous ceiling, covered in streaks of glowing azure. The blue hues were obviously the shimmering which he saw from a distance. It was bright enough to light the entire space, though some shadows remained hidden on the outskirts.

A vast lake filled most of the enormous landscape. The body of water beached at his feet but otherwise lapped at stone walls encompassing the majestic grotto. The otherworldly lighting reflected off the gentle ripples, creating a brilliant radiance. A waterfall poured over the rear wall of the chamber, its splashing echoed in a soothing rhythm. Except it failed to soothe him. He remained on the precipice of panic for no discernable reason. The vista before him alone should have infused him with a sense of calm, yet he felt the opposite. One could easily consider the view postcard beautiful were it not so menacing.

Menacing?

Why should a pool of beauty cause discomfort? Why did he experience a sense of foreboding at the mere presence of the body of water? At first glance, there was nothing special about the area besides its location and his dire circumstances, yet it frightened him. He could not explain other than feeling it had bad juju.

The lake produced waves, gentle though they were. Standing on shore, he wondered whether the earlier sloshing was that of the tide lapping against the beach. He attempted to attribute the distorted propagation of mud smacking sounds to the literal echo chamber, but it made little sense. Not even ocean waves crashing created the squelching which initially greeted him. With no discernible source, he parked those thoughts to focus on the mystery of the shimmering cobalt glow.

Bioluminescence.

In the incident's aftermath, Joe struggled with his sanity as a town of people he thought were his pals all feigned ignorance. Law enforcement claimed Denise perished by car crash alongside Granger. All bullshit. Joe and his buddy knew better. The cops suggested the teens suffered from the Mandela effect, remembering an occurrence as something different. Joe raged at that diagnosis. When confronted with it, he stated he understood there was only Jif peanut butter, not Jiffy, and that the Monopoly Man never wore a monocle. The cop didn't understand what Joe was talking about. That led him to ask the officer whether the man even knew what the Mandela effect was. The officer did not.

Joe's social life soured as he became a pariah of truth in a gaslighting community. His isolation resulted in a newfound appreciation for book learning. Never the best student, (unless classroom shenanigans was a major) He turned his studies around, if only to ignore classmates seated alongside him. Liars, the lot of them. Finding faith in science helped Joe move past the traumatic event. The scientific knowledge he gained would come to serve him well in his chosen profession. (If inheriting the family farm was a choice. Of this he often wondered.) A concept he learned back then came to him now.

Bioluminescence meant life.

After identifying the reason for the glow, it raised a tantalizing question. What kind of life could exist so far underground? Something plopped to the ground behind him, wet and sloppy. He turned to find a fist-sized glob at his feet. He looked up for the source, noticing how the stalactites seemed to drool.

The blob formed a jiggling mass, beading like Mercury. He touched it with his shoe. It rippled. That helped him understand the true nature of the grotto. There was a strange pallor to the 'water'. He thought of it as the color of Milk of Magnesia, (a medicine stocked in his house since childhood). The shimmer on the surface was almost white, bordering on silver. Now that his eyes had adjusted to the unique lighting, he studied the expanse, noting how every visible wall dripped with a slickness of the same shade, feeding into the body of the lake. The waterfall in the distance ran so thin and stood so far away it appeared normal. There was no way to determine if it instead was only a diluted version of the milky liquid.

A loud splash echoed along the furthest side of the cavern. He could not identify the source. Chemical runoff could have affected the so-called water. Some farmers cut corners, possibly using banned pesticides. Nasty stuff, but cheap. Taking a dip was out. The answer to what splashed remained elusive from his vantage point. No paperboy kid waited with a spinning headline that might explain all.

Joe deemed it a good time to move on. Having found no loved ones so far, he decided it best to seek the surface. The lake should have offered a clear tributary to follow. The water came from somewhere, yet he could identify none. He considered going back, following one of the many unexplored avenues along the way until he spotted an opening at the far end of the beach. A wide-mouthed egress beckoned. That was his answer. He turned to leave.

"Joe."

Rebecca's voice. Police settled on two overriding theories in her disappearance. Joe harmed her, or she left with a lover. The law felt nothing else lined up with Jenny remaining unharmed (physically at least). Joe often defaulted to the other man scenario, but when he searched his heart, he did not believe it. First, she loved him, warts and all. Second, she would never leave her children. Since her absence, he heard her call his name, whispers in the night or his mind. Now it rose above a whisper.

"Rebecca?"

Joe's voice echoed as if to punctuate his loneliness. Nothing but the splish-splashing of an underground waterway. Foolish the thought. Had it not already proven false at the fair. He wished to further apologize to the individual, but felt no right to visit her again and re-traumatize the poor woman. Better to let her slink off into the night with the folding of tents, left to tell tales of the crazy fan who ripped free her mask. The same man who even now still talked to his likely deceased wife.

Stepping to the water's edge, he noticed the reflection of a broken man. Once he looked past the pain, he recognized an unnatural clarity to his own image. The organic illumination radiating across the hollow was no match for the sun. The brilliance of his reflection appeared too perfect for such conditions. A high def resolution in an analog world. He attributed the purity to the liquid versus the lighting. What was that silver tinge? Model paint. The metallic sheen he applied to the plastic car kits as a child almost matched that which lapped at his feet. Yet it failed to stain the shore in the same shade, leaving only the blackened touch of a moisturized surface.

He dipped a toe. His reflection danced through the resulting spiral. The doppler effect acted as expected. If the liquid comprised anything other than good old H2 of O, he could not visibly identify the difference. Something splashed violently again. Joe scanned the lake. The ripple he started reached its zenith, then faded. With but a touch, he disturbed the surface. Yet an object producing a violent splash failed to cause a stir.

All remained still. An oasis. Physics appeared to have left the building, Joe thought. He turned his flashlight on and pointed it into the dark crevices over-head beyond the tips of the stalactites where the bioluminescence held court. His efforts cast shadows of teeth across the far side of the cavern.

A black mass dropped, passing through his beam too quickly to follow. Like a bad videographer, he aimed his light in every direction except the action. The object approximated the size of a Great Dane. That much he noticed.

Smack!

The thing exploded into the water with the concussive force of a world class belly flopper. He sought the touchdown spot, but the pool remained still. Im-possible. The world fell silent. The omnipresent dripping ceased like bird chirps in the presence of predators. His own heartbeat worked overtime to fill the void.

Radial waves should have traveled out from the splash. Then the still water ex-ploded as something breeched the surface from below. It vanished just as quickly, leaving bubbles in its wake. He aimed again where two limbs broke the surface (tentacles or arms?) and flailed. It eventually settled into a swim, moving in his direction. The swimmer beelined toward him as fast as an Olympian athlete. He lit up the area.

The light.

Joe realized it guided the unidentified individual. Rather than a lighthouse warning ships from shore, he was drawing something closer. He fumbled while trying to turn it off. The individual (or thing. Why did he keep seeing tentacles?) swam so near that water cascaded over him. Attempting to retreat, he lost his footing, dropping onto his rear.

The flashlight tumbled toward the lake's edge, shy of rolling in. He stabilized himself from his position on the ground and noticed everything return to stillness. Ripples vanished, and the lake surface shimmered peacefully. Whatever occurred until then, he wanted no part of. He leaped to his feet and reached for the light. Then something reached for him. An arm exploded from the depths, grabbing him with a grip that felt familiar.

The hanger on appeared female. He realized Cassie was in the caves, somewhere. She could swim fast. Was it her? Joe grabbed and pulled. The liquid sluicing off the woman's body as he pulled her free confirmed a silver sheen. A drenched woman rested in his arms, though her hair plastered against her face hid her identity. He set her down on dry land and swiped the strands away.

"Rebecca!"

He dropped alongside her and pulled her into a cradled position, feeling for signs of life. She showed it, hacking up voluminous amounts of the silver fluid. Once expelled, she sucked in a deep breath. Then she panicked, frantic, reaching for solid ground, trying to identify her surroundings until she discovered the arm across her chest. She looked up at him, whispering through unpracticed vocal cords.

"Joe?" She struggled with even the single word, touching her throat to massage atrophied muscles. "You're here?"

"Don't talk. Don't... I. Ah Baby, I found you. I found you,"

He pulled her tighter. She collapsed into a whimper and into him. She sobbed at the sudden freedom. Joe's tears joined in and he rocked her, shushing her, promising all would be okay. His commitment to safety went unheeded. She leaped up and staggered on unsteady feet. She noticed the open tunnel nearby and started for it, but fell. Joe rose in time to catch her.

"Run. We need to leave!. There are these horrific, unspeakable things down here. They defy description. Abominations of nature. The vilest of beings."

"I know. But we've got this. You and me, we got this."

Joe steadied her, tried to corral her. If she believed him, she failed to show it. She eyed the exit as if mentally counting the steps needed to make it there. Joe pulled her into another hug. Her resistance faded. They gazed into one another's eyes.

"Now isn't this sweet," someone announced in a powerful baritone.

Joe's blood ran cold upon hearing a voice he long thought extinguished. From where he stood, he could view the lake over Rebecca's shoulder. Rebecca reacted to the words by burrowing her face into his chest, trying to hide from a world which held her captive. Then Joe saw him. He wasn't sure if he thought the name or said it out loud.

Granger!

The supposedly dead classmate sported a thick black beard absent in his youth and was nude other than a pair of jeans rolled at the legs. Joe struggled to determine Granger's age. The individual somehow looked eighteen, but then again did not. Possibly he never was that age. Either way, facial hair or not, the individual seemed timeless, wizened, yet youthful. One more impossibility for Joe to wrestle with. Then it hit Joe. What was the man standing on? Granger began walking across the water from the opposite side of the lake. The blasphemous move stunned Joe.

The man of indeterminate age put on a show, spreading his arms wide then spinning in a quick circle. He showcased a dancer's grace but wore a lascivious smile. Granger licked his lips, looking from him to her. "Such a reunion. My. My. Mine!" Granger's voice rose, amplified further by the underground acoustics.

Joe's legs went weak. The solid rock beneath his feet not strong enough to hold him up as everything he ever knew felt suddenly unmoored. This was part of the Other he feared. He had passed through a border, proving actual ones existed. This was no longer Joe's world, it was one belonging to an individual who entered his life and changed it forever. Was the strangely youthful miscreant planning to do the same now?

Joe could not silence his thoughts. "How are you alive?"

Granger splashed three steps forward, almost a skip, one leg at a time, barely making a splash. The last movement exposed a stone pillar beneath the man's feet. Granger's smile softened, busted. He lowered his arms, dropping the crucified imagery. "We all have our cross to bear. Now prey tell me what you hope to accomplish? Surely you do not plan to abscond with that which belongs to me?"

"She's my wife!" Joe's anger carried through the cavern.

Drops of water feeding into the lake answered Joe. The sound had ceased earlier. Now it returned with a vengeance. Tiny droplets fell like rain in pockets through the underground bunker. Combined, the patter sounded like an army of cockroaches scuttling across tile flooring. The disturbing noise appeared to center on Granger. The man took another step.

"Something familiar about the way you are holding her. Oh, yes, reminds me of her in my arms earlier. While naked, the jeans are for guests. Would it pain you to know I entered her about the same time you entered these caves? My humbling home."

Joe launched forward, ready to walk across the lake himself. Rebecca held him back, shaking her head to ward off the notion. Joe felt the feelings from the day of the music festival times a hundred. He let it go and positioned himself to protect her.

"All these years and no one in town would even speak your name. They had us thinking we were crazy. But you killed Denise."

"So pedantic. Sacrifice is the proper word. Yes, the virgin served her purpose well. I designed the follow up subterfuge as an insurance policy against agents of the cloth arriving to perform certain ceremonies of their own. Would not want snooping by those who might be pre-disposed to purifying that which I unpurified."

"The blood. Everything gone by the time the police arrived. How?"

"He asks the man walking on water. You disappoint me if that is your sole question. Fine, for your small mind, assume my army returned the trappings of our rite to the way it was before. There were enough of them. So many willing followers in this pathetic zip code. Or expand your worldview and consider that Denise fed her existence fluids not into turf but into a realm awaiting a signal. That would explain why nothing needed cleaning."

"Joe, please, let's just go, just run. We never have to look back. I love you!"

"Don't believe the whore. She's tugging on heart strings, but she was tugging on something else earlier."

Joe clenched fists again. Rebecca kissed him. The pair staggered with the desperation of the too long separated. She looked in his eyes as they broke the kiss.

"It's always been you," she said.

"Ah, true love. It is so sickening. Really churns my guts..."

Granger gripped his waist and bent over, moaning. He rose back up, revealing an undulating stomach. When sucked in, the man appeared malnourished, so skinny that ribs showed through paper thin skin. A swirling mass filled his belly like snakes seeking escape. Despite the revolting display, every movement highlighted the man's physique. A rock star at his peak.

Granger bowed once more before rising like a head banger. Vast amounts of milky white liquid sprayed with the force of a firehose. The silver spew split into multiple globules midair before plopping on shore into egg sized masses.

The lake churned as if boiling. The pedestal under Granger's feet ascended, lifting him into the air, confirming the absence of one miracle while simultaneously producing another. How could a rock formation move in such a manner? The blobs that made land also bubbled while the dribbling slickness covering the cavern walls did the same. The world came alive with motion.

Clack! The blob nearest the couple split in the middle. A football sized crablike creature emerged, favoring one side with an oversized claw. The beast appeared half mammalian, possum like. A shell crested just above the creature's eyes, and the snapping pincer (longer than its body) was that of the traditional sea creature. The crab leaped for Joe's face.

He shoved Rebecca away and pulled the meat cleaver from his belt. With one slice, he separated the thing's claw. The beast landed in a tumble, screeching and hissing. The loose appendage writhed nearby, still snapping. Rebecca shouted a warning as another egg split and a second crab launched itself at her husband. He impaled the squealing creature until it stilled and dissolved into its original liquid.

Granger leaped from his platform and advanced along a rising series of stone pillars, each one timed to meet his footfalls. "You asked what purpose the virgin served. The ceremony produced my family, which you see before you. I beg forgiveness. They are a handful, a little wild. Might say they take after their father."

"I'm taking Rebecca home!"

"I believe you think you are. What is a blade against my talents? You do not understand what you are dealing with."

As if on cue, every bubble took the shape of an eye. Hundreds formed, each watching the couple. One by one they blinked out of existence with a pop only for another to form. A massive tentacle erupted from the depths, stretching high enough to caress stalactites. It wavered in view momentarily before sliding back underwater.

Joe pulled Rebecca toward the exit. A tentacle erupted closer this time (a different one?) and timbered at them. Joe shoved Rebecca even as he leaped clear. The enormous limb slammed into the ground, forcing the pair to separate.

Rebecca's screams rose above the din. She cried out, reemphasizing the nearby tunnel. Joe nodded. Then froze. As he looked across the lake, something (Oh God!) looked back. Within the waterfall at the rear of the grotto, an eye the size of the cavern wall gazed upon him. Joe felt a pull, as if the stare influenced him. He fought to look away, but gazing into the eye, he felt the absence of his world, and a sudden presence somewhere different. Chilling, cold, a place where dysmorphic creatures thrived, where the vilest of thoughts took form with glee. A place anathema to human condition and biology. Joe suddenly questioned whether they were trespassing on his or he on theirs?

The rise of multiple tentacles in his peripheral vision brought him back. They danced like snakes ready to strike. The one that already made ground rose again, ready to strike. Joe raced below its shadow, grabbed the flashlight, then swept up Rebecca and made for the cave. He switched off the beam to reduce their presence as targets of the otherworldly cephalopod. They narrowly escaped as the massive limb struck, followed by a second, shaking the ground so hard they nearly stumbled. They left madness behind and leaped into darkness.

The bubbling dissipated. Every set of eyes formerly open, closed. Tentacles receded into the deep while the remaining crabs liquified. Granger waded to shore, eyeing the couple's escape route and broke into a smile. A man with a plan.

CHAPTER 30

Slivers of moonlight cascaded across the cornfield in a staccato rhythm timed to breaks in the misty cloud cover. Silence ruled the land. A subtle breeze whipped the feathery tipped stalks of corn heavy in their husks, ready for harvest. Suddenly an isolated grouping of cornstalks jerked wildly. The fertile soil at the base of the disrupted crops crumbled away as the ground shifted. A circle formed in the earth, manipulated by underground forces, as something subterranean fought for the surface. Dirt clods rolled off the sides of a growing barrow. A clenched fist punched through, spreading into an open hand. An arm (caked black with grime) rose to elbow height before a second limb joined the party through the same tight opening. A head emerged between the two, Mother Nature giving birth. Matt spit out dust and gasped for breath.

He squeezed through, then dropped onto his back, gazing into the heavens. Stars shone down as if flirting, winking from perches in the brilliant night sky. The promise of peaceful slumber beckoned, but Matt rose to his feet. He staggered at the sight of open land where his house used to be. The barn seemed larger without its two story neighbor.

The storage shed and adjacent pumpkin patch loomed in the opposite direction. He calculated the distance of the farm versus that of the transporter. The vehicle was closer and would get him back quicker. He headed for it until something snapped loudly in the corn. He abandoned plan A and ran for the barn.

In his haste, the dozen red eyes staring at him from within the green went unnoticed.

B rad maintained his Samurai stance, pressed against the wall, waving the pipe while waiting for, well, anything. A belch of liquid announced an imminent opportunity to test his skills. Water frothed near his feet just ahead of a massive splash which soaked him through. He braced himself for the unknown and found it.

A conjoined twin version of the pig creature thrust through the surface with dual heads squealing in orgiastic delight at the sight of food. Deformed clawed hands sought their intended victim. Two minds sharing a single thought. *Kill the big guy.* They snorted in a horrific echo and advanced.

"No way!" Unable to choose a face, Brad slashed the pipe in between the two skulls, splitting the creature along its center! The metal sank into flesh pulled taught from the twins battling for dominance. Silver blood spurted as their necks drooped from one another, separating their partnership by a few inches.

Brad fought to pull his weapon free except the wailing beast (beasts?) yanked it away and tossed it into the water. The act of tossing the object hastened the damage. The pigmen leaned too far from one another, and their collective weight did the rest. Flesh tore loudly like a massive strip of Velcro being ripped apart.

Once the divorce began, they went along with it, deciding to split everything fifty fifty. The sickening crunch of bones joined in on the tearing flesh beat. Soon they were one no more. Rather than fall and splash, (as any torn in half organism should do in a polite society, Brad thought) they continued swiping at him with their individual arms. Now he faced dual instruments of terror. Neither could walk, but still they lashed out. The minimal island refuge kept him precariously close to their claws. One leaped from its solo leg, making land.

Brad kicked its face, then danced away when the claw went for ankles. The second halfling dragged itself forward. With no alternative, he grabbed a flashlight and crawled into the tunnel. And regretted the move immediately.

The walls were tight to begin with, but to someone with his phobia it felt even tighter. In shop class, kids sometimes placed their hand in a vice, urging others to turn it. Each wood-shop braggart started fine, the victim pretending to be stronger than the device, but inevitably all tapped out. The exercise in futility never failed to reach a point where the "viced" kid screamed bloody murder under pressure that left unchecked would crush the limb beyond repair.

Brad felt like those idiots while wriggling over cold stone. The walls on either side acted as plates and some jerk on the outside cranked the handle to the vice surrounding him. He wished to tap out, but clacks of claws on cement at his rear reminded him of what waited at the point of entry.

"Matt? Matt, are you alive? If your trapped corpse is blocking my way, I'll never forgive you!" Inching forward, he focused on rage to mask his surging fear. "Not only that, but I vow to eat your skinny ass if we both get stuck! After everything I've been through, you think a little cannibalism will stop me?"

Then something did. He found himself wedged tight with one arm stretched before him, the other trapped at his side. He struggled to dislodge himself. The free hand waved the flashlight wildly in desperation.

"No! Just let me out!"

He froze.

Rustling sounded ahead, followed by scratching. (Claws on stone?) A wolverine creature moved into the light where, unlike him, it had plenty of room to maneuver. Its teeth overlapped outside the confines of its mouth. Drool flowed at the sight of a prepared meal. Brad yelled at it to go away but it did not, in fact, he believed it smiled.

"Oh shi..."

It leaped at him.

CHAPTER 31

Joe and Rebecca ran until the luminescence faded, and darkness enveloped them. Because they were running blind, Joe stopped. Despite that, Rebecca fought to continue moving, tugging at him frantically. He held firm and turned the flashlight on. She squinted in the light, reacting to a world of brightness long denied. As she fought her way through adjusting to the light, Joe watched her and gasped in disbelief. Squeezing her hand tighter to ensure she was real, he then grabbed her waist and pulled her close. He tried to gaze into her eyes, but they raced about as if seeking escape.

"I knew it. I heard you. So many times I heard you."

She brushed away a lock of his hair plastered to his forehead with sweat. He looked down on her, smiling, hungry. She recognized the look.

"You cannot be serious. Don't even think of doing anything down here."

He bumped her playfully but shook her off. "That wasn't on my mind. Well, until you said it. And you know me."

"I do." She stared back as if reconsidering the offer. Something fluttered. "Did you hear that?"

The sharp flap of a sheet fluffed for bed making sounded close by. They scanned the area with the flashlight but saw nothing. The rustling grew louder. Overhead. Joe tilted the beam onto the cavernous roof, heavy with stalactites.

As he tried to examine the odd structure of the dangling formations, one opened its eyes! Others did the same until dozens of fiery red orbs glowed overhead as the source of the fluttering became clear. The dangling objects were human sized bats. Silver liquid dripped from around the nestled bodies. The monstrosities dangled upside down, cocooned in wraps thick with veins that came to life with a burning crimson matching their eyeballs. The massive wings struggled to unfurl from their tight grape leaves style wrapping.

The first to open all the way revealed a membranous six-foot wingspan. The extended arms exposed a head with partial bat features blended with a person's face. Its nose emulated a bat's closely though the mouth leaned human other than the overflowing jagged teeth. The body represented and amalgamation of both species. Human arms stretched wide and ended in palsied fists of sharp claws from which the wings draped like capes.

The loathsome biological blended fiend hissed and screeched. Soon the others joined in, spreading open themselves. They remained anchored to their perches while they lashed out at the intruders. Joe swung the cleaver, tearing a wing off the nearest attacker. The creature shrieked in annoyance, mostly unbothered by being clipped. Joe gasped in sudden recognition.

"Arden?"

Joe thought he recognized the features of Arden Jones who worked at Hanrahan's Butcher Shop? The man graduated with him. Joe saw him recently. The man bragged about an upcoming barbecue competition at the fair. How could the citizen have become part flying rodent? He identified another he knew. Chelsea Rowe, alive for sure, at least a week prior. The woman taught English at the high school. Both were from his class. All the right ages to have been at the killing field. Was it all somehow related?

A swipe from a beast sliced his cheek, drawing a thin line of blood. Stupid and lucky. Stopping to identify faces which could not be those of people he knew almost got him cut. Joe swung again, severing one of Arden's hands. The thing howled in pain. (Limbs more sensitive than wings. Check.)

For some unknown reason, the overgrown vermin did not depart from their mooring overhead. Had they done so, the fight would have ended quickly. Rebecca fared better than he so far, only because she stood pressed against a cavern wall beyond their reach. A closer examination of the Arden bat revealed human legs (albeit covered partly in black fur) stuck all the way to the knees in a thick layer of the silver goop. Were they being birthed? Not yet ready? That had to be it, he thought. He and his wife had survived only because the monstrosities had not fully cooked.

"We need to run."

"They are everywhere," Rebecca said.

"Stay low and near me. This is our best chance. Let's go."

They crab-walked their way through. Claws slashed at them, so Joe kept the blade raised while they traversed the gauntlet. The metal clicked and clacked against hardened talons. Hisses of frustration echoed in the tight quarters, but soon the couple escaped the danger zone.

Once clear, they ran without looking back until Joe once again faltered. Sweat washed over him from their efforts. Rebecca appeared fresh, dried off from her time underwater, almost invigorated. Joe winced in embarrassment. He favored a stitch in his side and hoped the cave proved too dark to reveal how flushed his face was.

"Maybe I haven't worked out so much lately."

"You look fine to me." She caressed his arm, testing the muscles.

"Stay with me, I won't let you go ever again."

"Do you know where we are going?"

"Home. We're going home."

"Which way?"

She gestured to twin tunnels. Joe remembered a story from his childhood and worried there was no lady or tiger option, only tigers. Or based on the half-cooked neighbors they left behind, maybe something far worse.

"Did you hear that?" Rebecca asked.

"No." Joe raised the blade, anyway. He waved it back and forth between the two openings, waiting for his ears to play catch up.

"I hear it all. Every noise. Every scream. The bubbling splash of every birth since I arrived down here."

"Births?"

"Granger. He's their daddy, the father of everything down here."

Joe noticed a look in her eye (a sparkle?). No, he refused to give into the jealousy monster in the face of genuine ones. What was this place? How could it deliver biological bastardizations? His head hurt. A deep fear overtook his wary bones as he remembered the worst of all of it.

The eyeball. The massive orb against the wall peered through him. It studied not his skin, nor his clothes. It saw everything. The presence of such a thing gut punched his sense of reality, filling him with an anxious dread of a world far beyond his control. He wished to further contemplate the existence of such a being, but that could lead to despair, and he refused to return there so soon after reuniting with his wife. He needed to focus on something else.

Home.

That was the answer. The road to recovery began there, he thought. It was the place with the building blocks to piece the family back together. All the rest he would figure out later. Left tunnel it was. She leaned into his ear, whispering so softly she could have been in his head rather than at his side.

"It's there. I hear it."

"Honey, you're scared. It is understandable after all you've been through, but nothing is there."

"You need to trust me. It's coming, you must strike it down. Kill it. You're supposed to protect me!"

The words staggered him as much as any blow. There it was. Had he protected Rebecca, she would never have ended up in the version of Hell they traipsed through. He failed before. He refused to do so now. Raising the blade, he followed her gaze to the left tunnel.

"Don't think, don't falter, just strike. Protect me. Kill it when you see it. Kill it!"

A blur leaped from the shadows. Joe swung. Cassie ducked, barely avoiding decapitation. The meat cleaver sliced a lock of her hair, which floated longer than the time it took her to drop and roll. His momentum against air caused Joe to strike stone. The weapon snapped off at the hilt. Cassie rose from the ground, eyes wide in wonder.

"Baby?" Joe's hand trembled at the point where he held the broken handle. He tossed it away in disgust.

"Mom?"

Cassie rose and launched herself at her Mother. Joe noticed his wife holding back, appearing distant as if afraid to wake up. He could only imagine the loss she felt while trapped, wondering whether she would ever see her children again.

Well, there was another child to see, and it was time to reunite them all. He joined in on the hug, completing the circle.

"Come on, let's get out of this hellhole. No more talk of Granger."

CHAPTER 32

The Fever 333 song "Burn It" blasted at a level designed to melt brains or announce a prize fighter heading to the ring. The warrior stepped before a dust covered mirror and examined his battle suit. Coil of rope across the chest, check. Tool belt with sledgehammer nested in the claw hammer loop, check. Timberland boots already caked with mud, check. Old school MP3 player with earbuds blasting the rock tune, check. Matt performed a quick shadowbox with his reflection to pump himself up.

"Oh, yeah!"

Then he turned his hands back in himself, tapping chest to stomach to pocket as if forgetting car keys. He realized what was missing and rushed off, returning with a pitchfork. He slammed the pole down and glanced once more in the mirror (used to keep livestock company in the years they owned animals). Satisfied he had everything he needed, he exited the barn.

He jumped on a nearby tractor and drove over to his home's former real estate. Moving at a slow pace, he felt the ground jolt under the weight of the vehicle as he grew closer. Hitting reverse, he backed away several feet and killed the engine. He jumped down on the side furthest from the hole and thrust the tines of the pitchfork into the earth. He stomped on the edge of the head until it merged with the soil, then he tapped the tip of the pole with the sledgehammer.

The tool stood erect and held firm when he tested it. He tied off one end of the rope midway along the handle, then pulled the line. The pole tilted slightly. He grimaced and vocalized his concerns to no one in particular.

"Please hold. Just need you as a backup in case the roof gives. I'll tie off on something more secure after I make an entry point. Don't want to tie to the tractor in case the ground gives way and takes me for a ride. An underground one." He made the motion of an object plummeting. "Tractor will take most of the weight anyway without anchoring me to a potential falling missile."

Matt fed the line through a gap in the seat and the chassis and circled around to thread it through. The ground trembled in aftershock and he backed away from the farm equipment. He waited for it to settle, then tied off the other end onto a tool belt loop. He lifted the sledgehammer, then stepped to the edge of the hole.

There was no mistaking the devastation. In a world where tilled land offered lush backdrops, the sunken ground loomed ominously. And precarious. The roof, resting several feet below the rim, had twisted at an unnatural angle. It filled the entire circumference of the sinkhole. To test the weight, he threw down the hammer. It landed with a loud thunk.

"Looks solid enough, I guess."

He threw the balance of rope, then leaped. It was a significant drop, but he rolled to absorb the blow. He took up a position at the center and raised the sledgehammer, striking home. The force caused bounce-back. The tool reared up and over him before slipping from his grip. He scanned the surroundings for anyone filming with a cellphone. Just his luck that even in the end of the world someone would spot his full-blown nerdism. It relieved him to notice he remained alone. He picked it back up and went to work, holding on tighter for round two.

K ate huddled with the kids on the couch while Roger paced. The area remained relatively well lit despite many candles having burned low. Roger's pace was so brisk that one wick flickered out as he passed. A wisp of apples and cinnamon accompanied the smoke. Roger noted the pleasant odor.

"Did you smell that?"

"What?" Kate asked.

"Apples. The candle."

"I prefer them scented. You can shop next time if it offends you."

"My point is, we smell it. We should have landed in the sewer. By rights we should be up to our noses in crap right now."

"Roger!"

"Gross, Dad," Tyler said, leaning forward with interest.

"No, it's not gross, but should be. The septic tank is near enough the house it should have burst. No matter where it spilled, we should have been awash in the stink. Unless everything fell intact underground. I don't see how any of this is possible."

"The monsters did it," Jenny said as a matter of fact.

"Yeah, let's mention how she was right. First order of business should be to talk with those who locked her up. Discuss their credentials, perhaps." Tyler answered the fist bump Jenny threw out.

"I do not know what is worse, monster talk or poop talk. Can we please stop discussing both?" Kate asked.

"Kay' but they dug the holes. It was a hole they dragged Mommy down. This time they dug a big one." The child crossed her arms defiantly.

Kate chose not to engage with the girl for fear of opening a Pandora's Box worth of tragedies. The child had, after all, woken from a violent nightmare only a short while ago. Jenny did not appear to remember the words she spoke in the fading remnants of the bad dream. Tyler asked his friend what she was talking about, but the girl's sleeping memories faded with the first yawn. Even as Jenny's anxiety settled, Kate watched it grow in her husband.

"Fine. I'll change the subject. I was only trying to distract myself from the fact I should not have let Matt go," Roger said.

"He'll be okay, he has too."

"I'm sure they are fine, Dad. Remember, he's with Brad. Have you noticed the size of the guy? He is as big as a creature. Or maybe he is one. Have we ever seen Brad and a monster in a room at the same time? I don't think so."

Suddenly a thud from above. Tyler moved to his friend. It sounded hollow, distant, rhythmic.

"They are trying to get in," Jenny said.

Wham! Something slammed the front door much louder than the strike from above. The parents pulled took up positions with the children in between them. They were under siege.

CHAPTER 33

While a ruckus continued both overhead and from the cave outside, the noise at the door settled into a soft knock versus pounding. Roger waved the others to stay behind him, even though they already were. Locking the entrance earlier seemed foolish but proved prescient. And lucky. A lifetime of memories turned upside down but *hey everyone, the locks still work*! Roger ditched formalities by not asking who was there, assuming whatever waited on the other side was anathema to dialogue. Machete at the ready, he yanked it open.

"Are you going to let me in, or leave me on your ugly front lawn?" Joe smiled.

Jenny rocketed to her father. "Dad!"

"I have a surprise kiddo."

Cassie walked into view. Jenny hugged her next.

Kate breathed in relief. "Oh, thank God."

"First, I can confirm monsters are down here. Big ones," Joe started.

"No one believed the kid," Jenny replied.

"I still haven't shown you the surprise."

Joe stepped further inside, allowing Rebecca to emerge from the shadows. A hush fell over the group as all took in the miraculous sight. The stunned silence soon gave way to gasps. And tears.

Kate's eyes welled up, and she choked back a sob. "Rebecca?"

"It can't be," Roger said.

"Cool," Tyler said.

Rebecca reached for her youngest, who remained glued to her sister in shock. "It's me, sweetie, I'm back." She embraced the girl.

Jenny's arms dangled loosely at her side. The others failed to notice the chilly reception, too caught up in the reunion. Rebecca felt the child's resistance and pulled away. She looked curiously at her frowning daughter. Rebecca stood and returned the frown. Before she could ask questions of the child, the others moved in, swamping the woman with affection. They marvelled at her return.

Once finished with the greetings, Rebecca took in the surroundings. "Your poor beautiful home."

"Who cares as long as we are all okay," Kate said.

"Besides, I hate to break it to you Honey, but our place looks like this and it isn't even underground."

Joe's joke landed flat, failing to rise above the weight of their situation. Cassie comforted Jenny, who had since wandered from the group. The siblings eyed one another in a shared unspoken language. Cassie's look asked what was wrong while the younger replied everything was. All with no words. Sister shorthand did the talking. Cassie looked concerned.

"Did you spot Matt?" Roger asked his friend.

"Sorry buddy, no, but..." Joe led Roger away, putting distance between them and the kids. "I saw someone else. Granger."

"What the hell are you talking about?"

"Exactly Hell. It's under us and he is in charge."

"That's crazy."

"No crazier than me finding my wife. That is not a tunnel at your door, it is a massive construct. One designed by a madman. These aren't only sinkholes, but gateways to a subterranean compound. You think your home just slipped into a crack and remained intact? It's all by design. An underground prison built for those who refused to go along with the psycho in his youth. And we are the prisoners."

Roger reacted with disbelief, wearing skepticism on his face. Joe waited for a reply, but his friend only coughed, signalling his unwillingness to argue. Joe grew agitated and chimed in.

"Will this be Jenny two point oh? First no one believes her, now you don't believe me? I have seen it. I was down there, you weren't."

"It's not that I don't trust you, it's just that I am battling to fathom how he could still exist. I know for damn sure he did not die in a crash. Neither did Denise. We hid the truth for so long, even from ourselves when we knew, Joe! Enough people feigned ignorance that we gaslit ourselves, or at least I did. You say he's there? I believe you. It also means we can get revenge. Together."

"No, I can't."

"What are you talking about? You remember what he did. How can you forget?"

"Not forget, never forget. But this is not my battle."

"You'd leave me to face him alone?"

"Joe is right. Why fight for a past love when Kate is here?" Rebecca asked.

Roger jerked his head, surprised their argument spilled into the open. The jab from someone recently rescued threw him even more. Kate stood by her husband.

"Roger has a point. If I accept there are mutations, and Granger is among them, it means he is responsible. Where else would they come from? Why else would a man fake his death other than to traffic in nefarious acts? We need to expose all his crimes, including kidnapping you, Rebecca." Kate looked to her friend a shot across the bow in defending her husband. "Don't we at least owe it to other potential victims to stop him? We're in the position to do so, we know where he is. What if he makes his way to town?"

"I finally have my family back. I won't lose them again. Ask yourself after what we witnessed, why did neither of us ever leave town? My parents are long gone. So are yours. What kept us here? Why did we never move when we cannot even trust our neighbors because we don't know which were in the killing field! I saw some of them down there."

"Saw who down there?" Roger asked.

"Arden. Some others. It may not have been them, but I swear some looked like them. Is it because they went along willingly? So many did. We knew this, and we stayed! It makes no sense how we never escaped this dust bowl. This isn't about one man. We remained here because something influenced us. Something beyond our understanding."

"Hogwash. We have roots here. It is as simple as that. There is nothing more to it There's no way he could influence us."

"Don't tell me you didn't hear him in your head that day too. Right here. Inside." Joe tapped his skull. "He corrupted the town. You saw what they were doing to one another. How many infants were born nine months later?"

"Impossible to tell in a place where everyone tries to birth farmhands. If what you say is truth, then why hasn't he been in our heads since?"

"Maybe he has. Think of bad thoughts you've had. We talked about us all getting together. A foursome. Where did that come from?"

Roger looked to the kids, grateful they did not overhear. "I make my own decisions, right and wrong, and I live with them. Don't put my weaknesses on another person. Yours either. I know your demons, and I know a good man who has kept them in check. No, this killer is only human, and we can finally get revenge. He had his chance before, and now it is our turn."

Joe shook his head. "I told you. We're getting out of here and I'm never looking back."

"I never took you for a coward."

"And I never took you for a fool."

Roger punched Joe. The blow staggered the injured man, but he leaned into it, ready to go. Rebecca winced as if shellshocked by violence. Cassie rushed over, placing herself in front of her father. Kate did the same with her husband.

Roger fought to break free and get at his former friend. "He kidnaps your wife and I'm the one who goes after him?"

"You question me protecting my family? Never mind the danger below, you've got me now. Let's go!"

The two men postured to fight.

Matt pounded with the sledgehammer. Sweat poured off him for his efforts as a pile of debris grew at his feet. The structure shook with every blow, popping and creaking. The blasting music in his ears drowned out all the ambient noises signalling imminent collapse. He wiped his brow with his sleeve, then continued the assault.

"Where's Brad when you need him?"

He struck again, and the ground shifted. Matt lowered the hammer and yanked his earbuds out. Boards snapped, groaning in defeat and with a pop the roof sagged where he stood. The movement created a funnel effect. All the debris slid toward him.

Matt danced in place, trying to avoid the larger pieces and exposed nails that poured in his direction. He found himself up to his ankles in accumulating shingles and shards of wood. Clods of turf broke away from the edge of the hole and tumbled down, joining the party. Before long he was up to his knees in detritus. He scrambled to gain a foothold to fight against the tide, fearing it might bury him as more and more soil spilled over and down, loosened by the failing structure. A muffled crack sounded below the collective pile and it vanished in a whoosh. He followed.

"Oh, sh..."

The coil of rope zipped into the new hole in the roof and chased the free-falling youth. An attic floor came into his view. The sledgehammer hit the attic floor in a cloud of dirt and shingles. Thin flooring groaned under the weight of an unexpected load. Matt jerked to a stop just above the mess. He spun in motion as clods continued raining down around him.

"Oh, wow."

Above ground, the pitchfork loosened, then pulled free in an explosion of soil. The tool rocketed like a missile. With a cling, clang, cling, it bounced across the top of the tractor, flying airborne before shooting toward the roof. The pole proved wider than the opening so it stopped short, but the fresh slack in the line zipped down at a furious pace.

Matt yelped as he dropped onto the pile with a thud. He lifted his face, stunned. He glimpsed above, noticing the pitchfork resting precariously across the expanse above. Then, as if in slow motion, one more clod, a rather modest chunk, soared through the air and landed alongside him. Everything happened fast after that. A fresh snap of floorboards and he went into freefall again.

"Wait, stop, he's hurt. Can't you see?" Kate said.

Kate's words struck home before Roger could hit his friend. Joe visibly favored one shoulder and grimaced under the pain of raising a fist. Roger lowered his own and lifted his chin, offering a clean target. Joe had no qualms. He readied to punch when suddenly a massive crash sounded from above.

The world exploded as the ceiling collapsed. Everyone dove from falling debris. The sledgehammer made a thunderous noise as it landed at the center of the destruction. Matt cursed while in freefall, but the accompanying din of chaos drowned out the expletives. The rope jerked to a stop midway above the floor, leaving the teen dangling upside down. The clouds of dust eventually settled.

"Hi everyone. Miss me?"

Cassie rushed over and kissed Matt. Gypsum fluttered like snow around the young couple. As they ended the kiss, she burst into laughter. She spun him playfully before bringing him in for a round two.

"How did this happen?" she asked.

"I never wanted to try bungee jumping and now seemed like the perfect time."

"Let's get you down," Roger said.

Matt spotted Rebecca. "It could be the concussions from crashing through multiple floors, but is that Mrs. Hennigan?"

They lowered Matt to the ground. Kate answered him with a nod before scooping her oldest into a hug. He did not fight it. Tyler punched his brother's shoulder. Cassie entwined her fingers with Matt's as everyone crowded around minus Joe, who nodded from a distance.

Rebecca hugged the youth and whispered in his ear loud enough for all to hear. "Looks like things have developed in my absence."

Cassie blushed and released Matt's hand, suddenly aware of the audience. "That was a glad he's alive kiss. Spur of the moment thing."

"I'd have a lot more near-death experiences if that was my reward." Matt grinned well past the shit-eating point. He gestured to the rope. "Obviously I found a way out, but not safe to climb this. Turns out pitchforks are not the best anchors."

"Hey, where's Brad?" Tyler asked.

"He hasn't returned? I thought he might have made it back to the door. He was not having the tunnel escape. Claustrophobia. We need to find him. Something already got Heather down there."

"I won't allow you to leave without an adult this time. Nearly lost my mind before. I'll go with you," Roger said.

"No. I will," Joe stepped up. "Can't let you have all the fun."

So not a coward. Roger nodded. Kate breathed in relief at the peacemaking. Matt, unaware of the feud, shrugged and started off.

"Cool. Let's roll."

They grabbed flashlights and headed into the corridor, leaving the others behind.

CHAPTER 34

Matt peered down the collapsed stairs and lit up his friend's last known position. The spot was ominously empty. The water reflected shadows in ever-changing patterns. Joe gripped Matt's shirt to keep the teen from falling in. The sound of water rippling suggested no one was present. While the world lay torn asunder overhead, the basement showed how far their world had sunk. In normal times, a burst pipe would cause them to rush for repairs before damage could infect their home. Now water gushed liberally, and it bothered no one. The whole situation saddened Matt, but concern for his friend kept him from lingering on such thoughts. He called out again.

"Brad?" After no answer, Matt dangled a foot over the ledge. "I need to go down and check."

"Let's be quick. Take my hand." Joe lowered Matt, then leaped down himself in a massive splash, soaking his shirt. He massaged his aching shoulder.

"You're hurt. Maybe my Dad should have come."

"I'll be fine, at least until the adrenaline wears off. Don't see that happening soon. The blood has mostly dried."

"Blood?" Matt inspected the man.

"I said I'm okay. Your friend?"

"Brad! Where are you?"

"He would have answered if he could. I encountered certain things that roam down here. They are not conducive to a breathing lifestyle for us humans. Sorry. You tried. No reason to keep you in danger. We should go."

"I need to know for sure. The big lug saved my life. And it is friends, plural I lost if I don't find him."

Matt took a step then screamed, sinking beneath the surface. Bubbles roared up from the spot where he vanished. Joe grabbed the youth, who came up sputtering and coughing.

"What is it?"

"A nail, and it went in my foot. Not too deep, I stepped away from it when I felt it. Still hurt like heck though."

"You scared the shit out of me. I thought it was something serious."

"It is. Between this and what I now understand was more than a rat bite, I've done a job on my legs this week. I can probably forget any dreams of ever joining the football team."

"I didn't know you were interested in that. But then I naively failed to notice how into my daughter you were."

"Actually, I'm more of a watch football on TV kind of guy. Except I'm not. Don't enjoy sports, not a fan. Fine, I have zero interest in playing, but something about having your house cave in makes you think about these things. Oh, and yeah, your daughter rocks."

Tyler tested the rope while Kate whispered to her pensive husband. "I had your back earlier. But what is the plan? Do you know what we are up against? Someone who we both thought dead is not. How do you fight something like that?"

"I am certain he never perished. It was all part of the conspiracy."

"Conspiracy? Is that what we're calling it?"

"Everyone in that field was in on it and pretended she died differently than she did. Then they lied about his death entirely. It doesn't get more conspiratorial than that."

"I prefer living in a world of facts. Earthquakes are real to me. We experienced one. Leave the conspiracy world for a moment. What can explain a supposed dead man still walking amongst us? And how do you explain the talk about monsters?"

Roger cupped his chin, thinking. His eyes widened in place of a light bulb appearing above his head. "Not monsters. Mutations. Like two-headed cows at the fair, you saw the pictures when Joe went in. A company chooses a remote town and tests unethical stuff hidden from the world. Even with a limited amount of residents, how do you get them to look the other way? You involve them in a murder so they can say nothing. A corporation with that kind of leverage over the population could act with impunity."

"A company run by an eighteen-year-old?"

"We don't know his age when he posed as a student. He always seemed older, more experienced than the rest of us. How many startups are running nowadays? Uncommon then, but no longer. He was ahead of the curve. He also had access to seeds unlike anything I have ever encountered."

"You've seen his seed?"

"Seeds. Yes."

Kate fumed. "Decades of your nightmares waking us both. Me suffering through your suffering and only now do you tell me there is more you haven't shared about your involvement with him? Did Joe know? Is that the real conspiracy? That the pair of you were hiding things from me?"

Rebecca monitored the argument from a safe distance, her arms cradled around her daughters. The woman smiled at her kids and mimed her intention to join the other adults. The kids nodded. Rebecca approached the fighting couple. She spoke quietly and gestured to Tyler swinging on the rope.

"Yours is happily oblivious, but mine are plenty concerned. I did not return from a nightmare just to watch my friends argue. While I can't stop either of you, I would ask you to consider maybe having this discussion another time. Or at the very least, Kate, stop dragging my husband in it until he is here to defend himself."

Kate took in the younger one's nearby and softened, but not before shooting one more glare across her husband's bow. "Agreed. This isn't over though. We're not finished."

Roger remained defiant. "Neither am I. We can stop him here. I'm sorry to have kept things from you, but I'm also done running from my past. It ends now, and that starts with gathering supplies. I don't know how he did it, but he tricked everyone. As awful as everything surrounding him is, Granger is just a man. We bring him to justice for everything. As for arguing in front of the kids, well, I have a solution."

The solution involved his retreating to the kitchen. Still on edge, Kate scolded her youngest for acting recklessly. He dismounted and suggested it would hold for a climb out. He invited her to test it. Kate complied, delicately testing it while Tyler conjured images of climbing to their rescue. Cassie played a hand game with Jenny, lightening her mood. With everyone occupied, Rebecca too entered the kitchen. Jenny crushed her sister's steepled fingers, ending the church gathering.

Cassie frowned. "What's wrong?"

"That's not Mom."

"What are you talking about? Sure, it is."

"It can't be. When the monsters got her, they bit her face off."

Cassie staggered. The image of her friend falling to the floor minus a face resurfaced. She shivered and crossed her arms. With the knowledge out in the open, the siblings glanced sadly toward the next room as if suffering their loss all over again.

CHAPTER 35

R oger shone the beam across the floor, searching for a bamboo knife block which no longer lived on the counter alongside the sink. He was unaware of the make of the steel set but knew it contained at least two large chef's knives that could come in handy. Something sounded behind him. The crunch of broken glass? There was plenty. He tested his own feet to see if it came from him. There was none underfoot, but he noticed a few exposed nails jutting from loosened boards. He was thankful to avoid a punctured foot, especially after already taking one partially in the hand earlier.

A flash of movement caught his eye, followed by a thunk. He spun the beam which landed on the leg of a chair which somehow migrated from the dining room when the world shifted. He traced it as far as the seat and cried out at the sight of someone sitting there. Rebecca sat rigid with hands folded in her lap like a scolded child.

"You scared the shit out of me."

She stood. "Good. You should be."

"What are you talking about?"

"Did not wish to talk in front of the girls, but I am curious to ask what you plan to do. Take the fight to him? Do you even know what that entails?"

"It means I get revenge for Denise. Finally, some justice."

Rebecca eyed him as if studying a foreign species. She searched his eyes before bursting into laughter. He jerked his head, offended. Cognizant of his reaction, she brought the boil down to a snicker only to look at him and burst into a hearty chuckle again. She placed a hand on his shoulder to steady herself until she finally ceased laughing.

"Glad you're enjoying this," Roger said.

"I am sorry but the boy scout vibe, it just... Wow!"

"Nothing boy scout about what I'm planning to do."

She nodded. "You believe you are about to murder an actual human. Okay, I can use respect that. Maybe there is something there in you."

"You've been through trauma, so it's difficult for me to end this talk so abruptly. But I've got work to do."

"You posture with the courage to slaughter someone, and yet you are afraid to tell me to shut the fuck up?"

The harsh words from a person he thought he knew stunned him. He grew defensive. "There is a difference between can't ask you to and won't. And I never said kill. I will bring him to justice. Not foolish enough to do so unarmed, however."

"You are right. I was out of line. I am so lost, Roger."

She moved closer to him, offering the gaze of a wounded bird. He sighed, releasing his anger, giving over to relief at her return. He shrugged off the bizarre behavior.

"I am so relieved to have you back."

Her hand never left his shoulder. She clasped her free one with his. He looked confused by the contact.

"Just a quick twirl? While captive, I wished for nothing more than to dance again. Dancing meant freedom. Humor me?"

Roger agreed, though he held the flashlight between their bodies as a modicum of innocence. They moved to silence with her taking the lead. She smiled wistfully.

"We've never waltzed before," she said.

"I reckon we haven't. Too much alcohol whenever we have been out together. Mostly two-stepping, if I remember correctly. Not sure if you can call what I do dancing."

"I love your moves."

"Really?"

"Yes. Well, the dance ones, not the chasing Granger move. But the whole white man overbite, you've got that down."

He examined her again, more confused than offended. She leaned her head on his shoulder. Lit from below, her beauty faded, replaced by an imposing visage. Roger grimaced at the sudden change.

"Thanks for the dance, but I think we're done."

"Or we're just getting started."

She lifted her head and kissed him. His body betrayed him as he gave in to her rawness and hunger. She finally broke away, and as they gazed at one another, her beauty returned to the fore. Roger breathed heavily.

"For so long we wanted that. You know it. After what happened to me, I am no longer afraid to go after that which I desire. I crave you, Roger."

"No. We can't. This was a mistake. Emotions are raw because of your return."

"Come on, Rog, do not be a downer. I am right here. You can have me."

She grabbed his crotch and rubbed. He groaned at the unfamiliar touch. She tore his shirt open with her other hand and kissed his bare chest, eliciting another moan. He appeared on the verge of caving. She smiled at his predicament.

"That's right. Give in. Free the flesh."

Free the flesh! The chant from the field. Roger lashed out in shock, shoving Rebecca away. He struck her harder than intended, causing her to stumble. She fell toward one of the jutting nails. He reached out, trying to catch her outstretched arms as she timbered straight back. Their hands touched, but he failed to grasp her.

Suddenly she stopped, falling short of the nail and the entire floor. She hovered in place! Roger spotlighted her impossible position. Her grin widened as he watched, stretching too wide, too far. It spread until the skin tore along the corners of her mouth. Blood poured from a twisted smile, taking up half the real estate on her face.

Her body shot back up like someone rising from a coffin. Once she reached full height, her feet no longer touched the ground, instead dangling loosely while she hovered inches off the floor. Her head tilted, which shifted the blood flow from her mouth, creating an obscene pattern of gore across her skin. Her eyes rolled pure white, the pupils busy inside her skull searching for the woman she used to be. She snarled and her hair seemed to melt, growing wet as if still submerged in the lake where her husband discovered her.

"Did Joe tell you that phrase? Free the flesh?"

"Oh, you pathetic small man. They always put the hot chicks to wave the flag to start a drag race."

A male or something audibly approximating one laughed in place of the woman. Roger shook his head, shocked at the revelation.

"No. I don't believe you. You loved Joe, period. I know you did. You loved us, your kids."

Rebecca fell slightly, but remained hovering, only a couple inches lower. As if his words hurt. She grinned wider. Her skin ripped further, like separating Velcro. Blood poured anew over places where it had dried.

"Was I slutty the whole time? Did I cavort with strange men and women, or did all this happen after they abducted me? There were so many times your wife and I kissed, made out. Touched one another inappropriately. Has she ever shared that with you?"

Roger ignored the line of taunting. "I can't believe Rebecca was under his thrall all these years because I knew her too well. I don't know who or what you are, but if you're occupied with me, it's because I frighten you. And him. Granger must be vulnerable."

"Blasphemy!" Rebecca's voice boomed guttural, deep and angry. "You and my dumb little hubby. The two goody two shoes he could not corrupt. Do you think the herald for the Timeless has been hiding? No. He has been harvesting."

"Harvesting what?"

"Sins to feed his army. He has worked the town for decades. All those folks unable to look you in the eye are not only reliving the ceremony but shamed over the vile acts he nudged them into performing. Conversely, others looked at you with hunger. Men and women. You could have had your way, you could have punished them and used them. The meat puppets would have cried out in a timeless ecstasy that began the moment flesh sprouted in the universe. Most very much enjoyed what he made them do. Even your wife."

"No. She would never..."

Rebecca swatted Roger. He flew across the room and crashed into a wall, but remained on his feet. The sheetrock buckled. He lifted his head to look at her while trying to shake off the blow.

"Maybe me. Maybe I could be a better man, but pedal your bullshit elsewhere. Kate is an angel."

Rebecca snarled at the mention of the word. "I belong to him and will never let you interfere. He needs a tad more time until he rises in glory to corrupt a new generation of chattel. Once the corruption is complete, the doors shall open, allowing our Masters to return."

"I wasn't afraid to tell you something earlier, was only being polite. Forget the niceties. How about now you shut the fuck up?"

She glided at him, arms reaching. Roger leaped away as her hands exploded through the wall. He grabbed for the board with the nail, but Rebecca floated back at him. Before he could reach the makeshift weapon, she grabbed him by his throat and lifted him effortlessly. He kicked frantically, fighting to escape and to breathe.

He punched her once, twice, three times. She tossed him into the same wall. He broke through what remained and fell unconscious, tangled in the cavity between studs, his legs jutted out into the kitchen.

Rebecca floated slowly to the ground and primped her clothes. Her eyes returned, and she jerked her head upright, bones snapping into place. Her bloody grin healed itself and the blood shimmered to silver and melted back into her skin. She reclaimed the look of a ravenous beauty.

She eyed her fallen foe. "Just like a man. As soon as things get exciting, you go to sleep."

She grabbed the weapon he failed to retrieve, then stormed the wall where she lifted his head by his hair, exposing his throat. Before she could jab the nail home, something sounded behind her. Rebecca jolted supernaturally quick to the kitchen door. Kate appeared, trying to look past her friend. Rebecca held the board behind her back.

"What was all that noise?" Kate asked.

"Things are a little... unstable in there. Roger told me to exit and not to let anyone else in. He is gathering supplies. He appears intent to after the big baddie. I failed to convince him otherwise. I am sure he will perform swell."

Kate nodded and returned to the living room. Rebecca dropped the board, and the nail thunked into the floor. The woman floated briefly then settled back done before following Kate.

CHAPTER 36

Rebecca approached her huddled daughters. She reached out, surprised when neither took up the offer. She tilted her head curiously, stopping shy of the point a neck might snap. Then she approximated a smile.

"What is it, Jenny? Come here."

Cassie gestured her sister to stay put. "You know, Mom, you look great."

"Thank you, honey."

"Too good considering how long you were missing. Who kidnapped you? The Kardashians?"

"Cassie! Your mother has been through a lot. Don't talk to her like that," Kate said.

"I sleep in my makeup one night and I can scare farm animals away. Yet you stand there looking botoxed AF. What's your secret?"

"I had to stay strong for my pretty girls. Nothing is wrong, you know that most of all Jenny. Come here, sweetie. Come to Mama."

Her youngest advanced with arms outstretched. Cassie soured at seeing her sister cave. Traitor. The girl embraced her mother.

"When we walked back here, Mom, I shared all the horrible things I saw. We agreed to keep quiet for Jenny. But it was Jenny who opened my eyes to what happened. A monster bit Lisa's face off. The fat man who killed her fits the description of the one she claims took you."

"Shush, no need to scare your sister. She was confused is all, did not know what she saw that day. You are glad Mom is back, aren't you, sweetie?" Rebecca patted her younger while smiling at the older. "See, you're being silly. Everything is fine."

Jenny pulled away and clawed her mother's face! Skin tore off like rotten fruit, a façade crumbled. The woman shot to her feet. A skin flap bounced on her cheek as she scolded her daughter.

"You bitch!" Rebecca's voice registered the baritone of an otherworldly voice.

She raised a fist to her child. Tyler pulled Jenny clear. Kate grabbed Rebecca's arm but could not hold it. The woman broke her grip so easily that Kate temporarily froze, shocked at the display of strength. Rebecca offered a follow up display by striking her friend in the chest so powerfully that Kate went unconscious before hitting the ground in a heap. Tyler raced to his fallen mother while Cassie squared off against her own.

"Please, Mom. I can't imagine what you went through. We never gave up. Dad never gave up. No matter what they did to you, I know you're in there somewhere."

Rebecca's voice returned to normal. "Ah, my sweet daughter, you've always been so beautiful, so innocent, so..." Suddenly the woman's visage morphed. Her eyes rolled white while every bone in her face battled for the surface, trying to acclimate to the body or escape it. "Stupid!"

Rebecca levitated inches above the floor and flew at Cassie, grabbing her by the shoulders. Without slowing, the woman carried her daughter in her grip, shooting across the room. Cassie glimpsed over her shoulder and spotted a splintered board jutting from a wall. Cassie screamed as the wooden fragment impaled her side. Rebecca released the girl, leaving her dangling just shy of tippy toes. Cassie's top bloomed crimson. Blood pooled onto the floor. The woman maintained a floating position close to her daughter's pained face.

"Smartest one in the group turned out to be little Jenny. You asked what became of me? Pleasure and pain, all the same. Free the flesh! I could teach you so much."

Rebecca traced a hand along Cassie's body. The teen squirmed in disgust. Cassie tried to jerk her head away but had nowhere to go. Rebecca licked her lips.

"These vessels of skin can bring immense joy when violated properly. Granger has the touch, unlike your wimp of a father. Never around when needed. Case in point. Where is he now in your time of need?"

Tears rolled down Cassie's cheek. Her physical pain turned to mental anguish over the cutting words. Rebecca gargled a laugh. Cassie stared into the face of a monster. One she knew intimately.

"Since I've already penetrated you once, how about I awaken you to new pleasures? Show you what you have been denied while living in your moral bubble." Rebecca slid her hand further down Cassie's body.

"Incoming!"

Tyler swung on the rope and kicked the woman in the back of the head. Rebecca grabbed one of his legs on the backswing. The youth struggled to maintain his grip on the frayed lifeline. His proximity to the egg white eyes, distorted face, and slimy hair caused Tyler to cry out in fear. The stench of putrid flesh sealed the deal. He wanted out of the fright fest, so lashed out with his free leg.

She easily caught the second and yanked both. Something snapped overhead, and the taut rope slackened and fell. Tyler smashed his face on the ground while she maintained the grip on his legs. Debris rained over them both, but she remained standing while he suffered the worst of the collapse. When the debris settled, one last object made ground. The broken pitchfork fell in two pieces. The tines stuck into the floorboards while the remaining half of the handle bounced nearby.

Descending back to earth, Rebecca released the boy's limp limb, which thudded to the floor lifelessly. She kicked the debris away to uncover his face, then raised a foot to stomp his skull. Suddenly a sharp stick burst through Rebecca's stomach near her hip. The woman roared and turned.

Cassie greeted her with vitriol. "Did you like that penetration, bitch?"

"Now you've pissed me off. You should show your damn mother some goddamn respect!"

"If ever I see her. I will."

Rebecca pulled the board clean through herself. "You should know your mom gave herself willingly to Granger years ago. Long before she vanished." She punched Cassie in the face. Cassie staggered but remained upright on the rubbery legs of an untrained boxer. "So many in this insignificant town lined up to be with him. Your mother no exception. Of all the little hangers on, your slut mother was always first in line." She struck Cassie again.

Cassie's lip burst, but she refused to go down. "Liar!"

"Don't talk back. Your true father would not like that. You should acquaint yourself with Granger since he is your real daddy."

Rebecca readied a last strike. Cassie raised her free arm. It would offer no kind of defense. Rebecca's body suddenly bowed, jutting at the waist. Silver white gel shot from her mouth in an arc across the room, and her growling segued to a sickening, high-pitched whine. Tines of the pitchfork jutted from her abdomen where more milky liquid flowed. Rebecca lowered her head to examine the damage. The movement allowed Cassie to spot the person behind the woman.

"Leave my daughter alone!" Joe yelled.

The woman turned and aimed her wrath at her former love. Spittle sprayed from her mouth as she raged. "Leave her alone! So pathetic. What did I ever see in you?"

"Rebecca loved me. Nothing you say to me will ever make me doubt that."

"I am telling the truth. Deep down in that sad little place you call a brain, you understand I have always belonged to him. I entered that field and groped my classmates as they too groped me. We consummated our darkest desires all while we bathed in the blood of your best friend's girlfriend. I am on the inside with Rebecca's secrets now. Do you want to know what she really thought of you?"

"I want only two things. I want my wife back. Since that can't happen, then I want you to shut the fuck up!"

Joe kicked her. She fell but stopped short, hovering over the hardwood. She grinned as if winning a move in chess. Check. Joe stomped down on the woman's throat. The force drove her into the floor, driving the pitchfork clean through her torso. Blood and gel spurted. Rebecca's imposter seized and flopped until finally going still. Checkmate.

"That was super gross," Matt said. He rushed to Cassie, who suddenly lost her legs. She fell into Matt's arms.

Kate rose to her feet. Roger leaned unsteadily in the kitchen doorway. Jenny rushed to Joe and buried herself in his body, looking away from the woman on the floor who melted into silver and puddled on the floor before seeping through the cracks. Jenny sobbed into her father's stomach.

Roger and Kate helped Tyler, who groaned but mentioned he was fine. Matt ripped off his outer shirt, leaving him in a tee. He used the fabric to bind Cassie's side. Kate touched Joe's shoulder.

"Joe, I'm so sorry," Kate said.

"Words. They were just words. I know what was in her heart."

"We didn't find Brad, but the way out is downstairs," Matt said.

"So, what do you want to do?" Roger asked.

Joe looked around the room at all the love remaining, then viewed the already fading puddle on the floor. "We get the kids to safety. Then we go after the son of a bitch."

CHAPTER 37

The group formed a human chain and waded through the water, moving in silent formation. Warriors on the march. One by one they broke off to enter the hole. Navigating the tight quarters elicited groans from each, as the effort amplified the pains of battle scars. Roger brought up the rear. He took one last look at his former life before joining the others.

The crest of the sun lingered along the edge of the horizon, hanging so low in the sky it threatened to wink out for the night. Widening Matt's original makeshift exit, the group rose from underground like the dead rising. The two youngest emerged first and dropped to the ground, arms outstretched, perfectly positioned to make dirt angels if they had strength enough left to do so. They did not.

Everyone else followed behind the children. Kate and Roger lifted their faces to absorb the last of the sun's rays. They sniffed the air of freedom, taking in the wide expanse of countryside. Joe joined them. They scanned the surroundings for threats. All seemed quiet.

Kate caressed her husband's chest. "We made it."

"We're not out of the woods yet," he replied.

"So, what's the plan?" Joe asked.

"We get everyone else to safety and then we improvise," Roger replied.

"Improvise? Rebecca was not human. All the monster talk is true. You're not considering going back down?" Kate frowned.

"Yes. We need to end this."

"We need to secure help," she said.

"The thing that looked like Rebecca was desperate to keep us from confronting Granger. Why? Because he is vulnerable. She spoke cryptically of the universe and timeless people."

"All the more reason to seek help. This is way beyond anything we can deal with. This is madness personified. A world of universal monsters."

"It is one of one man's creation. He's more than human, yes. Probably always was. But I think the energy used to create leaves him weak. Why was Becca so intent on stopping me? She knew I was going alone and still considered me a threat. If he is so strong, why send his fang filled lackeys above ground rather than face us himself?"

"Because they're doing a bang-up job. We're lucky to be in one piece. We can't say the same for everyone. The kids have lost friends. I don't know how they are keeping it together right now. Thank God, they have each other," Kate said.

The adults eyed Cassie and Matt as the pair consoled one another in the distance. It pained them to see the teens so weary. The younger ones also commingled. Tyler somehow made Jenny laugh. Youth appeared resilient even in the face of horror. The parents lowered their voices, hoping to allow their children a break while they plotted their next move.

Roger stood firm. "Becca was a spy in our midst. Without her, he is blind. We can catch him by surprise."

Joe chimed in. "You want us to get help, Kate. But who? Who do we trust? They either corrupted my wife after abducting her or years earlier if we believe what she said. Things were strange when I met with the police recently. I assume they have fallen to his sway. Our entire lives we tried to hide from the memories as much as the man. How has that turned out? It is time to fight."

"Man? Listen to you. You think he is a man? Rebecca floated! How do you fight an army that can do that?"

"I don't know. Faith that we will figure it out. Faith that by defeating whatever Rebecca became, it means we can do the same to Granger. She lied to me prior to the attack, with words designed to plant doubt as deeply as we bury seeds. By not asking you certain questions raised by her diatribe tells me I am in the right, that I am strong enough to finish this. My starting point on how to proceed begins with refusing to give into despair..." Roger couldn't finish his sentence. Cornstalks exploded nearby. Something leaped from the field.

A hideous deformed version of a chimpanzee charged Joe. Its head rested atop massive shoulders with no neck. Its arms flailed high. The muscular limbs culminated into twisted, thick fingers capped with edged talons. It pounced on Joe's back.

Its lack of neck kept the creature from biting Joe. It struggled to position itself to where its bared teeth could explore flesh. Roger yanked the grotesquery off even as Joe spun, attempting to dislodge it. The combined momentum propelled the unwelcome guest into a sea of green suddenly bustling with motion.

"Move!" Roger yelled.

Everyone raced toward the barn. Corn stalks trembled alongside their escape path. Flashes of massive forms appeared through breaks in the stalks. The creatures whined in tones that suggested communication. And because the creatures chose not to break out into the open, it appeared their communications related to their true goal. Don't kill yet, herd them all to the farmhouse. The group had no choice but to comply.

"They're everywhere," Cassie yelped.

"One is right behind us!" Jenny screamed.

A ghastly spindly beast broke free and tracked Jenny's path running on all fours toward the smallest prey. It raced along on clawed paws, which faced away from its torso rather than straight. The legs bent at the knees opposite the direction of known bipeds. While the creature was the true physical threat, its gait offered a second threat. That of mental trauma. Having such abnormalities visited upon an unsuspecting group opened a gateway to madness. The freakish being confirmed existence of a world where sanity no longer ruled as king.

The quilled wombat sized creature found its groove, closing in on the girl. The beast huffed air loudly through nasal passages as crooked as the being's bony limbs. It built up steam. Would not be long now.

"They will get us, just like they got Mommy!"

"Not while we're here." Cassie pulled Jenny clear of the galloping predator.

Joe kicked the oncoming monster, landing a blow to its side. An enormous quill sliced through his boot between foot ware and toes. The kick did the trick.

The creature rolled out-of-control back into the field. Joe extended his arms, and each daughter grabbed one in flight.

The families charged the looming barn. Once there, they regrouped, forming an outward facing circle to monitor any advancing dangers. The missing house in the near distance stood as a symbol of how torn apart the world had become. Joe's pickup remained parked on the road.

"I have a shotgun and fuel container in the truck," Joe said, hurrying toward his vehicle. His girls accompanied him.

Roger turned to his sons. "Gather what you can from the barn while I get the gas canisters stored on the tractor."

The brothers rushed in and slammed the doors closed. A gunshot drew their attention. They glanced through the massive hole in the wall and spotted Joe shooting at something out of view. Despite the drama, they returned to the task at hand.

Outside, Joe lowered the rifle and herded the girls into the pickup. He jumped in, then spun donuts along the dirt road and front lawn, taking out some advancing monstrosities. Each galloping creature appeared stranger and more macabre than the next, all fluid in form as if trying to learn their own species.

Roger and Kate unhooked a large plastic gas container strapped to the rear of the tractor. Kate screamed as something resembling an inside out dog advanced on their position. Roger lifted the engine cover and yanked free the metal rod used to prop the hood for servicing. He skewered the beast with it. It melted into silver liquid and faded into the dirt. The frightened couple scrunched noses at the foul smell.

Matt and Tyler, weighed down with supplies, rushed from the barn. Matt yelled as they ran toward their parents. "Critters! Lots and lots of critters!"

Whatever they witnessed inside remained there. Nothing followed them. Joe pulled up alongside the tractor, leaped out and dropped the tailgate. Roger set the gas canister on the bed while Joe hopped in the back and opened a side compartment housing another can. He retrieved some flairs and a first aid kit. He handed off the kit to Cassie through the rear window of the truck. She attended to her injury. The boys dropped their assembled war chest comprising a shovel, rake, hoe, tool belt, and a mixture of gardening tools. Matt spread them out on the tailgate.

Tyler opened a burlap sack inside which was saw blades. "These are my personal favorites."

Matt peered through the window and noticed Cassie partially undressed as she dabbed alcohol on her wound and winced. Matt initially looked on in sympathy, but mostly stared at her exposed bra. She smiled until grimacing as the sting kicked in again. She pulled out a large gauze pad and pressed it tight. It sucked to her skin, already wet with blood. She took an Ace bandage and wrapped it tightly around her abdomen.

Joe and Roger simultaneously grabbed the handle of the plastic gas canister, eyeing one another in a standoff. No one else noticed, too busy prepping the weapons stash while watching their flank. Joe held the shotgun in his free hand.

"What are you doing?" Joe asked.

"One of us needs to stay to ensure everyone gets out of here safely."

"Agreed. Sound plan, now let go of the canister."

"Your family has lost enough."

"And yours hasn't so how about we keep it that way?" Joe emphasized the rifle as if a threat.

"Are you going to force me to make the case in front of my wife? Denise was my girlfriend back then. I did nothing."

"Because you couldn't. WE couldn't."

"And now I can. I will not run anymore. It's time for some payback."

"Anger? Revenge? You don't think that might feed into what our undead friend wants?"

"Maybe, but it doesn't change the situation."

Joe handed over the shotgun. The group suddenly noticed the end of the standoff.

"Honey?" Kate glared at the gun.

"Dad?" Tyler did the same.

Matt stepped to his father. "I'm coming with you."

"No. It will take two men to protect everyone. You've got this, son."

"Dad..." Matt trailed off.

Cassie pressed her hand to the glass, reaching for Matt, who appeared on the verge of tears. Instead, the teen steeled himself and joined Joe as if in a competition to see who could arm Roger the fastest. Joe accessed another compartment and retrieved a coiled rope. As if sensing, he grabbed a wrench and spun. A furry quadruped resembling a badger leaped onto the roof of the truck.

Joe batted it through the air. It landed with a squeal and retreated into the corn. "We've got to move."

Roger strapped the plastic gas container to his back, then put on the tool belt and attached the metal can to a loop on its side. Matt dropped extra shotgun shells in the sack with the saw blades, tied it off and handed it to his father, who attached it to the other side of the belt. Roger approached the tractor.

Joe looped rope through the wrench and tied it off on the tractor. The wrench dangled against the chassis of the farm vehicle, serving as a makeshift alarm. Joe lifted and released the tool, checking the loud clang. Roger fed the other end of the rope through a loop at his waist.

"When you are ready for us to pull you up, give it a tug. We'll hear it," Joe said.

"If I make it back."

"When you do." Kate hugged her husband.

The younger ones joined the party. Growling in the distance took on a more sinister tone when something hissed wildly. The stalks rustled anew, spreading in a wider pattern. With danger fast approaching, the group broke their huddle as Roger bade goodbye.

"Matt, look after your brother. And for heaven's sake listen to your Mother for once, huh?"

"Sure, give me the impossible tasks, Dad." Father and son shared a nod.

"Good luck, buddy." Joe patted Roger's shoulder.

Roger walked out onto the fragile roof and lowered himself into the dark.

CHAPTER 38

The rope stopped several feet short of the living room floor. Roger dangled while searching for a safe dismount strategy until his arms gave out. He slipped and fell, landing in a push up stance just shy of cracking his face. He laid in a plank position, trying to regain his strength.

"About to take on an army of monsters and can't even stand on my own two feet."

From his lowered position, an object swiped the underside of his chin. He grabbed at it instinctively, as if clearing a spider web only to find something more substantial in his grip. And slimy. What filled his clenched hand rose above and below his grip. The few inches rising from his fist nearest his face wiggled. A tongue! The appendage stretched to a gaping maw of a hideous being a dozen feet away.

The beast's jaw rested on the floor. Its proportions appeared out of whack with anything found in nature. While the skull appeared no larger than a racoon's, its body stretched into a massive tear drop shaped blob whose hindquarters rose as tall as a man. Large muscular rear legs supported the torso while its tiny front paws barely touched the ground. The back feet took the form of knobby basketball sized stumps. Talons sprouted from each foot at irregular intervals like a severe hyperdontia smile.

The creature raised its haunches and pushed off from the back limbs, following the path of its own tongue, sucking it back in as if a reverse clown trick. How the lengthy organ fit in such a compact dome Roger could not fathom, yet it continued to retract as the beast rushed his position. Its head remained low the entire run, spraying hungry spittle as it advanced, driven by the massive rear engine. Roger reached for his belt. Thunk! He impaled the tiny head with a screwdriver. The red vanished from eyes which stared straight into his own.

Roger rose to his feet. A knock at the door drew his attention. Then something fluttered over his shoulder. He spun. Nothing. Another thump at the entrance, a visitor for sure. He advanced. Snap! Something behind him.

A debris pile toward the back of the room shifted. He raised the light. Two red eyes peered from the shadowed doorway of the kitchen. A rottweiler from hell emerged. Any deviation from the earthbound version mattered not. It was big, angry, and running right toward him. He rushed to the front door and yanked it open. A pig man squealed in surprise.

Roger ducked, and the hellish dog leaped, missing him but connecting with the swine. The two monstrosities battled, crashing about the threshold so violently it threatened to bring the house down around them. Roger aimed and blasted through both with one shot. He stepped over them and into the cave.

Roger moved deliberately with the shotgun ready. Soon he reached a fork in the underground road. Moans echoed through the cavern, a mix of pain, pleasure, and desperation. The inhuman warbling blended into a blistering symphony of despair. *The perfect soundtrack for hell*, he thought.

The moaning informed his decision. He entered the left tunnel. Joe warned Roger about ghastly furry hunters that lurked the corridor and spoke of bats elsewhere ahead. The description did not do justice to the monstrosity Roger spotted waiting for him. He aimed.

Too late.

The beast leaped. Roger instinctively raised the stock of the gun to block the attack. The monster clenched the weapon in its jaws even as its claws sought purchase. Its powerful head jerked, easily dispatching the rifle, then the animal bared teeth, eager for flesh. Roger braced himself for the inevitable.

Clang! The creature fell unconscious.

Roger breathed in relief and offered a slight grin. "You never listen to me."

"Obviously. I'm a teenager," Matt replied, lowering the shovel he used to dispatch the threat.

The wrench clanged loudly. Joe pressed it tight to stop it. Just another test of the emergency monster system. He tugged, then dropped the rope like recasting a fishing line after no bite. While the kids watched the perimeter around the tractor and truck, Kate sidled up.

"Earlier I'm considering a divorce because my husband allowed my son to wander off. Now I sent him to join his father. It leaves me thinking marriage is complicated," she said.

"No kidding. Who do you think you're talking to?" Joe replied.

"I am open to listening to your plan. Anything to distract myself from my lousy decision."

"It was the right thing to let him go. We couldn't stop him. You know that."

She nodded, grateful for the acknowledgement. "What if these things have attacked the entire town? What if we're not ground zero?"

"I doubt it. If he had the strength to do so, he would have decades ago. If we had only stopped him in the field that day. Done something, maybe…" he halted. His turn for a guilt trip.

"There was nothing you could do. One thing to kill these beasts, another to do the same to your classmates, wouldn't you say?"

"I've been thinking about it. About how long it's taken. Like we plant seeds for crops, I believe he did the same but in us. All of us. Think of what everyone did that night. How well do we know some of our neighbors? So many shied away from me after Denise's funeral. Old friends just faded from my life. I think a shame spiral overtook some participants. Others? Who knows what they have done since? The amount of citizens who are mean and ornery are plentiful around here. Maybe the correct word is evil. Granger planted corruption, darkness of the soul, and now is the reaping."

"What saved us from the same influence?"

Joe looked to the kids. "They did. There were moments though with Rebecca and me where things could have gone dark. We're less innocent than we think."

"Because we are human, Joe. We all falter. It doesn't mean it is Granger's handiwork, it's just..." She paused, considering her own demons. She leaned against the tractor, a world-weary woman. "The fears I have over whether Roger can succeed? That is on me. Only me. I will not cede those feelings to the work of the underground bastard. These fears and doubts are my own. They come with being a family. Lots of frustration and doubt, but there's everything else, isn't there?"

"Everything else," Joe agreed.

"Mom!" Tyler yelled.

The kids scrambled to the parents as the stalks shifted in a central area. Something coming. Or things. Then they appeared. An army of soldiers, identical as clones, terrifying in appearance despite their diminutive size. They stood no taller than Tyler or Jenny, but the reach of their arms was so long, their hands brushed the ground as they walked. Their skins were the color of extinguished charcoal briquettes. Fiery red lines covered the entirety of their bodies and showed through the skin. Their rudimentary circulation system suggested fire in their veins. Eyes were the only features on the otherwise blank faces. The recessed orbs burned as bright as their blood. Dozens advanced in lockstep minus the random deformities which so far defined all other underground dwellers.

Jenny pointed. "Those are the same ones that got Mommy, except they had a bigger one with them that bit off her face."

Joe raised a rake like a baseball bat. "Get everyone to the truck. Now! I'll hold them off long as I can. If something happens, hit the gas and keep on hitting it."

Kate rushed the girls away. Tyler grabbed a hoe and joined Joe, back to back.

"Don't even say anything Mr. Hennigan because I'm not going anywhere."

"It will piss your father off if you do not get in that truck."

"What's he gonna do? Send me to my room?"

"Excellent point. In that case, it's Joe then."

"Got it, Mr. Hennigan."

Kate climbed into the front along with Jenny. Cassie took the back. Kate performed a quick head count and came up short. "Tyler?" She spotted her son outside. "Shit!"

"Language Mrs. Whatley," Jenny said. A drone appeared and pounded at the rear window. Jenny screamed, then rose, recovering from the surprise. "Shit!"

The window remained partially open, so Cassie pulled it close only for the creature to smash the glass. It reached through and grabbed for her. The army lined up between the vehicle and the others, cutting them off from one another.

The dark, featureless creatures performed a strange, synchronized maneuver. Every second drone turned the opposite direction. Then on cue they advanced. Half destination truck, half marching on the exposed humans. The rogue troop in the pickup caught Cassie's hair and pulled her toward the jagged glass with startling speed and strength. Cassie screamed.

CHAPTER 39

The defeated creature lay in a heap at their feet. Circumstances above ground limited how much time Joe had to convey details of the layout. The thrust of the conversation revolved around following the main pathway, but many offshoots along the way caused him to worry he inadvertently strayed off track. When a constant murmur rose in the distance, it convinced him he was heading in the proper direction. He followed the symphony of despair which comprised sharp notes of agony, ecstasy, pain, and misery, all crying out at once. His ears would be his guide, or at least that was the plan.

Once Matt dispatched the fanged beast, a hush descended upon them. They had not killed it, which left the possibility its mind remained connected to something greater than itself. That thing would be aware visitors were on the way. He lost the element of surprise. "*Great! Mental links. Just one more unfathomable danger on my shit sundae,*" Roger thought.

Then he remembered another clue Joe offered about following one's nose. A powerful stench suddenly greeted them. Roger scrunched his face and coughed. Matt did the same.

"Lots of gym socks?" Matt asked.

"Sulfur. Not sure if it is occurring naturally or a byproduct of farm chemicals. Either way, it could be our secret weapon. I wish we had our fertilizer for real fireworks, but there is no way to transport it here, and nowhere to run if we used it. I'm hoping the existing fumes might supply our firepower with a kick."

"How exponential? Are we talking we fly to the moon alongside him? Or turn our back and walk away as if the explosion doesn't exist like they do in action movies?"

"My plan is to end him. How it goes down I can't say which is why you should not be here."

"But then monkey king would have eaten you, leaving me to grow up without a Dad which might negatively stunt the last remnants of my childhood development. And let's face it, I'm already insufferable. Minus one more guiding hand, look out world."

Matt stepped alongside his father and tapped the handle of the shovel against the ground. The pair looked like a twisted version of the painting *American Gothic*.

"You're wrong about something. I think you have grown up."

He ruffled Matt's hair. The two walked on. Roger swept the rifle in an arc as they moved. Soon the world of sound opened for them again as water crashed to shore ahead. Bingo. Joe supplied that information. The father and son navigated the tight exit until emerging into the enormous, cavernous lakefront.

The space appeared empty. Gentle waves lapping at rock offered a false sense of comfort, a vacation setting in a place far removed from such a scenario. The pair set the gas canisters down. Matt noticed it first, freezing with nervous wonder. Roger followed his son's gaze, only to find himself gazed upon.

A massive eye covered a full wall across the lake. Groundwater cascaded over its surface in a thin waterfall. Eyeball met stone met water. Distance made examining the orb, leaving them uncertain whether it belonged to a larger beast made of rock or existed only in liquid form, using the flow as a conduit. It appeared to look upon them from some other place, or some other world. Roger attempted to allay his son's fear while ignoring his own.

"That is only one variant of many things we have defeated so far."

"It's a pretty freaking enormous variation, Dad!"

"Granger is still human, I believe. It must be the reason he has not returned to the surface all these years. We've got this, right?"

"Not phrasing it as a question might help."

"We have. Where are you, Granger? Afraid to show yourself in a fair fight?"

"There are two of us and one of him. Not sure we're talking fair, but then again he has a giant eyeball at his disposal. Hopefully, the odds give him pause."

The lake bubbled under the waterfall building to a full boil until suddenly a geyser erupted. Granger tore through the surface from below. He leaped high into the air before landing in a three-point stance atop the water's surface. He rose, mystically dry. The man appeared exactly as in high school except possibly taller, leaner, more dangerous on the surface. Despite decades having passed, the man looked the same age as in his class photo. Roger aimed the shotgun.

"Dad? Walking on water? That's next level compared to wearing a pig head!"

"It's a trick. Joe warned me about it. He's standing on stones."

"Many tricks up my absence of sleeves. The latest of which will explain the reason for my missing presence when you first arrived."

"You're here now and so are we. It is time we end this."

"You have NO idea!" The ferocity of Granger's voice visibly startled the visitors.. Granger rushed across the water obscenely fast, stopping midway along the lake where he cracked his neck. Crick, crack, crick. Multiple snaps from a single head jerk. Not normal, maybe not human. "I have been busy. Where you might ask? On the surface."

Roger went pale even as he steadied the rifle. "You lie. That's what you do."

"Dad?" Matt looked to his father for reassurance.

"That is exactly what the youngest boy yelled when I pierced his flesh. Well, he said it before all the screaming began. There was much screaming. Annoying, really. It makes it harder for me to focus on the work."

"No! I don't believe you."

Granger paced in a tight circle, placing a thumb against his mouth, mumbling as if baffled. "Well, he does not appear to trust me. Strange, that. How can I convince someone? Ah yes. Evidence. The proof is in the puddles, one might say." He extended an arm, palm down. The lake bubbled below his hand. A pale grey body rose from underwater, struggling to rise through the murk. The water sluiced away, revealing Tyler!

Matt dropped the shovel. Tears welled in his eyes. Roger rushed across the shore, wading into the surf, splashing to get to his youngest son.

Tyler appeared to be a living corpse. He reached out from the watery grave. "Dad? Daddy? I think something is wrong with me..."

Matt leaped in and grabbed his father, fighting to hold him back. Roger raised and lowered the rifle, torn, biting into an arm to muffle a scream of agony. A hand clamped onto Matt's ankle, forcing him to scramble, but the grip remained firm. In his retreat, he pulled someone along. Cassie! Her bloated form surfaced, dangling from his leg. The teen froze in horror, his legs rooted to the spot where his world ended as he knew it.

Roger glimpsed the fresh new terror off to his side. "No, this can't be happening."

"It is. All because you had to be the hero. I have nurtured and tended my crops, comprising so many denizens in this county. Spent so much time nudging their moral compasses away from true North until they carried out the most glorious vile acts. Most reveled in their excesses, despite some feeling shame. Those who tried to change, who developed a sense of unease over their new character, were the very individuals who yearned to taste the darkness again. They longed to feel—dirty. Eventually shamefulness lost all sway." Granger clasped hands over his heart, smiling at the memories. "The things, oh what they did in my name. And I am only the messenger. The weak townsfolk violated their oath to humanity all to pacify the Ancient Ones. But for all the lustful, greedy, violent, backstabbing deeds they committed in the service of a higher order, you did far worse than they. You abandoned your family!"

"No, I..."

"They cried out for you. Screamed your name. At first, at first, at first. The longer I violated them, the quicker they evolved. I taught them more about living than you ever did. I offered the pleasure of pain, the ecstasy of suffering. Any coherent speech eventually gave way to wailing until they grew skillful in the language of the Ancient Ones. By the end, none even remembered who you are. I freed their flesh."

Roger screamed and pointed the gun.

"Shoot him, Dad. Shoot the bastard!"

Joe rose from the water before Granger, blocking the shot. He appeared less a corpse and more himself, wearing the weight of Granger's words on his face. The man stood waist deep and struggled to free himself. His legs remained rooted as if stuck in mud.

"I'm sorry, buddy. I did what I could, but he was too strong. He hurt Kate, badly."

As if on cue, Granger dipped a hand in the water and came up holding tufts of hair belonging to the woman. She bobbed up alongside Joe, her face half gone as if melted. Only a single working eye remained.

She focused on her husband. "Roger? Roger, please save the kids. It's too late for me now." Kate attempted to step forward, but Granger kept hold of her scalp.

On noodle legs, Joe listed to one side. It gave Roger a shot, and he took it. Roger fired. The blast blew Granger's arm off at the shoulder. Even though the force staggered the brute, he maintained a grip on Kate's hair. The man eyed his damaged body and nodded as if impressed.

"Ah, finally a rise from you."

"Next is your head unless you release them."

"Release? I am the only thing keeping them animated. But since you have pissed me off, what say I remedy the situation."

The man's clavicle undulated as a growth formed. A whiteness appeared, sprouting from the wound. New bone! Tissue stitched around the shoulder, forming fresh flesh, but before that process could complete, Granger gripped the growing arm and snapped it off with a loud crack.

Granger jerked in painful ecstasy during the act of breaking his own bone. He raised the jagged skeletal piece and jabbed the edge into Joe's neck. Joe registered confusion before his hands went to his throat, too late to stop the gushing flow that quickly sapped him of his strength. He tipped over and vanished beneath the lake under a crimson puddle.

"One down and several to go. Prepare to watch everything you love die."

Granger pulled Kate's hair, exposing her throat. He raised the bloody bone. She stared at her husband, tears pouring down her only eye. Jenny rose from the surf waist deep, followed by Brad, Chet, Heather, and Lisa. The collection of tortured souls moaned wistfully, resigned to a horrific fate, the line between dead and living erased, leaving only suffering. Matt cried out at the sight of his friends even while he tended to his own fallen loved one.

"No. Please. Leave them alone. Don't hurt them anymore. This voodoo stuff, whatever realm you're channeling this madness from, can you un-ring that bell? Bring them back? My soul. I'll give you mine if you free them."

Granger licked his lips. A drip of saliva splashed into the water, sizzling on the surface until hissing into steam vapor. The moaning stopped as the townspeople froze in place. The man steepled his fingers.

"Dad, do not make a deal with him," Matt said.

Cassie moved closer to him. "Don't interfere. I wish to return home. Surely you want me to."

Granger released Kate's head. She sloshed forward, reaching for her husband. "A fair trade, it means the kids will be safe. You would do that for me, Honey?" Kate reached the shore. Roger set the gun down and they clasped hands together.

Matt reached out to Cassie. She yanked him toward the water. The teen yelped in surprise at her strength, falling into a tug of war, a struggle over land versus lake.

Kate's horrific face grew more so. Her features shifted and twisted until becoming only a massive mouth with descending layers of jagged teeth filling the void like that of the Fat Man. Her huge maw snapped open and shut repeatedly, drooling in anticipation of a meal. Roger slipped on the slick surface and stumbled onto his back. She fell atop him, maintaining control of his arms, then opened wide. It would take only one bite. Roger closed his eyes, understanding there would be no deal with the devil.

Something whizzed by unnaturally fast. A loud thunk and choke of surprise prompted Roger to reopen his eyes. A saw blade jutted from Kate's mouth. She fell off him before doing the mercury roll, returning to the silvery mess and joining the lake. Roger glanced over his shoulder.

"Dudes! Get out of here. Those things are not real. I know because that handsome devil in the lagoon is not me!" Brad yelled, pointing at his twin in the distance.

Brad stood on the shore, clothes torn, battle scars on full display. The teen's duplicate snarled and charged unnaturally fast toward his doppelganger. Brad grabbed the shotgun and fired as it leaped at him. His twin's face vanished in an explosion of gore. The body slumped to the ground.

"At least he died pretty," Brad said of the mess at his feet.

Tyler sprouted tentacles in place of arms and whipped them through the air, grabbing Roger's ankles. Roger scrambled to grab anything on shore to keep from being pulled in.

Matt and Cassie continue their struggle, hands clasped together above their heads. She jerked her shoulders back and forth as something rippled beneath her breasts. Her chest opened as if someone were unzipping a dress, revealing a small four limbed creature. Her body fell limp to one side, though she somehow still gripped his hands, leaving him exposed as the creature stepped out of its host.

Brad tossed a blade to Roger, who sliced himself free of the tentacles. Brad then used the shovel to impale the monster attacking Matt. He lifted it away and dislodged it into the murky waters.

The three men regrouped. Roger removed the cap from the large container and poured fuel along the shoreline. Matt lifted the metal canister and shouted to his Dad, who nodded in understanding. An unspoken pact only understood by family.

"Just don't miss," Matt said and hurled it through the air.

Roger grabbed the rifle and aimed. Granger reacted, attempting to bat away the hurling object. Too late. Roger fired. The container exploded in a hellish ball of flame, engulfing Granger and setting the surface of the lake on fire. The flames quickly spread to the shore, bursting into a wall so intense it forced them all back.

The entities posing as their family and friends burned with wails of despair. Their formerly human sounding voices gave over to the screeching of the undead. Roger peered into the blaze.

"Go. Pull the rope, they will lift you up."

"What about you?" Matt asked.

"I need to stay. Long enough to know for sure. I'm worried about the sulfur down here, so run!"

The teens ran off. From within the hellish blaze, tendrils of flickering fury danced on increasingly turbulent waters. The burning took on a pulsing pattern of intensity. A vortex formed into a whirlpool of fire sucking fuel from elsewhere in the conflagration. The wall of flame whirled in a pattern which revealed the man inside before obscuring him again. The effect mimicked that of an intense orange strobe light.

Granger lifted his head, revealing eyes burning brighter than the flames. The man basked in the glow, unfazed by the destruction. He stepped forward, building speed, eventually falling into a side-to-side gliding stance like a skater on ice. Before Roger could flee, Granger reached the shore. Roger aimed the gun.

"Born of fire and cold were we, risen before the Gods, birthed in despair and hopelessness. We fed on misery of destruction's creation. Upon the rise of sin that you call humanity, we discovered a never-ending banquet with which to satiate our hunger. You believe you have any chance to stop me? It would take more resources than what you brought to the dance today."

"We will stop you."

"You and what army? Because I have one. Do you know how much corruption it required to bring my troops to life? How many collected souls as you called them? That is not how the whole thing works. I would explain, but it is far above your cosmic pay grade and by that I mean your understanding. Fealty is currency to the Ancient Ones, however. I ask again if you can fathom how long it took to create my empire?"

"Yes. Since I was in high school. But I'm not a kid anymore."

Roger fired, knocking the devilish man back. Silvery gel spurted from a massive chest wound, which quickly healed. The 'blood' formed puddles like model kit paint, each droplet sprouted a tiny waving tentacle, too small to do harm but unnerving Roger long enough for his foe to recover.

Granger advanced as Roger shot again. Click. Empty. Sharp needles ripped through Granger's gums, pushing his original teeth free, each plinked to the ground. A tooth fairy bounty. Roger used the rifle like a club, smashing the man's face.

He spit out his last tooth. Roger swung again. Granger caught the weapon on the upswing and easily yanked it away. He flipped it in the air and gripped the barrel and swung. The strike launched Roger across the beach. Roger grabbed his chest and wheezed. The blow so powerful it interrupted his heart's rhythm.

Granger looked at his downed foe. With the sickening sound of tendons and muscle and flesh rippling, his limb reformed again, or deformed. The bone grew longer than his arm and culminated in a sharp edge. "You tried to destroy my family, so it's only fitting I return the favor. Do you get my point?"

Granger pressed the length into Roger's shoulder. Roger screamed in agony. Granger quickly yanked it out, aimed and jabbed again. This time he punctured Roger's calf, sticking it in deep and twisting. Roger tremored under the pain. Granger pulled the bloody mess free and placed the point at his victim's throat.

"Do I have your full attention? I will not end you yet. I plan to ensure you do not move while I visit your family for real."

Granger morphed into a nude version of Roger. The weaponized arm reformed to normal. He appeared as an exact replica of the family man. Silver liquid poured off the imposter like sweat until even the clothes matched. A mirror image of Roger stared back at himself.

"While it bothers me how your annoying friend exposed my earlier ruse designed to imbibe you with despair, I enjoyed your anguish. Now I can proceed proper. After your wife watches me tear her children apart, I will violate her with glee. She will scream the names of unknown Gods in her moment of ecstasy and will forever be mine. Lost to you, a blip on the radar of life, not even a memory. I intend to violate them in your name, in your guise with glee. If you refuse to walk on my side, then I will devour yours. The fresh bounty will replenish the Ancient Ones and further open the doorway. Why do it in front of her? The joy is in the sharing. Now if you will excuse me, I am off to enjoy some soul food."

Granger as Roger shifted from angry to jolly, all but skipping away whistling an eerie tune. Roger struggled to rise and fell. He slammed a fist in agony, screaming as the music faded in the distance.

CHAPTER 40

J oe and Tyler battled the dark army, but there were too many of them. While their weapons proved effective against their foes, the pair grew weary. Their foe's diminutive size suggested they might be slightly less lethal than their sharp-toothed cousins, but with so many of them assembled, numbers threatened to succeed where brute force failed. (Not that the smaller ones appeared unwilling to kill given the opportunity.) The guys fought back to back, a last desperate move of fighters out of options.

Inside the pickup, the women battled the lone troop at their rear. The attacker's clan surrounded the vehicle, rocking it to tip it over. Cassie remained focused on the immediate threat. She grabbed a shard of broken glass and jabbed the eye of her attacker. It screeched and vanished. Blood poured down her palm, a victim of her own defense.

She spotted an old tee in the truck bed and reached for it. One Eye reappeared, somehow hissing despite an absence of mouth. The glass jutted from its socket. She instinctively shoved it deeper. With a grotesque 'urk' the creature fell dead. The body seemed to melt into silver and rolled away, dripping through a gap in the tailgate. She retrieved the shirt and wrapped her injured hand, cradling it to her mid-section. Bloody cloth pressed to bloody cloth. She was past wincing.

Jenny rocked in place while covering her ears. "Make it stop!"

Kate noticed Tyler's predicament. She ignored the violent rocking of the cab and stomped on the gas. "Hang on!"

Dirt spun as Kate mowed down multiple monsters while driving toward her son. She yanked the wheel at the last second, causing the truck to slide until the tail came to rest next to the two men. They leaped in and she sped off, aiming for the cornfield.

"You okay, honey?" Kate asked her son.

"I will need more time to process an answer, Mom."

Cassie screamed. "Hole!"

A massive sinkhole appeared dead ahead. Kate turned. The rear tire danced along the edge of the abyss just as the others caught, allowing the truck to speed away. The near miss jolted the vehicle, bouncing everyone high in the air. Tyler almost tumbled off the tailgate. Joe grabbed the boy's belt and pulled him back.

Joe yelled through the broken window. "There will be more. The ground isn't stable. It's a labyrinth down below."

"You want me to stop?"

"No. But we've got to get out into the open where we can see oncoming hazards."

Tyler chimed in. "Have we forgotten we need to pull a rope of for Dad?"

"We're leading them away," Kate replied. "After we lead them elsewhere, we can return and..."

Wham!

A massive monstrosity rammed the passenger side of the pickup. Despite the blow, the truck continued moving. A bastardized version of a minotaur, one with a boar's head rather than a bull's, chased the vehicle. The beast had two eyes instead of the single of lore. A large tusk rose from its lower lip. It possessed oversized legs with equally impressive forearms. They lost sight of it as they sped away.

Wham!

The Minoboar found them again, ramming the passenger door, which buckled. Kate swerved only to encounter another sinkhole. She jerked the wheel. The violent motion bounced Tyler through the window into a gap behind the seats in the cab. He exchanged a quick fist bump with Jenny.

"It's trying to lead us into a chasm. How can it be so fast?" Kate asked.

A horrific creature with a raven's head appeared in front of them. The human sized biological oddity stood with arms spread like a scarecrow minus a post. It flapped its limbs, which sprouted feathers. If it intended to take flight, it never made it. It fell under the wheels of the truck with an epic squawk.

"They are everywhere," Cassie said.

"Dad's back there, we need to get back!" Tyler yelled.

Kate hit the brakes, tossing the passengers forward. After a quick search for the threat, they found nothing but an angry mother. One who gunned the engine while appearing content to remain where she was.

"Uh, Mom?" Tyler prodded.

"I am not moving this car if everyone does not let me be."

"It's a truck, not a car," Jenny said.

"Jenny!" Kate scolded. Joe placed a finger over his lips to shush his daughter. "Feel free to get out and walk any who don't give me time to think. I'm under a lot of pressure here."

The stalks shook more violently. The minions broke through and advanced on the pickup. Tyler gestured wildly at the advancing army.

"Mom?"

"Kate," Joe said.

The Minoboar stepped into the clearing huffing with the satisfaction of discovering a disabled vehicle. With the stomp of a hoof, it prepared to charge.

"Is everyone going to cool it?" Kate asked.

"Cool, yes, super. Chilling in the non-Netflix way," Tyler said.

Affirmatives all around as the Minoboar charged. Kate floored it. The wheels spun, but the truck failed to move. They all screamed as the beast advanced. Kate gunned the engine, but the wheels remained stuck. The Minoboar smashed into the tail of the pickup, dislodging the trapped wheel. The vehicle caught solid ground and sped away.

Kate navigated around various sinkholes, each seemingly larger than the last until they finally broke into the open. The truck barreled down the road, heading toward the town. She scanned her surroundings. It appeared as if they were in the clear.

"Mom?" Tyler pleaded, looking back at the vanishing farm.

"Getting out while we can. It's the responsible thing to do," Kate said.

"What about Matt?" Cassie asked.

"She's right. We can't help anyone if we can't help ourselves. It is better to go into town for help. Let me in?" Joe spoke through the window. The truck stopped and he leaped out of the back and into the passenger seat.

Kate turned to Joe. "You said you knew. You knew she wasn't gone."

"I was wrong, Kate."

She nodded. Oh yeah, that. She shifted back into gear, drove a foot and stopped. She adjusted the rearview mirror. "You might have been wrong, but I'm not."

She shifted again and hit the gas, driving in reverse toward the farm.

CHAPTER 41

Matt leaped for the dangling rope in the living room but could not reach. He moved the couch underneath but bumped an end table which tipped a candle. The flames lit the arm of the couch. Matt quickly slapped out the flames, then lifted his arms and breathed, calming himself. There were enough baddies around without one of their own adding literal fuel to a literal fire. He felt the burned surface to ensure it had cooled, and no sparks remained in play. He turned to find Brad standing cross armed and annoyed.

"Are you three done?" Brad asked.

"Three?"

"Moe, Larry, and Curly."

"Funny. Help with the couch maybe?"

"No. You still can't reach with that. I'll give you a lift."

"And what about you?"

"Once you are up, lower it for me and your father."

"Thanks," Matt said.

"For what?"

"For not even pretending he might not make it back."

Brad laced his fingers low to the ground. Matt looked at him questioningly.

"The Three Stooges? How old are you?"

"I could know them. You don't know my life."

"Yes, I do. You're my best friend. I totally know your life."

Brad rolled his eyes. "Uncle Elmer is a fan."

"Ah. I knew I liked your Uncle Elmer."

Matt stepped on his friend's hands. Brad lifted him easily. Matt gripped the rope and climbed high enough to get his legs in on the action. He kicked until the cord looped around one leg, which absorbed some weight. Once stable, he gave the line a shake. The wrench clanged above.

"What's that noise?" Brad asked.

"We tied a tool off to signal to lift us. They should have pulled already. Not a good sign. I'll attempt to climb."

Matt climbed with youthful vigor despite the recent battle. It did not last long. By the time he ascended to the top of their old home, he found his energy depleted. He struggled not to release the cable and fall back into the darkness. His arms were spaghetti, and his aching fingers burned.

Kicking wildly, he tried to throw a leg over the edge but could not find purchase. Something snapped, and the house dropped several feet. A small section fell away, narrowly missing him as it tumbled into the open hole. The fresh break exposed a beam. He anchored himself on it and scrambled onto the roof.

Below, Brad heard a thunderous sound overhead. His eyes went wide in concern.

"Oh, no. I'll catch you, Matt!" He held his arms out and suddenly realized the error of his ways. Debris rained down. He ran off and leaped into the threshold as part of the ceiling collapsed into the living room with a massive crash. Brad shook his head.

"They always said, use a doorway in case of Earthquakes. They never mentioned doing it when a so-called FRIEND dumps a roof on you!"

Brad waited until the destruction settled. As the world returned to silence, he heard oncoming footsteps echoing in the cavern. He retrieved the flashlight and aimed it into the dark stone corridor where someone stepped into the beam.

"Lower the light?" Granger (as Roger) said.

"Mr. Whatley! Hells yeah, you did it! You kicked Granger dude's butt? That tool is such a loser. I mean as far as monstrous God like demon scum go. Not clear what his deal is. But humanity, baby, am I right?"

Brad threw a fist out for a bump. Roger ignored it. Brad shrugged off the dis and pointed at the opening in the living room.

"Matt's fine. He went topside to and will lower the rope within reach. Unsure why he hasn't pulled it up yet, though. Then my supposed friend tried to drop a roof on me. Not what I would call a friendly thing to do."

"What are you rambling about?" Roger asked.

"Am I? Well I'm still pumped we won. How did you do it? I mean, you couldn't get too close to that gross loser. Have you smelled his breath? What does the dude have against mints? Would it kill him to chew some gum, is all I'm asking? Hey, you know what? You can lift me. Once I'm up, I won't abandon you like some people have."

Brad positioned himself. Roger approached and placed one hand under Brad's foot and the other gripped on his neck. Before Brad could protest, Roger raced across the room at a stunning speed. He slammed the teen face first into a wall. Brad remained standing despite the harsh blow. He shook his head, trying to understand what happened. Then he spotted Roger's red glowing eyes as the man left him for the center of the room. Granger as Roger peered up at the opening.

"Oh crap. All those things I said? I'm such a kidder." Brad suggested.

Roger prepared to leap for the dangling cable, but Brad beat him to it. The youth ran across the room, launched himself off the corner of the couch and caught the rope. He quickly lost steam while climbing the line and yelled to the sky in desperation.

"Matt. Pull me up!"

Roger jumped impossibly high, grabbing the cable at a point above the teen. Granger glanced down and hissed, his features briefly shifting back to that of his original form. Granger kicked Brad's face, dislodging the boy who crashed through the living room upon impact. He fell through to the basement, landing on concrete just shy of the water, out cold.

Roger climbed, whistling an eerie tune.

CHAPTER 42

The wide road allowed Kate to navigate effortlessly as the truck roared backward at a high rate of speed. The passengers scanned the surroundings for further intrusions. Beside the screaming engine, the rest of the world appeared calm. Corn stalks showed no signs of having ever been a battlefield for unimaginable beasts with an army of minions. Silk tufts, capping off near bursting husks of bounty, danced in a wind of promise. She drove parallel to the postcard scenery. It was as if Dorothy clicked her heels and everyone was suddenly home.

Kate was not having it. "Where did they all go?"

"Who cares? As long as they're gone," Tyler said.

"I'm with your Mom. Something weird is happening," Cassie scanned the field.

"I don't want them to take anyone ever again," Jenny chimed in.

What appeared too good to be true was. Joe spotted them first. The horde surrounded the sinkhole, nestled so close together they almost formed one organism. The person on the roof would be in a terrible spot.

He pointed them out. "I found our little hellions. Hurry!"

The barrier of bodies blocked the view of whoever was at their mercy. Kate sped up. She raced backward as if planning to enter the hole. The howling engine drowned out the passenger's cries of worry. She looked in a mirror and frowned at the sight of the scurrilous dark entities circling the house. HER house! The protests in the cab increased in intensity as the sinkhole grew closer. She was going too fast.

The truck barreled toward the edge. At the last minute, she spun the wheel, striking down a stretch of the evil troops. One tire encountered the lip of the opening and surely would have dragged them down were she driving any slower. Once clear, she hit the brakes.

Matt stood on the roof swinging a board to keep the predators at bay. He had been there for only moments when the cavalry arrived. The horde hissed collectively as they appeared to assess the damage from the surprise attack. The relieved teen took advantage and rushed through the break in their line and leaped into the back of the truck.

The two brothers touched, confirming the other alive. "I've had a lot of time to think. You can go in my room whenever you want. If you can find it."

"No thanks. Mom's crazy, by the way," Tyler said.

"What about your dad?" Kate asked. The troops advanced. She gunned the engine as they drew closer. Closer. "Matt! Your father?"

"Told you," Tyler looked to his sibling.

Inexplicably, the underground denizens broke away from the pickup, marching into the cornfield like miners ending a shift. The group watched the retreat with stunned amazement. Clang! The wrench jangled against the tractor. Kate turned off the engine and raced to the hole. The others followed.

"Mom, it's Brad, he..." Matt appeared suddenly confused. "Dad?"

"A little help?" The father pleaded while dangling from the roof's edge.

Tyler instinctively prepared to jump down, but Joe stopped him. "Too dangerous. We need to pull him up."

Everyone pulled like tug of war. Once they got the man to solid ground, Kate leaped into his arms. The couple kissed. Roger returned the kiss passionately. Lots of tongue. Kate leaned away, flushed, eyeing him with surprise. She gestured to the others nearby, silently urging him to stand down. They failed to notice.

Cassie finally took a moment with Matt and gripped his hand, leaning her head on his shoulder. Joe slapped his friend recently reformed arm. Granger, in the guise of Roger, winced.

"I'm sorry. Are you okay?"

Roger offered a winning smile, one which melted away years of lifelines earned from farmwork. "Nothing three months in a hot bath wouldn't solve. But I am good. Never better."

"Is it over, Dad?" his younger son asked.

"Soon it will all be over."

Joe watched the last of the army vanish into the field. "This should be epic news, but it feels weird."

"I think they leave when Granger does," Roger said.

"Is he really gone?" Cassie asked.

"Do you see him anywhere?" Roger winked at her.

Matt frowned at the flirt. Cassie flushed in embarrassment. Everyone moved in on the man, celebrating the victory, except for Matt who peered down the hole.

"What about Brad?"

"Time I go on a diet. Poor guy hurt his back helping me. Said he could not use the rope in his condition, so he planned to exit another way. Last I saw of him, he headed for the basement."

Someone shook Brad awake. The teen blinked through the fog and raised a fist. "Stay away, you son of a bitch!"

"It's me, Roger."

"Let me smell your breath."

"What?"

"Allow me to sniff it, you probable demon twin!" Brad lit up when the man complied and huffed in his face. "Oh, I want coffee. Okay, fine, you're not him. Besides, much like me, you appear to have received an ass kicking so I'll assume you are the real Mr. Whatley."

"You've been noticing sulfur, not his breath. Never mind. My injuries are slowing me down. I need you to run ahead and warn everyone." Roger gestured across the basement.

"Aw man. Not the hole. There were critters earlier. I freaked and broke through a shallow wall into another cavern. That's how I found you guys."

"I will follow you. Do you know which route to take?"

"Yes, the one tight enough to squish my ball sack." He climbed into the dark.

With the danger passed, everyone tended to wounds and prepared an exodus. Tyler and Jenny helped assisted Kate in cleaning glass from the interior of the truck. Joe sat atop the tractor trying to start it. Matt fiddled with the engine while suggesting Brad would likely balk at facing the hole and return for the rope. They needed to lower it. The farm equipment had other ideas. It sputtered with every turn of the key.

Cassie and Roger walked to the distant barn. Matt observed them entering the structure and frowned when his father closed the door. A blast of steam from the engine caused the teen to refocus on the task at hand.

Inside, Cassie watched the man she considered a second dad take in the place as if lost. She breathed through pain while cradling her side. The ache failed to abate. She cleared her throat.

"Everything okay, Mr. Whatley? I really need that first aid kit."

He turned his grin on her. A million-dollar smile belonging to someone else. "Yeah, sure. Just a little unsteady. Rough day. Obviously."

Then it was her turn. Cassie stumbled, and her eyes fluttered. Roger caught her. He pulled a footlocker from under the bench, then sat her down. "Seriously. How are you?"

She lifted her shirt partially open to reveal blood soaked bandaging. "Could really use a fresh wrap."

"Such a sturdy girl. So hard to break. Full of hope even while lacerated."

Cassie's head lilted, falling into his hands. He brushed a strand of hair away and examined her features. Her lids drooped, and she leaned into him, battling to remain conscious. Suddenly aware of the closeness, she jerked upright, more alert.

"The first aid kit. Please. I already used up what I could from the truck."

Roger made a show of searching the workbench, pulling open various drawers. His face lit upon discovering a sharp gardening trowel. He gripped the handle like a dagger.

"Do you need help to look?"

He dropped the tool and turned, staring at her lasciviously. "Looking? No. I have been doing that since the walk here. You're lovely."

"Mr. Whatley?"

"Making the observation that you've grown."

"Maybe I'll get your wife. She knows where it is."

He placed his palms on either side of her. "We do not require Kate's presence."

Cassie rose. With him leaning in, her breasts brushed across his face. He snarled in erotic delight, but released one arm to allow her to step away. With a flourish, he opened the footlocker.

"Ta-da!"

Roger emphasized the find with jazz hands, then retrieved the kit and slammed the chest closed. He helped her sit on it.

"Guessed where it was, but here we go."

"A guess? It's your barn."

"Kids move stuff all the time, always getting into things they should not. Little rebels, all of them, from cradle to grave. At least they did not drink the alcohol."

Roger lifted the plastic bottle and set it aside. He unbuttoned her top button. Cassie grabbed at the second to keep it closed since all the lower ones were already open. He shrugged over her modesty.

"Just trying to make it easier to get at them."

"Them?"

He lingered before answering. "Your wounds."

Roger gripped the edge of her blood-soaked dressings. She reached to stop him, but the motion caused him to press against her wound. She gasped in agony.

"I never say this to women but try not to move, it will hurt less."

The unexpected contact shook her. She bit her lip and nodded, a silent gesture for him to be gentle. Roger slowly unwrapped the bandages, leaning in each time for the sections behind her torso. Every reach around her back caused his face to brush her body. She sat up straighter, trying to keep her chest above him. The wrap came free, a bloody mess of fabric. Her side looked grim. Skin flaps dangled over a blackened hole that wept blood.

"Oh my, my, my, how that must hurt. Horrible job on the triage. Looks like you could use someone with more experience. One who knows their way around the human body."

That was enough. She struggled to close her shirt. "I'm fine, actually. I've got this. You can go assist your family."

"But we're not finished. I have known you since you were a child. In case you failed to notice, you are far from that any longer. Let Daddy help."

She suddenly spotted the bottle of alcohol at her side.

"No, don't..."

He poured it directly into her wound. Her eyes shot open in surprise and the world slipped into slow motion. The liquid flooded cold into her. Then it hit. She attempted to scream. Nothing came out. Her gaze rocketed through the room where it locked onto a rooster clock mounted on a wall. Then the pain magnified tenfold. She kicked out, her body jerking in pure agony. She shook as if in a seizure. Her hair went slick with sweat, dropped across her face and sucked into her mouth as she finally gasped for air. Before she could choke on the strands, she passed out. Roger caught her as she fell off her seat.

"Brad!" Matt yelled into the abyss. "Why won't he answer? Probably angry I dumped a roof on him earlier. I didn't have time to warn him because suddenly those minions were everywhere. Maybe my actions hurt him, not him helping my dad. It's my fault."

"I understand your concerns, but this differs from before. We know he is relatively okay. There is no reason to doubt your father. He was with him. Even if your friend is claustrophobic, he would likely chance the tunnel versus being trapped indefinitely."

"Yeah. I'll go look for him in the field. What's taking Cassie so long?"

"With the threat over, she is getting bandaged up proper. I'm thankful Roger is tending to her. She is the first-aid wiz but needs help. He can handle seeing her in so much pain better than you or I could. He'll prep her to ensure she is in a condition to make the trip to the hospital."

"Why close the door?"

"What?" Joe asked.

"Nothing. Yeah, I'll go wait for Brad."

Matt started off. He walked a few feet and looked back at the barn. Something nagged at him. He shook it off and continued walking.

Cassie woke on a bed of hay. She lifted her head, groggy, trying to remember. Pain in her side refreshed her memory. Reaching down, she discovered herself bandaged perfectly, as if attended to in a hospital. She breathed in relief until noticing her top fully open exposing her bra. She pulled it closed and buttoned. Then his legs stepped into view.

"Sorry about the shirt, but I needed room to work. Hope you do not mind."

She tried to shake off the fog. Something else felt off. She touched the bandage again, wincing but feeling okay. She quietly tugged at her bra and found some comfort in it being intact.

"Thank you," she said.

"For the bed, the bandages, or the pain?"

Roger leaned in. Cassie struggled to determine how long she was out. She remembered the clock. It was the last thing she saw before her world went black. Mere minutes had passed. How had he accomplished so much? She rose and continued with her shirt.

Flashes of memory flooded her, of agony where alcohol descended onto her exposed nerve endings. She looked at him, confused. "Why? Why did you do that?"

"I determined it would prove easier to bandage you if you were not so squirmy. It worked. You can see how better you are."

Then she noticed her pants loose, the button unbuttoned. She quickly fastened them and reacted in shock toward the man she thought she knew. She tilted her head quizzically.

He shrugged. "You were kicking everywhere. It was so cute. Who knows how that happened?"

"Mr. Whatley, I can't believe you would..."

He was suddenly on her, tight against her. She never saw him move. He whispered in his ear.

"Do not fret, my dear. Had I visited you in such a manner, you would be a different woman now. That item of loose clothing is of your making. Wish fulfillment, perhaps. You danced with the demon of pain. Tell me little girl, do you long for more? Because I have plenty to give. I understand my friend intrigued you. A certain female officer. You do not think for a minute I have been loyal to my wife, do you?"

Cassie bolted for the door. She opened it and rushed outside. She screamed as someone grabbed her. How had the man moved so fast? Her fear provided a vision of the older man's face in front of her, except it was the younger version. Matt tried to coral her as she fought him off.

"Hey! Whoa! Are you okay? What is it?"

"Nothing. He's been through a lot. Forget it."

Roger stood in the entrance to the barn. "We had a chat is all. Shared dreams of the future." He winked at Cassie, who shuddered.

Matt stepped protectively in front of her, but she shoved him aside, standing her ground alongside him.

"You want to talk, Dad? Fine. I was going to go find Brad, but thought maybe I would check in first. Glad I did. Let's reminisce. Remember when we snuck away to Dundee Lake? We were seeding the corn, but it was hot. You said Mom would never know. Father and son, just a little swim time?"

"Sure. I suppose you'd like to return there now that we're out of this."

"Why not? We had such a fantastic day, didn't we?"

"We did."

"I cramped up because we went straight from the fields. I nearly drowned! We've never gone back."

Granger's face morphed into a split between that of Roger and his own. "You'll wish you drowned when I am done with you."

"Where is he? What did you do to him?"

Brad raced across the field in the distance, shouting. Matt charged his father's doppelganger. Granger easily swatted the youth away, launching him through the air several yards. Granger morphed fully back to himself and clenched his fists. He jerked his hands up, disturbing the soil as if pulling at an underground string.

The landscape rumbled. Cassie tried to get to Matt, but something gripped her legs, locking her in place. Claw tipped arms rose from the dirt, clenching her. Her trapped stance kept her facing the man responsible for her pain. She struggled to free herself, to no avail.

Matt remained on his back, fighting to breathe. The force of the blow robbed him of oxygen. He reacted to Cassie's cries by lifting his head and attempting to rise. A clawed limb subdued him, forcefully pressing his forehead down while other hands joined the party gripping legs, arms, and torso. They attempted to drag him under.

Kate and Jenny cleaned the truck, oblivious to the new threat. Joe and Tyler yelled down the hole for Brad. Once they gave it a rest, the cries from across the plain reached everyone. Kate instructed the girl to stay in the vehicle. She glimpsed Matt flailing from a prone position. She ran a short distance when sprouting arms grabbed her legs, stopping her so abruptly she face planted. Her skull bounced, and she lifted her head in a confused stupor. She attempted to push off from the ground, but two more hands gripped hers, trapping her on all fours.

Joe and Tyler witnessed her fall and rushed to help. Joe yelled for the youth to attend to his mother while announcing he was going for Cassie. Before he could finish the thought, the denizens of the deep reached through the turf and anchored the man's legs. Tyler narrowly escaped his attempted attacker. Joe bent over. Tyler got the message and jumped onto the man in a piggyback. Jenny yelped from inside the truck where a dozen hands ripped through the ground and shook the vehicle.

"No eyes visible. Granger must supply them with sight. He can't focus on everything. Do you see the hoe?"

"You bet!" Tyler leaped off and dodged a gauntlet of new thrusting limbs, the deadliest of crops. He stomped on the metal head. The handle sprung into his grasp. He tossed the tool to Joe as his luck ran out. They grabbed the youth in a grip so firm he winced at the pressure.

Granger focused on Cassie. "Now I lay you down to sleep. May the Ancient Ones all souls keep! We are ready to begin your descent. You and I will finish what we started and do so in front of your family. Oh, the things we shall achieve. The bed of hay is ceremonial. On it is where we bring you to a point where you no longer beg me to stop, but scream for me to continue. That is when we know you forgot the world you once knew."

"No. Please. Haven't you taken enough?"

"I take what you flesh vessels eagerly give. It is what I do. Before long you will offer yourself to the Ancients. Soon your being shall merge with what your kind call sin. The pleasures shall turn you, like I turned out your mother. I understand if you remain resistant to my current form. Maybe you prefer the touch of one of my many lieutenants?"

In an instant the man vanished, only to become Officer Baker. The woman's breasts were on full display, her blouse hung open. Even though the real woman was not present, Cassie felt ashamed at her nakedness. A woman exploited. The act was one more violation from the monster of a man, no matter how unscrupulous the target.

Cassie quickly dispelled any sisterhood thoughts about the exposure when the cloned woman grabbed her by the throat. The choking was something her captor would be unaware of unless Nadine offered details. The two were in cahoots. Lisa relayed a sickening tale of the officer's antics. Had the cop always been such a horrible person, or had she fallen under the influence of the evil man? Was he the gin to her tonic? Cassie struggled to breathe, locking eyes with the demon before her. The resemblance was uncanny. This was the twisted officer, and if not, she failed to distinguish between the copy and the real thing, except for a firmer grip.

Nadine grinned, licking her lips. "I see a change in you. I think you enjoy her. Looks like we're about to have some fun."

"Step away from the hot chick!" Brad yelled.

The officer's head sagged in a 'don't these people ever die?' frustration. The woman's chest deflated before Granger morphed back to himself, down to bare body except the jeans as he first appeared in the underworld. Brad threw a punch.

Without looking, Granger caught the oncoming fist. The teen registered fear upon realizing how easily the man held him in check. Granger pulled the boy forward before palming him hard in the chest. The boy rocketed through the air before crashing through the barn doors, disappearing somewhere inside.

Granger licked his lips with a tongue slightly too long and too dark. "So many damn pests on a farm. Now, where were we?" He turned around.

Joe stood ready with the hoe. "Not. One. More. Of. My. Family!" He swung it like a baseball bat.

The metal hook struck home. Granger's head snapped sideways, but quickly returned with a heavy scowl. Joe struck again. Granger caught the handle, and the two fought for the weapon. Joe released his end, causing the other man to stumble from the unexpected move.

Joe punched him once, twice, three times, but he did not fall. Joe hit harder and his fist exploded into his foe's face as if a gourd. The man's features dissolved into a skin cocoon wrapped tight around his hand. Joe tried to yank himself free.

Granger's twisted flesh followed the trajectory of the retracting arm, pouring up and out over his skull like a candle melting in reverse. Teeth appeared within the fleshy wrap and bit into its prize. Joe screamed and tugged while being bitten by an outward facing mouth. The fangs snapped off, and he finally wrested himself loose. Granger returned to his former self.

Joe circled, drawing the man away from his daughter. Granger glanced toward the others while the men danced. Tyler battled to free his mother with a rake. Matt appeared on the cusp of losing his fight. The arms criss-crossing his torso held him partially underground. Granger refocused on Cassie. Joe took note.

"You'll get to her over my dead body,"

"Something we agree upon." The predator circled his prey. "So easy it was to turn this town upside down. They served as a succulent buffet, allowing me to feed on all their wickedness as each chose enlightenment."

"You mean darkness," Joe said.

"Naivety. Perhaps that is the sole reason you and yours escaped my grasp. Stupidity masquerading as nobility. Enlightenment is the correct word. The former innocents of your burg followed the righteous path of character destitution, embraced wantonness, succumbed to the truth that is corruption. They fed at my teat as surely as I did theirs, spurred by the mighty Elders. The Dark Masters who stand outside time witnessed the destructive forces and violence that birthed this realm and declared it good. The Ancients existed well before the Gods and will continue long after. We are timeless."

"And we are family!"

Brad stood nearby holding two hay bale poles. He tossed one. Joe caught it and bashed Granger in the face. The teen used the other to battle Cassie's captors.

Joe saw his daughter break free. "Run, Cassie. Help the others!" She ran, keeping ahead of thrusting hands, seeking her recapture. He struck his foe. "They are all part of you. Your power wanes the more you send out into the world. I watched you falter as your army attacked. Your numbers make you weaker while ours strengthens us."

"Enough!" Granger waved, and all the limbs slithered back into the soil as if snakes.

"They're gone. The freaky grabbers left," Brad announced.

The teen joined Joe and raised his pole. Granger transformed. His body shifted as dark bubbles appeared under his skin. They traveled along his legs up into his torso like pitch black tennis balls.

His arms dissolved into roiling tentacles until changing to heavy crab pincers and then furry paws matching those of the Rottweiler beast. A rapidly shifting anatomy. His face did the same, running through the gamut of beasts on the loose since the terror began.

Joe recognized several variants in the mix. The nature of the changes dawned on him. "He's absorbing them, reclaiming his creations. We must fight now!"

The pair stormed the mutating figure. The shapes reacted as themselves, with each variant responding to the attacks accordingly. A monkey head spit at Brad when the teen poked out its eye. That guise gave way to the tear drop headed beast. It's long tongue lashed out like a bullwhip slicing Joe's cheek before vanishing, replaced by other terrifying biological anomalies of combined species.

When its face segued to a featureless drone, the two men poked tips of the poles into each eye and pressed hard, maintaining contact. The bubbles under Granger's skin popped loudly, turning into a visible flow of darkness, evil blood rushing into his veins. Then it happened.

Granger grew taller, his bones crunching audibly, while tendons twanged like broken guitar strings after stretching beyond breaking points. The poles dislodged from the eyes of the long-gone drone and fell to the ground. Joe and Brad stepped back in shocked submission. The growth spurt continued as the circumference of his biceps morphed to inhuman proportions. Something raised slowly from his now oversized skull. Legs stretched to tree trunk thickness and sprouted a fine fur coating, resembling those of an enormous goat.

The men retrieved their weapons and struck as a unit. Granger caught both sticks with ease. With a flick of his wrist, he snapped them midway, leaving himself armed. He clubbed Brad. The youth's head cracked like a cheap melon and he fell flat on his face, instantly unconscious. The remaining combatants swung at the same time.

The force when they connected flung Joe's weapon away. Granger threw one aside and lifted Joe by the throat. The father kicked impotently while fighting for air. Granger placed his victim against the barn door, then raised the hook side of the pole.

Thunk!

Granger impaled the man through his shoulder. Joe dangled, blood dripping into the soil. He blinked, trying to remain conscious. Granger squeezed his cheeks as one might a child.

"Now I secure what is mine. You will watch helplessly as I defile. Though you beg for mercy, there will be none. Wither hope as it rots on the vine. The acres of this land have long gone sour. You think your wife begged for you in her moment of torment? You believe she ever considered your memory while curled in my arms? No. she screamed only my name. At first in terror, then in pleasure until both mingled into an ecstasy she never experienced at your side. Oh, how I enjoyed converting her into my little pain princess! You doubt my path. I have seen it in you. You question the strength and glory of agony and defilement. I vow to prove you wrong. It may shock you how quickly they forget your existence by the time I am done with them."

"To my last! To my end, I know they love me!" Joe raged, spittle spraying, and then tremors of pain washed over him.

"We shall see. Love is a construct easily deconstructed."

The monstrous figure departed, supplying an unobstructed view of the deviant's final transformation, including twisted horns curling away at the forehead. The beast stomped a hoof, the legs elongated, muscular. He stood so high off the ground he could have been on stilts. With such a stride, a single step drew him dangerously close to the others. Nearer to the objects of his salacious desires. He would be upon them in no time.

Joe struggled to keep his head upright as his daughter ran, unaware of the monster on her tail. Joe's world faded, but he summoned enough energy to warn her. "Cassie! Behind you!" Then, as much as he wanted to, he could not muster the strength to cry out in pain.

R oger grabbed his leg and winced upon returning to the surface. He lost track of Brad some time ago. The youth panicked in the confines of their escape route and scrambled off too fast for Roger to keep up. The boy followed the original plan to race ahead to warn the others, even if panic provided the incentive. It pleased him to discover the teen already gone. The last thing he wanted was for the kid to wait for his aged ass.

And old it felt. *What a year the past day has been*, he thought. He arrived at the shed which took him further from the farm, but he had no choice, he needed the first aid kit inside. He ran his hand along a lip above the door and retrieved the key to open it.

Stumbling against a pallet of fertilizer bags, he opened the kit and quickly wrapped the wound, aiming for too tight. Someone screamed toward the home. Blood spotted through the gauze, but it allowed him to stand despite the leg turning numb. It proved enough to allow him to walk again. He had work to do, but he needed to hurry.

Somewhere in the distance, another scream.

CHAPTER 43

The ground thundered behind Cassie's feet as she fled from the unknown. Screams from loved ones pleaded for her to hurry. She sensed something closing in and launched into track star mode, finding her next gear while running the opposite direction of the others. She could not help Matt when monstrous hands fought to pull him into an early grave, but she could assist by leading the new threat away. Though they released everyone, he still struggled to free himself of the soil. Cassie worried an underground chasm might swallow him whole. He cried out with concern for her despite his own predicament. Matt had her back even while in peril, so she planned to do the same for him.

She did not look behind herself. There was no reason. The fear in the voices of her loved ones made it clear the pursuer was horrific. How deadly she knew not, but wished to ensure it remained her threat only. She continued drawing it away. Whatever IT was. The pumpkin patch became her destination.

A tear rolled down her cheek in understanding of the sacrifice. The protests faded into the distance as she ran so far that she was soon alone. She would face her hunter solo. The shaking ground acted as a proximity alarm. It would not be long now. The earth shifted under every thunderous step of her predator. (Were those horse's hooves?)

The power of the force at her rear felt so strong she feared she might freeze up in fright. A part of her desired to submit and get it over with. But she ran. Where there was hope, she would run. Still, it terrified her to think she would soon join a club no one ever wished to belong to. Her Mother was also a member. That club? Death. And like her mom, her hazing would be painful.

Despite what a bevy of unholy beings suggested about her mom, Cassie believed her mother fought to the end. Cassie vowed the same. They could take

Cassie's life, and likely would, but she refused to allow them to pervert the memory of the woman who raised her. Cassie vowed to fight with everything she had. She would call the beast on its lies in the face of gaslighting. She vowed to remain silent in the face of torture, to deprive the attacker of satisfaction. The unstable ground announced imminence. *Oh God, it's here, I can hear the rumble of its heart, so loud now*, she thought.

Matt hit the brakes and threw open a door. "Get in!"

She jumped in just as the behemoth sideswiped the pickup, ripping the passenger door off at the hinges. Cassie grabbed for the seatbelt as Matt drove off. The truck roared through the field while Granger paced the vehicle off to one side.

"Where were you going?" he asked.

"Trying to lead him away."

"Good idea. We'll do it together."

Wham! The truck bounced as Granger rammed it with the force of an oncoming car. The collision caused Cassie to bounce through the doorless opening, but the strap did its job, stopping her shy of feeding into wheels. She fought her way back into the cab. Matt spun into a donut, kicking up a massive dust storm. The young couple coughed as the particulates designed to blind their pursuer also invaded the interior.

Wham!

A large shape flashed through a break in the cover. They struggled to spot the man, hoping he too suffered the same visual limitations. Matt shone the high beams, which fell on red eyes in an opaque sky. He yanked the wheel and hit the gas.

Wham!

The truck spun again, forcing the teen to fight for control. Dust eventually faded in the wind. The pickup settled after rocking violently. Matt removed his foot from the accelerator.

"Why are you slowing?" Cassie asked.

The vehicle rolled slowly, with Granger changing his pace to match. The fiend fixated on the families ahead. Matt gestured to their loved ones.

"He could have tipped us over but hasn't. He has been repositioning our trajectory to force our return. That's his plan. Suffer the little children. He requires witnesses to the misery he induces. There is no running. But we have a chance."

He looked sadly at her for permission. Her nod sealed their unspoken plan. Matt gripped the wheel and sped toward home. Granger ran parallel, maintaining enough distance to ensure compliance. A few hundred yards from their destination, Matt hit the brakes. Granger overshot them, surprised by the sudden stop.

Granger stood equidistant between the family on the backside of the hole, and the parked truck. He twisted his neck, determining which path to follow. He announced his decision by squaring off against the pickup. The mutated man grinned wickedly. Matt roared the engine. Granger roared himself, stomping a foot for emphasis.

"Cassie, I want you to know..." Matt started.

"No. Tell me after."

"Sure. After," he lied.

Matt floored it. The pickup fish-tailed before straightening. Granger kicked off, the two partaking in the ultimate game of chicken. The distance closed quickly with neither side blinking.

Granger planted himself. The truck smashed into him like hitting a pole at full speed. The rear of the vehicle lifted as the front crumpled into what was once a man. Glass shattered and airbags exploded. The back of the truck settled onto the ground and went still. The collision launched Granger airborne, his arms and legs flailing. He bounced across what remained of the roof, rolling toward the hole at its center.

Matt coughed and looked to Cassie. Neither appeared well. Matt sported facial bruises from the impact despite the airbag. Cassie's hair frayed wildly while tiny lacerations covered her body from the broken glass shower. Cassie dangled out the open door, held in place by a distended seat belt.

Matt pressed the button to release her. She crashed to the ground with a groan. Matt pushed his door open and fell out himself. Steam gushed from the front of the truck, though the engine continued running. An uneven clunk pinged under the crumpled hood. Fuel leaked from the vehicle in a small rivulet where it pooled nearby.

Granger held onto the roof by his fingertips, trying to shake off the force of the collision while mustering enough strength to pull himself up. The already stressed structure struggled under his weight. Pieces broke off and tumbled into the void. The massive legs kicked wildly to gain hold. He appeared unconcerned with the distance below and more concerned with maintaining a view of his prey.

The weight of his current form acted as an anchor, so he morphed back to human form. Now lighter, he easily caught the ledge with a leg and pulled himself up. He spotted Kate and the kids huddling nearby, then turned to learn the fate of the teens.

The crumpled truck rested near the hole. Granger chuckled with glee at the sight of the couple damaged but alive. Promises of pain were back on. Cassie reached for something inside the truck before pulling her hand back and leaning on the hood. Granger raised his arms in triumph.

"Your effort failed. Death would have been merciful. Now I will teach you the ways of the Ancient Ones. Their methods prevail. We will visit Timeless gospel upon what remains of your skin. You tried. You failed. Your optimistic insanity and pride have proved to be your downfall. I led you back to torture you in front of your loved ones. Now you are right where I wanted you."

"Really? Because last I checked, we have you right where we want you."

Matt leaped into the truck. Cassie grabbed the lighter she had pushed in. Matt drove straight toward the surprised-looking man. Cassie lit the puddle of gas and a line of fire raced after the fleeing vehicle. Matt leaped out at the last second. The truck roared over the edge of the hole. Granger crossed his arms over his face as the truck smashed him head on. It drove through the roof, taking the man with it like a prized hood ornament.

Debris thundered down alongside the pickup. The vehicle exploded deep underground, sending wood shrapnel through the air and into the yard of their beloved lost home. The force of the explosion knocked everyone off their feet.

Matt rose first, happy to spot his mother tending to the children. All apparently okay. He then trekked on unsteady feet to Cassie, who was down on her knees. He dropped alongside her and gazed into her eyes.

"So that thing I wanted to say to you?"

She pointed to her ears. "What? The explosion, I can't hear."

Her words sounded like cotton in his own head. He mouthed 'never mind' then pulled her close. They laid down in the tall grass to rest as the world underneath them burned.

CHAPTER 44

Blackness. Followed by pain, enough to bring the world back into focus. Joe roared in agony as the door swung wide, slamming him into the side of the barn, driving the pole deeper.

"Sorry! My bad!" Brad yelled and dragged the gate away from the wall, drawing a renewed cry of protest from the impaled man.

"What are you doing?"

"Trying to get you down, sir."

"Sir? How old do I look exactly?"

"Old. More gnarly than old, but, yeah, tired too. Like Wolverine in that last movie."

Brad grabbed the end of the pole and pulled, only to flinch under a thunderous explosion. The resulting jerk on the rod would have prompted further cries from the impaled man had the destruction in the distance not drawn his attention. Fire rose from the pit.

"Jenny! Cassie?" Joe closed his eyes in silent prayer.

"You were out and missed the action. I think everyone is fine, that barbecue is for big ugly."

Brad yanked in a quick fluid motion like the tablecloth trick, though with blood, lots of it. Joe dropped to the ground. The wound bled freely, so Joe pressed his hand tight against it to stem the flow. Brad pushed the adult's hand away and took over. Before freeing the man, he had quickly prepped items for triage. He tore a quilt into strips and utility rope into sections.

"Someone used up the whole emergency kit. This is all I could find, but should do the trick. I studied first aid class in school. You are in a condition they have trained us to call nine-one-one for immediately. But no phones."

The teen proved an excellent student, efficiently wrapping the bandages around the worst of the damage. The river of blood did most of the work, soaking the material in place. From there Brad tied off strips at key points, providing a tourniquet of sorts. Once fully bandaged, he fashioned a sling. Joe nodded in appreciation before shoving his medic off.

"Thanks, but get away from me, kid. I need to check on my daughters." Joe attempted to rise, pushing off from his one good hand only to fall on his ass.

"See? Old." Brad helped the man to his feet. "Speaking of, Mr. Whatley should have been back. I hope he wasn't still in the tunnel when that blaze started."

"Let's not think that. We'll gather everyone together, then search for him. Now that this is over and..."

The ground shook at a level exceeding that which originally swallowed the home. Its epicenter spread from the burn in a visible Doppler wave. The rumble knocked Kate and the children over as clouds of dust engulfed them. Disturbed soil gave visibility to the energy pattern, which quickly reached Matt and Cassie. The initial bounce launched them from their resting posture onto unsteady feet. They danced in place while trying to remain upright. The overwhelming cacophony of the rumbling earth drowned out their startled cries.

The motion reached all the way to Joe and Brad where it crested. The pair rode it like surfers. As the world settled into an aftershock, the two raced to join the others. Suddenly the blackness of a new sinkhole opened at their feet. They course-corrected themselves clear of the danger. A tentacle shot through the opening, rising high into the air. The monstrous, thick appendage quivered wildly. The ground erupted again, this time exploding out rather than collapsing as another feeler jutted thirty feet into the sky, waving about in exploration. Hunting.

Two more ruptures appeared on either sides of Kate and the kids. Enormous clouds of dirt exploded all around. Kate threw herself over them as a dust cloud engulfed them, thicker than the last. Twin protuberances slithered excitedly, appearing eager to hunt. They swayed in the night sky. Kate gestured the children to remain silent within the cloud cover. Through the dusty veil, they watched and waited for the colossal twins to make a move.

A new hole emerged underneath Matt and Cassie. It burrowed up and out rather than collapsing inward, resulting in an enormous variation of a molehill. It carried the young couple in its wake. Once the incline grew too steep, they rolled down the slope on either side. An erect tentacle burst through the opening before slamming the surface with a thunderous slap. The muscular appendage cut the two lovers off from one another.

"Cassie, get Jenny!" Joe yelled to his daughter while running.

Another ungodly feeler ascended from the depths, inches from the fleeing father. Joe watched with awe as it rose before him. Up close, the tubular flesh looked like a whale's skin, and glimmered with a slimy coating. The gloss shone a faux rainbow like motor oil on asphalt after rain. Odors of the sea and sulfur crossed the open plains.

More appendages appeared, transforming a once tranquil farm into a horrific vision. Writhing tentacles danced before the fading moon. The surreal image loomed as if from a fantastic planet rather than one from Earth. Brad roused Joe, and they continued running.

Matt and Cassie faced one another from opposite sides of the living barrier. The predator squirmed before sliding in a wide arc, scooping soil while sweeping toward Matt. The teen ran, but it closed on him fast. With no escape route, he turned into faced it and leaped, landing atop the squishy tactile member.

The limb reacted violently, swatting the air, hoping to catapult its rider to oblivion. Matt withstood the beast's initial movement and jumped before being swatted away. Matt landed into a run alongside Brad and Joe. They rushed in the direction of the fire pit that was once a home. Cassie ran well ahead of them.

No time for a reunion for the best friends. They circumnavigated the major hole while attempting to reach the others. A massive eye gazed out from within the wall of flames. The blaze fluttered wildly in the wind and the watchful orb vanished if ever there at all.

The ground rumbled anew. A volcano waiting to explode. Explode it did, but not with magma. Instead, the largest intruder of them all rose like an obelisk so high it threatened to touch the moon in the sky. Twenty feet, thirty, forty. Its girth at the base increased exponentially as it neared a hundred feet. The expanding width of the beast's lowest portion widened the original opening. The group retreated from their positions as the edge cratered, threatening to take down the whole yard.

Suction cups traversed the length of the monstrous tentacle. Above the fire line, the suckers opened, each revealing an eye. They glanced in a multitude of directions, scanning the surroundings. The act appeared to supply the other slithering limbs with the gift of sight. The limb closest to Kate swooped low to strike. She grabbed the kids and ran.

The tentacles slithered back below ground, only to reemerge much closer to their prey. Several exploded to the surface perilously near the assembled men. It forced them to scramble from one another. The feelers sought them out.

As the closest to the massive fire pit, Cassie ran to escape its growing circumference. The monolithic limb rising high appeared oblivious to the flames licking at its lower section. Dark smoke wafted from the base of the monster. The odor of rotten fish cooking rode on the breeze. She glimpsed over her shoulder to notice a wall of eyes blinking furiously, an unholy, sight. The only thing more terrifying and what drew her back to the reality of her current situation was the ground crumbling near her feet. She kicked into a higher gear until mercifully the land settled. The beast had reached its apex. She found herself cut off from both her sister and her father.

The earth exploded beneath Kate and the children, lifting them high into the air, the victims of a direct hit of an emerging limb. The airborne trio performed unintentional acrobatics that would have made any circus performer proud. Gravity took hold, and they landed with sickening thuds. Soil rained down, burying them completely. Nothing moved under the makeshift graves. The otherworldly denizen leaned down and used its tip to flick at dirt, searching for the hidden prey to confirm death.

Fresh ruptures kept coming. Cassie fell victim next. A slimy appendage rocketed from the ground and caught her in its trajectory, wrapping around her waist and lifting her in its flight. Once it reached its apex, it shook her wildly into submission. She hung as limp as a rag doll in its grip high above the plain. Its prize subdued, the beast began a slow descent, attempting to return from where it came.

"Cassie!" Joe yelled.

The yell roused her, and she cried out weakly. Matt caught Cassie's hands as she descended, but the futile tug of war ended immediately when the powerful limb easily shook him off. The tentacle ascended again, straightening as it went. The move put distance between itself and the circumference of the hole, placing Cassie out of reach. Matt paced the edge, yelling for her to hold on.

Kate rose from her shallow grave and sucked in air. She noted the proximity of the monstrous arm digging in the wrong spot nearby. Trying not to signal it, she rolled over and dug for the children.

The sound of a motor pushed to its limit cut through the screams. Roger drove the utility vehicle, pulling the tow behind. A blue tarp covering the trailer whipped in the wind. A corner sprung loose and flapped, revealing a payload of fertilizer and gas containers.

Roger yelled for everyone to run as he sped toward the fray. His cries were too weak to rise above the fog of war, so he waved wildly, flashed his lights, and honked the horn.

Kate freed the young ones. Then she spotted the fresh commotion. She understood her husband's intent. Giving the kids no time to rest, she screamed for them to run. They maneuvered past the nearby digger and made for the open road. Once there, they kept going. The wide dirt expanse left them in the open but also allowed them to move faster. They did not look back.

Brad, Joe, and Matt all converged around the opening in the ground above which Cassie still dangled, the beast taunting them with its prize. The base of the creature holding Cassie filled out the circumference of the hole but tapered toward its tip. She danced involuntarily over fifty feet above her boyfriend and father.

Cassie battled to remain conscious. Every herky-jerky motion of her dance partner shook her bones, rattled her brain in her skull. Her teeth snapped together with each sudden jerk. The grip at her waist strained her breathing and pressed painfully against her wound.

In a haze, she noticed the oncoming vehicle and pointed. Her captor suddenly noticed the same. An ungodly cry shrieked from somewhere below the mother limb of the beast, (or beasts?). All eyes of the main feeler fixated on Roger. The pitch of the shriek shifted, possibly sending a signal.

One after another, the limbs slithered below ground in quick retreat. The one holding Cassie uncurled from her waist, but not before flinging her higher in the air than she already was. All the men converged to break her fall collectively, but the effort knocked all of them off their feet. The ground rumbled as furious movement below them passed by like a rolling freight train in one clear direction. Destination Roger.

He drove for the fire pit. The group finally recognized the warnings and rose on unsteady feet. Cassie leaned into Matt, barely able to walk. Joe tried to assist but struggled with his solo arm. Brad took her other side, and the teens dragged her. They headed toward the pumpkin patch in the distance, trying to put space between them and the old home.

The first of the submerged tentacles reemerged directly in front of Roger. He yanked the wheel, avoiding the obstacle causing the hay trailer to tip on two wheels, but it settled back down. The tentacle reached a peak, then slapped the ground with thunderous fury, barely missing him. Even though the force bounced the vehicle into the air, he continued.

Kate and the kids passed him off to one side as they ran away. They shared a quick look, then a scream as another feeler burst from the earth between them. It paid no mind to the escapees, swiping instead at Roger who ducked. The motion dislodged the tarp. The fabric became entangled with the limb. It smashed the blue foe into the ground as if battling a living thing. The distraction allowed Roger to pass.

Another ascended, rocking Roger's world but missed. Then another and another. Each grew closer to the target. So too did the vehicle. The lights strung between the poles over the hay-bed clanged like a wind chime, dancing furiously over the area of a missing pole. Roger retrieved the pole from the passenger seat and wedged it between the seat and gas pedal, then leaped out. The eyes on the mother tentacle ahead blinked wildly. Roger hit the ground and rolled, rose, then ran.

All but the alpha retreated down their holes. They reappeared along both sides of the vehicle like an upside down spider. The alpha protuberance emitted another dreadful screech from somewhere below, a cry of warning to its own independent limbs which failed to get the message on time. They interlaced and thrust down, encasing the vehicle at the edge of the pit. The collective grasp brought the load down with such force that it swallowed what remained of the yard.

The vehicle vanished into the newly created trench. The blaze at the base of the alpha arm sucked underground with a raucous whoosh, rivalling the decibels of the creature's call. A high pitch whine sounded deep below, energy building, then boom! A world shattering explosion lifted the battered landscape. Flames erupted from every opening and engulfed tentacles which rose from the depths seeking escape. Each one burst into flames. The rainbow colors of their skin bled into one shade. Black. Inhuman wailing overtook the night.

Everyone ran as the world exploded. Lengths of topsoil vanished as the underground caverns collapsed. The alpha tentacle opened all its eyes. The orbs widened with a look of terror. A thunderous crack sounded and the structural integrity of the limb faltered. It waved about as if drunk before timbering down straight at Roger!

He glimpsed over his shoulder and spotted what might as well have been a building collapsing. Ignoring immense pain, he sprinted and leaped as the organic obelisk crashed to the ground at his rear. He landed roughly and covered his head, waiting for the inevitable. The rumble of the collapse shook him where he lay, but spared him a crushing.

When the world settled, he rolled onto his back and looked over. The defeated cephalopod raised its tip just enough to reveal a single eye which focused on him briefly before glossing over. The limb slithered away, not of its own accord, sliding into the hole, dragged by the weight of something heavier than even itself.

Roger breathed in relief until a geyser of fire ripped open the turf to one side of him, then the other. He rose to run again. Matt greeted him and helped lead him to where the others had regrouped.

Everyone hugged in reunion. Warriors returned from the battlefield. Tyler rushed forward and embraced father. Kate staggered toward her husband, gazing at him in disbelief. She took his face in her hands.

"Is it really you?" Kate asked.

He nodded while Brad stepped up, accusatory. "Hey, how do we know after, you know."

Matt approached cautiously. "Hey Dad, do you remember that time at Dundee Lake?"

"Yes. My worst day ever until today."

Brad raised his hands. "Amateurs. Even Granger knows that now. We need another test."

"I have something. Remember what I said the night we finally got together?" Kate asked.

"I believe it was shut up and..." Roger started.

Kate leaned in and kissed him. He winced under the contact but pulled her tighter. They continued to kiss. Tyler stepped away, allowing his parents a moment. Jenny giggled while Joe pretended to cover her eyes.

Tyler rolled his eyes. "Gross. Get a room." Then he noticed the burning hell that was their home. "Oh yeah, never mind."

Cassie spotted an SUV nearby on the edge of the cornfield. "Whose vehicle is that?"

Brad raised his keys and grinned. "Parked there so as not to get busted by Matt's parents. Guess that didn't work."

"Perfect, though. God knows we need some medical attention plus we can see how the town fared," Joe said.

The group eagerly marched toward the vehicle. Brad lifted his keys and be-booped the lock. Suddenly the ground beneath it collapsed, taking the SUV with it. It landed upright somewhere below, its headlights shooting into the sky like a spotlight. The alarm beeped incessantly.

Roger pointed to the moon overhead. "Pleasant night for a walk, huh?"

"It would be if you didn't live so far from everything. I swear I don't know what she sees in you," Joe said as the adults merged into a trio leading the others down the dirt road. The children paired off on either side. Cassie and Matt held hands with Brad third wheeling alongside them.

"Does this mean that Matt is off the hook for his party?" Tyler asked.

Matt made a fist and a shush face before offering innocent doe eyes to his parents. His mother was not buying what he was selling. Matt deflated at not receiving a pass after everything.

"Not at all. We'll deal with that later," Kate said before turning back to her husband. "So, what now?"

"Could be time to make a change. Maybe move somewhere safer, like Los Angeles," Roger replied.

"Yes!" Matt started a merry dance, twirling Cassie under the moonlight. The rest of the group carried on, leaving the young couple dancing alone. Adolescent love with nothing left to fear. Until...

Something rustled in the cornfield. The moonlight caught eyes in the stalks. A racoon emerged, corncob in its mouth, a sign of nature getting back to normal. The young lovers smiled at the interruption before falling back into an embrace. They began a slow dance as crickets returned and struck up the band.

SALEM PREVIEW

Water cascaded over rocks in a creek bed. The gurgling of the pristine flow gave way to heavy breathing, guttural, animalistic. Splash! A wooden bucket dipped into the water under the shaking hands of Sarah Goode. Despite the pitched black night sky dotted with pinpricks of stars in ever random patterns, the temperature had not dropped precipitously from the earlier temperate New England day. Her tremors related to something other than a non-existent evening chill.

The water flooded into the container as with minimal spill. Her full-length apron (tucked laboriously into her petticoat) absorbed any stray splashes. She faced more dampness in her daily kitchen routine than her adjacency to the burbling brook. The sweat on her brow produced more dampness than even that.

Heat. She was flush with it as if the death's fever knocked on the door of her soul, announcing an invitation to visit God's realm. Yet, she was not the one sick. She turned her head toward the way she came. The act of looking back caused her hands to shake more violently, and she almost lost the bucket to the current. An owl hooted nearby, watching from somewhere in the dark. Sarah gripped her waistcoat tight, modesty in all things, even beasts. Especially beasts.

There it was. So far was she from her home, from her church, from the nearest cross. Vulnerable and alone in the night, her coif over her hair not enough to provide cover, to keep her hidden from the reach of evil. The thing danced in the starlight high on a ridge high above her. A dog. Large, black, fangs bared, glistening even in the darkness, growling deeply. (A familiar sound?) It raised itself on its haunches, eyes reflecting red as if under a moon despite there being none visible in the sky. It was as if the beast burned from within, using an animal only for its eyes. Far too bright were the staring orbs for her to see them on such a night, but see them she did. It barked.

Sarah ran. Bucket in hand, racing for a distant house. An upper window glowed under the flickering light, matching that of the dog's eyes. A lower window offered a more certain glow, warm, stable. God, she thought. There, in the room housing her cross, the one she now wished she carried with her.

Yet how could she have? So heavy was the bucket now filled, she struggled to move. Her initial flight of fear gave her strength beyond her norm, but the distance traveled stole her stamina from her limbs. They ached; her heart ached. The upper room, the flickering light, a place once welcoming, danced in an unholy red. Was God there in that room? He who was everywhere? No, sadly it appeared God perhaps had a blind spot, for how could he allow his sheep to suffer so?

A bark. In her ear. The beast upon her? She turned, splashing in a circle, droplets ringing her in an involuntary Pagan ritual. Nothing there. No beast on the ridge. Maybe there never was, for certainly she knew where one truly resided all along. The upper window flashed brighter, as if sensing her stare. She continued toward the soft glow of the lower level.

"You do my job Mum?" Haddy asked as Sarah burst through the door into the kitchen struggling under the weight of more than water. Haddy stirred a large boiling pot resting atop the stove.

Haddy did her best to relieve the woman of her burden, taking the handle and freeing the woman of the house from her burden. Sarah fell against the wall, the one holding the cross on its face. She looked over her shoulder, taking comfort in the sight. She wiped her brow with her cinched sleeve, clearing a sweat brought on as much by worry as her activities.

Thump! Obscenely loud from above. Sarah eyed the ceiling. Haddy eyed her employer. The older woman stirred more vigorously. She raised her stir spoon to the air.

"Oh, how children can play," Haddy said.

"Were it so. I would welcome such rambunctiousness, would tolerate their insubordination of house rules, were things only so simple," Sarah said.

"Do not bring lies into the home, missus. Never a day would you tolerate such a scandalous bout of play, nor will you in days to come, for surely after ceremony life will return. The old ways will return."

"Do you believe that?" Sarah asked.

Wham! Did someone drop a new house atop their existing one? How else to account for such a loud noise, Sarah wondered. She attempted to smile at her charge, offer a reassuring agreement, but fell short. Her mouth crimped into further worry.

"I have been called a fool. I prefer the term resilient missus. Do I believe boxes opened can be closed? My frailty of character deems it so."

"You bring me strength, Haddy. For that I thank you," Sarah rubbed the arm of the woman.

Haddy poured the bucket into the pot. Steam exploded into the air under the combined liquids. The vapor enveloped the two women, vanishing each from the view of the other. Sarah waved away a cloud which appeared that of a demon chasing its tail, one circling her in a bemused fashion, enjoying the distraught woman's plight. The reappearance of Haddy drew a gasp from Sarah.

The older woman appeared as if melted under the remnants of the steam bath. Haddy deftly moved tongs to pick up one white rag, then another, dropping both into the boiling vat. She stirred with the same device before using it to pull one from the pot, shaking it out and placing it in a tight bunch onto an ornate silver platter. She repeated with the second, then handed the tray to Sarah. The two women nodded.

Wham!

More noise overhead. Sarah steeled herself and moved in that direction, exiting the kitchen into the living room where a narrow staircase awaited. The heavy breathing from outside moments ago filled the air again, clearly emanating from above. She climbed the stairs; the tremor returning to her hands as she held tight to the steaming cloths.

Upon reaching the landing, three doors lay ahead. Growling sounds from the end of the hall, guttural, violent. Hungry. The sounds are unnatural and feed off each other from the nearest door and the furthest. An echoing symphony of raspy abhorrence, the sounds of violations of flesh, truncated by overpowering noises of forces striking at the walls within each room.

"As the Lord is with me, I beg thee for strength. I beg thee clarity of sight, to see the true nature of these lost souls. Through me show mercy, in my presence offer the afflicted comfort, allow those who gaze upon me to return to mindfulness of God's power and love."

Sarah balanced the tray and approached the first door. All fell silent, as if birds in the forest detected a predator. She touches a door that opens so effortlessly she can only imagine it did so on its own. She steps into the room, looks at the sight before her and screams. Something inhuman screams back.

Also by Paul Carro
The Salem Legacy

Between 1692-1693, innocent women were hanged as witches in Salem under mysterious circumstances. Why did friend turn on friend? Why did crowds cheer the death of neighbors? And the biggest mystery, why did the executions finally stop?

Centuries later on the California coast, Linda Hunt became a teacher at the same orphanage she was raised in. Resigned to a life without family, her world turns upside down when a mother she never knew dies in a nearby nursing home leaving more questions than answers about her lineage.

Inheriting a deed to a house in Salem along with an antiquated key, Linda and her friends travel to the infamous town in search of her family name. But some mysteries were never meant to be solved, and some secrets were meant to stay buried.

With the aid of a local historian, Linda pulls at the threads of the past, waking ghosts of a tragic time. Soon the group is subjected to unspeakable terror as they find that uncovering the truth comes at a price.

As history reveals itself, Linda learns witches were not born in Salem, they were made.

Available here: https://www.amazon.com/Salem-Legacy-Paul-Carro/dp/B0B1C7Q1BF/

In 1692 residents of Salem began a hunt for witches
In 1693 they found one

PAUL CARRO

THE SALEM LEGACY

A HORROR NOVEL

Also by Paul Carro

The Little Coffee Shop of Horrors Anthology

Two generations of writers from one family get together for twelve terrifying tales. The writers visited twelve different coffee shops across the country to craft stories as dark as any drink served by a barista. Stories include: *A killer who keeps his eyes on the prize. A divorced couple face unspeakable aquatic horror when they hand off their child for shared custody weekend. A creepy cafe customer gets as good as he gives when he picks on the wrong barista. A group of influencers learn the hard way what a side hustle really means.* Read these and eight more shots of horror. Welcome to our coffee shop where the shaking does not come from the caffeine and the chills do not come from iced drinks but from the twelve tales of terror. You will never look at coffee shops the same again!

Available here: https://www.amazon.com/Little-Coffee-Shop-Horrors-Anthology-ebook/dp/B09HT253HB/

Also by Paul Carro
The House

The day began when Sheriff Frank Watkins found two bodies and three heads. Then things got strange. Paranormal TV host Charlie "Thunder" Raines has spent a lifetime seeking answers to the unexplained. When he spots a woman no one else on his crew can see, it appears he will finally receive his answers but at what cost? Yoga instructor Suzy Potter thought she left her past behind by moving cross country and changing her identity. When a door that previously did not exist creaks open in her studio, she discovers the past can never truly die. Before the day is over more doors will open before slamming closed, trapping residents of Tether Falls, Maine in a place seemingly existing between two worlds. The mysterious event brings together nine strangers with nine secrets so dark they plan to take them to their graves, with one house willing to accommodate them all. Welcome to The House–Where secrets go to die. Enter if you dare!

Available here: https://www.amazon.com/House-Horror-Novel-Paul-Carro/d p/1735070106/

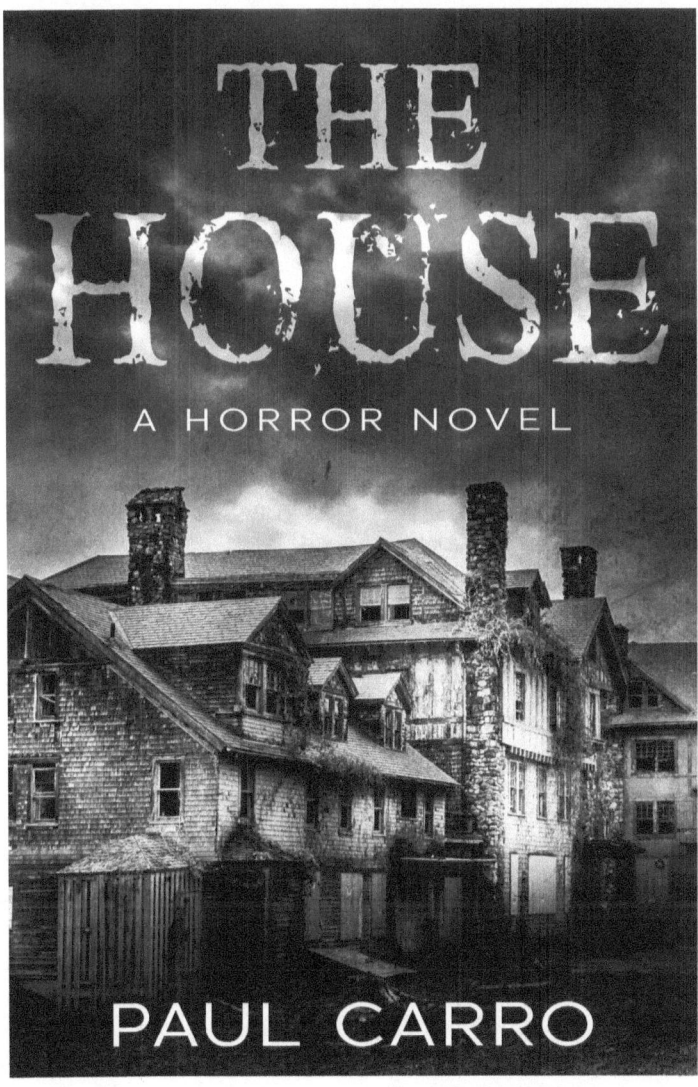

About the Author
Paul Carro

Paul Carro was born in Maine and fell in love with writing at an early age. He was first published during fifth grade in an anthology of Maine authors alongside a horror icon. Soon after college Paul moved to Los Angeles and worked for years in TV and film.

"Nolan Walker And The Superiors Squad" is the first novel from Paul Carro. A long time comic book geek, Paul has created his own YA superhero world with the first book in the Nolan Walker series.

A horror fan from the age he could walk, Paul now writes in his favorite genre. The House was his debut horror novel. The Hand Off is a novella length eBook offering a sneak peak at an exciting soon to be released new project. His latest release The Salem Legacy is now available.

When not coming up with new epic misadventures for his hapless hero, Nolan Walker, or cooking pasta extra creepy in the world of horror, Paul can be found hiking in various places around his Santa Monica, CA home.